the Storms of Tarshish

Drew Harmon

Trespass Island Books

trespassislandbooks.com

Storms of Tarshish

Formatting by Polgarus Studios

polgarusstudio.com

ISBN 978-0-692-90406-0 (print)

Acknowledgements

I'd like to express my gratitude to the following people for their support, encouragement, and inspiration in writing *The Storms of Tarshish*:

To my beloved wife Karen and my children Ian, Kelly, and Rowan for keeping me going.

To the veterans of the Armed Forces of the United States of America, particularly those with whom I have had the pleasure of working. All similarities to characters in this book are coincidental.

To Mark Cudworth, Beth Lovell, Ana Garcia, and Benjamin Russell whose particular attention to detail and storytelling helped me to make *The Storms of Tarshish* much, much stormier.

To my beta readers: Karen Harmon, James and Arthella Lacey, Alice Morgan, and Christopher Ryder. Your feedback, encouragement, and contributions have been truly invaluable.

In Memory of
Victor Augustin Garcia de la Cruz
Son of Borinquen,
Who told me tales of his beloved Puerto Rico,
And of his seafaring ancestors:
Pirates and slave traders.

Glossary of Sailing Terms

You don't have to know anything about sailing to enjoy *Storms of Tarshish*, but it will help if you become familiar with a few of the sailing terms found in the back of this book.

Jardines de la Reina
Cayman Brac
CUBA
HAITI
DOMINICAN REPUBLIC
Puerto Rico
Vieques
St. Croix
JAMAICA
CARIBBEAN SEA
LESSER ANTILLES
DUTCH ANTILLES
Aruba
Curacao
Bonaire
Margarita
TRINIDAD & TOBAGO
Barranquillia
Chichiriviche
COLUMBIA
VENEZUELA
Orinoco River
Orinoco Delta
Isla Cangrejo

1

In a little backwater of Chichiriviche, Venezuela the last brick of cocaine was packed into a long steel torpedo, and the hatch was bolted down. Its tow cable was secured to the back of a tired old fishing boat by a thick rope that could be severed quickly, if the authorities showed up. The GPS beacon, disguised as a log, was tested along with the motor-winch that would allow it to surface, if the torpedo lost its way.

It was a reasonably low-key and cost-effective smuggling technique. A scout boat would radio any contact with the authorities back to the tow boat, and the crew would cut the rope. The torpedo would glide on its stabilizing fins to the bottom and, after a time, extend its beacon-log. The back-up boat would come along later, pick up the tow cable, and continue with the delivery.

A tense foreboding among the men dampened the usual laughter and well wishing. That seemed to be happening more often these days. Scouts, tow boats and narco-torpedoes—each worth twenty million dollars—were simply vanishing on the dark ocean. There was talk of the rival Suiza Cartel, the Devil, and the wrath of their boss. There wasn't much difference between them.

In Colombia, the mood was different. Just after midnight on a Barranquilla wharf, men scrambled to ready a little fleet of battered fishing boats—and two brand new Picudas, each one thirty-eight feet of sleek radar-invisible fiberglass, sporting a trio of two hundred horsepower outboard motors. A score of experienced guerrillas, armed for the big catch, stowed their gear aboard. Word of the convoy had been circulated through the Caribbean grapevine. Whatever was out there preying on their commerce would have a fight on its hands if it showed up tonight.

The scout boats set out, their crews selected specifically for their inexperience, unaware of the certain fate that awaited them. The courier crews, drilled and ready for anything—they told themselves—passed a bottle, invoked a blessing from Santa Muerte, and toasted their valiant enterprise as they chugged north into open water. Finally the Picudas fired their engines and headed out.

2

Black ice stretched into the distance like an onyx highway, and Blake's little iceboat was burning it up at a mile a minute. He streaked across the lower lake, flat on his back, in what amounted to little more than an open coffin with a sail, on a trio of skates the size of machetes.

Frigid air seeped in one corner of his goggles and stabbed his watery eyeballs like frozen needles. He blinked his vision clear and saw that the last patch of pale sky had been swallowed up by a gathering pall of cloud. A light snow now wrapped the next race marker in a shroud of white haze and, worse yet, hid the dark patches—the thin ice he'd noticed on the previous lap. He had nightmares about the thin spots and about things under the ice— ominous shadows stalking him as he crossed the dream-lake. He loved iceboating but he *hated* the ice.

A peacock-blue boat whooshed up from behind. As she passed, the skipper slapped a hand on the name painted on the hull: *Sari 'Boutcha!* It was his girlfriend, Mia Devlin.

Griffy can't be far behind, he thought. Much to his annoyance, a black boat with a red hourglass on the side zipped by in pursuit of the blue.

"Stoof it in yer Pookits!" Blake yelled through his scarf, in his favorite Scots brogue. "I'll get ye on the windward leg!"

Stinging eyes and third place weren't the only things aggravating him. Nobody had heard from Uncle Carson for two months, and his schooner, *Tarshish,* had not been back to her home port in six. No one seemed terribly worried about it, but it gnawed at Blake and it made him resentful. Just when he needed him most, his uncle was nowhere to be found—as usual. Blake was sure he could handle his problems at school, but Nanna's new man-friend was going to require a level of intimidation that *this* fifteen-year-old could not deliver. And then there was the situation with his girlfriend.

The flurry became a white out. A sudden gust heeled the boat, lifting the starboard outrigger and runner four feet in the air. "Parasite!" Blake shouted as he leaned to hold the boat down. "Snake! Gold digging Jerk!" The gust passed, dropping the boat with a jolt and a sound like breaking glass. In an instant Blake was plunged into painfully cold, suffocating darkness. The boat rolled as it popped back to the surface, casting Blake off. He felt an upward rush as the flotation in his dry-suit sped him toward the surface. He hit a solid black wall. *No! Not under the ice! Not under the ice!* he cried in his mind. He clawed his goggles off, desperately seeking any light to guide him back to the breech. *Which way? Where am I?* Blake flailed wildly. Something jerked his arm. He knew instinctively it was the mainsheet. He caught hold of it, and pulled hand over hand. Now he could see a blurry white wedge ahead, moving downward with a slow eerie grace—like the fin of a ghost whale. He stopped pulling for a moment, startled by the phantom. Then he realized it was the mainsail and knew he was going to make it. He pulled with renewed vigor and burst out of the water with a groan. He struggled to get his bearings. The iceboat was upside-down and everything was white blindness. Blake labored to get a leg up on one of the outriggers and hoisted himself onto the belly of *Ice Scream*. He pulled a little air horn out of his chest pouch and bleated out three rounds of SOS. Blake pulled off his water logged scarf and helmet, and listened. They were coming—the scraping, rumbling sounds of the remaining five boats were growing louder. "Seriously, guys?" he panted, "Full tilt in a white-out? I thought *I* had adrenaline issues!"

He considered swimming to the far side of the breech and hauling himself onto the ice with his life-picks, before the big crash. He would probably have to anyway. He clenched a yellow plastic whistle in his teeth, pointed the horn in the direction of the fleet, and started his SOS again—ready to leap off the gently bobbing hull. He paused after thirty seconds of signaling. It took a moment for his hearing to recover from the din. The fleet was not moving. There was a motor running to the south. Excited voices drifted across the lake.

Finally the voice of his friend, Doctor Trudeau, called "Hallooo" out of the white abyss.

Blake shouted back and blew several more blasts on the air horn. Three shadowy forms appeared a few yards from the edge of the hole.

"That you, Blake?" said Trudeau.

"I wish it wasn't! The dry-suit was definitely worth the money."

The engine sounds grew louder and shortly Cezar Pagán appeared, driving a small ATV with a Jon boat in tow. The men, shoulders hunched against the cold, flocked to the boat. Trudeau brought an aluminum extension ladder and laid it on the ice, sliding another eight feet out of it. He pushed it across to Blake, who scurried over the makeshift bridge without delay.

"Let's just leave it. I want to get ashore."

"Sure you're okay?" said Trudeau, noticing the scratches on Blake's face.

"Just a little freaked out, that's all. I went under the ice."

"Yikes! Let's have Cezar take you back to Gunn's. We'll pull your boat out."

"No, you don't have to do all that. I'm fine. Let's pull her out and get off the ice before the killer whales show up."

The snow squall passed and a bright spot opened in the clouds. They got a line around one of the outriggers, flipped *Ice Scream* over, and dragged her out. Cezar tethered her to the back of the Jon boat while Trudeau pulled the sail down. The men gave him a slap on the back as they headed to their boats.

"Where you want to go?" said Cezar. "Back to Señor Gunn's, or the sailing club?"

Blake climbed into the Jon boat. "Tahiti."

3

Sunday morning, Blake and Mia sat in the back pew at St. Rowan's Episcopal and waited for the recessional parade of priest and acolytes to rumble by, as the choir belted out Dixit Dominus. They popped up and trailed the white-robed throng to the vestry room. Father Cameron finally emerged, having exchanged his holy attire for a sport jacket and faded blue jeans. He flinched when he saw them.

"Can we speak with you in private?" said Blake.

"Can I get some coffee first?"

"No," said Mia opening the door to his office suite.

"So be it," said Father Taylor, with a sigh of resignation. "Follow me!"

He led them through the waiting room and into his little office. It smelled of books and brass polish. He rolled his big leather chair out from behind his cluttered desk, plunged into it and propped his feet up on an end table. He was tall and young. His pointy red beard glowed against his electric blue shirt. Blake and Mia sat on a short couch opposite him.

"This is about your arch nemesis, again?"

"Nobody will listen to us," said Blake. "He's taking advantage of Nanna. She doesn't see it."

"What do you want me to do?" he said. "Your grandmother seems happy enough."

"We're supposed to take care of the widow and orphan. Isn't that what Scripture says?"

"Does it?" countered Taylor. "This is our third meeting, Blake. Is it possible you're a little jealous? It would only be natural to feel like your territory is being invaded—to be a little resentful of a new authority in your home. Maybe it appears to *him* that *you're* the one taking advantage of Clarissa. Let me ask you, does he make your grandmother happy?"

"He's a letch!" objected Mia.

"Kids, whenever you have social organizations of hominids, you'll always have conflict. It's natural! Just like school—you will always have your insiders, your outsiders, and your special characters."

"Has he hugged your wife, yet?" she retorted.

Father Taylor shifted his weight as if bitten by a flea. He hooked one finger behind his white clerical collar and extracted it from his shirt, then tilted his head and smiled. "Whoever is without sin, let them cast the first stone."

"What the hell is that supposed to mean?" Mia snarled.

"Well, you know, you're not the only ones raising concerns about morality in this congregation."

"Now you've either said too much, or you've said too little," Blake replied.

"I wonder, are you two keeping your relationship pure?"

Mia stood up and bristled. "I am not even going to dignify that! Kiss my..."

"Don't you see?" Blake interrupted as she stormed out of the little office. "Now he's trying to split me and Mia up."

"You didn't answer the question," said Taylor, with a smug smile.

"We aren't the only ones who see this going on!"

"Are you and Mia keeping it clean?"

"As a matter of fact we are! We don't even make out, if you have to know."

Father Taylor put his feet on the floor and leaned forward, resting his elbows on his knees. "Brett Turlow does a lot for this congregation, Blake. He shares his talents, and dedicates his time to maintaining the building, and the grounds. So what if he's a boob man? He serves tirelessly. What do you do? Sure, you made a big splash up in Freeman and did some good things for the community, but that was two years ago. What have you done for this congregation except attack the character of a respected man? It has to stop. Now. You understand?"

"Thanks for your time," Blake said as he stood up. "I won't bother you anymore."

He found Mia waiting on the front steps, under a dreary gray sky. It matched the gray stone facade of the medieval-looking church. It was beginning to snow.

"Well, did we get kicked out again?" she said.

"Doesn't matter. We're not coming back. You up for some target practice at Mr. Gunn's? He loaded a bunch of nine millimeter for us. You can shoot the Uzi."

"Tempting, but I gotta bust my hump on school stuff if I want to graduate on time. We *are* going to beat this jerk, Tux."

He smiled doubtfully. "I love you."

***

Mia was relieved to find that her Aunt Serena had decided to spend the afternoon knocking around an antiques mall.

She fixed herself a sandwich and went to her spacious bedroom, where a stack of textbooks waited on her desk: Anatomy and Physiology, Chemistry, Intro to Nursing and Health Sciences. On top of the stack rested several sheets of an opened letter. It shed purple glitter when she picked it up, and smelled of lavender. It was from Fiona, that little rascal who had latched onto her two years ago, when she and Blake had gone on vacation with old Tripper Gunn. Mia smirked at the kooky illustrations scattered through the text, particularly the masterpiece on the final page. A queasy, drunken unicorn with a large blue beer can impaled on its horn, stood beneath a flaming rainbow of putrid melting colors. The can's big red F in a gold circle, and a pool of neon green unicorn vomit told the rest of the story.

Fiona wrote:

My Ever Loving Mimi-devil,

If your dearest old dad ever offers you a drink of warm Foster's Lager, you must under no circumstances accept it. This poison must never pass your lips or you will immediately turn into a heaving gurge-

beast. This most vile Aussie concoction is collected from the bathroom drain beneath the lair of an evil mountain dwarf!

It's like chemo in a can! I thought my hair was going to fall out all over again! It tastes exactly like my mom's hair spray. Exactly!!! (Don't ask me how I know that.) Half of the unicorns in my kingdom have been turned into HGBs by this stuff.

The letter continued in the same vein for several paragraphs, then suddenly shifted gears.

Great news! Doctor Whackenstein says the evil King Lou Kemia has been defeated and driven from my kingdom. I'm in complete remission! You may now refer to me as Her Majesty, Queen NED. As in No Evidence of Disease! Daddy thinks it was the chemo. Mommy thinks it was all the crying and praying. I think it was both. But who cares! I'm Queen NED! Mimi-devil, as my loyal subject, you may now osculate the royal donkey!!!

Mia smiled, then sighed in relief, "Best. Christmas. Ever." She thought she should call the brat to celebrate the good news, but that would be at least a two hour investment. She already wished she'd given in and gone to shoot guns with Blake, at the old marina. *I'll call her before bed,* she thought, opening her chemistry book.

Her phone chimed. "Saved by the dumb belle!" she answered, rolling her eyes. "Whazzup, Shay?"

"Close your books, open your eyes, and imagine you're in a tropical paradise."

"Your florid elocution arouses my suspicion. *What* are you up to?"

"Me? Up to something? Mia, you've known me since second grade. When have I ever been up to something?"

"C'mon. I'm not in the mood," Mia droned, impatiently.

"I'm up to Christmas vacation in Myrtle Beach with my best bud, who desperately needs a break from school before her head explodes."

"OMG, Shay! Do you know how behind I am?"

"You went to school all summer!"

"Yeah, 'cuz I didn't bother to go to school for most of my junior year."

"But you got straight A's last quarter! You deserve it. You *owe* it to yourself, woman!"

"Lay off, for the love o' Pete! Fiona's parents already invited Blake and me up to Wisconsin."

"Ooh lah lah! So, it's romance on ice?"

"Shay, for a friend, you really suck. You know that?"

"As a matter of fact I do. That's what besties are for. So, have you figured out how you're going to let him down, yet?"

"Who said I am?"

"Hi, my name is Mia Laurentia Devlin of Sigma Epsilon Chi, I'm a hot nursing major, and I'm betrothed to an awky sixteen-year-old coffin builder from Fort Wayne who's never been to first base."

"He has, too!" Mia protested.

"Not with you!"

"That's not for a lack of… And he isn't awky! Ya know what? Shut up, Shay!"

"Myrtle Beach. We're going."

"No, we're not. And I'm not going to Wisconsin, either. I am trying to get my act together so I can go to college."

"Act is the key word, here. I.U. just loves you for your money," insisted Shay.

"Hi, my name is Shay Ryan, and I'm a slackaholic," taunted Mia, in return. "It's been ninety days since the last time I did anything productive. My friend, Mia, is trying to get me hooked on this stuff called 'maturity,' but I'm afraid if I try it, I might make something of myself."

Shay laughed. "You are just a savage cramp-a-thon, today! I think you've got a vitamin D3 deficiency. You need some sea and sand. Sun your buns, bake your,"

"You know," Mia interrupted, "you *could* come over here and help me with my Chemistry."

"The only chemistry I'm helping you with is chemical dependency. Seriously—about Blake—you've got to jump him, or dump him."

"Dang, Shay! You're like a female Griffy Williams."

"Who's he?"

"One of Blake's incorrigible sailing friends. Beyond that, I'll let you find out for yourself. You deserve each other."

"Is he on Facebooger?"

"Banned, actually."

"I'm interested, already! Well, I gotta bounce. Think. Myrtle. Beach."

"Call. Griffy. Williams."

Mia hung up, and looked out the window. The snow was coming down hard, in big flakes. The woods *would* be lovely. With a thermos of hot cocoa. And Blake. She wished everyone would just mind their own business about him. She knew they were right, up to a certain point, but it just wasn't any of their business. They had no idea what Blake had done for her. They knew nothing of his sincerity. His honesty. His loyalty. She'd never run into anything like it in her life. It was everything a woman was supposed to demand from a guy, but few really seemed to want. She felt undeserving of those treasures. Somehow they frightened her.

She looked back at the outline in her open book. Organic Chemistry: Substituted Hydrocarbons: Alcohols. She shook her head and said, "No comment."

***

The snow was also falling heavily on Highland Creek Reservoir. Blake crouched on a strip of gravelly beach outside Gunn's harbor, and kindled a fire using honey locust thorns. He added another log to the pulsating orange coals and watched scions of blue flame sprout from its bark. He leaned back against the cold dirt bluff, the acrid smoke stinging his nose. Trespass Island was a dark, indistinct hump in the white distance. The horizon had vanished behind the veil of snow, and the frozen lake spoke mysteries to him from the twilight solitude. It divulged its oracle of the future in eerie pings and twangs that sounded like a laser battle, and occasionally emphasized some startling point with a crack like a bullwhip. It settled down as the wind eased, thrumming and hissing to itself. In the distance he thought he saw five shadowy figures running across the ice, and it made him think of a scene from Moby Dick—Fedallah and the Parsees. He quelled the impulse to dash out and warn them about thin spots. After his fall through the ice—and journey under it—no inducement or reward could compel him venture back out there.

The complete sense of defeat he felt tugged at him. It tempted him into its easy embrace, and that of its comforting companions: rationalization and fatalism. He was no stranger to the trio; his first twelve years having been a domestic dark age, where he learned well the art of the self-fulfilling prophet of failure, under the mealy-mouthed tutelage of his obsessive-compulsive father. Yet suddenly, that winter of discontent had been gloriously enlightened by one unexpectedly transformative summer.

Two years before, his father had gone to France on business, taking his mother and sister along for the ride—but not Blake. Owing to the additional expense, he was left behind with his Uncle Carson Urquart, with plans for his grandmother to claim him upon her return from North Carolina. And return she did—several months later. In that time, he learned to buck up in the face adversity; to take action, yet be responsible for the consequences; to be optimistic in spite of his experience and common sense; to be useful, and forward thinking. He had learned to be a young man. He had also learned that defeat was not an irrevocable cosmic decree from a god who had it in for him. He learned that defeatism and fatalism were curable mental illnesses. Yet now, under this growing blanket of reversals, he felt himself getting sick again.

The crash through the ice was just a portent, a summation of his fear that this renaissance was a fluke that wouldn't—or worse yet—couldn't last. Everything he had invested his love and confidence in was on the verge of vanishing, like those figures in the snowstorm. The writing was on the wall. His grandmother wouldn't live forever; and Tripper Gunn, his beloved mentor—every bit the surrogate grandfather—was getting *very* old. He had appointed Blake as his heir, but Blake couldn't contemplate life at the old marina without him. The mere imagining of it was a painful emptiness that bordered on anxiety. The new state-run marina had finally opened last year, and had all but killed the little boat rental business and camp store Blake ran with the Pagán family, there at Gunn's old boatyard. The coffin and cabinet building enterprise he co-owned with Sylvio Pagán had continued to expand, leading Sylvio to move the operation into the empty half of Gunn's waning Freeman Flea Market. Once the old Scotsman was gone, his marina, his workshop, and his house would be achingly desolate. "He shall return no more to his house, neither shall his place know him anymore," Blake whispered. The wind gusted, and the ice responded to the words of Job with a baleful spirit-moan that sent a shiver down Blake's spine.

He blew on the chunky coals, making them flare and roar like dragon's breath that seared his cheeks and stung his eyes. He considered his prospects in the little tourist town across the lake. His exploits that wild summer had made him the golden boy of Highland Creek Reservoir, the savior of the sailing club, and the town hero of Freeman, Indiana; but his luster was fading. He was old news, about to disappear into the scenery. His reservoir of clout and social capital was running dangerously low. His inheritance would leave him with considerable property in Freeman, but the thought of managing it all bored him. Without his friends, without Mia, the town would be nothing but a mausoleum filled with the rank bones of long-lost summer nostalgia.

In Pemberton, home of the Urquarts, he had lost ground too. Adversaries had risen in his grandmother's home, in school, and at church. And soon his chief ally, Mia Devlin, would be gone—moving into other spheres of influence, changing, becoming someone else. *Going away.* He thought. *Everyone is going away. Everything is changing. Except me.* He flung a rock and tried to recall Starbuck's resolution, from Moby Dick—something about fighting grim, phantom futures.

4

Blake stuffed his English books into his locker, and slapped the door shut with a noisy rattle. Seventh grade at Pemberton Academy had been a breeze—so much so that he had been skipped forward to the ninth. And that was going alright, except for Accelerated Literature and Composition. Mr. Ranski and Moby Dick, it seemed, had it in for him. And then there were the rumors.

After the novelty of being the Hero of Highland Creek had faded at Pemberton Academy, a contempt bred of familiarity began to ooze among the more malcontented and malicious cliques. The cafeteria drama queens naturally focused on his relationship with Mia. They would snicker furtively to one another and call him "Studley" with lascivious moans and lewd winks, whenever he passed by. They called her "killer" once—and only once. The events that followed nearly resulted in Blake's expulsion. And it wasn't long before it was discovered that the poster-boy of the local anti-drug crusade had a secret identity: The Coffin Pimp of Freeman. It started in the Chess Club with a friend of a friend of Griffy Williams—his old "frenemy" and consummate prankster. It made its way to the Goth kids, and now rumors slithered through the halls about Mexican coffins containing gutted, drug-stuffed corpses; of how he was really part of a Latino coven in a turf war with the Mangrave catfish cult; and how he had buried alive one of the rival warlocks, in the grave of an ancient black holy-man. Worse yet, these tales were not confined to the academy, but had spread to the township schools where the former denizens of Voodoo Jack's Party Shack still lurked. Griffy

Williams steadfastly denied any knowledge of the situation.

Blake looked down the long hall to the exit. Now it was back to Nanna's to shovel snow and chip ice under the watchful eye of Brett Turlow. He thrust his hands deep into his coat pockets and trudged down slushy sidewalks toward the chocolate brown bungalow, thinking about Mia the whole way. She had just received a letter of preliminary acceptance from the Indiana University School of Nursing in Indianapolis. Her astonishing financial statement, along with letters of recommendation from the Mayor of Freeman and Doctor Trudeau had flagged her for special attention—even before she had taken her SAT test. *This time next year* he thought bitterly, *and she'll be gone.* Everyone, it seemed, was trying to prepare him for this bleak future. Her new classmates would undoubtedly ask if she had a boyfriend. Guys would hit on her. How long would she be able to stand the embarrassment of admitting that her steady was only sixteen? There would be no hiding it either. They had been big news once upon a time, and someone was bound to remember. He just wanted to go back to Gunn's and forget about everything. But now the Pagáns were a constant presence at the old marina—running the camp store, keeping house and cooking for Tripper. Sylvana even stayed overnight to keep a caring eye on the old man. It was all tedious frustration.

***

Blake lifted the shovel and chucked another load of snow. Brett Turlow lifted his flat-cap and smoothed his dark gray hair. "When you finish that, you can salt the front steps and the walks. And you mind that shovel around the cars."

"When is the snow blower coming back?"

"The shop's backed up with 'em. I wouldn't figure before Easter, pal. Besides, you're not getting anywhere near these vehicles with a snow blower!"

"It was brand new! There was nothing wrong with it."

"Needed a tune up. I could hear it." Turlow snickered, "At any rate, old chum, that's way too much machine for a little boy. Shoveling builds character. Gives you time to think about getting your grades up."

Blake stopped shoveling. "I've seen you talking to Mr. Ranski at church. I've overheard. I know what's going on."

"Oh do you, now?" Turlow said with a sinister look. "Maybe we just need to have a little conference with Mr. Ranski, your grandmother and I."

"What business is it of yours? When my uncle finds out…"

"Your uncle is in the bottom of a bottle in Davy Jones' locker, Blakey boy. I think I'll go set up that conference right now." Turlow walked away. "See if your uncle can stop me."

Blake sucked it up. He stared at Turlow's little red MG Midget for thirty simmering seconds, then started shoveling. A half hour later, the last patch of the red car disappeared under a mountain of snow.

Blake thumped the back door shut, stomped the snow off his boots, then levered them off his feet using the top step of the basement stairs.

His grandmother appeared at the top of the steps to the kitchen. "Blake we need to have a little talk. Father Taylor just called."

"As if it couldn't get any worse," Blake muttered.

"I don't understand this rivalry, Blake; you and Brett."

"What did his eminence want?"

"Someone changed the letters around on the message board in the foyer at church. Someone you know."

A smile began to take hold on the corners of his mouth.

"I assume you know what it says," she scowled.

"No. But I'd like too."

"After your meeting with Father Cam, Mia changed the sign. It's on the security tape. Just disgraceful."

"What did it say?"

"The sign should read Reverend Cameron Taylor, Church Rector. She changed the 'or' to 'um.' I am very disappointed."

"Yeah, she was a little frustrated with Father Cam. Nobody seems to care that Brett is taking advantage of you, and driving a wedge in our family."

"Brett is a good man. A little set in his ways, but I think his heart is in the right place."

"I'd get an X-ray and a second opinion."

"To your room, Blake! You are turning into your uncle. I won't have any more of this."

He gladly retired upstairs, flopped down on his bed and stared at the slanting walls of his homey attic abode. "Turning into my uncle," he said to himself. "And whose fault would that be?" He recalled the blustery day when his family left him with his uncle on that windswept hilltop, before they flew off to France for the summer. "Who was supposed to come pick me up in three days? Who left me to fend for myself on the ragged edge of the lunatic fringe for—drum roll please— four months? I don't mean to seem ungrateful, Nanna, but…"

Blake took a small stack of post cards from his nightstand. His mother had sent them from France, during that summer on the lake. They had been a lifeline, and an unexpected introduction to a side of his mother he had never known; the artistic, whimsical, free-spirited traveler who had, for his entire life and longer, hidden herself obediently beneath a pall of needlessly repressive fundamentalist propriety.

He shuffled through the cards: the Eiffel Tower at night, a Guillotine, a stone gargoyle, a luminous glass pyramid, Napoleon rampant, a fantastic landscape by M.C. Escher, and his favorite: Chirico's surrealist painting of two horses standing side by side on a stormy beach. One was white, with a long gold sash draped across its back, the other a blood bay red with an insanely voluminous mane and tail of wavy black hair—just like Mia's.

He was her white stallion, he knew. But she was his strength. His confidence flowed from her. She was now the one constant in his life he could trust, the anchor to which all of his feelings of personal security were moored. She had been all things to him: big sister, best friend, protector, ally, and love. He could not imagine her becoming someone different; someone who looked the same, but whom he did not recognize—and who no longer recognized him. Blake was beginning to worry about it to the degree that Mia was using terms like "high maintenance" and "co-dependent," whenever his anxieties bubbled to the surface.

He jerked himself to his feet and went to the window, looking down with satisfaction on the heap of snow that entombed Turlow's little car. The words of Haraguchi, Mia's impish old karate teacher, came to mind: *Is this your battle? Do you have to fight it now? Do you have to fight it here?* He closed his eyes and sighed. "Time for a tactical retreat."

***

Blake appeared in the living room wearing his coat and big trail backpack. Turlow squatted at the hearth and poked the fire. He still wore the brown tweed flat cap, a long straight pipe clenched in his teeth. Blake glanced at the pictures on the mantel, and scowled. There was his grandfather in the same flat cap, grinning behind the same pipe. Clarissa sat in her recliner, talking on the phone.

Turlow smiled at the blaze. "It was pretty cold out there. Your Nanna might make you some warm milk, if you say 'pretty please.'"

After the ice-boat accident, Gunn had congratulated Blake and given him a snort of brandy. And here was this jerk taunting him in his own home— with warm milk, no less. He resisted the overwhelming urge to put his foot between Turlow's shoulders and shove him screaming into the inferno he'd just kindled.

"Is that my mom?" said Blake.

Clarissa smiled and nodded.

"Please tell her I'm moving in with Mia and Serena."

Clarissa frowned, and held up a finger.

"Please, tell her. I'm leaving now."

"Your grandmother is on the phone, Blakey," snarled Turlow in his smarmy, condescending way.

Blake glanced at the curio cabinet across the room, and balled his fists. He could see the red scabbard of his grandfather's clan dirk behind the latticed doors.

"Ava, your son wants to speak with you." Clarissa handed the phone to Blake.

"Hi Mom. No, not fine. Look, I'm moving in with Mia and Serena. Yes, now. I just wanted you to know so Mr. Turlow can't report me as a runaway." Blake shot a snarky smile at Turlow. "I'll have Serena call you. Thanks. Love you, too." He handed the phone back to Clarissa, who was trying her best not to cry.

"Brett, drive Blake up the street to Serena's," she said, voice trembling. Blake's chest filled with squirming, gelatinous guilt.

"It's alright. I need the exercise," he countered.

"Lookout for thin ice!" sneered Turlow.

"Fire's the devil's only friend," Blake replied, opening the front door.

"Stop it! Both of you!" Clarissa demanded.

"Sorry, Nanna. I love you," Blake said pulling the door closed as he left.

***

While the Urquart bungalow was cozy and somewhat close quartered, Serena's house was open and airy—the star on her Christmas tree nearly touched the eleven foot ceiling. It was an old house, like all of the homes in Pemberton, and its interior décor reflected Serena's middle-aged eccentric chic. Mia's mother had inherited the family's no-nonsense go-for-the-throat business instinct, but her aunt Serena Krakow favored breezy, free-spirited forty-something impulsiveness, and the notoriety of being the black sheep of the clan. The soothing aroma of evergreen and baking cookies filled the air. Blake, Mia, and Serena sat before the looming boughs of the tree and held their war counsel. Blake recounted a litany of Turlow's increasingly bold incursions into Clarissa Urquart's life, ending with the latest outrage.

"He's wearing my grandfather's hat now, and chews on one of his pipes all the time."

"That *is* creepy sick," said Serena.

"Tell me about it. I overheard them talking the other day. He told her the lease on his apartment is about to expire and he can't afford to renew it. I called the rental office. He's got another five months!"

"What did your grandmother say to that?" said Serena.

"That she wouldn't let him go without a roof over his head."

"We've got to find your uncle before that camel gets his nose in the tent—permanently!"

"Ya think?" Mia interjected. She fiddled with her digital tablet. "The only thing I've been able to dig up is a cruising blog that mentions that Carson's boat was at Chaguaramas Yacht Club in Tobago, headed for Isla Margarita. And that was October."

"I thought they were based out of Puerto Rico?" said Serena. "What are they doing way down on the coast of Venezuela?"

"Ecotourism, supposedly," replied Blake.

"Well, at least we know they were sailing west," said Mia. "Maybe they were headed for the Dutch Antilles, then back up to Puerto Rico."

"Then Puerto Rico is where we'll start," said Serena. "I'll call your moms and then we'll make the reservations."

Mia and Blake looked at each other and said, "For what?"

"Our flight and hotel!"

Blake grinned, but it faded quickly as Mia rolled her eyes and groaned.

"Why not?" Serena objected. "You guys could use a break anyway. I don't know about you, but my Seasonal Affective Disorder is just killing me."

"But," said Blake, "if we leave, Turlow takes over. Completely."

"Then we'll take them with us!"

Mia got that slit-eyed look of disbelief. "OMG! You are *not* serious?"

"I hate to burst your bubble, but after Voodoo Jack she won't leave the house without a sitter that's been cleared by the FBI. Not to mention, I don't have a passport."

"Don't need one. It's Puerto Rico, hunny. Kids! It's me, Aunt Serena! I've got this!" she beamed.

"That's what worries me," said Mia. "You're like the crazy cat lady, only without the cats."

"Oh no, hunny; I'm terribly allergic."

5

Deep in the heart of Venezuela, a gleaming black Mercedes-Benz S500L armored sedan and four SUV's passed through a high chain link gate, as rain poured down on Guyana City. The motorcade made its way through the waterfront industrial park like a State funeral procession, to a large warehouse by the Orinoco River. The vehicles stopped by a massive concrete ramp that sloped from the building's giant corrugated steel doors down to the dark water. Lightning silhouetted cranes which loomed like gallows over the ramp.

Light suddenly splashed from a side door in the building, and a man hurried down to the sedan. Eight little red laser dots danced on his jacket like fire flies as he approached. The driver's window went down halfway, and the chauffeur spoke.

"Tell the Russian that El Emperador has arrived."

"I'll get him, but I wouldn't call him Russian if I were you. El Arquitecto is Chechen."

"What is the difference?" said the chauffer, in languid condescension.

"Call him Russian to his face, and find out." The man returned to the building, red fireflies dancing on his back.

Behind the tinted bulletproof glass, Manfredo "El Emperador" Suiza smirked. "No laser sights on Señor El Chechen." The chauffeur radioed the security detail. Five minutes later, light splashed from the door again and a short, wiry man made his way causally to the black Mercedes, the orange coal of his cigarette flaring in his curled palm.

Suiza rolled his window down."Salam, Señor Varayev."

"Good night to launch a submarine, eh?" said Varayev, exhaling a river of white smoke out one side of his mouth. He leaned against the car, face close to the open window. The smell of alcohol and sweat wafted into the immaculate interior.

"Indeed. I am anxious to see your masterpiece."

"Let's do it, then!" He fished a radio out of his back pocket and turned toward the great doors. "Okay, let's see if the fat lady floats!" The sound of heavy machinery rattled the metal walls of the building and the great doors began to slide apart. Suiza ordered the SUVs to line up abreast and turn on their high beams.

"Russian savages," mumbled the Chauffer.

"I am not paying Señor Varayev for social refinement, but technical genius, Maceo."

Varayev turned back to the window. "Yeah, you bet that's genius! Kevlar and fiberglass. She'll go down thirty meters, and I ran the exhaust under the boat to cool it, so you don't see her on thermal image scopes. Carry fifteen, I bet twenty tons of coke. Even got a nice crapper. And her big sister has air conditioning!"

"Allow me to join you, Señor Varayev," said Suiza, as he exited the car, opening a capacious black umbrella. The sound of a powerful engine bellowed from the building, like a dragon waking in its lair. Slowly, the tail plains and cylindrical shrouds of the twin propellers appeared in the massive portal, riding high above six wheels of an oversized flatbed trailer. A pair of spotters waving red light batons walked with the behemoth, as if herding the monster down to the water with magic wands. Four more men carried her tethers. The hull crept into the fan of light, the heavy rain washing over its multi-hued blue ink-blot camouflage scheme. The conning tower with its radio mast appeared, followed by the gracefully tapered bow. Lastly, the mighty snarling Russian Kirovec K-701 semi-tractor backed onto the ramp. A company of men scrambled out of the warehouse and took their places on a long pier at the base of the launch ramp. The black river began to swallow the massive rig and its ponderous cargo, the chauffer's eyes widening as even the hood of the

Kirovec disappeared, its headlamps blazing eerily beneath the murky water. The signal was given and the berthing crew hauled on the tethers, pulling the sub up to its dock. "Now, watch this!" grinned Varayev, motioning with his cigarette. The Kirovec roared and thrashed its way out of Orinoco like the Biblical Leviathan, giant tires throwing spray as it clambered back up the ramp, plunging into the warehouse with a recklessness that bordered on abandon. El Emperador allowed himself a genuine, but restrained laugh. "You know how to entertain, Señor Varayev!" He turned back for his car. The Chechen lit another cigarette in his cupped hands as he followed.

"That was Venganza. Espada will be ready in two weeks, easy. What about sea trials?"

The chauffeur had gotten out and opened his employer's door. Suiza handed him the umbrella and slipped into the back seat. "The crew will arrive in a couple of days. Sea trials will have to take place en route."

Varayev blew another river of smoke. "Have it your way."

"I always do! Buenas Noches, Señor."

6

Serena obtained the necessary parental permissions and made the travel arrangements. The conspiracy was formed, and the plot laid; they would do this thing. But in spite of Blake's enthusiasm for the adventure, something had been nibbling at the corners of his conscience ever since he'd moved in with Serena and Mia. He picked up the phone and called his mother. To his surprise, his father answered the phone. Blake caught his breath, and bluffed.

"Ah, yes, is Ava Barber available?"

"Who is this, please?"

"This is… Mr. Alan from Pemberton Academy, just returning her call."

"One moment. Ava! Mr. Alan, from the school is on the phone!"

Blake hadn't spoken to his father in two years. The fact that he didn't even recognize his voice rekindled unresolved anger from their last encounter—on the day his family returned from France.

"Your son is an excellent student, Mr. Barber. You must be very proud."

"Hold on a second, Mr. Alan. Ava! Phone!"

Blake's temper began to smolder. "It's hard to keep track of all of his accomplishments. I hear he takes after his mother."

"Just a minute, sir, she's outside," his father sniveled. "I'll have to go get her."

Blake ground his teeth together and tried to remember the powder keg of trouble Mia's anger had ignited when she'd tried to ruin her dad.

His mother took the phone just in time to hear "Is it true they're naming the baby after you?"

24

"I'm flattered, Mr. Alan!" his mother chuckled. "Getting an early start, aren't you?"

"Mom. Great. He didn't even recognize my voice."

"Let's not go there, dear. What's up? Excited about the big trip?"

"Yeah, that's what I wanted to talk to you about."

"What's on your mind?"

"Well, I dunno. I…"

"It's about you and Mia?"

"Yeah. Alone."

"You two spend lots of time alone in secluded places. You live in the same house, now. What's bothering you, sweetheart?"

"We're going to charter a boat for a couple of days."

"And?"

"Serena's not coming along. It just feels different."

"What am I supposed to say, Blake?"

"I don't know. That's kind of why I was asking."

"We raised you with a strong sense of right and wrong, young man. Do you think there's something inappropriate about it?"

"Well, not if we have separate cabins, I guess."

"Do you think something inappropriate might happen?"

"I… I'm not really worried about that, either. I guess it's just how it looks."

"Seriously? In this day and age? No one will bat an eye. Look up bundling. It used to be an Amish thing. I'm okay with it if you are."

"I wish you could come with us."

"Me, too. But someone has to take care of your father, and you already have plans for your sister."

"Oh, well…"

"Blake, I'm confident that you'll both make good choices. As long as you are safe and sound, and have a good time, I'm fine with it!"

"Okay. Thanks."

"I have to get dinner on, kiddo. Give the girls my love."

"See you at the Christmas party?"

"Of course!"

"You think Agatha will go for it?"

"It's a fair bet. Don't worry. Start packing. See you soon, sweetie."

Blake said goodbye, and cast a long look at the mirror on the back of the bedroom door. His mother had explained it a hundred times. His father had changed. He hadn't always been like this. The distant, hair-splitting control freak didn't begin to emerge until shortly after they were married. His father had developed some kind of obsessive compulsive disorder, and then social anxiety piled in on top of that. He refused to take medication. He became utterly devoted to, and fixated upon his first child, Agatha. Yet he barely noticed the birth of his second. He lavished love and attention on Agatha, but Blake learned early on that paternal micromanagement was as much as he could ever hope for. And so he grew up doing his best to please his dad's maniacal punctiliousness. At least until he was twelve. But he'd still catch himself doing it subconsciously, and it drove him nuts.

7

The Highland Creek Sailing Club was radiant with holiday cheer. White lunch-bag lanterns glowed warmly on the hillside steps. The man-sized anchor in the center of the circular hill-top driveway was wrapped in red, white, and blue chaser lights, as was the big club house. Curtains of strand lights hung from the eves, and all of the windows were outlined with twinkling bulbs. From Trespass Island, it looked like a casino.

Inside, more than one hundred cordially inebriated sailors and their families feasted on the best that Tyner's catering had to offer. The dinner line snaked out of the galley and down the narrow wing off the great room. Blake was on his own turf, and easily avoided his grandmother and her escort. Brett Turlow was busy coercing every female in the place into a sturdy full body hug.

Tripper Gunn's joyous laugh rolled over the din of the crowd. Blake figured that his mother and sister must have just come in the door. He stood up on a window ledge and spotted them sharing hugs with the old man. Turlow made his way over to get his share, and when he released Agatha Blake saw her mouth a choice word and clutch her chest, eyes bulging. He hopped down and disappeared into the crowd. He resurfaced behind Gunn, who was still talking to Turlow.

"Hey Mr. Gunn, did you hear the news? Serena is taking Mia and me to the Caribbean for winter break!"

"Blakey, how many times..." Turlow began.

"Don't interrupt the lad, man," Gunn said. He clapped a gnarled hand on Blake's back and gave him a fatherly squeeze. "That's what yer mother said! I'd go with yeh if I did'na have to spend all my time fishing people out of holes in the ice! Mr. Turlow, this is one of the finest lads yeh'll ever meet. Single handedly brought this club back from the dead."

Turlow struggled to maintain his smile. "He's something, alright."

"We leave on Monday," Blake beamed. "We're hoping we get lucky and find *Tarshish* in the Yucatan. I've just *got* to tell Agatha." He excused himself and vanished back into the crowd.

"Pardon me, Tripp, but what is *Tarshish*? Is that like hashish or something?"

"Heh! No, it's the schooner his uncle crews. He's the dive master."

Turlow looked truly vexed now. "If you'll excuse me, I'd better see if Clarissa needs anything."

Blake waited ten minutes, then surfaced by the fireplace where his grandmother was chatting with the club commodore's wife. The middle-aged woman grimaced politely, discreetly readjusting her plunging neckline.

"Hi Cheri, I see you've met Mr. Turlow?"

"You could say that. Clarissa was just telling me you're all going to the Yucatan together? That's awesome!"

Blake feigned surprise. "Really, you guys are coming, too?"

"Oh, I don't know, Blake," Clarissa said. "Your grandfather always wanted to take me to the Yucatan, but we never made it. Brett thought a nice cruise might be the place to clear up all of this tension and misunderstanding. But I don't want to leave the house empty. Honestly, I don't know what to do. Serena's already made our reservations. I'd hate to disappoint her."

"Good old Serena!" Blake agreed, cheerfully. "Let me see if Agatha would be willing to watch the house." He looked over his shoulder and nodded to Mia, who was lurking nearby. She headed for her objective. "I'll be right back!" he said.

Agatha hovered close to her mother, scanning the crowd for one particular bear-hugging celebrant.

"Hey, Goldilocks," said Mia, as she passed by. "Come with me. I've got a proposition for you."

Her mother smiled with sly approval and encouraged her to follow. Mia led Agatha through the dinner line into the galley kitchen, squeezing between servers behind the long counter, and down to the little pantry at the far end. Blake was waiting inside. Mia shut the door behind them.

"I can't say much for the company, but at least it's quiet," said Agatha. "This whole place smells like rum breath."

Blake cut to the chase. "Look, here's the bottom line. We need your help."

"Yeah right. What are you trying to pull?"

"How would you like a place of your own for two weeks?"

Mia chimed in, "Cable. Wi-Fi. No dad. Slumber parties. No curfew. *Liquor Cabinet.*"

"What are you up to? Spill it!"

"We've got to get rid of Turlow," said Blake.

"You mean that walking talking mammogram machine? If he hugs me one more time,"

"The very same!" said Mia, folding her arms across her chest.

"But we can't do it without Uncle Carson," continued Blake. "Which means we have to go to the Caribbean and find him."

"So, what do I have to do with it?"

"We can't leave Nanna alone with Turlow. He'll take over completely. So we're taking them with us. But Nanna won't go unless we have a reliable house sitter."

"Oh, I get it. This is about getting me back for Europe."

"We need you to help us save your Nanna from that gold-digging bazoobie-buster," said Mia.

"Maybe she doesn't want to be saved. Ever think about that?" said Agatha. "Maybe you just conned them into taking you to the Bahamas, and you're..."

"Your inheritance is on the line, sis," said Blake.

"Say what?"

"You didn't notice the shiny new stove in the kitchen?" said Mia. "Scandinavian. Has two little ovens you can't even get a cookie sheet into."

"Ten thousand bucks. Turlow buffaloed her into buying it," added Blake.

"Brand new Buick Enclave," Mia continued. "Forty thousand."

"Sleep Number bed," said Blake. "Another ten thousand. King size. But Nanna sleeps alone. Starting to get the idea? Mom doesn't want to interfere. Mr. Gunn tried to talk to her. Mia, Serena, and I have all tried. The more things we point out, the more she just digs in her heels and pushes us away. She thinks we're out to get him. I couldn't stand it anymore. I had to move out."

Agatha frowned, doubtfully. "My inheritance?"

"We both get a quarter of the estate," Blake explained. "If there's anything left."

"We've already cleared it with your mom," said Mia.

Agatha, still suspicious, thought about it. Yes, she'd noticed the stove and the car. Two weeks of freedom and a slumber party on a ten thousand dollar bed were tempting. "Sell me your birthright. Sell me your birthright and I'll do it."

"Fine. It's yours."

Mia was astonished. "Wait, Blake!"

"I'm heir to the Gunn estate, Mia. How much more do I need? This is about Nanna."

"Swear to me!" demanded Agatha.

"I swear."

"Swear to God."

"I swear to you, Agatha Barber, in the name of Yahweh my God, that I give you my inheritance from Nanna Urquart. Mia is my witness."

"What if you can't find Carson?" taunted Agatha. "What if you can't get rid of Turlow?"

"What if my head explodes and your ass catches fire?" Blake replied. "It won't matter."

Mia opened the slatted door. "Thank you, Agatha. You may go now," she said, in that polite tone that really meant *get lost, you little witch!*

Agatha stepped into the noisy galley, feeling satisfied. She paused, and looking over her shoulder said, "By the way, I'm glad you didn't get hurt when you went through the ice."

8

Serena timed their arrival at Indianapolis International Airport perfectly. On the way, she had managed to stop at every red light that Turlow drove through, putting a good fifteen minutes between them. She dropped the kids off in front of the gleaming new mid-field terminal. They hurried past the ticket counters into the big circular plaza. Mia spotted Clarissa and waved energetically. Turlow, trailing her with a heavily laden baggage cart, shrugged impatiently and lifted one hand. They caught up to them at the entrance to the security checkpoint.

"Hey guys!" said Mia.

Before Clarissa could smile, Turlow barked, "Where have you been? Our flight is boarding in a matter of minutes! We still have to go through security. And *where* is your luggage?"

"Serena's parking the car," said Blake. "She wanted us to make sure you knew we were here."

Mia's cell phone chimed, she answered. "Speak, woman! Where? You idiot! Can you find it? Honestly, Serena if… Yes, I'll be right there." She gave Blake a look of disgust. "She lost a contact lens."

"Oh good god!" said Turlow. "If we miss our flight because that ditzy…"

"Brett!" Clarissa scolded. "I'm sure it will be alright. You two hurry back to the car. Mia, help your aunt find her lens. Blake, you get the luggage and get through security ASAP."

"Yes ma'am!" he nodded.

31

"You can board without us, it'll be okay," said Mia, as she took Blake's arm and hurried off at a trot.

When they got to the car, Serena was putting on lipstick in the rear-view mirror, humming merrily. "Did they buy it?"

"So far, so good!" said Mia.

"What did he call me this time?"

"Things even I've never thought of."

"You're too cute, Hunny Bunny." Serena glanced at the dashboard clock. Time for phase two!"

Mia dialed her phone. "Shay-Lo! Do your duty!"

Turlow scoured the boarding area with angry eyes as they shuffled through the line for Flight 714. A buxom young woman caught his attention. She waved anxiously, and jogged over from the restaurant across the concourse. He watched her bounce the whole way.

"Clarissa! Mrs. Urquart!"

"Shay, how nice to see you!" said Clarissa. "Working today, I see?"

"Yes ma'am. Mia just called me. She wanted me to make sure you catch your flight. Serena thinks she scratched her eyeball. She may need to see a doctor. They'll be on the next flight to Miami. They'll meet you at the cruise ship."

Turlow sighed with dramatic disgust. "That woman!" Someone cleared their throat in line behind them. "We're holding up traffic," he said. "Just get on the blasted plane."

***

It was 2:30 AM when Blake, Mia, and Serena stepped out of the Luis Muñoz Marin International Airport and into the balmy Puerto Rican night. Serena observed aloud to the agreement of her wards that the roof of the gleaming glass terminal looked like a flying saucer. They boarded a shuttle bus and headed for the waterfront Sheraton, in Old San Juan. Serena had reserved a three-room suite, sparing no expense—which was totally Serena. Blake stood on their balcony looking out at the festive harbor, full of gargantuan cruise ships and small fishing boats all decked out in Christmas lights. His winter blues began to warm to a rosier hue. The flight down was his first time on an airplane of any sort, and he thoroughly enjoyed it—adding flying lessons to his mental bucket list.

They hit the sheets and didn't rise until eleven. Serena was the last up. She meandered puffy-eyed into the living room in her robe to find Blake sunk deep into an overstuffed chair, glued to his tablet. Mia was on the phone. She drummed her fingers on the table and scowled at the ceiling.

Serena ambled into Mia's line of sight. "Hunny Bunny, will you tell room service to send up some cucumber slices for my eyes?"

Mia held up a silencing hand and shouted into the phone. "Thanks very little, Layton! No, you shove it!" She slammed the handset down on the cradle.

"Who was that, Bunny?"

"An old friend of the family."

"Her dad's reputation precedes us," said Blake.

"And that was the last bare-boat charter I could find on the east end of the island," Mia griped. "They all know the name Devlin."

"Why the east end, Bunny?"

"'Cuz that's the end with all the American islands, duhhh! We came here to find Carson, remember? Tux ain't got no passport—kinda limits us to American destinations."

"Oh," said Serena, a little baffled. "You were serious about that? Wouldn't you rather see the old city, and El Morro, then hit the beach?"

"*Really*, Serena?" said Mia in disbelief. "What the heck did you think we came down here for?"

Serena wilted a little, and pulled her robe close around her neck. "Well, I just thought it would be nice to escape the Hoosier Tundra and get you guys away from old Turdlow for a while."

"Then why did we bother to ship Turdley and Claire off to the Yucatan?"

"When people spend time with each other outside of their normal context, they begin to see each other for what they really are. I thought that a cruise would give him plenty of rope to hang himself with, while we have fun in the sun."

"O! M! G! That's Hurricane Serena for you—sucks you into the whirling vortex of her life and it's anybody's guess where you'll land."

Blake came to Serena's rescue, before Mia could finish shredding her feelings. "You know what, Serena? You're right! What are the chances we're going to find Carson today, anyway? Mia, why don't we do the town this afternoon, then plan our mission tonight? Tomorrow *I'll* make the phone calls, and we'll rent our boat under Serena's name—no problem."

"There, see?" said Serena, perking back up. Now, can you get me those cucumbers?"

***

Florida sunshine glinted off the windows of the Carnival Cruise Lines terminal, as an official from the ship found Clarissa and Turlow casting uncertain glances at the crowd. He delivered the news that Clarissa's grandson had called to advise that there were "complications." He read from his clipboard: "Tell Nanna that we will meet her in Cozumel. Tell her not to worry, have a good time."

Turlow squinted toward the giant ship, and smiled craftily. "We're going to do just that," he said. "Aren't we Claire?"

***

In spite of the charm of Old San Juan, Mia remained sullen and crabby well into the afternoon. Serena feigned exhaustion after touring El Morro fortress, begging the kids to leave her in a little cafe where she could phone Clarissa, then poke around in a strip of quaint little shops. They wandered along narrow brick streets through canyons of ancient Spanish houses with their little balconies and friendly pastel facades. They came out into a wide intersection, one corner of which was shaded by a small deciduous tree. Its branches hung over a sculpture in a fountain—three Taíno natives gracefully drowning one Spanish bishop named Salcedo.

"Well," said Blake, "that sort of sets the tone, doesn't it?"

Mia gazed around the square, and finally broke her pensive silence. "I didn't want to say it, Blake, but it's going to be like totally impossible to find your uncle."

"I know," he said with an air of resignation. "And Turlow is going to clean Nanna out. I'll have to go back to Gunn's. And you'll go off to college. And that will be that."

She studied the statue for a long moment. "What are we doing here, Blake?"

He smiled. "The question is what do you *want* to do here?"

She sighed, almost huffed. "I've got so much crap I need to get done for school, and now Serena…"

"Mia I am so sick of snow, and ice, and cold, and school, and not seeing you. You know there's a bio-luminescent bay over on Vieques? It…"

"Glows when you splash. Yes Mr. Professor, I was there when I was eight."

"I want to see that. And frigate birds, and dolphins, and go snorkel the reefs. Don't deny it. You know you do too."

"Come on. We better go find Serena before she buys up all the 'Three Kings' figurines on the island."

9

Blake thought the three hour technical lecture and chart debriefing at the Punta Alegria Marina would never end, but he had to admit that it was important information. He had no idea that ocean cruising would be so different. *A boat's a boat,* he'd thought. True: but the ocean, he learned, with its one-way currents, and steady breezes that rarely changed direction, was not in any way like Highland Creek Reservoir.

Serena fidgeted the entire time. Mia was sure she was going to open her mouth and spill the beans that *she*—the responsible party—wasn't going along for the ride. Even if she didn't blow it, Mia worried that someone at the marina would surely recognize the name Devlin on the crew list and liability paperwork, then all bets would be off.

A decade before, her father had attempted to establish a resort and yacht chartering company of his own on the east coast of the island. When the venture began to fizzle, he resorted to his usual strategies of corruption and treachery to win the day. But he lost it, and no one in the boat or resort business from Punta Tuna to Cabo San Juan had ever forgotten the name Devlin. Miraculously, through a few monumentally severe looks from Mia, Serena managed to keep mum.

They finished stowing groceries and gear aboard the brand new thirty-five-footer, hugged a teary Serena, then started the engine.

"Cast off fore and aft!" called Blake.

"Are you talking to me?" said Serena, with a surprised look.

"Untie the spring lines," growled Mia, "and throw them on the damn boat."

"What are those, Bunny?"

"Here, I gotcha!" called a lanky, fellow hurrying up the dock. He freed the lines and tossed them onto the boat. "Lemme help you aboard!"

"Oh no, hunny, I'm not going!"

"Oh crap," said Mia. "Hit it Tux, before it's too late!"

Blake throttled up, and they pulled away from their berth.

"Bye, kids! Have fun! I love you!" Serena waved as Blake steered *Chupacabra* around the end of the pier and down the long jetty, their inflatable dinghy trailing behind.

"They look like they know what they're doing. I mean, what could go wrong on a boat named *Chupacabra*?" said the man. "Was that your sister?"

Serena blushed, and gave him a knowing, if not gratified smile. "Aren't you *precious*, hunny? That's my niece and her boyfriend. And who are you?"

"Sorry! Everybody calls me Newly."

"Well, Newly, I'm Serena, and I've got to get going. If the charter agent finds out I'm not on that boat, I'm in big trouble."

"I hear ya! Say, I need a lift to Old San Juan. Not headed that way are you?"

"You get me past the charter desk, and I'll take you to dinner in Timbuktu!"

***

Blake took a deep breath of salt air and exhaled. It felt good to be on the water again, to be gliding over the waves on this deep blue day with the dolphins racing alongside like gray torpedoes, and the gulls and the frigate birds, and that beautiful young woman with the long black curls who was finally beginning to smile.

Mia trimmed the sails. "East and a point southeast, eight miles to Isla de Vieques, Tux!"

She slouched on the high-side bench, braced her feet on the helm column, and spread her arms out on the rail. As the coast of Puerto Rico receded behind them, and Vieques began to rise ahead, Blake gazed into the distance and smiled placidly.

"It's good to see the horizon again," he declared.

"How's that?"

"It's been two years since we saw the horizon on the *Badger*. We've been so busy with work and school. It's like I don't even remember who I am. I've felt so hemmed in. So landlocked."

"Well, it's wide open out here buddy!"

Blake laughed to himself, and grinned.

"What?" said Mia. "What'd I say?"

"I was just remembering Fiona."

"OMG don't even say her name, or she'll magically appear!"

"Fiona!"

"Stop it! Somehow that kid has got to be related to Haraguchi."

"I still think you should have kept up with the Karate."

"I told you. I'll never use it again. Not after what happened."

"Fiona! Fiona!"

"I might make an exception for you, idiot!" she laughed, sliding back to where she could kick him.

***

Newly guided Serena around the back of the Marina's main building, hustling to a hedge at the far end. She let him lead, relieved that he didn't seem to notice that she had her right hand wrapped firmly around a can of pepper spray, and her left thrust deep in her shoulder-bag, clutching a mini stun-gun she'd purchased in the hotel gift shop, of all places. He dropped to one knee and reached between the bushes and the wall. Serena backed up and prepared for action. She liked Newly and thought he was probably harmless, but you could never tell. He extracted a well-worn duffel bag and, to her great delight, coaxed a scarlet macaw out of the hedge. She relaxed and holstered her weapons.

"'Rena, meet Nebuchadnezzar!" beamed Newly. ""Nebby for short." The bird squawked, stretched his wings and set straight to putting his brilliant red, blue, and yellow plumage in order.

"Does he talk?"

"Does he ever! You speak French?"

"Mais oui!"

"Then I apologize in advance."

They hurried on to Serena's rental—a red SUV—and departed for San Juan.

"Where're the kids headed? Culebra?"

"Oh, they're just cruising around. Probably spend a day or two on Vieques. Blake's looking for his uncle. He's on a schooner down here, somewhere. It was a nice excuse to get away from the snow and ice."

"Missing uncle? Schooner you say?"

Something tweaked Serena's intuition. Something in his voice sounded a little too... excited, a little too interested.

"Oh I don't know. It may be a catamaran. Tell me about yourself, Newly Dewly. What were you doing all the way over in Punta Alegria?"

"Uh, well, I signed on to crew a big yacht to Spain. They never showed. So the kids are cruising? It's not far to Vieques. They'll have a nice sail."

Satisfied that she'd put him on the defensive, Serena pivoted the conversation completely. "Let me hear Nebby say something!"

"Oh, no 'Rena you don't..."

"Bon Jour, Nebby! Quel beaux oiseau, n'est-ce pas?"

The macaw, who had been happily enlarging a hole in Newly's duffel, exploded with a barrage of profanity that made Serena laugh so hard that she could barely keep the SUV between the lines. She kept him going all the way back to the city, dropping her passengers off at a little park along the shore.

Newly leaned in the open passenger window, and ran his fingers through his windblown hair. "I'd sure like to see you again, 'Rena. Where you stayin'?" he said, with a smile of hopeless resignation.

"Tell you what. I'll pick you up here tomorrow at a quarter 'til six. We'll go somewhere nice and chit chat."

"Really?"

She gave him an inviting look. "Really! Be ready to talk. I want to know *all* about Newly Dewly!" Serena drove away, chiding herself for mentioning anything about Carson and his boat. She wanted to know why Newly seemed so interested. Still, beyond this mystery, she thought there was something attractive, even endearing about him. He was a 'fixer-upper' to be sure, but that was her favorite kind of project. She would just have to get to know him and his uproarious bird a little better.

Once Serena's SUV had vanished in the distance, Newly dug his phone out of his ratty duffel bag and texted as fast as his thumbs could fly. His message was received far across the Caribbean, on the island of Trinidad and Tobago, in the opulent private lounge of a popular night club. The petite ebony proprietress glanced at the reply, then speed dialed. While it rang, she swiped through pictures of several Latina women and a little girl; each fettered, and much the worse for wear.

"What's up, Lulu? It's P.K… Don't screw with me, boy-toy; let me talk to the Man…" Her voice was silky, and filled with bored disdain. "Hallo Boss. I like the new merchandise, but you're keeping me waiting. When do I take possession? You always say that. Listen, I've got some news. Newly picked up an easy mark in Puerto Rico. She's got kids with her. They're looking for a missing uncle and… his *schooner*! They're headed to Vieques. I have a hunch they'll settle there. Shall I release the hounds? Okay, then. I'll send Arco. Au revoir."

P.K. swiped through her contact list, and selected another. "Arco, sober up and get over to Vieques. Time is of the essence. You're looking for two American teenagers—a boy and a girl. They chartered a sail boat from Punta Alegria. They're searching for their uncle. He works a schooner. The boss wants you to keep an eye on them. Find out anything you can by whatever means necessary. I want an appraisal of the girl. Keep me posted."

***

It was an easy passage on a beam reach. The wind was pushing eighteen knots from the northeast, and the swell was manageable. *Chupacabra* cleared the long reef at the west end of Vieques in under two hours. Blake brought the boat hard onto the wind. Another hour of spirited tacking, and they found themselves in Esperanza Bay. Only a few other yachts were moored nearby.

He brought her straight into the wind, and fired up the engine. Mia started the windlass motor, dropped the anchor, and yelled back to him. He throttled down slowly, and let *Chupacabra* drift backwards as she watched the windlass feed anchor chain out of a port in the deck. "Okay, that's about eighty feet worth!" she called. Blake killed the engine. Mia furled the genoa sail, and returned to the cockpit. "If I remember, the agent said the holding ground really sucks, here."

"Seems solid enough to me."

"Give it a half hour," she replied, as they lowered the mainsail and lashed it to the boom. "We'll wake up in Venezuela tomorrow, if we're not careful."

They boarded the gray dinghy, fired up the little outboard, and motored over to the forlorn town pier. Blake had climbed out, and was mooring the dinghy to the dock with a chain when a young man came running down the planks, screaming angrily in Spanish.

"Look out, Tux! The natives are hostile!" shouted Mia.

He let go of the dinghy, and stood up as the assailant rushed toward him. The young man wore an eye-patch, and seemed livid beyond the capacity for rational thought. Blake caught a little about 'stupid Americanos,' and a lot about cutting. Blake snatched his six-inch spring-assisted knife out of his pocket, whipped it open and assumed a defensive stance. The lunatic stopped well short of the gleaming blade and threw his hands in the air. The screaming didn't stop though. Blake understood enough of his raving Spanish to get that the problem lay in the fact that he, and possibly his mother, was a "damn stupid Americano Gringo bastard pirate," and not a local fisherman, which meant that he had to tie up on the *other* side of the empty dock.

Blake folded his knife and clipped it on the rim of his pocket. His remaining adrenaline turned to anger. He seized the erstwhile harbor master with a move he'd learned from Sensei Haraguchi, chucked him headfirst into the water, and shouted "You are not the only one with rage issues!"

"Holy Crap!" shouted Mia. "Blake, get in! The anchor's pulling!" She buzzed the dinghy in a tight arc past the end of the pier, and he jumped in. They ran *Chupacabra* down as she drifted away with the wind and current. They boarded and fired up the engine, and while Mia steered them back towards Esperanza, Blake thumbed through a cruising guide. He directed her around the little islands of Cayo Real and Cayo de Tierra, then on into the welcoming half-moon expanse of Ensenada Sun Bay.

"We should've started here," said Blake. "It's good ground all around, and you can pull your dinghy right up on the beach."

"What's it like on the far side?"

He checked the navigation chart. "Fairly shallow, pretty far out. Around the middle it's two fathoms at Mean Low Water, some places three. It's hit or miss. But there's a super shallow spot right in the middle of the east end." He climbed up on the cabin top. "Probably that really light blue area over there."

"I see it. Good job! Let's go in another two hundred yards and drop the hook!"

The anchor bit solidly, and Blake let a good hundred and thirty feet of chain pay out before he told Mia to cut the motor. Suddenly there was no sound but the breeze, the lapping of the sea against the hull, and the quiet clink of the spinnaker halyard against the mast. Blake gazed in wonder. The sea was the most amazing blue he had ever seen. Along the beach, tall palms stuck up above the surrounding deciduous trees, giving the forest an unkempt look. They stared at each other blankly for a moment, then started to smile.

"Are we there yet?" said Blake, hopping down into the cockpit.

"Yeah, I think we are," she said with a laugh of relief. She slipped around the chrome steering wheel and threw her arms around him. "Get the snorkel stuff. Let's check the anchor set," she said, giving him a good squeeze.

"You say the most romantic things," Blake replied.

"That's the rule, bud. It doesn't get serious 'til you're out of school."

They jumped off the bow and followed the anchor chain hand-over-hand, twelve feet to the bottom. The set was good—the anchor was buried deep and wouldn't drag in anything less than a gale. Mia tapped Blake's shoulder and pointed to a spot in the short sea grass just ahead. He scanned the bottom as they swam to it, but there didn't seem to be anything there. The slightest shift in the sand caught his attention, and then he spotted two big, yellow eyes atop an odd tan lump. They edged closer until a small octopus lifted itself from the sea bed and darted off, settling twenty feet away. Mia signaled him to surface, and his lungs happily agreed. He emerged into the sun and air with an exuberant shout. "That was totally worth the whole trip! We have got to get some scuba gear!"

"You gonna talk, or you gonna swim?" Mia put her snorkel back in her mouth and started off across the surface. As they headed in the direction of the shallow spot, the grass beds gave way to an alien landscape of black rock and fans of coral in purple and yellow. Schools of bright fishes of every color and shape scattered before them, as Mia pointed out sea stars and a puffer fish. Just when Blake thought it couldn't get any better, he was startled by a huge black thing covered in white spots as it swooped across the bottom like an enormous bird of prey. He realized it was a spotted eagle ray. He squeezed Mia's hand and shook his head in sublime awe. She understood, squeezed back, and winked behind her goggles.

By the time they got back to the boat, Blake could hardly haul himself up the swim ladder. The sun hung low over Monte Pirata at the far end of the island, throwing long shadows of palms down the strand. Three horses stood on the beach and considered, at a distance, a small clutch of tents which had just appeared on the sand near the trail to Esperanza. The largest horse put her nose to the ground and sniffed for clues, while her mate kept a wary eye out for the intruders who had so rudely obstructed their customary route. A short pot-bellied Spanish pony, with a long shaggy blond mane, stamped a hoof impatiently and snuffled as if she had already decided on a less-than-courteous course of action. The big horse decided not to risk it, so they took the long way to town.

Blake and Mia retired to their separate cabins to change into long-sleeved jackets and jeans, after which they rubbed liberal quantities of insect repellent on each other's faces and hands. It was a short hop to shore in the dinghy. They dragged it up to a lone palm not too far from the water, and started to chain both boat and motor to the tree.

"What's this guy want?" said Mia. A man in a red polo shirt and neatly pressed khaki shorts was strolling toward them in the fading golden light.

"He doesn't look local," replied Blake. "As long as he doesn't tell us this is his bay, I'm all good."

"Evening, kids! It's like the Garden of Eden, isn't it?" said the man, as he came within speaking distance.

"Don't know," replied Mia. "Haven't seen any serpents. Yet."

A little twitch at the corner of the man's smile was the only indication he'd felt the jab. "Name's Joseph Huckey," he said, extending a hand. "Louisville, Kentucky."

"Blake and Mia, from Indiana," said Blake, as he stretched over the dinghy to accept the handshake.

"Why that makes us neighbors! Tell me, how do you pronounce the capital of Kentucky. Loo-ee-ville, or Loo-uh-vull?"

"Frankfort," answered Mia, without the slightest hint of amusement.

"Very good!" he chuckled, warily. "You're taking kind of extensive precautions here. Expecting trouble in paradise?"

Mia pulled the dinghy closer to the tree, to give Blake a few more inches of slack. "Considering that our welcoming party amounted to Quasimodo on crack, we decided not to leave it to chance."

Blake closed the combination lock. "Guide books say that there is literally a thief behind every bush."

"Well, I take everything those books say with a grain of salt. We trust the Lord to watch over our tents."

"Your first time in the Caribbean?" said Mia.

"Matter of fact it is. I'm leading a youth evangelistic outreach team. The kids are all in town."

"Well, the wise man sees danger and hides himself," Blake said. "But the simple pass on and are punished."

"Good luck!" said Mia. "C'mon Tux. Nice to meet you, Mr. Hickey." She hooked her elbow in Blake's, and they headed toward town.

"It's Huckey. But, don't worry, I get that a lot. Say, son, you seem to know your scripture. You mind if I walk with you? I'd like to meet your parents."

"Spectacular," said Mia. "They're about two thousand miles that-a-way."

"You say your folks aren't here? You kids aren't on that boat alone are you?"

"We're Amish. Ever hear of bundling?" said Blake, noticing the hoof prints in the sand. "She sleeps in the bow cabin, I sleep in the aft cabin, with bulkheads and two doors between us. If it's any of your business."

"Well, I think you know the Bible says we're to avoid even the appearance of sin."

"No, it says the appearance of *evil*," returned Blake, as they detoured around the tents.

"What's your uncle always say about that, Tux? Error is what the Bible defines as wrong; sin is whatever the preacher and his wife don't like."

"Young lady, it is my duty before the Lord to warn you that the wages of sin is death!"

She spun in her tracks and took two steps toward him. Huckey froze. "Then cast the first stone, and collect your pay, Jojo!"

"Looks like you've had visitors," said Blake, as she stormed back past him toward the trail. Indeed, the flap on each of the twelve tents was wide open. Blake zipped his jacket as Huckey yelped and slapped himself on the neck. "Enjoy the sand flies!" They left the pastor to contemplate camp security.

After a brief trek across a wooded trail, they emerged at the end of the main drag, in front of a bizarre white building. It stood like a curvaceous, four-story chunk of coral. The upper two levels were completely peppered with holes, and glowed like a lantern in the balmy night. Music and the smell of cooking drifted down from the open second level.

"That's new," said Mia.

"Looks like," Blake began to say.

"The last place they'd allow Crackamodo. Let's go."

The second level of the hotel was a wide-open concrete space with tables, and a huge planter of cacti below an oval skylight. Just beyond the free standing bar, people were mingling on a long balcony. Strings of holiday lights spiraled up supporting pillars throughout the room, and a silver Christmas tree decked out in shiny blue ornaments stood near the entrance. Mia chose a table near the cactus garden, just in case anyone needed to be pitched into it. As they perused their menus, Blake began people-watching. A middle-aged couple at a little table on the far edge of the balcony caught his attention. They were laughing raucously and flicking bits of their dinner at each other. The woman had clay-red hair; the man wore an ample and well-curled handlebar mustache, and a mischievous twinkle in his eye. His twang was unmistakably Anglo-American. Blake thought the man would have looked natural in a cowboy hat and spurs. There were three empty champagne bottles on the table between them. The man stopped a pretty, young black woman with intricately braided hair on her way to the bar, and flirted with her. A waiter finally showed up at Blake and Mia's table, visibly annoyed, and definitely local.

"Buenas noches," said Blake. "Por favor, me gusta…"

"You don't have to show off. I speak English," said the young man, casting a red-hot glance at the noisy gringos on the balcony.

"But, Señor, we are from Tierra del Fuego!" Blake contested.

"Yeah? You just kiss it, Fuego. Now what do you want?"

They ordered two whole rotisserie chickens and salad. The waiter stalked off. The woman with the terra cotta hair took her last gulp of bubbly and flashed the black woman the kind of polite 'I-hate-you' smile that Mia often used. Blake's eyes stayed on the black woman as finally she swished over to the bar. The odd couple rose and all but staggered out. While Mia inhaled her dessert, budin de guayaba, Blake munched his churros and kept a furtive eye on the ebony goddess at the bar.

"Hey!" Mia barked, kicking him in the shins. "Show's over! Let's get back to the boat." They had barely crossed the street before they heard the rowdy couple from the restaurant yelling and laughing on the fourth floor. One of the Swiss cheese window louvers flew open and expelled a large floor vase, its contents on fire. It smashed on the pavement, belching flaming rolls of toilet paper and the smell of rum in every direction. The woman was laughing uncontrollably in the depths of the room. The mustachioed man appeared in the window, shook his fist in the air, and shouted "Remember Albizu Campos!"

"Any Questions?" said Mia.

"So that's why everyone hates Americans," Blake mused.

***

Blake slumped on the built-in couch in *Chupacabra's* saloon, hands on his belly, already beginning to doze. Mia sat in the wrap-around booth and put her head down on the table.

"I can't believe it's eight thirty and I'm ready for bed," he said.

She groaned, affirmatively.

"I freaking hate Pemberton Academy," Blake yawned.

"Where did that come from?"

"The bottom of my heart. I thought it would be cool people who were interested in learning and doing cool stuff. Turned out to be a bunch of phone-addicted Emo kids and vicious Wiccans. And Mr. Ranski's in cahoots with Turlow. I know it."

"Takes all kinds." She got up, slogged into the forward cabin, and rummaged in her backpack.

"And that Hickey, guy," he continued. "You know, I knew a girl who got pregnant at Bible Bowl. Snuck away during lunch."

"People will find the opportunity if their minds are set on it," she replied through a luxurious stretch.

"Not like we haven't had plenty of opportunity, already." He paused, then added impishly "but there's still plenty more…" Blake heard her flop on the bed and slam the narrow cabin door shut with her foot.

Mia turned on her phone and dialed Serena. It went straight to voicemail. "Hey, it's me. We made it. See you in St. Croix on Tuesday. Do NOT forget to call Clarissa." She hung up and let a moment pass, before calling, "Good night, Tux!" But he was already asleep.

10

Arco Boerman steadied himself and simmered impatiently as the small motorboat drifted toward the town of Isabel Segunda, which sat like a glowing crown on the otherwise dark brow of Vieques.

The trip from St. Thomas Island, a mere forty miles, had taken eleven queasy hours. He hated ocean travel and would have flown, but the next plane out of West Charlotte Amalie wasn't until 9:30 that morning. Still, he grumbled to himself, it was better not to have your name on a manifest, or face on a security video when doing this sort of errand; though at the moment he thought it would have been worth the risk.

His courier, seemingly the only one available on such short notice, was a withered fisherman, wary of pushing his motor or his seamanship too hard. Right off the bat they had to turn back, as old Lionel Joseph had forgotten to fuel up. Then, just to be on the safe side, he insisted on leap frogging to Savana Island, and then across to Culebrita Island, before making the "big hop" south to Vieques. How he had ever made a career as a casual smuggler was beyond Arco. It was on "the big hop" that the motor conked. When Lionel Joseph pointed to the twinkling lights of Isabel Segunda and cheerfully averred that the wind would blow them across to their destination, Arco had come within a hair's breadth of shooting him in the stomach and throwing him overboard. Half a day lost. It was the sort of thing he'd come to expect, lately.

The Caribbean branch of the nameless criminal organization Arco served had seen better days. The ascendant Suiza Cartel had pushed them almost completely out of Venezuela, and continually pressured their remaining narcotics trade in the Dutch Antilles. Local gangs chipped away at their manpower in The Leeward Islands. Now a phantom was swallowing up the convoys that managed to escape their vindictive competitor. The last disappearance, fifty miles off the coast of Barranquilla, Columbia, had consumed twenty of their experienced guerrillas, along with nine boats. A loss they could hardly afford. His employer, who hadn't set foot in the Caribbean in years, simply compensated by scaling back on narcotics production, while shifting the focus of operations in the region to human trafficking. It wasn't like him, at all. The boss had gained a chilling reputation among his adversaries in the old-order cartels through small but demonstrative personal acts of such extreme horror that they had nick-named him "The Assyrian." But times had changed. Recent years had seen the rise of the "super cartels," whose ultra-violent, para-military syndicates posed a salient threat even to local law enforcement agencies. It was thought that the Suiza's were even assisting Islamic terror interests.

Arco had been the Assyrian's chief enforcer in the Virgin Islands and Puerto Rico, answering only to the man himself. But now, a failed "palace coup" in the home-office had prompted a reorganization of the local syndicate, and he suddenly found himself reporting to P.K.—that sawed-off little sadist down in Port of Spain, Trinidad. One day he was calling the shots, the next he was doing grunt work—kidnapping, drug muling, and tonight: hopping into a leaking tub to chase teenagers on American soil. He encouraged himself with the thought that this job would pay just enough to settle his debt with the boss and allow him to retire to South Africa.

Lionel Joseph bent over the outboard motor and ran his hands over its cold features, once again. Suddenly he slapped his knee and guffawed, then mashed one part into another and started it right up. "Spark wire! I knowed it!"

Arco fondled his pistol, and ground his teeth. The aged craft finally flogged toward the meager shelter of Puntas Mulas as the eastern sky turned pearly gray. Arco adjusted his shoulder bag and tried not to stagger as he made his way up the long, narrow dock that led to the cheery blue fish market, the

Pescadería Angelyz. Not three hundred feet away, the Vieques ferry was pulling out on the day's first run to Fajardo.

He headed straight for Super Mercado Morales and picked up a roll of antacids and a Three Musketeers candy bar. He cursed the place for being out of Dramamine, and dragged himself a few doors down to the Buen Provecho deli. Fresh-squeezed grapefruit juice with Tito's vodka would have to do. The place had been open ten minutes, and was already packed with tourists. Arco took his drink to a corner table, and tapped the contact on his phone for Punta Alegria Marina. "Hey Freddy, it's Arco. I'm calling in that favor you owe me. Charter left out of there yesterday. Couple of teenagers. Americans. Boy and a girl. Need anything you can get me. Sure. Ciao." Arco polished off his drink, lit a cigarette and headed for Coqui Car Rental.

***

Blake jolted awake and nearly rolled off the couch. In the haze of sudden wakefulness, he realized there had been a huge bang and a jarring impact. He heard a small motor humming away, then growing louder. Bam! Something slammed into *Chupacabra* again, and scraped down the length of her hull. Now he could discern hysterical shouting from outside, and from Mia's cabin. She bounded through the narrow door, still in her clothes from the previous night. "Don't just stand there, Tux! That stupid son of a…"

Bam! Another direct hit knocked charts and the guide book out of their rack. It sounded like the hull might have cracked.

"Booger eater!" She darted up the companionway and into the cockpit. Crackamodo was wheeling his small green and yellow fishing boat in a wide circle for another run. She grabbed the telescoping boat hook, extended it to its full eight feet and calculated where he would strike next. It looked like a straight drive amidships. Blake came on deck, wielding a fire extinguisher. Captain Crackamodo saw Mia moving to fend off his attack, and adjusted his angle for a shot at the bow. She sprinted to the fore deck, dropped to her knees and planted the hook in the nose of the marauding craft. She shoved with all her strength, deflecting the collision. Blake bellied over the bow pulpit and blasted the ranting Ahab with the fire extinguisher, as he passed below.

The tirade stopped suddenly as the chemical fog sucked the oxygen from his lungs. The little boat swerved away sharply as the skipper slumped over and collapsed.

"Oh, crap!" Blake said, and bolted aft. "Radio the police. I'm going after him."

"Wait!" Mia replied. She held her breath and watched the enemy vessel speed toward the preacher's tent city on the beach. "C'mon...C'mon jerk-wad!" she murmured nervously.

Blake pulled the dinghy up to the transom and prepared to jump in.

"Yes!" Mia shouted. "He's back up!"

Blake returned to the bow. Indeed, Crackamodo had resuscitated. Now enraged by the colorful circus of dome tents before him, he turned his wrath on the foreign encampment. A half dozen young evangelists and Huckey were already on the hot sand, anxiously watching the skirmish with *Chupacabra*.

"This may be well worth the price of admission," said Blake.

"Ain't it nice to see it happen to someone else, once in a while?" Mia was beginning to smile.

The wild-man beached his boat and leapt out. Quite a merry shouting, screaming game of chase ensued. The evangelistas fled before him seven ways and when there was nobody left to chase, he pulled up the poorly anchored tents and dragged them into the light surf. The ranting never stopped for a second. Satisfied with his handiwork, he climbed into his boat and headed back to Esperanza through a narrow break in the sand spit which connected Cayo de Tierra to Vieques Island.

***

Blake and Mia surveyed the damage from their dinghy.

"At least the hull's not cracked," he said, running his hand back and fourth across its mutilated surface. "Scuffed, scraped, gouged, and splintered, but not cracked."

Mia was on the phone with the police department in Isabel Segunda. "The Navy blew up his father's farm? I don't even know anyone in the Navy!" she shouted. "Who the hell is gonna pay for my boat? Local problem? The whole freakin' island is local! What do you mean, local problem?" The police officer hung up.

"Did you hear me say he didn't crack the hull? We're good."

"Get out of the way, so I can take pictures for the insurance claim," she snapped. "Why does this crap always happen to us?"

"You know there's a cafe right in the middle of this beach? Oh, wait. It doesn't open 'til eleven."

"Let's go into town and get breakfast," she snarled.

***

They chained the dinghy to their favorite tree and took pictures of it, just in case. Down the beach, Huckey and the young evangelistas were reclaiming their tents from the sea.

"Hey, Jojo! Mia sniped, as they passed by. "Why don't you cast the Devil out of that guy?"

"We tried. I don't think Satan could hear us, the way that fellah carries on."

Blake stopped. "I think the horses like to walk through here. Maybe that was what he was upset about."

"Those animals are just like the Canada geese back home," replied Huckey. "Can't let 'em boss you around."

"Except," Mia added, "maybe when the geese weigh a thousand pounds, each. C'mon, Tux!"

They passed a couple of girls under a palm tree, one comforting her distraught friend who was blubbering uncontrollably about thieves, maniacs, mongooses, and vampire flies from Hell. Mia couldn't resist, and declared, "You're not in Kansas anymore, Jojo!" as they walked on.

"Kentucky," he said, under his breath. "It's Joe Huckey, from Kentucky."

Down the main drag, Blake chose a colorful restaurant that was open for breakfast, which seemed to help Mia's mood. The sign, decked out in Christmas lights, announced that this was Santina's Mongo Mango. Blake tactfully asked the hostess about the excitable one-eyed fellow.

The hefty Viequense woman smiled softly. "You mean El Campeon?" She sat down with them. "How do you like our little island?"

"It's paradise. If you don't mind being attacked by maniacs," said Mia.

The woman looked her in the eye. "Well said! You know, they used to do bombing practice here on our precious Isla Nena? One time—it was Mother's day—everyone is having a picnic over in Sombe; you call it Sun Bay. Well, here come four warships from Europe, and they drop the anchors. Some of our men go out in their fishing boats and ask them to leave. You know the answer they get? The water cannons! But our people see they can't shoot straight down, so they get paint, and rocks, and take their boats out to fight back. We go under the water cannons and attack the big numbers on the nose of the ships, because we know if we can mess them up, they have to go back to base and get them repainted. El Campeon is a little boy in his daddy's boat. A little boy. The sailors throw beer cans, and junk from the ships. One of them throw a wrench. Hit him in the head. He lose the eye, and now always he is yelling. The ships pull up their anchors, and leave."

Mia felt a twinge of compassion as she pulled out her phone, and called up the pictures. "Would you like to see what he did to our ship, this morning?" She handed the phone to the woman. "How many more boats can you afford that happening to? You know how fast stuff like this gets around on the Internet?"

"We moved to Sun Bay hoping he'd leave us alone," said Blake. "I mean, we're really sorry about what happened to him, and all, but…"

The woman swiped through the photos, with a concerned look on her face. "Let me bring you breakfast. It's on Santina."

***

They strolled down the renowned Malecón, the brick-paved sea-side walk with its low, yellow balustrade, and wandered through a mini mall of tiny shops. Blake purchased a pair of fine choker necklaces of white shell, accented with turquoise. He fastened one around Mia's neck, and fluffed her hair out. She smiled and kissed him on the cheek. From there they ambled, hand-in-hand, to The Island Stables Tour Company and signed up for the next available private horseback excursion.

By the time they returned to the dinghy, more cruising boats had anchored in Ensenada Sun Bay, and the beach was beginning to buzz with activity, heralding the arrival of the Christmas crowd in earnest. They hoped this would provide El Campeon with more friends to play with. The little tent city was gone. In its place was churned up sand, hoof prints, plenty of manure and the strong odor of horse whiz. They checked on the boat, picked up some beach stuff, and passed the afternoon in the water.

***

Blake left Mia to loll in the gentle swell, and made his way back to their spot on the crowded beach. He took a long swig from his water bottle and saw through the plastic the distorted image of a man heading straight for him. He took one last gulp. The fellow wore faded yellow gym trunks, and his wrinkled orange shirt was wide open, revealing a gray, hairy chest.

"She's quite a looker, that girl of yours," he said, in a cheerful baritone voice.

"Hi!" Blake replied, cautiously. Over the last couple of years, he'd learned to ask himself what people wanted from him. This guy had a strange vibe, and a manner that seemed too loose; and he didn't really want to talk to him.

"McNeary's the name. Dr. Charles Tipton McNeary the Seventh."

"Seventh? Wow, is there an eighth?"

"Yup! And you can bet he hates me for it, too. She looks a little older than you."

"Yeah, she's eighteen. I'll be sixteen."

"When?"

"July."

"Aha! Not bad, you lucky dog! How are you going to keep her when she goes off to college?"

"By not keeping her waiting now. Nice to meet you." Blake started away, but McNeary followed, touching him on the elbow.

"Hold on, I didn't get your name!"

"My friends call me Tux, but you can call me Blake."

"Blake, Just humor me a moment, will you?"

"I don't know any jokes."

"Well played! Look, Blake, I'm a Psychologist. I have an interest in what people are thinking. Imagine this..." Something caught his eye in the distance. "Two fine specimens, over there!"

Blake looked over his shoulder. He was sure McNeary was talking about a pair of guys who'd just entered the water. "So, I was saying; when I saw you, I thought 'this kid's different. He's got to be interesting. I wonder if he'll talk to me. I wonder if he'll talk to the Sphinx.'"

"C'mon. What do you want?"

"Fair enough. Imagine you're on one of these glorious, white-sand beaches, the tropical breeze whispering in the palm fronds above, nothing but blue sky and sparkling, turquoise water. Suddenly, what materializes but a giant black cat with glowing emerald eyes, floating in the air before you! And the cat says "I am the ancient Sphinx! You may ask me one question, and I will answer truly. What will you ask the Sphinx?"

Blake resigned himself to the fact that answering was the only way to get rid of McNeary. He thought deeply. "What is my purpose in life?"

"Really? You'd ask *that*?" said McNeary. "Most people want to know who shot JFK, or if aliens are real, or if Elvis is still alive—crap like that. Why did you ask that question?"

"Because I get two answers for the price of one. It tells me if there really is a supreme being and what he expects me to do."

The old shrink was amazed. "Are you really that shrewd?"

"Apparently."

"So, we're having a crisis of faith? You look like a good Baptist boy, to me."

"Once upon a time. Does the Sphinx have an answer for me, or do I get my money back?" said Blake, heading for the water.

"No refunds!" McNeary waved. "I'll see you around, Blake!"

He waded back to Mia, who'd gotten roped into a game of catch with a group of tourist children. Blake joined in, and soon the kids were asking if they were married, and making facetious and daringly indecent inquiries. Mia answered by turning 'catch' into 'target practice,' and 'drown the rats.' It only spurred them on.

"You miss her, don't you?" said Blake.

"Serena? Don't be stupid."

"Fiona: Demon child of Manitowoc."

"I warned you about using the F-word!" She body-slammed him, and took him under. Together they swam after the children, pinching legs and tickling ribs. Blake began to have hope that she might actually have a good time on this vacation. They had lunch at the sea-side cafe, where several of the beach rats tracked them down and demanded to be taken on a hike across the sand-spit out to Cayo de Tierra. As they tramped across the narrow key, Blake couldn't help but wonder how El Campeon had gotten his fishing boat through the shallow gap in its middle, at low tide.

Blake and Mia led their troop through the lush forest, past the lagoon, to the seaward cliffs while fielding all of the random, personal, and generally inappropriate questions their little minds could dream up.

Blake was having fun, and suspected that Mia was secretly enjoying it, too.

"How can there be cactuses on an island? Cactuses are in the desert!" said a little girl named Bryn.

"I guess there are things about cacti you don't know," Mia replied.

"Are you gonna get married?" said Zander, a mouthy nine-year old.

"Are you gonna sprout wings?" replied Mia. "Cuz I'm gonna throw you off that cliff if you ask me that again."

"What if I ask it?" said Blake.

"Are you proposing?" said Chelsea.

"Not if he knows what's good for him," sniped Mia.

"Do you guys kiss and stuff?"

"Ugh! Why does everybody want to know that? Why are you so nosy?"

"Cuz you're all grown up and stuff. So do you guys, like, you know…do it?"

"Do you?" retorted Mia, with a shocked laugh.

"Noooo! I'm just a little kid!" blushed Chelsea.

"How come some people speak Spanish?" asked a boy named Bracken.

"There you go, Tux. Save us from this inquisition."

"Do you want the biblical model, or the Indo-European dispersion model?" Blake responded.

Chelly, the only local child in the entourage, spoke up as if giving a report in front of a class. "Viequense people speak Spanish because our island was taken from us by Christopher Columbus in 1493. The Spanish made our Taíno ancestors their slaves. Then in 1898 the United States came and took our Island from the Spanish, and turned our beautiful home into a bombing range."

"And there you have it!" chuckled Mia, "I think this kid is related to you, Tux."

"No, Santina is my grandmother. I live with her."

"I should have known."

Blake pointed suddenly and said, "Hey look at that bird! What kind of bird is that?"

"Friggit!" cried Zander. There was uproarious laughter from the children. "That's what my mom says all the time!"

"F-r-i-g-*A*-t-e," said Mia. "Check your spelling. There's an important difference."

"Don't look up with your mouth open!" quipped Bracken.

"Can we play on your boat today?" asked Bryn.

"Certainly not!" Mia objected.

"I think it's weird having Christmas stuff on palm trees," mused Bryn. "How can you have Christmas without snow?"

"Have you seen that crazy guy?" said Bracken.

"You should have seen it! Mr. Tux got him with a fire extinguisher!" bragged Zander.

"Damn, that's awesome!"

"No!" said Blake. "Not awesome! Dangerous. I could've killed him. And watch your mouth!"

"Is he like, a pirate, or something?"

"Chelly," said Blake, "would you please tell the others about El Campeon and the Battle of Sombe?"

"It was on Mother's Day, 1997," she obliged, "and all the Viequense people were on Playa Sombe for a celebration..." It was clear that the little girl had spent many an hour at the feet of her grandmother, soaking in the history of her people. The mini-lecture went on for five minutes.

"Jeez! Like how do you know all that stuff?" said Bracken. "Are you super smart or something?"

"My Abuela teaches me. She says if you don't know your history, how can you know who you are?"

"Something smells like Vicks!" piped Bryn.

Chelly spoke up. "That is the eucalyptus tree. Abuela uses the leaves for medicine."

"Well, well; Mr. Professor has a little sister," said Mia.

As the trail looped back around the big salt lagoon, a familiar chirping skipped across the water.

Mia looked back over her shoulder and said, "They're playing our song, Tux!"

"What's that supposed to mean?" said Zander.

"That's an osprey," said Blake. "Our kayak back home is named Cry of the Osprey. Chelly, does your Abuela have any words of wisdom about our friend, the osprey?"

"No. It's just a big damn bird."

***

Arco was over it. He had hit all the tourist attractions, checked the popular beaches, and finally slogged to the end of the mile-long Mosquito pier; though he knew that if the kids were still on the island, they would be in Esperanza. No one in their right mind anchored on the windward shore with the Christmas winds coming on. But he had to perform his due diligence. Finally, his phone rang—it was his contact at the marina. Serena Krakow, Blake Barber, and Mia Devlin from Indiana. *Chupacabra.* Destination St. Croix. He relayed the information to P.K. as the sun touched the distant hills of Puerto Rico, igniting the sky with a blaze of golden splendor. Arco set his heart on steak and lobster. Esperanza could wait until morning.

***

The courtyard at Santina's restaurant was filling up fast. The air was thick with the sound of happy chatter, and the smell of good food. Sunset over the sea was spectacular as always. Blake stole another glance at the young black woman, two tables away—the one he'd seen in the hotel, their first night on the island. He was sure she'd noticed, but he couldn't help himself. There was something compelling about her, yet he couldn't find the word for it. *Gorgeous? Definitely,* he thought. E*xotic? Oh, yes. Hot?* he dared. *Mia sooo hates that word!*

"So, you like the *dark* chocolate, eh?" said someone behind him. He turned to see McNeary settling in with his supper, on the other side of the big round table. "I prefer white chocolate with nuts. But dark without is fine in a pinch."

"What? Oh," he blushed. "Yeah uh, she's…"

"Buxom. Fertile. Forbidden. Why aren't you over there talking to her?"

"Because my girlfriend will be back from the restroom any minute." Then it occurred to him what McNeary had meant about the chocolate, and it totally grossed him out. He looked back at the ebony beauty. She saw him and tilted her head in that irresistible way, blinking languidly as she sipped at her straw.

"Good heavens, man! Go over there and talk to her! She's practically *begging* you!"

"I told you, Mia will be back anytime!"

"All the more reason! Blake you don't want your girl taking you for granted, do you? When I was your age, I had eight girlfriends up on Cape Ann, in one summer."

Mia had just come out of the dining room into the courtyard, and nearly collided with a young man returning from the bar with a drink. He stopped short, lifting his glass to avoid the disaster. She saw his face and was immediately captivated by his disarming…everything. His smile and bright blue eyes radiated good will from a boyish face framed by a short, immaculately shaped beard, and thick brown hair combed straight back. He was just a little taller, just a little older. His muscled arms were tattooed with Marine Corps insignias and romantic sentiments.

"Hey, sorry!" he grinned. "Almost got a tequila shower, there!"

"Uh, yeah!" she said, catching her breath, and blushing. "Ah,"

"I'm Jayce Mitchell. Can I buy you a drink?"

"Well, I'm…thanks, but um, well I'm, uh, with my boyfriend." She felt her cheeks flush and a wave of giddiness flutter through her body like a cloud of girlish butterflies.

Jayce looked over the patio crowd. "That kid over there? I thought he was your brother."

Mia grasped for focus. "That kid is *not* to be underestimated, let me tell ya."

"Sorry, what was your name?" Jayce beamed.

"Mia. Mia Devlin. You're welcome to join us." *Gosh, what am I saying? Get a hold of yourself, woman!* she thought.

McNeary was still urging Blake on, when he realized that Blake was staring straight past him. He looked over his shoulder and spotted Mia and Jayce chatting as they headed toward the table. Mia was positively incandescent.

McNeary looked at Blake and raised a gray eyebrow.

Blake got up and strode over to the woman's table. She smiled and stood up as he approached.

"Hi, I'm Blake Barber, from Indiana."

"Pleased to make your acquaintance! I'm Saranda Manchester, U.K. Call me Randi." Her heavy accent made it sound like she'd said 'surrender' and 'Wandy.' "It's so sweet of you to come over! Would you like to join me? We can wedge you in, here."

"Hey Tux, soup's on!" called Mia.

Saranda looked at him from under her long eyelashes and smiled mischievously. "Uh oh, you've been caught flirting, naughty boy! Sowwy!"

Blake felt completely out of his league, but he determined on the spot he wasn't going down in flames on *this* one. "Actually, I was just about to invite you to sit with us."

"I'd love to!" She collected her plate and water bottle and followed him.

Mia had just taken a seat. The rowdy couple from the hotel had joined their merry little ensemble. They appeared to be in their late forties; the woman had her clay-red hair pulled back in a short pony tail, her partner sported a comb-over and perpetual five-o'clock shadow.

"Everybody, may I introduce Saranda Manchester, late of the U.K.," Blake declared, gallantly.

The revolutionaries looked worse for wear, but the flaming-vase bomber revived a bit when he saw Saranda. "Oh, we know Miss Manchester!" he said, extending a hand. His wife's smile still said *Hello, slut-puppy*.

"This is my beloved, Mia Devlin; and…" he gestured to the chocolate connoisseur.

"Charles Tipton McNeary the Seventh," McNeary said, reaching to shake her hand.

"Gil Moreland! And this lovely creature is my spoose."

"Hi, Donna Viney. Nice to meet you."

Blake pulled the chair out for Saranda, then tossed Mia a smug smile. Jayce extended a hand over Mia's head and introduced himself.

Blake sat down between the young women. Saranda winked at Gil. "You two had quite your own little shindig, last night didn't you? You look like you slept on the beach."

"We did," said Viney, brushing a patch of sand off her husband's shoulder.

A passing acquaintance stopped and traded words with the Marine. He left the table for a couple of minutes.

"Haven't seen you kids, before," said Gil. "Where you from?"

"Indiana," replied Blake. "We're looking for my uncle Carson. He's dive master on the schooner Tarshish."

"Don't know any Carsons, do we babe?"

"Nope," said Viney. "Don't know anyone who wants to hire an Osteopath and a massage therapist, do you?"

"The hotel cut you loose?" said McNeary.

"Eh, they're stodgy like that," said Gil.

"Totally," said Mia. "Who doesn't love a big vase full of flaming toilet paper pitched out the window?"

"Indeed," said Viney, clearing her throat and looking like she still might be nursing a headache.

Gil turned his attention back to Blake and Mia. "So I'd say you're in college, and you're a high school sophomore?"

"Freshman," said Blake. Mia's a senior. She's going to IU for Nursing."

"Cool!" said Saranda. I'm in Pharm-D at Virginia Commonwealth."

Jayce returned and took his seat, scooting a little closer to Mia.

"I bet you're just back from someplace hot and dusty?" said Dr. Viney.

"Afghanistan," replied the Marine. "Two years."

"Kill anyone?" sniped Blake.

"Not today. But, the day ain't over yet," grinned Jayce. Mia gave Blake an annoyed glance.

"What of *your* future, Mr. Barber?" said McNeary.

"Ah, I'm undecided."

"The Coffin Pimp of Freeman is going to college," Mia interjected. "For business management, if nothing else."

"Coffin Pimp?" McNeary laughed. "See, I knew you had to be interesting!"

Blake's cheeks flushed, and he smiled sheepishly. "Yeah, I'm part owner in a cabinetry shop."

"Which hasn't turned out a cabinet in who knows when," said Mia. "He fell in with a family of Mexican coffin builders two years ago, and life hasn't been the same since. He can tell you anything you need to know about the green-burial industry. Drags me along to funeral trade shows. It's totally creepy."

"I do not! We ran a booth at one convention."

"Once was enough. And he's partner in a little marina, and he's heir to a small rental-property empire. Somebody please tell him he needs to go to school."

There was unanimous agreement. He was about to protest when a loud jabbering rose above the sound of the dinner crowd. El Campeon had entered the courtyard and was moving from table to table greeting familiar diners, getting louder as he went. Blake got to his feet. El Campeon caught sight of him and went ballistic. Blake thrust a hand into his pocket and whipped out his knife as his attacker started for him. El Campeon threw up his hands as soon as he saw the blade, and began a melodramatic retreat, wheezing and coughing. Someone from the kitchen rushed out and presented him with a cheeseburger platter heaped with fries. He gave the noisy interloper a hearty pat on the back, shuffling him out of the courtyard and on his way.

"I think that was my flippin' order!" said Mia.

McNeary laughed. "Did you see that? That kid was ready for action!"

Jayce flashed his sweet grin at Mia and lilted his eyebrows. Mia blushed.

"Will you stop!" she protested, barely suppressing a giggle.

Jayce shrugged his shoulders and flashed his perfect teeth again, adding a sly wink.

"Gosh!" she laughed, turning to Blake.

He tossed a dour glance at the Marine and sat back down, scooting closer to Saranda. She draped a languid arm across the back of his chair. Dr. Viney, taking note, subtly elbowed her husband.

Gil swallowed and cleared his throat. "You must've met Champ, before?"

Mia's rational side, happy to reclaim some dignity, asserted itself with natural surliness. "I don't even want to talk about it."

"See, the trick with Champ is you gotta make friends with him," said McNeary. "Offer him some cash to guard your dinghy or something. That's what most folks do."

"How about locking him up for everybody's safety?" said Mia.

Gil dabbed mayo off the ends of his mustache with a napkin. "This may still be the States, Miss Devlin, but they do things different, down here. Way different."

***

Serena took Newly to dinner at the Sheraton's restaurant and casino—the Sheraton across town from her own. Once seated and greeted by their waiter, she excused herself and flitted off to the ladies room, stopping at the bar on the way. She slipped her waiter fifty dollars, asking him to make sure that all of *her* drinks were made without booze, and that all of *Newly's* were given an *extra* shot. For all of her flightiness, she could carry herself with a regal air that was endearing, yet commanded respect. The bartender smiled professionally and assured her it would be done.

Serena rejoined Newly, deflecting his insistent questions until they were well into their entrees—and he was suitably sloshed.

"Hey, you know, on the way over here you were talking about the kid's uncle, well I was just thinking, uh, what was his name?"

"Lawrence. Lawrence Devlin," Serena lied, enthusiastically.

"That's right! What was the name of his boat, again?"

"You never told me what you do, Newly Dewly!" She waived to the waiter for another round.

"Beach bum. Got tired of the rat race. Dropped out. What'd you say he named the boat?"

"Butt Naked and Drunk."

"Riiight! How could I forget?" He took a swig of his fourth strong Long Island iced tea, and looked like someone had just hit him between the eyes with a pool cue. "Which ain't a bad way to end an evening, don't you think? It was a schooner, you say?"

"Trawler. Big ship. They make canned tuna, hunny."

"What do they call home port?"

"Something like Sugar Mama's Yacht Club."

"Rena, I know every yacht club in every gunk-hole in the Caribe, and there ain't no such place."

"Chigger Llamas?"

"Chaguaramas!" Newly cried, triumphantly. "But thass Trinidad and Tobago."

"You mean like the hot sauce?" she teased.

"Thass tobasco, silly!" They both laughed like lush drunks.

"No factory ships out of there. Just tankers."

"That's what I said wasn't it? Tanker?" replied Serena.

"I remember in the car. You said schooner."

"Nuh-uh. Tanker."

"You're the one who's tankered!"

"Where'd you get that awful bird, hunny?"

"Who, Nebby? He belonged to an old boss of mine. Taught him everything he knows. Then he got religion. Ya can't have the bishop over with an animal that talks like that."

"The bird got religion? Must be Episcopalian!" They roared with laughter.

"Wherever you find four Episcopalians you'll find a fifth!"

"I never seen a gal who could put it away like you, Rena; P.K. can drink anyone under the table, but she don't hold a candle to you."

"Is that you're girlfriend, hunny?"

"Hah! Business associate. Short little thing. She'd shank you... Shank you as soon as look at you... Wicked little... I gotta pee. You mind?"

"If you mean here, yes!"

He laughed through a hoarse cough.

"Goodness, Newly Dewly, that sounds terrible!"

"Nah, juss a li'l asthma."

Serena motioned for her waiter, and asked him to assist her sozzled date to the facilities.

"Call him a cab, would you, Señor? There's a little park near Puntas Las Marias. Drop him there," she smiled. "I'll see you tomorrow, Newly Dewly. One o'clock." Serena settled the considerable tab, basking in the admiration of the bartenders and wait-staff, then returned to her own hotel.

***

Blake lounged in the cockpit of *Chupacabra*, vacantly watching for the occasional meteorite to streak across the heavens. They reminded him of the night when Voodoo Jack's gang had attacked the old marina. Tripper Gunn stood in a second-story window of his home and blasted tracer rounds into the hood of their pickup truck, mere feet from where Blake had been standing. "Like the shimmering arrows of angels," he reminisced. That summer marked the beginning of seismic changes that rocked his world and overturned twelve years of childhood misery. He had left home, and never looked back. He had met Mia, and turned thirteen. He had found a family and a place where he belonged. Then things settled out and looked like they'd stay comfortably the same, forever—as long as he ignored the distant rumblings from the future. Their evening at the Mongo Mango was another loud peal, warning of yet another cycle of upheaval. He had the sinking feeling that the cosmic pendulum was about to swing back into negative territory.

Mia lay in her cabin. A small fan wedged in the forward deck hatch above her bed blew warm, salty air across her body. Blake had been silent almost all the way back to the boat. She knew she had hurt him, and completely validated all of his fears. She couldn't figure out what had come over her, or how Jayce had completely robbed her of her self-control with nothing more than his sweetly mischievous face. She had never had any trouble being a temperamental hard-ass, never allowed herself anything less than total control—until the moment she laid eyes on him, and discovered it was all self-delusion. *I was a total freaking idiot!* she thought. *And everyone knew it.* But she couldn't stop thinking about him. The vibe he gave off! The chemistry! He was a willing rogue, but not a wolf. A man full of life and experience, and very flexible discretion. She knew he could take her as far as he wanted, yet she trusted him. *So this is what college is going to be like? Oh. Damn.*

11

Ruman Varayev, the Chechen engineer, stood in the tiny space behind the helmsman in the sub's conning tower. "Alright, Zamir. Give her a little more throttle. Put one hand on the red valve-handles and get ready. Okay, ten degrees up on the stern planes, blow the ballast!"

The young man at the helm eased back on the control yoke, and pushed two red levers flat. A hissing sound filled the space, and the distinct feeling that they were surging upwards tickled the pits of their stomachs. Varayev held on, unlit cigarette protruding from a puckered smile as the blackness in the view ports became dark green, then glowing brown, then sudden brilliant blue as the bow broke the surface and lunged toward the sky. The sub made and impressive splash as it settled, putting flocks of frightened birds to flight, and startled caimans from their lazy repose on the muddy banks of the river.

"I want to do that again!" Zamir laughed loudly, his trainer proudly slapping him on the shoulder.

"Okay! Who said you suicide guys don't know how to have fun?"

Zamir turned and looked sharply at Varayev.

"Okay, I know. True believers. I'm infidel scum. Start the compressor, and get ready to vent the ballast tanks."

Zamir turned back to his instruments.

"When the air tanks are full, flood the ballast and take her down to twenty meters."

They repeated the operation four more times, and Zamir was smiling again. "I wish my little boy was here, on my lap!"

Varayev considered his response carefully. "He could throw the levers and blow the tanks. He would love it."

Ismael, the diesel mechanic appeared at the base of the ladder, and voiced his disapproval. "The commander would not be happy that we are playing in the water like children."

"Then screw him!" Varayev shouted, down the ladder. "What does he know? Did he build this damned sub! No, I did! We need to shake her down, see what comes loose. Zamir, how old are you?"

"Nineteen," he replied, taken aback by the engineer's sudden rage.

"Nineteen? Nineteen! Holy freaking crap!" he cried. "You can't even drive a car, I bet! Nineteen, and you're taking my freaking sub across a thousand miles of ocean? Do you even know how to use a compass? Let me off now! You're all freaking crazy!"

"You had best contain yourself when we meet the commander," scolded Ismael.

"Screw your commander! This boy is the one who knows how to drive the boat. He's your commander, idiot! What is your commander going to do if the GPS quits in the middle of the Caribbean?"

"*What* have you done to the GPS?" said Ismael, in an accusing tone.

"I haven't done anything to the GPS, you stupid Paki baboon! Things fail! Especially at sea, and always at the worst possible moment!"

"Allah will…"

Anticipating the impending blasphemy, Zamir throttled up full, pulled back hard on the yoke, and threw the valve levers forward. Ismael tumbled out of sight with a shout, as Varayev cursed and clung to the ladder for life. Zamir let out a whoop as the sub vaulted from of the murky Orinoco, and belly flopped on the surface, throwing a massive plume of spray.

In the late afternoon they reached the river village of Curiapo, running just below the surface. They had covered almost one hundred and fifty miles since leaving the warehouse pier in Guayana City. Varayev coached Zamir into a cove at the east end of a large island. "Where are you from?" he asked the young helmsman.

"Albania."

"What the hell, why don't you go to the States? Go to university?"

"Because," Zamir said, pausing a moment. "I serve a greater purpose. What purpose do you serve, Chechen?"

Varayev lit his cigarette and started up the ladder. He opened the hatch, and looked back down at Zamir. "My own. It's a shame. You're a damn good pilot."

The *Venganza* was towed backwards up one of the channels that carved the island into oddly shaped slices, and secured her at a staging site. Her spring lines were snugged up and tied to trees. A crowd of distinctly non-local young men stood on the shore in the oppressive afternoon heat, slapped mosquitos, and watched. Varayev stood halfway out of the conning tower and assessed them coolly, as he puffed away. *So that's what passes for jihadis, these days, eh? University kids! Not one knows his head from his ass. Come all this way to make holy war on Uncle Sam. African. Arab. That guy's from Indonesia, maybe the Philippines. Look at the white kids! That one's Ukrainian, I betcha. Throwing it all away. God, I need a drink.* "What the hell is this? A field trip? School outing?" he taunted, as a gangplank was extended to the sub's round back. "Anybody bring a bottle? Somebody told me there would be seventy-two virgins? I was expecting virgins, not you bachi boys!"

A grim looking man in camo pants, utility vest, and cadet cap pushed his way through the midst of the young men, and trundled down the gangplank. He, too, was young. Sweat-drenched black locks framed an olive-tan face.

"You are Varayev, the engineer? What is your evaluation?"

"It'll hold together, if you keep that baboon Ismael away from the controls. He grounded us twice! Who the hell are you, the ghost of Che Guevara?"

"Commander Abdelhak. If everything is in order, you can go." The commander pulled out a radio and returned to the shore. "Command to Base. *Venganza* is secure. Begin loading, at once. Strike Team will report for injections. Send a boat around to pick up the *Russian*."

Varayev climbed down the metal rungs on the conning tower and crossed the gangplank. Zamir poked his head out of the hatch and smiled. "Take care of that kid, Commander," he said, jerking a thumb over his shoulder. "He's the only hope you damned *Turks* have."

Commander Abdelhak turned back to his team, ready to explode. "Report to the infirmary! We embark at sunset!"

12

The news of the miracle had traveled quickly from Isabel Segunda. A little girl, blind from birth, had received her sight during a beach-side baptism held by a group of teen-aged missionaries from America. Santina, the portly proprietress of the Mongo Mango, had served the news with breakfast.

"Jojo must've held his mouth just right," quipped Mia.

"Don't blaspheme," Blake replied. "Seriously, miracles happen."

"Then why couldn't he fix Crackamodo?"

"You're not asking the right question," Blake said through his last mouthful of eggs. Mia didn't bite. Blake left a tip and got up to leave. "The question is *who* does the fixing. And what's the difference between the two situations. Remember the line 'your faith has made you well?'"

"So it's all in your head?"

"I don't know. But that little girl can see. That's what you have to deal with."

Mia said nothing as they walked down the street toward the Malecón, her mind still swirling in eddies of confusion and guilt from the night before. At least Blake was himself again. He'd done well, she had to admit, picking up that British babe in retaliation, then flagrantly flirting with her until Jayce left.

"Let's go see her. You can ask her yourself," Blake suggested.

"Who?"

"Duh! The not-blind-anymore girl, that's who."

"Let's not."

"Let's do! You said you wanted to go to Isabel Segunda, anyway. Guidebook says there's a fort, a cool cemetery, and this dude who feeds all the stray cats at sunset. Like hundreds of them."

Champ wandered around the corner and almost straight into them. He cried out, then jumped back, pointing and shouting for help. Blake was ready. He whipped out a sheaf of twenties and fanned them out for Champ to see.

"¡Espera, nos rendimos! Wait, we surrender! El Campeon, I need your help!" Blake pleaded. "Give me a minute, here!"

Champ stopped the hysterics and walked right up to Blake and took the money. Mia slipped cautiously behind her beau.

"Guard my little boat. The one on the beach, okay? Over in Sombe, chained to the tree. You watch my boat."

"I watch the boat? You pay?"

"The little one tied to the tree. Okay amigo?"

"You pay?"

"I pay. You watch. Amigos?" said Blake, holding out a hand.

"I watch." Champ smiled, and trotted away.

"Why didn't we just do that to start with?" mused Blake.

"Just the sensible types, I guess. Now what?"

"We rent a moped!"

Isabel Segunda turned out to be a pleasant escape. No screaming maniacs assailed them. No creepy oldsters solicited them. No irresistible men teased. No randy Europeans flirted. Nobody chucked anything out of upper-story windows. It was just them buzzing along, Blake driving with Mia's arms wrapped around him, her hair blowing in the breeze. She knew that was part of his revenge, too; and she indulged him lovingly. The oddest thing they encountered while meandering through side streets was a Jeep Cherokee encrusted with figurines of the Virgin of Guadeloupe and assorted action figures. It was parked, strangely enough, outside of a stark gray Masonic Lodge.

They ate lunch in a little lime-green panaderia, where the proprietor crossed himself, grinned and blessed God when Blake asked about the little blind girl. "It's true!" he said. "I've known her all her life!"

They visited the Fort Mirasol museum, and the spiffy Punta Mulas lighthouse. In the interest of sustaining the illusion of temporary sanity, Blake forsook his plans to visit the cemetery, and the man with the stray cats. Instead he diverted to Playa Cofi, where Mia filled her pockets with colorful bits of sea glass; intent on sending them and a spool of copper wire to a certain brat named Fiona, who delighted in making jewelry out of such things.

Early in the afternoon, they said goodbye to Isabel Segunda, and sped their red moped back down the blazing asphalt ribbon that wriggled across the green island like an enormous black millipede. Mia was smiling, and feeling appreciative. They crested a hill and saw, in the shimmering mirage at the bottom of the next valley, a figure like a stick man prancing on tiptoe to the middle of the road. There was mischief in his step, like some trickster from a native legend. The apparition held up one arm as if hitch-hiking. As they approached, a filthy yellow-and-green tie-dyed shirt became evident. Ratty dungarees hung precariously from his bony hips, and a horrific pile of dreadlocks in variegated browns enveloped his bearded, white face.

"Hippies are worth fifty points today, Tux!"

Blake swerved back and forth across the road, but the hippie pranced to match him each time, signaling his intent to obstruct their way. Blake stopped ten feet from the trickster.

"You need some help?" said Blake.

The hippie tiptoed up to the front tire, his smile a disconcerting grimace; lips barely parted and pulled back in a straight line, revealing teeth clenched on edge like a kindergartner on picture day. He cocked his head to the left, then right. Without moving his mouth, he piped in a creepy falsetto "Hello! Hello! Ha-ha!"

"Run him down, Tux!" commanded Mia.

Blake revved the motor and declared, "I'm counting to three."

The tie-dyed trickster suddenly transformed into a dejected vagrant. "Dang, man! Does anybody on this island get performance art?"

"C'mon, what do you want?" demanded Blake.

"Migo was *supposed* to be on guard duty," he sniveled, "when someone ganked our gear."

Mia cast about warily for this dilatory sentinel. She spotted a young woman cradling a baby in the poor shade of a scrubby tree. Any other time, she would have told Blake to drive on. But something in her intuition tugged urgently at her better nature. "Is that Migo?"

"That's herself, babe."

Mia dismounted and went to the edge of the road and called, "Hi! I'm Mia."

Migo looked up. She was very young, Mia thought. Migo smiled timidly as Mia waded through knee-high grass to join her.

"Can you help us out, man?" said the trickster. "It's not like I'm asking for a handout. I'm an artist. I gave you a performance."

"I got what I paid for. You *may* owe me a refund," quipped Blake, rolling the moped into the grass and pulling the key. He ambled toward the girls.

"I told you we got ripped off! Mosquito houses and all. I got nothing to sell you."

"What's a mosquito house? Is that like a roach motel?"

"It's *folk* art. Tiny houses. For mosquitoes."

At last, Migo broke her silence. "Astral whittles 'em, then hollows 'em out with an old dentist drill he found." She had a pleasant southern drawl.

"It's called a burr," said Astral, sourly. "But the locals don't want it and the tourists don't get it."

Mia leaned over to peek at the baby. "Can I see?" It was apparent neither mother nor baby had had a bath in a few days. Migo shifted the infant, exposing her face. Mia almost gasped. *Even without the bug bites and heat rash,* Mia thought, *that is the ugliest baby I've ever seen!* "Awww! What a cutie! A girl, right?"

Migo nodded, smiling a little. "She don't make no trouble. But them flies come out at sunset and eat her up somethin' awful."

Mia gave Blake a look, and he returned to the moped, Astral following expectantly.

"What do you call her?" asked Mia.

"Astral calls her Gwok, on account of the sounds she makes."

"What do *you* call her?"

"I like Misty."

"Then I'll call her Misty, too. What do you call *you*?"

Migo hesitated. "Taylor."

"Taylor, I don't know if you noticed, but Misty looks a little hot. And I'm worried about those bites."

Taylor only gave a forlorn smile. "Astral says that the universe will give us everything we need."

Oh, god. Mia thought. *Clearly underage, and dumber than a box of rocks. And the guy with elephant crap on his head is running the show. The perv must be thirty!*

Mia pulled a bottle of water out of her backpack and emptied a packet of sweet fizzy vitamin powder into it. "Here. Drink this up." Immediately, Astral came prancing over with his freaky smile and creepy laugh. "You want some?" said Mia.

"Uh huh! Uh huh!" he squeaked.

"Then you can drink her urine, Elephant Man."

Blake walked up, pulled a bottle out and tossed it to Astral, who scurried off and guzzled it in private.

"Everything okay?" said Blake. Mia gave him a look which he understood clearly.

"Taylor, town is just a mile that way. The main street runs right along the ocean. Follow it to a restaurant called the Mongo Mango. I want you to go in there and ask for Santina. Can you remember that? You show her your baby, and she'll take care of you." Mia showed Taylor a twenty dollar bill and slipped it into the baby's diaper, sure it was the one place on earth Astral would stay farthest from at all times. She gave her another bottle of water. "This is for *you*. Keep Misty out of the sun. Find Santina. "

Taylor smiled. "Thank you, Miss Mia."

"Let's go, Speed," she said to Blake. "Our work here is done."

***

Back in Esperanza they returned the moped, collected the deposit and were strolling through a little neighborhood on their way to the Mongo Mango, when Blake stopped at a trash can along the road. To Mia's consternation, he daintily extracted half a dozen yard-long lengths of tack strip, and a tattered piece of carpet, in which he rolled them for easy carrying.

"Explain, weirdo," Mia demanded, arms akimbo.

"It's just a cruising tip I picked up from Joshua Slocum's adventures in Tierra Del Fuego. You'll love it."

"I don't even want to know."

They ambled down the Malecón, making plans for their trip to the glowing waters of Bio Bay that evening. Blake paused along the way to consider the bronze bust of a man whose resolute gaze kept eternal vigil over the fisherman's dock and waterfront. The plaque identified him as Ángel Rodríguez Cristóbal. He read aloud, "When the cause is just, there is no need to fear."

McNeary called out from an open-air bar, across the street. "There you are! Been looking all over for you!"

"What's up, Doc?" replied Mia, as he crossed the road to meet them.

"Where've you been all day?"

"Going to and fro upon the earth, and walking up and down in it," said Blake. "You look like you're hiding something."

"You want the good news first?" said McNeary, tentatively.

"Why not?"

"Champ tried to tow your boat, using your anchor chain. When your keel hit bottom, the chain snapped taught and the anchor tore the transom out of his dinghy. He sank like a rock."

Mia swallowed hard. "And the bad news?"

"The surf washed your boat up. You're hard aground. And the railing around the bow pulpit is bent up a little."

Mia took a deep breath and mumbled to herself "Tell me someone got video of this." She smiled one of those sarcastic *this-is-just-great* smiles, and said, "where is our little helper, now, Mr. McNeary?"

"Santina called his relatives. They're looking for him. Say, now that you're back, I've got some people lined up to pull you off."

"Thank you Mr. McNeary. We are *leaving* tonight, Tux."

"Why don't you just move to another bay?" said McNeary.

"Because we shouldn't *have* to move!" barked Mia. She pulled out her phone and dialed as she walked away.

A few minutes later, she returned and relayed that the police had already spoken with El Campeon, owing to a complaint filed by a witness. The authorities had it that a white kid paid Champ $100 to move his yacht, but didn't tell him it had a keel. They chalked it up to a misunderstanding, and asked if she or Blake intended to pay for the loss of Champ's fishing boat. The officer noted that she and her boyfriend were becoming a *molestia grande*—an epic nuisance.

"We are so *freaking* leaving," she declared, loudly.

"It's too late," countered Blake. "And anyway I'd rather wait and see if she springs a leak overnight."

"That's a great idea," added McNeary. Mia shot him a look. "Okay, it's not a *bad* idea. I'll go let the gang know you're here. Meet me down on the beach. Don't give up the ship, kids!" He ambled off toward Sun Bay.

Arco lounged on the hot sand and watched the effort to free *Chupacabra*. Getting her off of her side in shallows was much more involved than anyone expected. He surveyed the girl—top dollar merchandise—and noted carefully the spot where they moored their righted boat. This final job would be an easy one. He smiled to himself and texted P.K.: *Eyes on merchandise. Top quality*. He laid back with his hands behind his head and thought of Cape Town casinos.

Once the battered yacht was back on her belly in three fathoms of water, Blake and Mia had another challenge—picking up below deck. Anything and everything loose had been ejected from its proper place, shuffled together and tossed randomly into a new place. On the exterior, her port side, where it had raked along a hard spot on the bottom of the bay, now looked worse than Champ's handiwork on the starboard. *At least they match, now* Blake thought—but he didn't dare say it. To his great disappointment, they had to abandon their plans for the Bio-Bay tour.

The bright side of the whole fiasco was that the grounding of *Chupacabra* unified the sailing tourists in their resolve to see El Campeon reigned in. They presented themselves en masse to complain at the Chamber of Commerce in Isabel Segunda the next morning.

Finally, the boat back in order, they lounged in the cockpit—the ever present Coqui frogs peeping in the distance. A soft breeze caressed their faces, and the stars sparkled brightly over the infinite expanse of dark ocean.

Blake descended into the cabin and returned with a plate of smoked salmon from a can, hot mustard, crackers, and dark chocolate.

"What are you up to?" said Mia.

"Me?"

"You're buttering me up. But without cherries, you can forget it. Dark chocolate alone won't do it this time."

"Well then," he smiled, reaching into the companionway.

"No! No way!"

Blake produced a slotted plastic carton full of beautiful cherries.

"You are a *total* jerk! Where did you get those?"

"Santina. She insisted. She really likes us, you know."

He opened a bottle of sparkling grape juice and poured two glasses.

"Seriously, what are you up to?"

"Do I have to be up to something? I'm up to having a nice, romantic starlight picnic with the love of my life."

"Who also happens to want to get the heck off Isla Whackatania at the earliest opportunity because she's already graduating late, and should be home studying her butt off."

"And who also happens to need to relax and pay attention to her gallant boyfriend and stop thinking about a certain Marine."

Is it that obvious? she thought, before pushing back. "Which boyfriend just also happens be on the hook for demolishing an eighty thousand dollar boat."

"But who was clever enough to make sure your aunt's name was on the paperwork! Besides, she would want her niece to relax and pay attention to her gallant boyfriend, too."

Mia bit into a cherry. "Ah! These are amazing," she moaned, following the sweet fruit-flesh with a bite of chocolate.

Blake reclined on his bench and looked up at the stars. "I am *so* coming back here next Christmas."

"You'll do it alone," she scoffed. There was a pained silence. "That… didn't sound the way I meant it. I'm sorry."

"You think we'll still be together in a year?" Blake said, hesitantly.

"I'm only smart enough to know that I can't tell the future."

"It's kinda quirky, but I like this place."

"Like home isn't weird enough?"

"It's not weird now. Not like the year we met."

"Don't remind me."

"Last year was normal. Just school and work. Maybe we needed a little weird to keep us from taking each other for granted."

She gave him a look of the utmost suspicion. "And I'm the one who needs to relax, Mr. Paranoid insecurity?"

He gave an embarrassed chuckle through a bite of salmon.

"Uh, huh! Busted. You're driving me nuts, Tux. If you love something let it go. If it comes back, its meant to be, right?"

"That's exactly what Kalijah told Voodoo Jack when he wanted to sacrifice me early."

"Tux, I can't…I don't know how to make you understand… You know, people change. They don't intend to but they do."

"And that changes everything."

"It *could*. Blake, you could change. You *will* change. Where will *that* leave us? Leave *me*?"

"What are we going to do?"

"Stop acting like me going to school in Indy next fall is the end of everything."

When Mia finally went below to get ready for bed, Blake retrieved the tack strips he'd found that afternoon, bristling with points as viciously sharp as any shark's jaws. He broke them into eighteen-inch lengths, carefully arranging them on the floor and benches of the cockpit, saving a couple for deck and bow. He returned to the cabin, replaced the hatch boards and stretched a ribbon of duct tape across the companionway. On it he wrote in fat letters: *SHOES!!!*

***

Jayce and Saranda wandered down the dark beach, on an unauthorized excursion to Bio Bay. The waning moon inched high into the December sky and all was quiet on Ensenada Sun Bay except for their small talk and provocative insults. Suddenly Jayce shushed her, and steered her to the tree line. He crouched, pulling a small night scope from his jacket pocket. Through it he spied a lone man who had emerged from the forest wearing nothing but swim trunks, and carrying what looked like a waterproof duffel. He walked straight to the water, casting cautious glances to either side.

"Who is it?" whispered Saranda. "It's not Rudi is it? You'll have to fight him if he catches us."

Jayce gave her an amused chuckle "Where are *you* going?" he said, under his breath, as the figure waded into the bay and began to swim. After a minute it was apparent that he was headed for the boat they'd rescued that afternoon—that girl Mia's boat. "Watch my stuff," he said, stripping off his jacket, shirt, and shoes.

"What the hell are you doing? Who is that?"

"Gonna find out." Jayce sprinted across the sand and slipped into the sea. He swam all-out, well below the surface, rising every thirty yards to check the distance to his prey. He had closed the gap with his quarry to ten yards, when his target disappeared behind *Chupacabra*'s stern. Jayce surged under the boat and surfaced by the swim-ladder on her stern. The suspect was just stepping aboard. Jayce had drawn his combat knife and taken hold of the ladder when a series of muffled groans and clumsy shuffling noises filled the air. He ducked under the boat as the dark hulk of the suspect lunged back over the stern and landed with a huge splash. The intruder thrashed his way back to the shore, and was crawling for the beach in two feet of water when Jayce landed on him. "Who the hell are you?" Jayce snarled. "What were you doing on that boat?"

"I'm bleeding! There are sharks in this bay, you fool!" The man had an odd accent, not quite German, Jacye thought.

"There's gonna be a lot more blood, if you don't answer me." Jayce shoved the man's face into the sandy bottom for a full thirty seconds. He jerked him back up by the hair and put his knife to his throat. "What's up with that boat?"

"Kiss my…" was all he got out before the next face full of sea bottom.

"You're not coming up next time. Cops will call it drunk and drowned."

"Alright! I was going out there to sell some weed."

"Who's on that boat?" He pressed the knife against his Adam's apple.

"I got the wrong boat. Some bastard scattered nails all over the deck."

Jayce mashed a foot down on one of his captive's bleeding feet. "You're lying. Why *that* boat?"

His prisoner grimaced in agony. "Kids. Looking for some family member. In trouble with the law."

"*What* family member?"

The man didn't answer.

"Have it your way!" Jayce began to shove him under, but stopped short when he cried out.

"Uncle! They're looking for their uncle."

"Why?"

"I don't know. Crewing a schooner. I was just going to sell them some weed."

Jayce was about to abuse him further when laughter and voices drifted down to the waterline—a group of campers coming out for a late night swim. "I've got my eye on you," Jayce growled, nicking Arco's throat as he plunged back into the bay. He emerged well down the beach, mind spinning. "I thought that kid looked familiar," he said to himself. To his surprise, he found Saranda, right where he left her.

"I watched you beat the hell out of that guy through your little scope thingy," she said in disbelief. "Are you CIA or something?"

"I'd tell you but… Give me my phone, and head back. I'll be right behind you."

She handed him the phone, with its weird, fat antenna. "What kind of…"

"I said I'll be right behind you."

Saranda felt the no-nonsense tone his voice had assumed, and she complied. Jayce placed a call. "Hey, it's Jaybird. You won't believe this."

13

Commander Abdelhak stood in the dim passageway to the forward hold, his arm on the bulkhead above. Sweat rolled down his stubbly cheeks. His shirt was drenched. The air was thick with the stench of unwashed men, and diesel fuel. He glared vacantly at the tightly packed wall of white shrink-wrapped bales.

Someone spoke in the shadows behind him.

"Commander?"

"What is it?"

"The electrics are failing, sir. The deck-plates are…"

"The deck-plates are *what*?"

"They are so hot, the men can hardly bear to sit on them."

"A martyr must endure many things, Ismael," he replied, grimly.

"The men are saying… they say the batteries will blow up."

"You talk like an infidel!" Barked the commander. "God is great! The belly of this vessel is filled with his fire. That is why the deck-plates are hot. Now, go and give the men some courage."

The commander ascended a narrow ladder, and slithered in behind the helmsman.

"Zamir," he said, quietly. "How are the batteries?"

"Very bad. Not good."

Ismael reappeared at the bottom of the ladder. "Commander?"

"What is it, now?"

"It has started. The fever."

"No, it is too soon. It must be as you said. The deck-plates are making the men too hot."

"Commander, Hamid is coughing up blood. They will not even make the rendezvous."

"Damn. They are contagious now," said the commander.

"That gives us two, maybe three days," said Zamir. His thoughts drifted to his little son, and then to the irascible, foul-mouthed Chechen, Ruman Varayev.

"Then *we* will complete their mission, God willing."

14

Jayce had walked Saranda back to town, then returned to a secluded spot on the beach where he kept watch over *Chupacabra* for the rest of the night. He smiled proudly as he spied Blake at sunrise, collecting his tack strips and rolling them up in a rug.

He tailed the kids into town, on their way to the riding company stables. Jacye had begun to meditate on Mia's fine form when somebody shouted at them from across the street.

"Hey Fuego!" called a young man as he strutted toward them. "I hear you're givin' my buddy a hard time! What's your problem, blanquito? Huh?"

Blake recognized the angry waiter from the El Blok hotel. He hoped Mia might be reconsidering her vow against using Karate.

"Sorry, I don't know who you're talking about," said Blake, picking up his pace.

The waiter fell in behind them, dogging their heels. Jayce picked up his stride, donning the lightweight jacket he had wrapped around his waist, and smoothing it over the pistol concealed against the small of his back.

"Why don't you bully me, huh? 'Stead of people who can't take care of themselves?"

Blake was hastily weighing his options, when it occurred to him that a little chutzpah might score a few points with this guy and, more importantly, with Mia. He steeled himself, stopped, and turned to face his adversary. "Do you mean El Campeon?" he objected, loudly. The waiter stopped in his tracks.

Blake closed the distance between them. "That guy has been at our throats since we set foot on this island! You should see what he did to our boat! We're just trying to mind our own business and enjoy our vacation!"

"Why don't you just take your boat and go back where you came from?"

"How can you say that, when there are more Puerto Ricans on the United States mainland than there are in Puerto Rico? Tell me that, genius!"

"Blake, c'mon. We'll be late to the stables," said Mia, walking backwards.

"What's your name, man? Why can't we be friends?" said Blake.

"Cuz, you're blanquito. And another thing: You better stay away from Randi! Now go ride your pony, little boy."

"Check please!" Blake taunted as he turned and rejoined Mia, who looked a little unnerved.

The waiter glared for a moment, nostrils flaring; then slowly, a spiteful, self-satisfied smile possessed his face, and he strode off.

Jayce noted the waiter's face as he passed by, and waved when Mia caught sight of him. She blushed, and rolled her eyes as he caught up to them.

"You guys sure know how to make friends, around here," said Jayce.

"Come to join our merry little band of stalkers?" Mia replied, looking straight ahead, trying desperately not to glow.

"You riding?" asked Blake.

"Say no," Mia interrupted, stealing a quick glance. "We've had our share of horse's butts this morning."

"Is she always this hostile?" Jayce smiled

"Only if she's crazy about you."

"It's a long swim to St. Croix, kid!" Mia retorted.

They started down a short stretch of highway. Jayce casually scrutinized every car that approached, still ribbing and flirting with Mia and making guy talk with Blake.

"I couldn't help noticing that you guys seem to attract weirdoes," he said, as they turned down the lane that led to the Isla Paso Riding Company.

"I was just thinking that, when you walked up. And Blake is the weirdo magnet, not me."

"Explain your aunt, then," Blake countered. "And your brother. And…"

"They're family. They don't count. They were here when I arrived."

"Listen, I got another one for you to look out for," said Jayce. "White guy. Medium build. Dark, thick hair. Funny accent, sort like Schwarzenegger. Walks like his feet are killing him. Bad guy."

"How bad?"

"Shoot-him-on-sight bad. Just keep an eye out."

Jayce dismissed himself when they got to the stable, and returned to Esperanza. After a quick breakfast he began scouring town for a man with painfully tender feet.

***

The tour guide cocked her leather Outback hat, and took a swig from her canteen. "I'm Trish. You guys ever been riding?"

"We ride at a park, back home," Mia replied.

"Good. Come on around and meet your mounts. You signed up for the private tour, right?"

"Yes," answered Blake. "Definitely."

"Island life getting a little weird on you?" smiled Trish, as she led them around the stable to the staging area.

"You could say that," Mia affirmed.

"Well, I can assure you that these horses are the sanest people in town. Blake, meet Comet. Mia this is Spray. She'll take good care of you. And this is my best buddy, Luca."

Mia was immediately charmed by the Paso Fino gait of the horses as they ambled along Coco Beach, and by the open and frank character of their guide.

"So, are you two a package deal?"

"Yeah, we stick together for mutual protection, don't we Tux."

"You guys act more like brother and sister, to me," said Trish.

"The little brother I never wanted." Mia turned back to Blake, with a smile and a wink. "Seriously, Trish, this guy has saved my hide so many times it's not funny."

They followed a short trail that meandered up into a small neighborhood, then onto the main drag, Calle Flamboyan.

"Any possibility we could pick it up a little?" said Blake.

"Let me guess—you've met Champ?" Trish replied. "Don't worry. He's scared to death of the horses."

"In that case, what would it cost to rent Spray for the rest of the week?"

Trish laughed as Mia sweet-talked Spray. "You wanna be my bodyguard? Huh, Spray? Take care of me and Tux? How are we gonna get you on that boat?"

"Don't underestimate her, she loves the water!"

They left the road near El Blok hotel and wandered through the forest, up into hilly country, with Trish pointing out items of interest along the way. "That huge mud ball there in that tree, that's a termite nest... Guess what that is—believe it or not, that's cotton... Grab one of those mangoes! These ponies are direct descendants of those brought to the island by the Conquistadors, five hundred years ago."

From the high ground they could see dark clouds in the hazy distance, piling up over the sea. Trish led them down into a deep, cool arroyo. Blake was satisfied to see Mia chatting casually with Trish. At last, they found themselves sloshing along in the surf on Black Sand Beach.

Blake trotted Comet up onto the sand ahead of the girls, sending ghost crabs skittering back into their burrows. Mia had just invited Trish to dinner on the boat when Spray and Luca startled. Champ came screaming out of a little cave, arms above his head, charging straight at Blake. Comet bolted headlong down the beach. Instantly, Trish had Luca in high gear in pursuit of the runaways.

Mia dug in her heels and cried "Kill, Spray! Kill!" fully intent on trampling Champ under hoof. Champ turned and froze at the sight of Spray thundering down on him. A young man sprinted from the cave, shoving him out of the way. Mia wheeled Spray around and chased them both to the cliff wall. They scurried up a steep crag and were gone.

"Bastardistas!" shouted Mia, furiously.

"You have to be faster than that, blanquita!"

Blake held on for dear life, Trish galloping up from behind. Just ahead, a small wave rolled in and rushed away, depositing a dead ray on the black sand.

Comet locked up the brakes, and Blake, overcome by the laws of inertia, flew over the horse's head. He landed flat on his back ten feet away.

When Trish reached him, Comet was nuzzling his face and snuffling apologetically. The horse looked up as if to say "It's alright, he's only stunned."

Trish dismounted, and knelt at Blake's side. "Are you still alive?"

"Tell me this has happened to someone else?" Blake groaned.

"Nope. But you are the first person who's ever stayed on Comet at a dead gallop! Can you move?"

"Maybe…Tomorrow."

"I know a couple of osteopaths, in town. They'll fix you up. If they're sober."

Mia brought Spray up briskly, Paso Corto. "It was that jerk waiter!" She jumped off, and ran to Blake.

"Rudi," Trish announced, rhetorically.

"I've had it, Blake. We're pulling out of here tonight."

"Thanks. I'll be alright," Blake replied, with a tinge of sarcasm.

The adrenalin levels began to ebb, and Mia came to her senses.

"Oh no, Tux! Oh gosh, are you alright?"

"Kiss me. It may be your last chance."

"Get up, Jerk," she scowled.

"Okay, now I see the romance," said Trish. "Help me get him on his feet."

***

Arco smeared triple antibiotic cream over the soles of his feet, and gingerly pushed his hand down the back of his swim trunks to slather his left buttock. Several horses milled around his rented Jeep, and peered hopefully in the windows. He'd pulled off and spent the night on a side-road, halfway between Esperanza and Isabel Segunda. He adjusted the rearview mirror and considered the slight cut across his Adam's apple—his opponent's calling card—and smoldered with anger. He never saw the man's face, but the man had seen his. *What do I remember?* he thought. *American. Shorter than me, I think. Strong. Well trained. Watching. Find the kids, and I find him.* A call rang in on his phone to the tune of Deutschland Über Alles. Little Hitler was calling from Trinidad.

"They're still here," he answered, testily.

"Good morning to you, too! The evening didn't go as planned, big guy?" P.K. purred.

"It was all a sure thing. Then I stepped on a scorpion fish."

"The Flying Dutchman stopped by a little sting? Good thing it wasn't a bumble bee!"

"I lost my balance when I grabbed my foot. I fell on the damned thing."

"Oh, poor Arco! *How* humiliating. Well, don't worry, big guy. Newly will catch them in St. Croix. He already has their Auntie eating out of his hand."

Arco was about to warn her that the kids were already under surveillance, but decided to let that clown Newly find out on his own.

"I'll let you know when they leave."

"You do that Arco. And bring me a note from the doctor, if it isn't too much trouble."

"Sieg Heil," he replied flatly. He hung up, and tried to remember the last time he'd had a tetanus shot.

***

Rain began to spatter the windows of an upper room at the Mongo Mango. Blake lay on a portable massage table, the two bodyworkers doing their magic.

"Bend the left knee and rotate his hip to the right," said Dr. Viney. Gil obeyed and, as he did, the woman with the terra cotta hair pressed his left shoulder toward the table. Blake imagined that they were wringing him out like a wet towel. "Okay; one, two…" They eased off slightly and on "three," applied sudden pressure that popped every vertebra in his back, and made him groan with a laugh of relief.

Dr. Viney flattened him out and gave him a moment to catch his breath. The room was dim and cool. Santina had bartered its use in exchange for regular treatments, and chores.

"Where'd your girl go?" said Gil, as Dr. Viney scooped Blake's head up in her hands, and began to apply subtle pressure with her fingers.

"Gil, sacrum and lumbar," said the doctor. Gil slid his hands under Blake's lower back, and behind.

"She and Trish are filing another police report."

"Another?" said Viney.

"Champ grounded our boat, yesterday. Mia's had it. If the cops don't do anything this time,"

"And they won't," said Gil.

"She'll want to leave immediately."

Viney gently turned his head to the left. "What about you?"

"I'd like to stay. I love it here. Lunatics excepted."

"I resemble that remark!" protested Gil.

"It's actually a really cool place," said Viney. "You just picked kook season. Champ goes nuts over the Christmas gringo-fest, and Rudi thinks he's the next Che Guevara."

"So what are you guys doing here?" said Blake.

"We're traveling the islands for tax purposes," said Gil.

"Oh yeah! Like doing charity work, for a massive write off? We do that with our casket business."

"Not exactly," said Gil. "Let's just leave it at 'tax purposes.'"

Blake realized that his body no longer ached, and that he had never felt so relaxed.

"So, wait," said Dr. Viney. "I haven't seen you with your parents. Where are they?"

"It's a long story. We're living with Mia's aunt. She's hanging out in San Juan while we look for my uncle."

"Intriguing *and* romantic! How long have you been together?"

"This makes three years. She'll be starting nursing school next year."

Dr. Viney tilted Blake's head back, and pressed her finger tips into the base of his skull. "That's got to make you nervous."

"Jeez, you were like twelve or something?" said Gil.

"It's complicated."

"You're just gonna let her go like that?"

"What can I do?"

"You saw how she was flirting with that Marine! Pursue her! You gotta get her out of the friend zone. Make her see you as a young man, not her little brother!"

"Don't listen to him, Blake," countered Dr. Viney. "The friend zone is where any lasting relationship begins. Sounds like you've got a solid foundation."

"Where did yours start?" said Blake.

Dr. Viney cast a doubtful glance at her spouse. "The Twilight Zone. Now, no talking for five minutes. Breathe. Clear your head. Gil—sacrum and iliac." Gil pulled his hand from under Blake's back and laid his forearm across his pelvis.

Viney squeezed his head a little. "C'mon on, kid; stop thinking."

It took a few moments, but for the first time in Blake's life there was complete silence in his mind. He was aware of every sound, every vibration in the room, every tiny movement of the doctor's fingers. Suddenly, his head popped out of the doctor's hands; then again, and a third time.

Gil smiled. "It's all moving down here, miracle worker!"

"Ain't never seen that, before!" exclaimed Dr. Viney, quietly. "You've got a lot wound up in there, buddy." She slowly withdrew her hands and let Blake's head rest on the treatment table. "Okay, I just bought you two more days in paradise, Bubba. Tell Mia that you need to avoid any strenuous physical activity for two days. Doctor's orders. Just lay there. Take a nap."

The doctor covered him with a white bed sheet, then slipped out of the room with her husband.

Blake's thoughts wandered slowly to the osprey they'd heard in the lagoon; to little Chelly and her history lesson; to the times he and Mia had shared on Cry of The Osprey, paddling together, gliding across the reservoir as one. A hint of movement drew his attention to the ceiling. There rested a brown butterfly, wings painted with orange bars and fringed with blue eye-spots, oblivious in its repose, to a ghostly little gecko creeping its malevolent way across its white stucco hunting ground. The lizard paused, then made a lightning sprint. It seized the butterfly head first. Its wings spread out flat, creating the illusion of a single, bizarre creature. The gecko managed one gargantuan chomp after another, slowly collapsing, and consuming the delicate masterpiece.

The doorknob clicked. Blake felt a ripple of air move across his face. He didn't move. He thought it might be the doctor or Mia, perhaps. Little Chelly appeared by his side. She put her hand on his forearm and stroked it sympathetically.

Blake closed his eyes and opened them again. She was gone. There was a subdued peal of thunder. He thought it might have been a dream, but for the tiny bits of butterfly wing on the sheet.

***

Mia was having a drink with Trish on the upper veranda, when Blake found them. It was pouring down rain. Mia was saying something about abandonment issues and co-dependency.

"Look who's back among the living," said Trish.

"You look stoned!" Mia seemed in unusually good humor. "They put you on Whackadone?"

He ignored the ribbing and stared into the distance. "Well, there goes Bio Bay, tonight."

"About that,"

"I came here to see the Bio Bay. I'm not leaving until I do," he said, quietly and matter-of-factly.

"Not unless you have…"

"A note from my doctor?" he smiled faintly, holding up a slip of paper. Mia snatched it away.

"To whom it may concern, blah, blah, blah…" she read aloud. "Two days?"

"Doctor's orders," he replied in smug serenity.

"Oh, well," she said. "We can't leave, anyway. Trish insists that she's treating us to dinner, at her place."

"Have you seen Chelly?"

"Washing dishes, I think," answered Trish. "Pull up a chair."

Blake fetched a seat from another table, and joined them. "Good news!" Trish beamed. "Champ's family finally rounded him up and took him home. You've become a local hero among the cruising set."

"But not the police?"

"Definitely not," said Mia.

"No quiet resentment among the locals?"

"You could say there's a quiet sense of relief among local business owners," said Trish.

"Got a text from Serena," said Mia. "Your Grandmother called. We're all dead meat."

"All the more reason to stay," said Blake, leaning back and gazing vacantly at the rain pelting the palm trees.

"What's up with you, boy?" chuckled Mia.

Blake sighed. "How would you know if you had a mystical experience?"

***

Trish's place was a squat, concrete-block house in white stucco with turquoise trim, a flat roof, and louvered glass windows. It was surrounded by an eight foot chain-link fence, in spite of being in a nice neighborhood. Luca grazed and nuzzled in the scrubby lawn, until Blake came out with a bag of carrots and apples. Insects whirred their evening chorus, punctuated by the loud peeps of the coqui frogs. Dogs barked in the distance. Somewhere, the familiar cooing of a mourning dove brought back memories of Gunn's Harbor, and his life a world away. As Luca munched on the sweet treats, Blake's thoughts turned back to that morning and the trap he'd set. Somebody had come aboard as they slept, but not who he'd expected. Champ and Rudi were obviously in fine running health. Whoever had left their bloody footprints all over the cockpit would be lucky to be back on their feet, this soon. He felt a pang of guilt for not telling Mia. He'd cleaned it all up before she awoke.

In the kitchen, Trish stirred a big pot of spaghetti, and popped the top off a bottle of beer.

"So, what you're trying to say is he's *safe*," she said.

"I guess that's it," replied Mia, as she leaned against the counter and sipped wine from a snifter.

"Safe is okay."

"But, is it just a cover for my insecurities? Am I just using 'safe' as an excuse?"

"I dunno. Are you? Do you love him?"

"Yes, I love him! But… I…ugh! I care about him. I have a lot of affection for him. I'm kind of crazy about him."

"But, you don't know if you can wait for him to grow up?" Trish added a heap of chopped onions and garlic to a large pan.

"He's more grown up than most guys his age. But sometimes he's still… *very* fifteen."

"And maybe you want to get out of the safe zone and live a little, play the field? Figure out who Mia really is?"

"There ya go! Figure out who Mia is. Who Mia could be."

"And that's why you chose nursing?"

"I want to make a difference. I want to give back."

"Ahhh. The great make-a-difference myth," intoned Trish. "Toss that colander in the sink."

"Uh oh. What am I missing?"

"What does 'making a difference' mean to you?"

"I… I'm not sure."

"Twelve-hour shifts of wiping butts and swabbing up vomit in the ICU, for hordes of mostly ungrateful people?"

"I was thinking more like neonatal, or Nurse Practitioner."

"Nice! How do want to make a difference in those fields?"

Mia got up and helped Trish pour the steaming pasta out of the big gleaming pot into the colander. "I feel like I'd be able to…"

"Save lives? Cure diseases? Control outcomes? Stir the veggies."

"Wow. You got me." Mia went to the stove and stirred the onions.

Trish rinsed the spaghetti. "Making a difference doesn't rely on controlling outcomes. It can, but not always. It's all the everyday little things you do for people, and the way you do them." She took a stack of plates from a cabinet, a handful of silverware from a drawer, and clanked them on the counter-top. "The spirit you do them in. It's not this whole I gotta-save-the-world, Super Man idea that we foist off on ourselves. Add the tomatoes. Now, *why* do you want to make a difference? That's the real question. Don't answer. Just think about it before you choose your career path."

Mia threw back the rest of her glass and held it out. "Hit me!"

Trish smiled and poured her another.

The screen door whacked shut, and Blake appeared in the kitchen. "This place is a lot bigger than it looks!"

"Which ain't sayin' much," Trish chuckled. "It's the bushes. They hide half the house. Wash your hands up to the elbows and set the table, bud!"

They passed the evening playing dominoes, and listening to classical guitar CD's.

***

Back on the beach, Jayce sprayed himself down with a double dose of insect repellent, settled back against a palm tree, and switched on his night scope.

15

Arco sat in the tan Jeep, and drenched his feet with Orajel Extra Strength, cursing the menthol and camphor vapors. "All I have to do is crap my pants and I'll smell like my grandmother's bathroom," he grumbled. He'd slept in the car again and woke with the sun, dashing through Isabel Segunda long enough to grab some medicine from the Super Mercado, and two grapefruit juice and vodkas from Buen Provecha. He rattled eighteen hundred milligrams of ibuprofen out of a small bottle, and washed the tablets down his remaining cocktail. He berated himself for coming so ill prepared for this job. Find two kids—how hard could it have been? He should have been back in Charlotte Amalie by now, with his feet up, watching Chevy Chase Vacation movies.

He reached into his bag and extracted the one thing he had remembered to bring: his Glock 9mm. Arco screwed on the silencer, and checked the magazine—Fiocchi 158, full metal jacket. He wanted to kill that punk that jumped him in the shallows. He wanted to kill those stupid kids, sink their boat, then fly down to Trinidad and Tobago and slaughter Little Hitler. The hate pounded in his temples.

He reached back into his duffel looking for a candy bar, but clutched a wad of cool leather. He recoiled a little, took it out and hung it from the rear view mirror. It was a black neck tie, oddly veined, with the word 'Ngandu' embossed in cursive along one side of its pointed tip. It had been a gift from the boss, two Christmases ago, and a grim reminder about unrestrained ambition. He scowled at it. P.K. had gotten the matching gloves, and took perverse pleasure in actually wearing them around her night club.

He looked in the mirror and considered the hard pale blue eyes staring back, the lined face with more than a couple gray hairs in the brows. *Thirty-eight and this is what I look like, already.* He thought. *You haven't lived this long by being rash or stupid. But you were stupid this time, Arco. Sloppy. You got lucky. Don't screw it up for yourself. Newly will get what's coming to him in St. Croix. Just sit back and enjoy the show, Arco. Who knows? Maybe they'll catch him and he'll squeal on P.K.* He smiled at that, and relaxed a bit. It was a pleasing thought, and not at all out of the realm of possibility. *Still got to make a report. Now, how am I going to…?* A car passed by, interrupting his thought. It had two kayaks strapped to the top.

Arco walked into a sports shop in Isabel Segunda within the hour. He pulled out with a neon-green sit-in kayak strapped to the roof rack, and a blue bucket hat and sunglasses on his head. He could barely feel the soles of his feet, and the new plan lifted his spirits. Lunch and a well-deserved drink were in order, after which he returned to the Super Mercado for all the Orajel they had left and a several of bars of chocolate Ex-Lax. It was a leisurely drive down Highway 201 to 997 near the south shore. Arco pulled off at the southwest corner of Esperanza, and followed a sandy trail through a small woods to a nameless beach. He dashed his Jeep along the tree-line, and into a thin spot at the edge of the Quebrada La Perla palm forest. He medicated his feet again. Next he took the paper wrappers off the of Ex-Lax and left the bars, in their gleaming foil, on the passenger seat; gifts for the thieves who would descend on the Jeep mere seconds after he hit the water.

***

On Sun Bay, preparations were in full swing for the Christmas Party. The band was setting up their gear on a deck of sorts, made of short risers. Awnings were erected and picnic benches were set up in rows under them. Kegs of beer and tubs of ice were wheeled in, and local restaurants prepared to feed hungry festival-goers from covered booths.

At the waterline, Blake loaded the last bag of groceries into the dinghy, along with one of the beach rats, and little Chelly—who had been following them around since lunchtime.

Blake watched Mia speed the dinghy across the sparkling golden bay, to *Chupacabra*. The sun hung above Monte Pirata, turning a narrow cloud bank that stretched over the bay into a bridge of scarlet billows. He breathed the warm salt air deeply and smiled; it had been a fine day. They'd played in the water all morning with the kids, snorkeled under a light surf that rippled like quicksilver as you swam under it. Then it was lunch, and the grocery, and tonight the party. It was all bliss. Except for the nagging question of who had stepped on his tack-strips, and why Jayce Mitchell always seemed to be lurking nearby. And Jayce's allusion to a bad guy with bad feet. He didn't hear McNeary traipsing up from behind.

"Uh, oh," said the old shrink. "I've seen that look before."

Blake gave him only a cursory glance.

"You can't stay here, son. You gotta go home."

"Why?"

"Because you can't just drift your life away in the Caribbean, that's why. You've got a greater purpose to fulfill."

"Is that the Sphinx talking?"

"What's that quote from Conrad? Explains a lot of people down here pretty well. Something about the eyes of dreamers and the temper of buccaneers—living in a crazy maze of plans and schemes that only winds them up dead, in the end. Then there are slackers, with that soft spot of decay in their souls. Determined to lounge safely through existence."

"You're talking about my uncle."

"It's in *your* eyes, too, Blake. It gets pretty boring, gunk-holing island to island, drinking your life away, bedding this girl then that. It's meaningless. Leads to depression. Addiction. Suicide. Makes a nice break, but you can't spend your life just doing that. You've got an empire to build. There are people out there who need Blake Barber to help them bear their burdens."

A minute of silence passed before McNeary spoke again.

"Listen, I know a little place…"

"I'm not interested!" Blake interjected.

"For you, and the girl," he continued. "Little bio-bay, just as bright as the big one. You can get your boat in there. Champ doesn't even know it exists."

***

Latin music rolled across the water toward sunset, as Arco picked his way through a luminous flotilla of cruising boats and motor yachts all decked out in glowing Christmas splendor. Strings of colored lights cascaded over their rails, spiraled up their masts, and outlined their rigging. People were grilling, drinking and dancing on their decks. It seemed like every sail cruiser on the island was there. All except one. He laughed and exchanged holiday greetings with boaters, smiled and waved at children—his gut tightening another notch with each passing moment.

***

The last rays of sun faded over the tangled tops of the mangrove trees, in the little backwater McNeary had suggested. *Chupacabra's* mast poked up just above the green canopy. Blake suspected that the old rascal was trying to do him favor, where Mia was concerned, and he resolved not to waste it. Mia locked the hatch boards and they left *Chupacabra* alone in the secluded cove. They buzzed the little dinghy across Puerto Ferro Bay, past the ruins of the old lighthouse, hugging the shoreline beyond the inlet to Mosquito Bay, then on around into Sun Bay. Mia beached the dinghy with a dozen other little boats. Blake was wrapping the chain around the prop when McNeary wandered up with an obese man who sported a crew-cut, no shirt, and thick eyeglasses with nerdy black frames.

"What luck! This is the guy I was telling you about, Jackie!"

"The coughing pimp?" replied Jackie, in a voice that sounded like it never quite made it out of puberty.

"Coffin," said Blake, over the back of the boat. He snapped the lock shut.

"Yes!" said McNeary. "The kid who beat the Sphinx! I see you took my advice?"

"Don't know what you're talking about," said Mia. "Tux, have fun with the guys. I'm going to go look for Taylor." She jogged up the beach, and into the crowd.

Jackie watched her go, with a look of bored condescension. "I bet she's your Gordian knot."

"Have sword, will travel," replied Blake.

"Hah. See you around, Charlie." Jackie waddled away.

"That was a man, right?" said Blake.

"You know, I haven't figured it out, yet," replied McNeary.

"So, did you hear about the miracle up in Isabel Segunda?"

"Yeah, little blind girl and all. But please, don't call it a miracle," grumped McNeary.

"She was blind from birth! She can see now! What would you call it?"

"A phenomenon! Cosmic rays! Mystical vibrations! Anything—just don't call it a miracle!" McNeary was clearly agitated and Blake, who generally went to lengths not to offend people, was genuinely delighted.

"Phenominaculous is too hard to say."

"Look, just because something extraordinary or unexplainable happens, we don't have to go jerking God down onto the stage, first thing."

"I don't think anybody jerked him down. I think the girl invited him, and he showed up."

"Okay, then her faith made her well. But it was all localized within her own psyche."

"A self-made miracle, then."

"Don't call it that, dammit!"

Blake couldn't hold back any longer, and chuckled.

"Oh yeah, you're jerkin' my chain, I see. I get ya. You better go find your girl before that Marine does, or you'll be sailing back to Indiana alone. See ya later Mr. Barber." McNeary trudged across the sand toward the crowd.

Blake felt an impish satisfaction as he set off to find Mia—or Jayce Mitchell.

The evangelistas were wandering like prophets through the pagan throng, handing out tracts and trying to win souls for Christ. Huckey had a bullhorn, periodically announcing the reason for the season and inviting everyone to the seaside baptism to be held in two hours' time. Mia spotted that nasty pile of matted hair meandering among the revelers, just before it vanished into the sea of bodies. She lunged through the mass searching for Taylor, for anyone with a baby. She exited the assembly on the far side, and headed along the tree line. She found the girl not too far away, sitting by a temporary pole light near the path to Esperanza. She was just staring into the night. Mia knelt before her.

"Taylor?" The girl didn't make eye contact. "Taylor, how is Misty?"

"She don't move too much, no more." Her voice was barely audible over the band, and generators.

"Let me see."

Taylor angled the baby toward Mia. One limp little arm fell aside.

Mia gasped. She stroked the arm, and Misty quivered, but didn't open her eyes. "Stay here! Don't move an inch," Mia commanded. She bolted for the crowd, following the sound of Huckey's bullhorn.

"Jojo Huckey-butt!" she bellowed. "Jojo! Jojo!"

He was oblivious to her yelling until she caught his arm and yanked the bullhorn from his hand. She put it to her mouth and blasted "You're coming with me! *Now!* It's an emergency!" She dragged him to the tree line and headed for Taylor at a run.

"Would you mind explaining yourself?" he protested.

"A baby is going to die, if you don't get her to a hospital."

"There's a hospital in Isabel Segunda!"

"That's not a hospital, and it isn't open!"

When they reached Taylor, Huckey bent down, took one look at Misty and said, "Oh, dear Lord! I don't know what *I* can do."

"You have a car! Drive her to the damned ferry, take her to P.R. and get her to a real hospital!"

"I gotta tell the kids."

"I'll tell the kids! Taylor, this is Joe Huckey. He's a *good* guy. He's going to take you to the hospital, okay?"

Taylor rose feebly.

"I'll get my car!" Huckey cried, taking off full speed across the sand. "Meet me in front of El Blok Hotel."

***

"Where's your girlfriend?" said Saranda, cozying up to Blake.

"I don't know. I'm beginning to worry."

"She's probably dancing with someone. Jayce Mitchell, like as not. But you don't have to worry, I'm here!"

She sipped her drink and gave him that maddeningly seductive look.

A beefy young man walked up and offered a little yellow pamphlet. "Hi, I'm Jared. Do you know where you'd go, if you died tonight?"

Blake thought for a moment and said, "Sheol. Now go away."

"Sorry, I didn't get that."

"B'reshit bara Elohim et ha-shamayim, v'et ha-aretz."

"I'm sorry, is that Spanish?"

"It's Hebrew," answered Blake.

"I don't speak Hebrew."

"Then how can you tell me what the Bible says?"

The young man looked at him blankly for a moment, then went on his way without another word.

"Wowzers, you're magic!" beamed Saranda. "Does that work on Jehovah's Witnesses, too?"

Mia made her way through the forest of bodies, Jayce Mitchell almost underfoot.

"You moved your boat?"

"Yeah?"

"Where?"

"You sound too interested."

"I am."

She stopped and turned so quickly that he almost slammed into her. "Listen! I didn't ask for this! I wouldn't even be here if my boyfriend wasn't trying to find his long-lost jackass uncle. You can have any girl here, so could you just please pretend you never saw me?"

"What's his uncle do down here?"

"Runs diving tours or something on a big schooner. It would be better if Blake didn't see us together."

"What the dude's name? If I run into the guy I'll tell him to call home."

"Urquart. Carson Urquart."

The wheels seemed to turn behind his smiling eyes for a moment. "Alright. We're cool. Sorry I spooked you. It was nice to meet you."

"Look, I... Thank you, Jayce." She broke away and resumed her search for Blake, face on fire, heart pounding.

Jayce pulled out his phone, and headed for the waterline. "Hey, it's Jaybird. Yeah. Affirmative. It's them." He fished out his night-scope and scanned the wide harbor.

***

"Hey, moped maaan!" Astral appeared, eyes fixed on the gorgeous Brit. She recoiled and, still sucking her straw, sidled up to Blake. He startled as she slipped her hand into his back pocket and gave a playful squeeze.

"Hey who's your friend? My name's Astral."

"What kind of name is Astral, for a boy?" said Saranda. "I've never heard of such a thing."

"It calls all of the essential energies of the cosmos to my aid, every time someone says it. Pretty cool, huh?"

"Tell me, Astral: do your friends call you 'Ass,' for short?" Saranda giggled.

"Heh. Heh. Hehhh," said Astral, with a nasal sneer.

"Where's Migo and Gwock?" asked Blake.

"Migo?" said Saranda. "You mean the like Fungi from Yuggoth?"

Astral brightened up. "Hey wow, you know about H.P. Lovecraft?" He took a step closer, and was suddenly knocked off his feet, landing with a thud. Mia towered over him as he tried to squirm away, and shouted things through Huckey's bullhorn that caused the crowd to clear a twenty foot circle around them. The profanity and death threats finally simmered down to a list of boiling predictions: "And presuming your baby lives, you are going to scrape that pile of elephant-crap off your head, and you are going to wash dishes for Santina, clean out the stables for Trish, and pick up garbage until you can buy Taylor and Misty a ticket back home!"

Saranda took her hand out of Blake's back pocket and put a full three feet between them. Astral crawled into the crowd, staggered to his feet, and was gone.

"Bye-bye, Ass!" Saranda waved, cheekily. "So Tux, I've got to hunt down my date. Nice to see you Mia!"

Mia glared at Blake.

His face flushed. "Well, hey, uh they've got roasted corn on the cob!"

Saranda found Rudi near the beer tent, with his arms around not one, but two very tan and curvaceous beauties. He was pontificating to several of his envious buddies about foreigners, and didn't notice her. Saranda grabbed a pitcher from a nearby table, scooped it full of ice from a trough full of beer bottles, and glided smoothly up behind him. With one fluid movement, she pulled out his waist band and dumped the frigid payload into his shorts.

Rudi's eyes bulged as he took a very long, very deep breath, clamped his lips between his teeth and held up a finger as if to say "hold that thought!" He started away in a pained shuffle, but broke into a dead run for the sea as soon as he thought his friends couldn't see him.

***

Arco's feet were on fire, the wet mesh in his trunks was rubbing him raw and his lower back continually threatened to spasm. *Chupacabra* was gone, along with his sudden manic hope of completing this job. He wanted a stiff drink and a soft bed, but he still needed to report in. Anger was pounding in his temples again. *They can't be gone. Doesn't make sense!* He thought. *What teenager ditches a Christmas beach bash to start a six hour night passage? No, they're not gone. They just went off for a little privacy. Probably skinny-dipping in Corcho Bay. You haven't given old Arco the slip. Not by a long shot.* It would be almost two miles back to the Jeep, if he returned the way he came—the safe way—but it would be less than a mile if he cut through that gap he'd seen in the sand spit between Cayo de Tierra and the shore. *It can't be more than five-hundred meters,* he thought. *I'm going for it.* He poured all of his frustration into moving that kayak.

***

"Miss Mia?" called Joe Huckey.

"What the hell are you doing back here?" she scolded. "Oh my god, you didn't leave them…"

104

"The ferry's down. Mechanical trouble. Won't be running for three hours, so I called the police. They ran her over to Fajardo in one of their fast boats. Baby's probably getting an IV right now."

Mia deflated in relief. She took a deep breath, and put out a hand. Huckey considered it for a moment, then clasped it. "Thank you, Mr. Huckey. I'm sorry I was such a... *witch*."

"Well, it usually isn't the best way. But sometime that's what it takes to get things done."

She smiled and handed him the bullhorn.

"I fixed her up with enough money to get home," he said, as she walked away.

He raised the bullhorn to his mouth and blared 'Miss Mia, do you know Jesus Christ as your Lord and Savior?'"

She looked over her shoulder and called back "I'm working on it!"

Mia finally spotted Blake talking with Saranda. They were facing each other, and she had one hand on his shoulder. Blake was beginning to look comfortable with the situation. Mia was about to change that when she spotted someone stalking up behind him. She shouted, "Blake! Duck!"

He turned and dropped to one knee just in time to miss Rudi's flying fist. Saranda hit the sand with an impressive thump. Someone screamed, and a general commotion ensued. Rudi looked at his fist, then his unconscious girlfriend. Mia grabbed Blake by the arm and ran for the dinghy.

They were already around Punta Negra when a siren began to wail its way up Calle Flamboyan.

***

Jayce ran along the edge of the crowd, making frequent checks through his scope. He'd had his eye on a lone kayaker for the last hour. His suspect was now headed for the sand spit, and he looked very familiar. Jayce poured on the steam, and reached the narrow canal two minutes ahead of his quarry. He hunkered down on the other side of the spit and peered through his scope. "Gotcha," he whispered to himself. He drew his pistol from his waistband, fished a long tube from his jacket pocket and screwed it onto the barrel. He held his breath as the kayak glided through the twenty-foot-wide channel. Arco passed by without even noticing the man prone in the sand not ten feet away.

***

Dr. McNeary was ambling away from the din of the party, set on returning to his villa, when Jayce came jogging up. "Well, Merry Christmas. What have we here?"

"Have you seen Blake and Mia?" said Jayce, wiping sweat from his brow with his forearm.

"Missed 'em. Lit out of here just ahead of the police."

"You know where they moved their boat?"

"Why don't you leave that girl alone, Mitch?"

"I intend to. I need to borrow your car."

"What's up?"

"Give me your keys. It may be life or death. Where are the kids?"

McNeary produced a single key on a fob. "Back of Puerto Ferro Bay. In the mangroves. Mine's the little yellow fart-car across from El Block. But listen…" Jayce said thanks as he snatched the key and sprinted off.

***

They floated beneath the night ocean in bath-warm water. Fish streaked like blazing neon comets beneath them, and every splash was a glowing plume of liquid blue fire.

"Thank you," said Blake.

"For what?"

"Coming to Vieques."

"You'll pay for it, later."

"Come on, you're enjoying yourself! You know, we've been so busy the last couple of years; we haven't had time to breathe. I remember back when I first came to the sailing club, like the second day, my uncle was yelling at me. He said, 'will you just take a minute and look around? What kid has all this in his grasp?'"

106

"Yeah, so?"

"Why go back?"

"Don't start!" Mia groaned.

"Seriously! We're just kids, but we have piles of money,"

"You're a kid. I'm legal. And you don't get your cash 'til Gunn kicks the bucket."

"Still, we've got all this, if we want it. Why go back to the rat race?"

"Because Tripper Gunn will kick your butt if you don't get a degree."

"Spend a hundred thousand dollars to learn how to make someone else a lot of money, like my dad did? I'm not going back. I think Uncle Carson was right."

"So, slack your life away until you wake up one day when you're fifty, and decide it's time to make something of yourself? I want to accomplish something. And I want to do it on my own merit, and not my old man's money, for once."

"I'm not going back," he said, smugly.

"Going!" She splashed blue fire at him.

"Not!" he cried, splashing back. The whole argument devolved into a phosphorescent mayhem of shoving, laughing, tickling, and dunking.

When it was over, they rested, hanging onto the end of the floating lounge. Blake strained to reach a flamingo-shaped drink floatie over Mia's shoulder, but it was just out of range. As he settled back, his cheek brushed hers ever so lightly, and he paused. Their eyes met, their breath flowed together with electricity. She whispered "you jerk," as he pressed his mouth to hers, and their lips slipped together. She returned his kiss deeply, sumptuously. A dolphin back-flipped fifty feet away, creating a neon blue explosion in the night. They startled, then laughed. Blake turned back to Mia, but she put her hand on his mouth and said, "I love you, but we can't do this." She let go of him, and swam backwards toward the boat.

He pursued. "What did I do?"

She hauled herself up the swim ladder, little rivulets of iridescence running off of her sleek body. "Nothing, Blake, It's not you."

"It's about the Marine, isn't it?"

She stepped into the cockpit and leaned over the transom. "Will you stop worrying about that? We just can't do this, now." Her voice quavered. "Keep swimming. I'll get us something to eat." She retreated to the cabin as he pushed off the transom, and floated away in a glowing blue cloud of frustration.

***

Arco finished strapping the kayak down on the roof rack, and climbed into the Jeep. Jagged vinyl and coarse foam abraded his bare legs and back. He hopped out, and turned on the dome light.

Vandals had shredded the upholstery. He shined an LED flashlight on the tires; they had not been slashed. The headlights were fine. A litany of Spanish insults and profanity were key-scratched across the hood and sides of the vehicle. He spread a towel over his seat, offended by the idle barbarism. He consoled himself with the fact that the Jeep had been rented using false ID, and smiled a little when he noticed that the chocolate bars were all gone. Arco grabbed his phone and pulled up Google Maps, switching to satellite view and scanning the south shore from Esperanza eastward to Ensenada Honda. *Maybe Playa Caracas, Maybe Playa Prieta.* He studied the channels and folds of the mangrove lagoons in Puerto Ferro Bay. *That's where they are. That's where a couple of pretty American kids would go.*

Jayce parked McNeary's smart car under a tree where Highway 997 bent north for Colonia Lujan, cut the lights and took up his night scope. He ran scenarios through his head as he waited. If the guy came up this road and turned into the National Wildlife Reserve, then he was definitely in pursuit. Probably checking all of the beaches and bays clear to the east end of the island. But where would he start? He'd have to search Puerto Ferro by boat. *I'd get the hard work out of the way first, if my feet were hamburger,* Jayce thought. *And I'd pick the access site on the east side of the bay—it's more central. Disabling the Kayak won't be an issue, but he could still swim for it. That's a lot of swimming, but he did it once before, right? Got to keep him out of the water. The dude was worried about sharks. He'd be more apt to run into a lionfish than hammerhead. That means I've got to wing him. Guns or Knives, Butch?*

It was twenty minutes before a Jeep with a kayak on top appeared around the next bend. Jayce turned the car around, and drove across a sandy short cut to Puerto Ferro Peninsula Rd., which ran parallel to the highway. He flipped his high-beams on and sped north to the intersection at the entrance to the Vieques National Wildlife Refuge—gateway to the eastern beaches. Sixty seconds later, the Jeep made the anticipated turn into the refuge. Jayce turned in the opposite direction, drove fifty yards, then switched off his lights and made a U-Turn. Driving the tiny car was tricky enough without having to do it in pitch dark, left hand on the wheel, while holding a night vision scope to his right eye, *and* trying to stay far enough behind the Jeep to remain undetected.

They'd wound through three-and-a-half miles of forest when the road made a hairpin turn to the northwest, and continued down a little peninsula. Jayce switched the car over to electric, and took the next three hundred feet at a silent crawl. He turned the little car around and put it in park. Arco dropped the kayak on the ground, and put one hand on the rear window to steady himself. He did not notice the little red dot of light creeping up from the tailgate. No sooner had he touched the cool glass than a searing pain shot up his arm and bits of glass stung his face. He ducked and ran in a half-crouch to the front of the Jeep and hunkered down, clutching his throbbing hand. He could feel that his right trigger finger was gone. A half-a-dozen thuds shook the kayak at the other end of the Jeep, then the front window began to disintegrate, the bullets chirping over Arco's head. And then it stopped. Arco tried to hear over his own breathing, and the coqui frogs. He cursed himself for leaving his pistol in the front passenger seat, as he hastily pulled off his tee shirt and wrapped his hand. *He would have killed me by now.* He thought. *Let him.* Arco braced one trembling elbow on the bumper and levered himself up. He flipped the glass-covered towel over on the driver's seat, climbed in, and struggled to turn the ignition with his left hand.

***

The police found him near the main park entrance, still behind the wheel, plowed into a big sign warning about the presence of unexploded ordnance.

A few hours later, P.K. received a call on a cell phone she reserved specifically for unsecured communication. A Doctor Gallardo of Caribbean Medical Center in Fajardo, Puerto Rico, was calling in regards to a "Mr. Pieter Visser," who had specified a certain "Ms. Princess Willamina Kingston" as his emergency contact. She was amused to hear that Arco a.k.a. "Pieter Visser" Boerman had been savagely attacked by a gang, had his car and boat shot up, and somehow managed to lose a finger defending himself. P.K. relayed the message to her boss, who seemed cheerfully taken aback and, to her complete shock, advised that he would release Arco from all obligations to the organization, and would be closing down operations in St. Thomas.

When Arco came out of surgery and saw that he had a voicemail from the Assyrian, his blood chilled and he nearly fainted. He listened to it twice. Tears welled in his bloodshot eyes as he began an almost frantic quest to book a flight with his smart phone. Lufthansa. Cape Town, South Africa via D.C. and Munich. $3395, one way. Arco ordered a Taxi and signed himself out of the hospital in ten minutes flat.

16

Mia stood at the bow pulpit in the gray dawn and called orders back to Blake, as he motored *Chupacabra* carefully back down the narrow mangrove channel, to Puerto Ferro Bay. The thick forest of trees with roots like tentacles finally withdrew, allowing a full view of the sky. Blake didn't like it. Banks of low clouds like purple bruises scudded in ragged chunks overhead, and he could see whitecaps rolling outside the narrow mouth of the bay.

"Gonna be a fearsome fifty to Frederiksted, Tux!"

"Glad I skipped breakfast," he called back. His stomach was already crawling at the possibility of being on the open ocean in a heavy squall. After days of brilliant skies, tranquil seas and sunshine, the overcast sky and choppy water felt claustrophobic, and malevolent. Even the gulls seemed to gaze around, nervously second guessing as they glided overhead.

As they passed the headland, something caught Blake's eye on the rocky promontory to starboard. He leaned against the wheel and looked through the binoculars. Two horses—a red, and a white—stood at the cliff's edge, below the crumbling ruins of the lighthouse. He was sure he glimpsed a gold sash draped over the back of the white horse.

"Do the words 'two fathoms under the keel and coral heads' mean anything to you?" said Mia, rejoining him in the cockpit. He snapped back to reality and adjusted their course. "How about 'life and death?'"

"You're very reassuring!" he replied.

"I'm serious as hell. And you're nervous."

111

"No, I'm not."

"Yes, you are. And I heard the weather report, too. I'd be lying if I said I wasn't a little edgy."

"Then why not wait it out?"

"Because I don't like your new friends, and we've worn out our welcome. Besides, I don't think the weather is going to be that bad. Now get us out to blue water so we can make sail."

He throttled up and they surged forth into the rolling sea.

"NOAA says the wind's shifted to the northeast," he called, as she went forward. "Sea's running ten feet and up, later today."

"I heard. It's the Christmas winds. At least we can reach the whole way. You ought to have a blast, Mr. Adrenalin!"

Now well away from shore, Blake rounded the boat into the wind. Mia raised the genoa sail, and he shut the engine off. Together they tied a double reef in the mainsail—just in case—and hoisted it.

"I think we ought to tether to the lifelines," said Blake.

"It's not blowing any harder than the day we sailed down here," she said. "Now, southeast and a point east by the GPS, Mr. Barber!" Blake spun the wheel to port so that *Chupacabra* would drift in a backwards arc. Quickly the rattling sails filled, snapping taut. Mia trimmed the jib sail, as Blake turned the wheel to starboard and eased the main. *Chupacabra* heeled and began to make way over the dark, emerald ocean.

A pod of dolphins surfaced to leeward, and raced alongside. "See? Guardian angels, Tux!"

"Trust and go forward," he said, uneasily. "Urquart family motto!"

The dolphins stayed with them for a good while, leaping and flipping, keeping pace effortlessly through the growing waves.

The wind had come up to almost thirty knots, and they took turns steering for an hour at a time. Blake was beginning to enjoy working *Chupacabra* up and over the eight-foot rollers. Mia checked the GPS, then the weather satellite feed. "Wow, we've made thirty miles, not bad! Looks like there's a little fun ahead. Probably miss us. I'm going below and dogging everything down, just in case."

"Now you're making me nervous," he said as she stepped down the companionway.

She turned and smiled reassuringly, but she knew he could hear the concern in her voice. "We did the run from Culebra to St. Croix the year before I met you. The thing is, out here you can see the storm cells coming from miles away. Sometimes you can steer around them."

"And the other times?"

"We'll be fine. I have faith in you, Blake." She sank back into the cabin and began stowing, strapping down, and tying up anything loose. Then she checked the survival gear, the radio, and pulled out the tethers.

Blake took a deep breath. *Faith in me*, he thought. *Where is my faith?*

When Mia returned to the cockpit a half-hour later, she found Blake standing with his feet apart, gripping the wheel with white knuckles. She got her footing. "Looks like it's kicked up a notch or two," she observed.

"Yeah? Well, look ahead!"

Mia assessed the ominous dark wall sweeping toward them across the swell.

"I brought your tether," she said, clipping one end of it to the lift ring on his life jacket, the other to the lifeline on the rail.

"Let's heave to, and put another reef in," said Blake.

"There's no time." She snapped her own tether to the lifeline. "Blake, fear has no place on a boat. That goes for both of us. We're good sailors, we can do this."

He steeled himself, and nodded.

"I love you," she said, confidently.

The black wall swallowed them whole. The wind ripped up to forty knots and screamed in the rigging. The rain roared down so hard they couldn't see beyond the mast. The dark sea surged angrily over the starboard rail. Mia braced one foot against the base of the helm column, and helped Blake steer. The waves were now pushing twelve feet in height, their tops blowing off as the gale strengthened its resolve, turning everything into a howling white infinity. Together, they steered *Chupacabra* up the faces of those heaving leviathans, and surfed down their backs. They worked desperately to manage their speed, so to keep from burying the bow in the next trough, and tumbling the boat end over end. They could feel the vibration from the rigging through the hull. They didn't speak—or think. They only felt: every surge, every roll, every yaw and pitch. They were completely absorbed in the anticipation of the ocean's next move, and their next adjustment to the wheel. It seemed to go on forever. After forty grueling minutes, the storm relented. The rain tapered off and the wind dropped to twenty knots. *Chupacabra* assumed a more hospitable angle, and her cockpit drained. They were soaked to the bone and shivering.

The waves were still big, and Mia's heart leapt into her throat as they swept up the face of a freak twenty-footer. Blake handled the boat with iron resolve and, as they crested its peak, everything seemed to pause—to catch its breath—in that weightless moment before the screaming rollercoaster dive into the valley of dark water, on the other side. She smiled at her beau in exhilaration and said, "You are still my flippin' hero, Blake Barber!"

There was no time to decode the sudden expression of shock that flickered across his face as they plunged down the back of the wave. There was a spine-jarring impact. A tumbling body-slam against the compass bubble and instrument panel by the companionway, a sickening rag-doll jerk as she collided with Blake, who'd been pitched over the steering wheel yelling "No, God no!"

Mia got to her feet, grabbed a lifeline and pulled herself to the rail.

They were on something. It was under the boat, and it was huge. Her mind raced to identify the bright blue monolith protruding like a fin from the water next to the hull. "What is that? We hit a whale? Blake, we hit a whale!" she shouted, frantically.

"We're broaching!" cried Blake, clawing his way back to the helm. "We gotta get off it before we lose the keel!" But the keel was buried like a giant meat cleaver, deep in whatever they'd slammed into, and prevented the gale from pushing them over. A terrifying groan rose out of *Chupacabra's* belly, the rig and hull shuddering from the unrelieved strain of wind and water. Blake, back on his feet, braced one foot against the helm column, and struggled to look over the side. A long tubular shape covered in blotchy blue camouflage lolled in the water beneath them. "What the? Mia, It's a…" With the next rising swell, the bow pitched up steeply and the ocean separated them from the object.

"Oh my god!" cried Mia. "It's a submarine!"

Blake came to his senses as they plunged into the next trough. He started the motor and jammed the throttle forward, just in time to take them up the face of the next mountain of water. "Luff the sails!" he shouted, yanking the main free. She jerked the genoa sheet loose, unsnapped her tether, and dashed forward.

"Mia wait!"

She clipped on to the twisted bow-pulpit railing, and watched as the next swell lifted the eighty-foot cigar above her head. The desperate screams of men flew like tortured seabirds from a savage gash in the sub's hull, right behind the conning tower. Just as it seemed that the ocean would cast the behemoth down on top of them, the bow of the sub slewed skyward, crested the wave and slid into the next valley. Tears streamed down Mia's face. She struggled to catch her breath as she watched the ocean pouring through the ragged wound in the sub's side. With the next crest, there came a horrible cracking. The whole front of the vessel separated and disappeared. With the following swell, the rest of the blue submarine was gone.

"Mia! Get back here! Now!" She didn't hear him. She was frozen, staring at the curious white bales that were popping up like hundreds of giant marshmallows in place of the sub.

"Dammit! This can't be happening!" Blake shouted. "Mia! I think we've got water coming in!" With that, she released her death-grip on the railing, and returned to the cockpit.

"Take the helm!" He leapt into the cabin, snatched the radio mic and dialed in the Coast Guard. "Mayday! Mayday! Yacht *Chupacabra* in distress, collided with submarine. We're taking water. Sub broke up and sank. Repeat we are taking water, and the sub sank. Over?"

"Roger, *Chupacabra*. This is United States Coast Guard Cutter Joseph Clinton. What is your position?"

Blake read the coordinates off the GPS screen. "We are still under motor, making eight knots on a bearing one-four-two degrees."

"*Chupacabra*, hold course for St. Croix. Intercept E.T.A. twenty minutes. Update this frequency every five minutes."

"Roger Coast Guard, Thank you and out." He emerged from the companionway, and secured his tether. Okay, they're coming to get us. Mia?" She looked at him with unblinking eyes and quivering lower lip. "Twenty minutes, Mia. We have to hold it together for twenty minutes. I can't tell how fast the water is coming in. I'm gonna pull the dinghy up and get the survival kit, Okay?" She gave a jerky little nod. "C'mon, take the wheel."

***

The seas had settled considerably, and the ten foot waves now seemed tame to Blake. Mia had just advised the Coast Guard that *Chupacabra* was riding a foot lower, making her a complete pig to keep right-side up.

She stepped back into the cockpit, and scanned the horizon with binoculars. "They said five minutes, where are they?"

"Four minutes and thirty seconds away," Blake replied.

"You're not funny. Are you mad at me?" she said.

"Why would I be? Are *you* okay?"

"No. Scratch that. Yes! God bless America! Here they come!"

The USCG Joseph Clinton was a glorious sight: long, sleek, and white, with a towering bridge, and a wide, slanting red stripe on her bow followed by a narrow white, and blue. She tore across the sea like a wild stallion. In a few minutes the gleaming ship hove to, a hundred yards from *Chupacabra*. She launched a large, orange rubber boat from out of her stern. It rocketed across the waves, and pulled alongside. Blake and Mia pitched their duffels to a man in her bow and boarded before he could offer a hand. The Coxswain grinned, and told them to hang on as he wheeled the boat around *Chupacabra* and zoomed back to the big cutter in a huge s-curve. He swooped the Prosecutor-class interceptor around the back of the Joseph Clinton and straight at a ramp in a narrow bay in her stern. Mia's stomach did a loop when she realized what was about to happen. Blake was grinning ear to ear. At the last second, the coxswain cut the throttle and the Prosecutor swooshed up the ramp and stopped.

They were met by a female petty officer, and several seamen who took their bags and helped them on deck. The Prosecutor slid back down the ramp and roared off to secure *Chupacabra* for towing.

"Are you alright, Ma'am?" said the officer.

"I may have peed a little," gasped Mia.

I'm Petty Officer Kristy Andrews. Let's get you to the Doc, then we've got an appointment with the skipper."

There was a loud bang from *Chupacabra*. Blake stepped to the railing and watched as she turned across the waves and rolled over. Her keel, marred by deep scrapes and streaks of blue paint, rose as if to salute as she rolled over and went down. Blake turned to Mia and said, "We are *sooo* not paying for that."

They got into dry clothes, were inspected briefly by the ship's surgeon, then seated in a small office for a meeting with the burly Captain Wexler, and petty officer Andrews. The proceedings were recorded on video. The captain was not amused by having to rescue two irresponsible teenagers who lost their yacht in treacherous conditions, and he expressed his feelings regarding their foolishness without reservation.

Blake respectfully countered that they were experienced sailors, and had weathered the storm admirably, having covered most of their passage without a hitch. Unfortunately, his tone was tainted with sarcasm by the time he mentioned that they couldn't have foreseen a collision with a submarine in the trough of a gigantic rogue wave. Captain Wexler scoffed at the notion, and launched into a bluster of penalties and punishments for making fraudulent accident claims.

Mia looked him in the eye and shouted sternly, "I will *never* forget the look on Blake's face when he saw that sub. I will *never* forget the impact. I will *never* forget the *screams. Ever!*"

Someone knocked at the office door.

"Come!" said the captain.

Another officer leaned in. "Captain Wexler, I have the initial recon on the accident site."

"Let's hear it."

"Two Jayhawk choppers were dispatched and confirm a couple of hundred bales of narcotics spread over the area. Five bodies were recovered; all males, several believed to be of Middle Eastern extraction. Some fiberglass flotsam. High degree of confidence that the yacht struck a narco-sub. Sir, I saw the scars on her keel before she went down. She must have cracked them like an egg."

"Dismissed." Captain Wexler crossed his arms and leaned back. "Tell me about it, Miss Devlin."

When Mia finished, the captain stood up, opened the door and said, "You've had a helluva day. You two did a *helluva* job. Andrews, complete the debriefing and get 'em ashore. Merry Christmas." He exited, shutting the door behind him.

"Charming," said Mia.

"Pardon, ma'am?" said the petty officer. "Did you notice the armaments mounted on this vessel? In case you were wondering, it's life and death for us—twenty-four seven. The skipper acknowledged your crisis and paid you a fine compliment."

Mia gave a conciliatory nod, avoiding eye contact. "Sorry. You guys *are* awesome."

Andrews leaned forward on her elbows. "Because of the sensitive nature of certain details surrounding this incident, and because there was a significant loss of life, you are hereby ordered to regard all details of this incident as confidential and secret. Breach of this confidence could endanger the security of persons and/or assets acting in the service of the government of the United States of America, as well as your own personal safety. Do you understand this order?"

They answered affirmatively. She pushed a form and a pen across the table to each of them. "I'll need you to sign this affidavit, certifying that your video-recorded deposition was true, then this form affirming your understanding of your orders of confidentiality." They signed the papers. "You will need to remain on St. Croix through mid-day tomorrow. You will meet with a special agent from the DEA for further debriefing. He will contact you with instructions."

Blake started to speak, but Andrews cut him off. "I assumed that since your lodgings are now under three thousand meters of water, you'd need a place to stay. Arrangements have been made for you at the Azure Haven Hotel. A taxi will pick you up by Emancipation Park. Your aunt, I believe, is flying in on a puddle jumper later this afternoon."

The Joseph Clinton delivered them to the big pier in Frederiksted, opposite a cruise liner the size of Vieques.

By the time Petty Officer Andrews finished with them and escorted them ashore, the sun was shining and the humidity was hideous. Blake looked for a rainbow, but there wasn't one.

***

"Okaaay, how are we going to do *this*?" said Blake, observing the single queen-sized bed and modest chair.

"Let me illustrate." Mia dumped her duffel bags on a long bureau and plunged face first onto the mattress. "As long as it doesn't sink, I doesn't care."

Blake tossed his bags on Mia's, and sank into the chair in the corner. He kicked off his damp shoes, and put his puckered feet on the bed. The digital clock on the night stand said three p.m. There was a large bowl of fresh fruit on the bureau. He was so thankful to be ashore. To feel safe in that dim little room with his best friend. He knew she felt the same way. He watched her back rise and fall in deep, steady waves; listened to the whisper of her breath like the quiet rustling of palm fronds. *You're my island,* he thought. *I have faith in you.*

***

Talking. She was talking. Mia was giving Serena the what-for. Blake dragged his eyes open. He rubbed the stiffness out of his neck, and peeked around the edge of the curtain—sunset over the swimming pool. A huge green iguana, clinging to the trunk of a nearby palm tree, noticed the rustling curtains. Blake's gaze met with that of the reptile, and instantly an almost magical comprehension dawned: The iguana knew a sucker when he saw one. He bobbed his head slightly, and leaned toward the window perceptibly, as if to signal his readiness to accept any offer to ease his own loneliness.

119

"Baby sitter? For his *macaw*? Are you serious?" Mia griped. "Not another charity case! Don't call me Bunny. And I don't *care* if it speaks dirty French! Do you know what we've been through? Ugh! We're in a hotel. Because, Serena! The boat! Is! Gone! Yes, I mean gone! As in an octopus's graveyard beneath the waves! No, I *can't* talk about it. Look, get rid of Flakey Jake and get down here. Better yet, stay put. We'll catch the plane back to San Juan tomorrow afternoon. I want to go home, *now*. Non-refundable my butt! Hey! Serena? Serena!" She slapped the phone down on the bed.

"What did I hear about a macaw?" said Blake, still groggy.

"My aunt has the unfailing ability to find the most pathetic males on the planet. She feels it's her mission in life to rehabilitate, and bring the best out in them. Her latest project happens to own a macaw with the dirtiest mouth in the Caribbean."

"Worse than yours?"

"You're not even funny." She looked dead serious.

"No, but I am hungry."

"What else is new?"

"Wait," Blake said, "you mean that guy that cast us off, back in Punta Alegria?"

"So I'm told." She got up and stalked into the bathroom, slamming the door behind her.

Blake picked up a menu from the end of the bureau. There was a neon blue sticky-note stuck to the front of it. He turned on a floor lamp. The note read *Order anything you like. Sky's the limit. Compliments of Agent Feral Cain.*

"Hey!" he called to her. "I'm calling room service!"

Blake heard the shower start. He dialed room service and, waiting for them to pick up, peeked around the drape again. The iguana was still lazing on the palm trunk like an old, tired dragon. Room service picked up. He ordered pizza and salad, and desert.

Blake hung up the phone and fetched a cluster of grapes from the bowl on the bureau. No sooner than he had pulled back the drape and opened the pane than the big lizard dropped off the trunk and bolted for the window. Blake tossed grapes frantically trying to slow the iguana's progress long enough to shut it again, but the lizard—through much practice—snapped up the fruit effortlessly at a dead run. Suddenly, Blake had six feet of scaly green beastie in the room. It leaped for the bureau. Blake snatched the fruit bowl, rebounded off the door, and leapt to the bed, the iguana in hot pursuit. They made three thumping, crashing laps around the little room before Mia's muffled voice called indistinctly from the bathroom.

"Nothing, dear!" Blake called back. He bungled the last hop to the bed, falling flat on his back. Grapes, kiwis, and bananas flew in all directions. "Just a big… flippin'…lizard… in my… hotel room!" He clutched a kiwi and a few grapes and slung them out the window, followed closely by two bananas. "Here boy! Fetch!"

The beastie sprinted across the bed, and launched itself back into the great outdoors. Blake slammed the window shut with his foot. The shower went off. Blake set frantically about putting the room to rights. Mia stuck her head out the bathroom door.

"What the *hell* are you doing out here?"

Blake slouched innocently in the comfy chair, feet on the hastily re-made bed.

"Waiting for room service. I got churros and flan!"

"What was all that noise?"

"Water hammer. Plumbing problem. Only happens when you run the shower."

She regarded him with deep suspicion before retreating into the bathroom.

***

Blake's heels hit the floor and startled him awake. He realized in a drowsy fog that Mia had kicked his feet off the corner of the bed, and she was saying something. The clock read two a.m.. There was a clicking against the window behind him, like a spatter of tiny pebbles.

"Is that hail?" said Mia.

"I don't hear anything," he said, almost innocently.

"Sounds like pea-sized hail."

He shifted in the chair and pulled his feet up. "Well, let me know when the poop-sized stuff hits, so I can take cover."

A very firm pillow flew out of the darkness, hitting him squarely in the face like a sack of potatoes. She turned on a light and sat up. "Open the curtain."

"Why? Sounds like it stopped." As if on cue the frantic clicking resumed, followed by a substantial clunk. "It's probably a mongoose," he said, rubbing his neck and looking guilty.

"You didn't feed that lizard, did you?"

"Lizard?" He was dumbfounded as to how she could possibly know.

Mia scooted to the edge of the bed and got up. A stray grape exploded under her foot. She winced, and cast a sharp look at the fruit bowl, which was damningly empty. She jerked the curtain aside and shrieked when the giant Iguana lunged out of the darkness and hit the glass.

"How could you be so stupid, Blake? Seriously!"

"I didn't know he was an addict!"

"There were signs everywhere! Don't feed Fritz!"

"That's not fair, you know iguanas are illiterate."

Mia snatched her pillow from Blake, and scooped her blanket off the bed.

"You two have fun. I'm sleeping in the tub."

"What if I have to use the bathroom?"

"There's one in the lobby. Pay close attention to the signs."

17

Most of Azure Haven's breakfast crowd had opted for the patio. Blake and Mia had taken up in the back corner of the square dining room. A short man wearing his flat cap backwards, and toting a shoulder bag, walked past the entrance sipping something orange from a tall glass. He quickly back-stepped to the door and looked straight at them, raising his drink in a salute.

"There you are!" he chuckled as he ambled over, digging laboriously in his back pocket. He extracted a black wallet. "Blake Barber and Mia Devlin, I presume?" He flipped open the wallet to reveal a gleaming silver badge. "Special Agent Feral Cain. Drug Enforcement Administration." He set his shoulder bag on the floor.

"Please, have a seat," said Blake. "Thanks for breakfast."

"It's the least I could do for a pair of true American heroes!" He turned a chair around and dusted it lightly with his flat cap before straddling it like a saddle. His head was wreathed with a crown of thinning blond hair, the amber lenses of his sunglasses seemed to compliment the color of his cocktail. "Captain Wexler said you guys had quite the adventure." A waiter walked up. Cain flashed the badge. "Do me a favor, we need some privacy here." He nodded toward the few other diners. The waiter winked, and moved them to the patio.

"You mean Prince Charming?" said Mia. "You know, that stuff isn't just for breakfast anymore."

"That's 100% pure carrot juice, Mia. I don't touch alcohol. Dulls the senses. Some people add spinach, but that's too swampy for me. So, the old man was a little crabby, huh?" He looked over his shoulder, and lowered his voice. "Well, imagine you're a Coast Guard lieutenant—they only *call* you captain because you command the ship—and you're hot on the heels of a narco-sub carrying two hundred million dollars' worth of blow, hash, and heroin. *And* a dozen wild-eyed A-rabs headed for your homeland. You lose 'em in a wicked squall…" he took a swig of his juice, and licked his lips. "Next thing you know, you get a mayday from a couple of kids claiming they just sank the best shot at a promotion you've had in a decade. You'd be a little pissed off too!"

"Terrorists?" Blake said, in disbelief. Mia looked out the window, visibly affected.

"Blake, you two have served your country in a way most never could or ever will. And I'm proud to know you. So listen, I have some paperwork for you to sign and we have to talk about secrecy and national security, and all that. So, you guys are just cruising the islands for Christmas Break?"

"Just the American Virgins," said Blake.

"I didn't know there were any left!" Cain laughed. Mia's jaw dropped in disgust. "Uh, present company excepted, of course." He pulled a manila envelope containing a sheaf of paperwork from his shoulder bag, and dropped it carelessly on the table. "Don't have a passport?"

Blake shook his head. Agent Cain produced a small camera, turned it on, and told Blake to sit up straight. "Just for the records. Don't smile. Okay, now Mia. Beautiful!" He put the camera away, and opened the folder. "The Coast Guard report mentions you're looking for your uncle, a Carson Urquart. You find him?"

"No," said Blake. "He's Dive Master on the schooner *Tarshish*."

"Never heard of it." The briefing lasted another twenty minutes. Agent Cain packed his things into the shoulder bag. "Alright, people are gonna ask questions. You can say that there was a catastrophic stress fracture where the keel joins the hull. Probably a manufacturing defect. Blake, Mia, it has been a pleasure. If I were you I'd enjoy the Carnaval, watch the fireworks, forget about your uncle, and catch the first flight home."

"We intend to," said Mia.

Agent Cain shook their hands and strutted out of the restaurant like a rooster, whistling *Stars and Stripes Forever*.

"Loose. Cannon," were Mia's only words.

"I still hate Sousa," added Blake.

*****

Blake had hoped that wandering the green and pleasant grounds of the St. George Botanical Gardens would ease Mia's mind. She often retreated to the park conservatory back home when things were too hectic, and she didn't feel like hiking all the way to Stony Hollow. In spite of the verdant beauty of the place—the stone bridges, the birds and butterflies, and lurid flora—her mind was fixed on those desperate few minutes of the accident. The fact that the history of the park, not to mention that of the Caribbean itself, was a monument to crushing slavery and human cruelty seemed to seep into her mood.

He felt guilty for her suffering, but oddly unaffected by the accident itself. There was only a certain lurking shame connected to the loss of the boat, such as a child might feel after accidentally breaking the cookie jar while pilfering it. But it was over; Cain would make sure the insurance company covered it. The bad guys were dead, and a ton of drugs didn't make it to the USA. *What should I feel guilty about? What am I supposed to do?* he thought. *Go to my room and think about what I have done?*

Strangely, it was Kmart that seemed to ease Mia's angst. Walking up and down aisles of familiar things, and the smell of floor polish and new clothes, gave the momentary illusion that she was home. They ate lunch at Little Caesar's, then caught the bus back to town.

*****

Mia leaned against a stuccoed wall, phone to her ear, her simmering temper about to break into a rolling boil. She shoved Fritz away with one foot as he passed by. He hissed, bobbed his head violently, then trotted after Blake.

Blake was perusing the goods of a street vendor a few doors down, interested in a small, tan backpack, stenciled with a seahorse design. She ambled up looking severe, phone still in her hand.

"Do you like it?" he said.

"It sucks." There was meanness in her tone, and he felt its sharp accusing edge. "Serena missed the plane. The afternoon flight's been canceled."

"What about that guy she picked up?"

"What about him?" she growled, rhetorically. "C'mon. You wanted to hit the fort." She walked on.

He hated it when she was in a punishing mood. Nobody was immune from her scorn, and it made him feel like a little boy—a little boy who didn't deserve to go to the fort. A little boy who was being indulged in his childish whim, who was getting his way to the high inconvenience of someone so much his superior. It made him angry because he knew that she was daring him to say something. Daring him to pull the last block out of the Jenga stack, to give her the excuse—the justification—to loose her avalanche of pent-up frustration on a deserving world.

Blake knew her game; knew she needed to play it. And he knew he would, for... his sake. Then it would be over, and life would go on. *How do married people put up with this all their lives?* he thought. He bought the pack.

The sunlight seemed pale and bleak, draping the afternoon in a shroud of quiet anxiety. Blake looked down and beheld Mia, surrounded by the red walls and white shutters of Fort Frederiksted. She scuffed her feet on the brick pavement and stared at an empty gun carriage with a broken wheel. From his vantage on the wall, he could also see the majestic white cruise ship standing solemn and aloof at the end of the long pier. Fritz squatted at Blake's feet, nuzzled his shoe and gazed up at him, hopefully.

"How am I going to get rid of you?" he said. "I knew better than to feed you. I gave you what you wanted, and now you're attached." It hit him like a punch in the gut. "And as much as I like you, I have to get rid of you because you're... holding me back. I have to get on with my life."

A single tremor shook his jaw, and his eyes misted. "Oh, no," he said softly, looking back to Mia; but the courtyard was empty.

He found her in the Fort's museum staring at artifacts from the Middle

Passage—iron manacles, a cat-o-nine-tails, the bell from a slave ship. He suggested that a nap in the air conditioning while he goofed off at the beach might be the ticket, then dinner somewhere nice. She said she didn't want to be alone. He decided that a nap was what he needed too. She insisted that she would sleep in the chair, and that he could stretch out on the bed for a change.

***

Blake entered the pool area with a large tray of fruit. Fritz was on him at the first squeak of the gate. He managed a controlled drop of his load, as the lizard attempted to climb up his leg.

A hoarse laugh roiled into a cackle from behind. "Fritz demands sacrifice! The signs are in English, for the love of Pete!"

Blake turned. Feral Cain floated in a lounge chair on water so clear that he seemed like a genie suspended in midair.

"There were signs?"

"There's one on that gate!" Blake opened it. Sure enough, there was a green plaque reading *Don't Feed Fritz!* "If you're going to be an agent, you gotta start paying attention!"

"I don't follow?"

"You can't spend your life building coffins and fishing boats, kid! Is that the extent of your vision?"

"How did you…"

"Your website! Young man, you have a digital footprint two axe-handles wide! You're fifteen-and-a-half and you've sunk four boats in combat actions, to date."

"Three, technically. I can neither confirm nor deny any other incidents."

"Now you're talking like an agent! Blake, my old man was the bombardier on a B-24 in World War Two. European Theater. Intelligence came in that Hitler and Mussolini were having a secret picnic, and Pop's crew was assigned to deliver eight sixteen-hundred-pound sausages from the big deli in the sky. Flew a thousand miles over hostile territory just to have cloud cover scrub the mission."

"Wow."

"Hell yes, wow!" Cain sat up, sending ripples through the illusion. "Blake, what if you could go through life saying 'my old man was the guy who stopped World War Two?'"

"I guess that'd be pretty cool."

"What if you could *be* that guy? The guy that saved his country?" Cain settled back in the lounge. "Saved the world?"

"I don't know what to say to that," replied Blake. "Who wouldn't, I guess."

"You'd be surprised."

"Well, Mia's...uh, probably wondering where I am."

"I hear ya. Just a tip. You've got a friend for life, now. It's easier if you just carry him around like a big baby."

"Great." Blake glanced at Fritz, then slipped back through the gate, casting a scowl at the sign.

"Listen, you ever need a favor, look me up," Cain called. "Sky's the limit, Blake. Remember that."

18

Mia opened her eyes. She was sure she'd heard a squawk. It was 7:30 AM. Again, a squawk—but closer. Tromping, and lugging that came right up to their door. A knock. A squawk with French profanity. Serena scolding with a laugh. Another knock. Mia jerked the door open, and glared.

"Bunny! I've been so worried about you!" Serena beamed. She hugged her niece and pushed into the small room. "Blake, hunny, come get my bags, will you? Oh, Bunny, it's so good to see you! This is Newly and Nebuchadnezzar." The macaw screeched.

"OMG! Is he freakin' gonna do that all the time?" balked Mia.

"Just when he's excited," said Newly, cringing slightly.

"Which is most of the time," added Serena. "So, what happened to the boat? Oh my, are you two sleeping together?"

"Hell no, if it's any of your business!" snapped Mia.

"I sleep in the chair," said Blake slipping past to fetch the suitcases from the hall.

"Where's the bathroom?" said Newly. "Nebby can perch on the shower rod. Makes clean-up a lot easier."

"I think not!" cried Mia. "Let 'im crap up *your* room."

"That's the problem, Bunny. St. Croix is all booked up for the Carnaval. I don't know what we'll do."

"I can sleep on the beach. I don't mind," said Newly.

"That's a good thing for you," snipped Mia.

Serena opened the curtains. Fritz threw himself at the glass. Nebby shrieked and flapped his wings furiously. Serena dashed them shut again. "What was that?" she gasped.

"Get that damn bird out of here before I let the lizard in. He eats parrots, buddy."

"Newly Dewly, do you mind?"

"No, babe! We'll just take a little stroll, grab a brew." Newly shut the door behind him.

"Newly Dewly? Babe?" Mia said, with a searing look of disbelief.

"Blake, hunny, what happened to the boat?"

"There was a catastrophic stress fracture where the keel joins the hull. Probably a manufacturing defect."

"What's that mean in *English?*"

"It means the bitch sank!" Mia shouted. "What do you think it means?"

"Sank? Like…Sank-sank?"

"Un, deux, trois, quatre, Sank!" shouted Mia. "Eighty thousand dollars beneath the sea! Davy Jones' freaking locker! Total loss!"

"Oh, dear! I hope the insurance will cover it."

"But we're alright, thank you for asking—Not!"

"Oh Bunny, you're right! I'm so sorry. It had to be terribly traumatic."

"You could say that. We're leaving tomorrow, right?"

"I don't see why not. We'll do the Carnaval this morning, a little sightseeing this afternoon, and the party on the pier tonight. We can catch a plane in San Juan tomorrow afternoon. This bed looks big enough for the two of us."

"Sadly."

Something occurred to Blake. "I'll be right back. I'm going to check on something." He had long ago figured that Agent Cain must have pulled strings to get them a room, and left standing orders to accommodate their every whim. He went to the reservation desk and asked the clerk if there might be any vacancies. Magically, a cancellation appeared on his computer and Serena had a room. He returned with card-keys and good news, and immediately started to haul Serena's bags out.

"Where are you going with those, hunny?"

"I was taking them to your room."

"Oh, no—propriety, darling! Newly and I aren't, uh, *involved* you know. Bunny and I will sleep here, and you boys can bunk together in the other room. How on earth did you get a reservation just like that?"

"It's complicated," Blake said, setting Serena's luggage aside and retrieving his duffel bag.

Mia followed him out and closed the door. She took his arm and turned him around. "Hey," she said softly. "I'm sorry I'm such a crank. Thank you for being so awesome. I love you." He smiled reassuringly and, to his complete surprise, she kissed him tenderly on the lips. "Let's rock this island and go home. Okay?"

"You bet."

She slipped back into her room. Blake turned pink, and nearly did back-flips down the hall.

***

Fritz saw Blake pass the pool gate, and was at his heels in ten seconds flat. He would not be shooed off. "Only one thing for it," Blake said as he picked up the weighty iguana. He shifted the beast around so he could rest his warty head on Blake's shoulder.

"I love Carnaval!" declared Newly, arms outstretched as if to embrace the whole island "St. Croix, where the soup of the day is rum and Coke! Maybe your uncle is around here, Blake. Who knows?" A sudden fit of coughing interrupted his festive mood. He dug in his back pocket, produced an asthma inhaler, and took six hits.

"Newly Dewly, don't you think you're over-medicating, hunny?"

"If you're not wasted, the day is, Rena!" he cried, with a wheezing laugh.

The Carnaval village was a cross between a state-fair midway, festival main-stage, and just short of a cheap strip club. Not to mention booths selling every kind of liquor known to man. It was loud, crowded, and reeked of sweat and alcohol.

"I have to apologize, Blake," said Serena, "I don't remember it being this raucous."

"What do you remember, Serena?" jibed Mia.

"There's the Captain Morgan tent. C'mon 'Rena!" said Newly, pressing ahead.

"Go ahead," called Mia. "We'll catch up to you later."

"You kids be sure to pick up some Jamaican Jerk," said Newly.

"One's enough, thanks," said Mia.

Blake hefted Fritz up for the umpteenth time as they made their way out of the Carnaval Village and down the crowded sidewalk. Every so often someone would shout with a grin, "De signs were in English!" or "Don't feed Fritz!"

A skinny, white college student with round glasses pushed past and quipped "An albatross would have been lighter!"

"Thanks, Coleridge!" Blake retorted over his shoulder.

"I'm going to punch the next person who makes a crack about that scaly abomination!" said Mia. "Tell me again why you wanted to do this?"

"Serena said something about experiencing other cultures. Broadening my horizons. Sounded interesting."

"It's gonna be an education, that's for sure." The sound of drums tumbled down the avenue, and cheering filled the air. Blake and Mia slipped into a gap that had just appeared by the orange plastic barrier fence. "Here comes the end of innocence, Tux, avert you eyes!"

A wall of neon-yellow and green feathers vibrated and shimmied to the beat of the drums, like psychedelic peacocks stomping backwards up the pavement. With a wild cry, they jumped up and spun around as the music exploded in earnest. Gorgeous faces, gleaming smiles, and more undulating dark flesh than Blake had ever seen, jiggled, rolled, loped, and shook past.

Blake shielded his eyes with his free hand, and glanced at Mia. She chuckled and said, "Now you can honestly say you have a pornographic memory!"

A tribe of Zulu warriors went by, menacing the onlookers, steering wide when Fritz turned and hissed.

Another wall of feathery female semi-nudity vibrated along, molested by a cadre of lascivious men in lurid body paint.

"Oh, crap! This is the most animalistic, pagan thing I've ever seen!" cried Blake, face now bright red.

"Aside from your thirteenth birthday party, I agree."

"It's our culture!" chided a woman next to him. "You don't like it, den don' look at it!"

"Ma'am, I fail to see what half-naked black women grinding their butts together has to do with the birth of our Savior!"

She opened her mouth to reply, but Fritz hissed and tried to lunge. She squeaked in terror, and slipped into the throng.

"I think I'm starting to like him," said Mia. "You think he'd really eat that bird?"

A couple of floats passed, and the sound of steel drums—an army of them—ping-ponged off the buildings, and more excited cheering washed down the avenue. A group of what looked like giant swaying puppets in colorful satin Coolie jackets and cone-shaped hats—their faces veiled in matching scarves—loomed over the dancers, tossing candy, dancing, and performing antics to the delight of the crowd.

"Moko Jumbies!" said Mia. "I hate these guys."

"Why?"

"*Clowns.* I hate *clowns.*"

"Who doesn't?"

Behind the Jumbies, a large green farm tractor crawled along, towing the double-decked float of the steel drum ensemble. A young mother pushed in next to Mia, anxious for her toddler to see the stilt-walking clowns. The little girl was gumming a banana, a wary eye on the approaching Moko Jumbies.

Blake was relieved to have something of interest to look at above the embarrassing spectacle, and marveled at their ability to manage such antics on stilts. The blue Jumbie strode up, bent over and, shaking his head at Fritz, said, "Ohhhh mon! Dot's de ugliest baby I ever see!"

The orange one bent as he passed, and said, "Dot baby look just like Fritz!"

"Dot so mean!" said the pink Jumbie, bending to look Mia over. "He look just like his mama!"

The Moko Jumbies slapped their knees, and burst into uproarious laughter along with all those within ear shot. Mia's eyes narrowed to slits. She snatched the pasty banana from the toddler's hands, stuck it under Fritz's nose, and said, "Here boy!" She chucked it—splatting the pink Jumbie square in the back. Fritz burst from Blake's grasp and darted into the next troupe of now screaming showgirls. Suddenly, the pink Jumbie began to hop in a tight circle on one leg, trying to shake something big, heavy, and green off the other. Fritz had just reached the clown's thigh when the stilt separated, and the pink Jumbie careened into the blue, on his way to the pavement. Fritz changed rides, leaping onto the blue's back who, flailing with an Olympic backstroke, plowed into the orange.

The crowd was eating it up. Orange, now in possession of the iguana, dodged precariously through a group of plumed dancers, and found himself in a head-to-head with the green tractor. The driver slammed on the brakes as the Moko Jumbie side-stepped, tripping over the big wheel and plunging into the drummers on the top deck. The drummers clambered up their kits to avoid the slashing tail of the panicked reptile in their midst. The trailer creaked ominously under the sudden shift in weight, and began a slow and inexorable list to starboard. Mia grinned in devilish anticipation as Blake tugged her shirt tail and suggested that it might be a good time to go. They slipped into a little alley and trotted off between stuccoed buildings. There was a huge metallic crash behind them.

"Did that make you feel better?" said Blake, as they broke into a full run. She didn't look back. "Best! Parade! Ever!"

They caught a bus to Sunny Isle Shopping Center, slouching low in the back seat. There they rented a scooter, went through the Wendy's drive-through, then zoomed down to the south coast and turned east. After seven miles they cut back across to the north coast, buzzing through the hilly and historic Slob District, where the island narrowed significantly. They admired, with passing curiosity, the gleaming white wonder of Castle Aura; which looked like a Moorish fortress perched on the island's highest summit.

"Reminds me of that weird little castle in Metamora, back home," said Blake.

"Don't even remind me of *that* freak-show!" she replied.

They rode in the shadow of St. Croix's low mountains all the way to Punta Udall, the eastern-most point in the United States—and the extreme opposite end of the island from Frederiksted.

The road to Punta Udall ended in a loop crowning a high dome of volcanic rock, a good two hundred feet above the ocean. The jewel in its center was an oddly-shaped monument of four stone wedges arranged symmetrically around a central metal column.

"What is that thing?" said Mia, as she parked the scooter at the curb. Blake stretched his legs, and ambled up to a bronze plaque.

"Short story is that it's a sundial. The Millennium Monument. Indicates the direction of the first sunrise of the year in the US on January 1, 2000. Supposed to be two M's intersecting each other."

"C'mon. Let's eat," she said, sitting down and leaning against one of the wedges.

He sat down beside her and stuffed several warm fries into his mouth. "Stolen waters are sweet, and bread eaten in secret is pleasant," he mused.

They watched a herd of majestic cumulus clouds, urged along by the trade winds over a dark sea that went on forever. They tore into their double hamburgers.

"Man, I hope nobody was hurt when that thing went over," said Mia.

He hummed in agreement.

"I gotta pull my act together, Blake."

"What's that supposed to mean?"

"Face up to things. Everything I do is just me running away from me. It's no good."

"I find your dysphoria unsettling."

"I knew you'd understand."

Blake remained silent for a while, then slurped his chocolate shake. "I bet there are whales out there."

She nodded, took a deep breath, and felt the breeze moving her curls.

"It'll be weird to be back up to our butts in snow, tomorrow night," he said. "Doesn't seem real. I mean to be sitting on the edge of the world like this, only to have to go back home and be stuck again."

"All you have to do is slog through a couple more years at Pemberton."

"If we can't get rid of Turlow, I'm moving back to Gunn's and finishing high school online."

"Sounds like a plan."

"Yeah, but then what? College? What's after that?"

"You're the one who's always saying 'what do you want to do?'" She slurped her shake loudly. "What do *you* want to do, Blake?"

"What am I *supposed* to do? What's it all about? I mean, look!" He gestured toward the ocean. "It just goes on! Remember what you said to me when we first met? About the trees?"

"Can't say that I do."

"You said that if you dropped dead right there in the woods, those trees would just go on standing there, and the sun would just keep shining. You know how long that bothered me? I look at that ocean and feel the same way. It's like...does anything really matter?"

"It's a little early for a mid-life crisis, isn't it?"

"There's something else. There has to be. I don't know what it is, and I don't know how to find it. I need someone to show me."

"Then you gotta figure out what it is. I want to be a nurse, because I realize that I need to give back. But I'm a control freak, and I'm selfish, and my temper jacks everything up. What am *I* supposed to do?"

They relocated to a lonely beach by Whale Point, where they spent the afternoon looking for shells and sand dollars in the shallows, and generally maintaining a low profile.

***

It was nearly sunset when they wandered back into the Azure Haven, wind-blown and wary. The clerk smiled as they passed the front desk and went to their separate rooms. There was a sharp, ammonia stench in Blake's quarters. He held his breath and tracked the odor to the bathroom. Nebuchadnezzar was perched on the rod. The mess was unspeakable.

Mia dragged into her room, smacking the television off as she passed. Serena was relaxing on the bed. "Bunny! They were just about to show the parade!"

"Shut up!" Mia trudged into the bathroom and closed the door.

***

"Where've you guys been?" said Newly, lounging by the pool with a drink. "You see that steel pan band bite it? Holy cow!"

"No, we bailed out and left town." Technically, this was not a lie, Blake told himself; they were well down that alley when the trailer had gone over. "Anybody hurt?"

"Nah, just bumps and bruises. Cops came looking for you. Some bald dude with a badge chased 'em off. What was that all about?"

"No idea. Your bird has turned the shower into a sewer."

"Yeah, somebody left grapes out. Can't tolerate 'em for some reason. Housekeeping will get it, that's what they're paid for."

Blake considered Newly's report and was beginning to wonder if Azure Haven might not be a front for the Drug Enforcement Administration. It seemed about half full, now that he thought about it. *Now that's my dad talking*, he thought. "Maybe it would be best if you two actually did sleep on the beach tonight."

"Whaaat! And miss out on a night of air-conditioned Posturepedic bliss? Look, I'll cop you some booze, you can watch dirty movies all night long! It'll be a great time."

Blake turned for the gate.

"Hey, where ya goin'?"

"I'm going to slap Serena."

***

The pier was packed with revelers grooving to Reggae versions of old Christmas standards, and cheering the parade of boats decked out with glowing palm trees, flamingos and—oddly enough—UFO's. Bikini-clad women in Santa hats gyrated on their decks. Mia and Serena had already seen enough and returned to their room to relax.

Blake was standing at the edge of the crowd, admiring the twinkling flotilla in the bay, waiting for the fireworks to begin. A man with a heavy New York accent spoke to him. "Young man, you know you've got the prettiest girl on the Spanish Main?"

"I think so!" Blake said, as he turned and smiled. The man, who Blake guessed to be about 65, extended a leathery, sunbaked hand.

"I'm Giotta, Frank Giotta." His New York accent was so thick that Blake thought he said Jawter. "But you call me Jotty. Who are you? Where you hail from?"

"Blake Barber. From Indiana."

"Indianer? Mighty cold this time of year! So, you and your girlfriend come down to the islands for the Christmas carnaval, huh?"

"No. We're looking for my uncle, actually."

"Are you, now? The Mrs. and I have a fifty-five foot catamaran. Sail all over this puddle. And I never forget a name. Who's your uncle?"

"Carson Urquart."

Jotty sucked on his lower lip, his brow rumpling up under his gray bangs. "Urquart, huh. Gimme a minute. "Hey Mrs. Giotta!" he shouted into the crowd. Be right back, Blake, don't move." He made his way back into the crowd of revelers, returning three minutes later, with a broad smile. "Urquart. Short fellah, muscles?"

"Yes!" Blake replied, hopefully.

"Bushy biker mustache, dark red hair? Fifty-something?"

"That's him!"

"Two weeks ago. Jamaica. He brought that big, beautiful schooner in for repairs. The Mrs. calls her *Hashish*, but I know that ain't right."

"*Tarshish*! I have to tell Mia—this changes everything! Thank you so much Mr. Jawter."

"Jotty, son. Call me Jotty. You go tell her!" he chuckled.

Blake ran back to the hotel. Newly was trolling for unattended drinks in the bar when he saw Blake jog past. He hurried after him. "Wait up dude! Where's the fire?"

"Where are the girls?"

"Freshening up. You got good news?"

"We'll see."

***

"That's great news," exclaimed Serena. "Our own Christmas miracle!"

"No!" Mia said sternly. "I'm not setting foot in another boat."

"It's too far to sail," said Newly. "We'll have to fly. I've got a friend with an old puddle jumper."

"You don't have a passport, Tux, remember?"

"That reminds me," said Serena. "Someone left a package for you, Blake." She retrieved a manila envelope from her suitcase, and handed it to him.

He carefully tore open the top, and pulled out a folded sheet of paper. Spreading out it with one hand, he read silently.

"Well, don't keep us waiting, hunny," said Serena.

"A token of appreciation for your gallant service to the United States of America. Best regards, F.C." He slid his hand into the envelope and pulled out a little blue booklet with silver lettering. "It's a passport," he said, utterly bemused.

"Oh, *hell* no!" shouted Mia. She got up and stalked out, slamming the door behind her.

In the uncomfortable silence that followed, Newly pointed to the birdbath-sized Piña Colada on the table. "Is she gonna drink that?"

***

Blake caught up to her along the waterline, and strolled next to her without saying anything. Finally, she broke her silence. "I do *not* want to go to Jamaica. Period."

"Who'd your dad rip off there?"

"Nobody, surprisingly. It's just the most beautiful, crime-ridden hell-hole on earth. That's all."

"I thought that was Mangrave," he replied, in an attempt at humor.

She stopped and shouted at him. "We killed a dozen people, Blake!"

"But they were…"

"I don't care if it was Hitler's freakin' mother! A vacation should not include a body count! You can go to Jamaica. I'll see you back home." She was about to storm away when someone hailed them.

"Hey, Blake! There you are!" Jotty hot-footed it down from the crowd with the Mrs. in tow. "Been lookin' for you all over! Say, she's even prettier close up!"

Blake didn't waste the social momentum. "Jotty, this is Mia. Mia, meet Jotty, and the Mrs."

A stale "Hi," was all Mia could manage.

"Miss Mia, would you mind if I borrow your beau, for a minute? You and the Mrs. get to know each other."

"Be my guest," she replied, flatly.

Jotty led Blake down the beach a way. "Blake, I gotta tell you something. Listen, I'm just sayin', a year ago me and Doreen were cruising twenty miles off Columbia, sun comin' up, when we see *Tarshish* a mile ahead. She's got all her canvas up, and she's moving *way* faster than a schooner's got a right to. *Way* faster. And so I look down at the radar, and you know what I see?"

He had Blake's undivided attention. "What?"

"Nuthin'. Not a solitary thing."

"Maybe…"

"I checked it three times. We were pinging everything for ten miles then all the sudden, nuthin'. Screen went blank, and the GPS quit."

Blake contemplated the possibilities. "My uncle isn't running drugs."

Jotty raised his hands, defensively. "Did I say anything about drugs? I'm just telling you. Your uncle's sailing on an unusually fast ship that doesn't show up on radar. When he brought her in to Jamaica, she had a big tarp nailed to her port side. If I had to guess, Blake, I'd say they took a few rounds of fifty-cal off some drug runnin' bastard."

"Maybe a scuba tank blew up. Or the propane stove," Blake countered.

"May be! I'm just sayin'. Trouble in the Caribbean is like walking into a spider web in the dark, Blake. You don't know it's there 'til it's stuck to your face. You want my advice?"

Blake took a pensive breath and reluctantly said, "Yes, sir."

"Fall in love with your girl, and go back to Indianer. Speaking of which, let's go see what kind of trouble the ladies have gotten into."

He slapped a paternal hand on Blake's shoulder and escorted him back to the women. Doreen had gotten Mia a plate of food, and managed to get her to eat a few bites. Blake claimed Mia, and after exchanging cordial goodbyes, they started for the hotel. Blake turned and called back to the old New Yorkers. "Jotty, where can I charter a bare-boat in Jamaica?"

"Don't know, Blake! But I hear Indianapolis has a nice sailing club!"

***

Agent Cain propped his feet up on the bureau and adjusted his ear piece. A couple of taps on the tablet screen and he was once again listening to the goings on in the room below.

From the sound of it, Mia had barricaded herself in the bathroom, Serena was consoling Blake—who wasn't having it—and Newly was half drunk.

"I can't believe we were this close, and we have to give up," protested Blake.

"Bunny's right, Blake," said Serena. "It's another eight hundred a piece for the flight to Jamaica. We've just about blown my credit limit. As it is, we'll be lucky to get home."

"Maybe I can help," said Newly.

"Please don't," called Mia, through the bathroom door.

"Why not call the marinas over there," Newly continued, "and see if they know anything... uh what was the boat's name?"

Before Blake could speak, Serena affirmed *Butt Naked and Drunk,* hunny."

"Right! So, maybe they could get him on the radio or something. I'm sure somebody can get a message to him."

"See, there you go!" said Serena.

"Why didn't I think of that? But if he's there, I'm going—one way or another."

"That's the Spirit!" said Newly. "Like I told you, if that doesn't pan out, I have a buddy with a puddle jumper. Speaking of which, is there a restroom in the lobby?"

"Yeah. But watch the signs," said Blake.

"And don't feed Fritz!" yelled Mia.

Cain got to his feet, and hurried to the stairs. He heard the door to 14 open and close. He hurried to the hall below in time to tail Newly to the lobby.

Newly entered the men's room. Cain tapped the tablet screen and returned to the stairwell. In a moment he heard, amid echoey fumblings, Newly's voice.

"Rubio? Newly. Listen, a kid's gonna be calling over there tomorrow looking for his uncle, name of Carson, from a boat called *Butt Naked and Drunk*. Tell him he's out on the Wishbone Reef doing a diving tour. You expect him back in three days. Got it? Spread the word, and let the boss know that I may have our ghost."

Cain grinned like death, and pulled out his phone as he returned to his room. "Captain Flint? File a standby flight plan for Ian Fleming International, arriving tomorrow morning. Two kids, their aunt, and a twerp. This is the twerp we've been looking for."

***

Newly snored rum and vodka vapors in the pale light of Blake's tablet. *If you lit a match over his mouth*, Blake thought, *you could use him for a Bunsen burner.* He shifted in his chair and shoved the mattress with his foot. Newly didn't roll over, nor stop snoring.

Blake frowned as he flicked through listings for every marina, yacht club, wharf, and dry dock in Jamaica, copying phone numbers and checking bareboat rates.

This was his last chance. He knew he'd pushed Mia to her limit. The accident was days ago, and it still bothered her consciously. The screams of the drowning men were always there, in the back of her mind, and the sound of the submarine breaking in half. But for Blake it was more surreal than it was anything else. He knew he wasn't a hero and didn't like Cain treating him like one. Making it through the storm had been courageous, perhaps heroic; if he had known it was a narco-sub and intentionally rammed it, *that* might have been heroic. But it was just an accident that happened to kill a dozen evil men whose faces he had not seen, whose screams he had not heard. Beyond the actual terror of the storm, and the accident itself, it affected him little more than if he had only seen it on the evening news.

His head jerked up. He yawned deeply, and continued to ponder. If they had left Puerto Ferro five minutes earlier—or later—if there had been one more or less wind shift or gust, or slip of his hand on the wheel, they would have missed it. How could it have been anything but destiny, a sovereign intervention by the creator of the universe, which saved countless lives?

19

He rose with the sun, ate breakfast in the hotel restaurant, and started making phone calls. His fifth contact filled him with elation. "Yeah, dey come in and outta here couple days, mon. Dey out on de Wishbone Reef, by Marley's Rock. Dey come for maybe three, four days an' pick up more tourist." Blake could hardly contain himself. He rushed back to the girls' room and banged on the door.

"Mia, I found him! I found him!"

"She's in the shower, hunny!" replied a very sleepy Serena.

Blake thought for a second, then dashed outside and around to the pool. Cain was floating placidly, sipping something blue from a tall glass.

"I need to ask you a favor," Blake panted.

"Sky's the limit, like I said."

"I need to get to Jamaica."

Agent Cain smiled graciously. "Learjet do ya?"

Mia was in a dark mood when the private shuttle bus delivered them to Henry Rohlsen Airport. The driver turned left at the terminal and proceeded to a group of hangars and offices at the far end of the complex. They drove right up to the waiting Learjet. The morning sun glinted in blinding spikes off its oval windows. By the cockpit, flamboyant script declared the plane's name: *Sky's the Limit.* Cain helped with Serena's luggage, Newly hauled Nebuchadnezzar awkwardly in what amounted to a clear acrylic tube with a perch, and grated doors at each end. Mia was sure Serena had purchased it for him, and scowled at the muttering bird. Once everyone was aboard, Cain called to the pilot. "Take it easy on 'em, Flint. The kid looks like a puker!"

"You're not coming with us?" said Blake.

"Got bad guys to bust, buddy. God bless America, folks!" He waved like a political candidate and scuttled down the steps. A short man sporting a closely-cropped black beard came from the cockpit and secured the hatch. He clapped his hands together, smiled bashfully and said, "Alright everyone, my name's Nello, I'm your copilot. It's a short hop to Jamaica, shouldn't take more than a couple of hours. Please buckle up. After we're at altitude, you'll be able to get up and move around. There will be a taxi waiting for you at the airport. Everything okay?" Everyone nodded except Mia. She was watching Cain through the window. He'd driven over to the hangar and was talking to someone. When he stepped out of the way, she did a double-take. Sure enough, it was Jayce Mitchell.

The engines whined louder, and the plane began to roll across the tarmac toward the runway. Blake was grinning from ear to ear as they received clearance from the control tower, and started their take-off run.

The white, dashed lines on the asphalt whipped past like darts. The cabin tilted up, the ground fell away, and in seconds they were over deep blue sea. The whine of the engines eased to a tolerable droning as the plane reached altitude and the pilot throttled back to cruising speed.

Mia reclined her seat and closed her eyes. Across the aisle, Blake scanned the sea for schooners. Soon, Jamaica, green and splendid, stretched itself before them, low clouds scudding among the inviting Blue Mountains. The plane banked and swept in a wide arc to make an easterly approach, and descended for a smooth touchdown. They taxied straight up to a very small terminal building. The morning was already sultry and the transition from the pressurized, air-conditioned cabin into the damp heat made their ears ache and their stomachs turn a little. Nello carried Serena's big suitcases inside, pointed out the custom's desk, then returned to the plane. Blake and Mia passed through without issue, but the Custom's officer was not happy about the macaw. Another agent asked Serena if they were together and, upon her confession, commanded her to open her luggage. She suggested that the kids find a charter while they got all the fuss sorted out.

They went to the passenger lounge, which amounted to a waiting room with a few magazines and a couple of vending machines. A custodian swished his mop around the floor. Mia dialed the Ocho Rios Marina and asked for the charter desk, identifying herself as Serena Krakow.

"Yes. Yes. The *same* Serena Krakow. Who lost the *Chupacabra*. Flagged for insurance investigation? No, this is my niece's phone. I understand. Thanks." She looked at Blake. "I hate to tell ya, Tux; buuut, we ain't gonna get no boat in these here parts."

"Pardon; I hear ya say you lookin' for a boat?" said the custodian. "You see Cappy Potenza. Just down de road, three kilometers other side of Oracabessa. Ya look for de sign for Old Jetty Road."

"Do you have his phone number?"

"Na, Cappy got no phones. Taxi out front take ya right over dere. He fix you up."

They returned to the Customs desk; over which was spread the whole of Serena's wardrobe, and an astonishing number of Three Kings figurines. "Hunny, they say I'm importing without a license. They have to have a supervisor to clear me, but he's at lunch in Kingston."

Mia sighed heavily. "You are the kiss of death, you know that, right? Every charter agent in the Caribbean knows your name, now."

"Hunny, I'm so sorry. Blake sweetie, I hope you're not angry."

"We got a tip on a bare-boat just down the road. Might as well check it out while we're waiting."

Newly, calming Nebuchadnezzar, said, "You can get some groceries in Oracabessa, then pick us up at the fisherman's wharf. It's right by James Bond Beach."

"See, there you go! You have a plan," said Serena. She smiled hopefully at Mia, who rolled her eyes and headed for the front door.

The customs agent answered his phone. "Yes sir. Very good, sir." He ended the call. "You can pack your tings, ma'am. Chief says you're okay."

"Did he say anything about me?" said Newly.

"You gotta wait for de veterinarian, mon. I take de bird, you wait in de passenger lounge."

Serena hastily repacked, huffing and fussing. The agent in charge offered to carry them, while the second asked Newly to put Nebuchadnezzar back in his carrier.

"Dis way, Ma'am." He led her back out to the Learjet, and ascended the steps with her bags. Nello followed him back out onto the tarmac.

"Ma'am, I'll need you to climb back aboard."

"I don't understand. If it's about that boat…"

He produced his badge. "DEA official business. Please step aboard, Miss Krakow. Everything will be alright."

Reluctantly, Serena returned to her seat. The hatch was closed, and the engines began to whine.

Newly was in the lounge scrutinizing the vending machines, and poking his fingers into the change returns. The big customs agent came to the door. "Hey! De veterinarian call. He say no problem. You free to go, mon. Welcome to Jamaica."

***

The filthy gray Subaru rattled down Old Jetty Road at an alarming rate, veered onto a rutted dirt lane, and came to a skidding stop in what appeared to be someone's front yard. A small house sat atop a slight rise. Chickens pecked casually around the porch.

"Cappy probably in back, mon. That twenny-fie dollah. Five for de ride, twenny for de trill!"

Blake paid up, and said, "Keep the meter running, we'll be right back."

"Okay, mon!"

Mia had barely shut her door when the wheels spun in the dirt, and the Subaru disappeared backwards up the lane.

"Hey, jackass! Our cooler's in the trunk!"

Blake sighed. "It's not that far to Oracabessa, we can hoof it if comes to that. Let's see the boat." Blake headed around the small house, Mia fuming behind. There was a broad deck attached to the back of the house and from it the land sloped down to a narrow channel of dark water. There a grubby sail cruiser baked in the sun.

"Looks like a Catalina 36," said Blake.

"Looks suspect to me."

Blake climbed the ramp to the deck. The house was not in bad shape, he thought. He knocked on the screen door and called "Hello? Cappy Potenza?"

"Yo ho ho, and a bottle of rum!" was the exuberant reply. A man in a wheel chair rolled into view, then careened through the small kitchen, and crashed out of the screen door. "Fifteen men on a dead man's chest! Drink and the devil had done for the rest!" He wore a black plastic pirate hat atop his very round head, and had slipped on a toy hook-hand as he blew through the door. "Ahoy maties!"

"Yeah, we're here about your boat?" said Blake, cautiously. The man jerked his head toward the sound of Blake's voice. His eyelids drooped low over milky whites. He looked Latino, and he was missing a leg.

"You're not here for the party?"

"No. The boat."

"How come there's never a party? Who sent you?"

"A guy at the airport."

"Slingin' a mop?"

"Yes."

"Marcion. Never trust him."

"So there's no boat, the taxi's gone, and our groceries with it," droned Mia.

"Hey, you know how I lost this leg?" Cappy thrust his hook-hand into the air. "Jock itch!"

"I really hoped we'd left this in Vieques, Tux. Let's go."

"Hey, I was born in Vieques! You know El Campeon?"

"OMG," she said, tromping down the ramp.

"Vieques is the cancer capitol of Puerto Rico," said Cappy. "All the chemicals from the bombs. That's what got my leg. Diabetes got my eyes."

"Sorry to bother you," said Blake.

"The boat'll cost you a thousand bucks, cash. No questions asked. Where ya takin' her?"

"I dunno, Mr. Potenza. Doesn't look seaworthy," said Blake as he backed down the ramp.

"The wife takes her out every night. I'll throw in the dive gear, and a dozen eggs I boiled this morning. And some bananas!"

Hearing this, Mia continued on to the boat.

"I've got five hundred in cash right here," declared Blake.

"You're lying," Cappy said, flatly.

Blake swiftly pulled the cash from his wallet and snapped the bills by the ends three times.

"Hey, those are brand new! Lemme see one."

Blake handed him one bill. Cappy rubbed it between his fingers, then touched it to his tongue.

"She's all yours, kid! Shallows are light blue, deep water is dark blue, brown you need wheels."

"If she passes inspection." Blake gently pulled the C-note from Cappy's grasp.

"Sure thing!"

Blake joined Mia aboard the boat. "Wow, it reeks. What do you think?"

"Looks sound. Probably sloppy refueling. We're not going to do any better for five hundred bucks. Go pay the man."

***

"Wot de hell you kids doin' on my boat?" demanded the angry black woman, tossing her well-kept dreadlocks over her shoulder.

"Chartering," replied Mia. "Why does the whole cabin stink like diesel? When was the last time this engine was overhauled?"

"Charter my eye! Get de hell outta dere!" She stormed up to the house yelling "Cappy! What dem kids talk you into?"

Cappy rolled out onto the deck. "What's that, my chocolatina?"

"Don't 'chocolatina' me! Dey two white kids say dey takin' my *Kristen Rachel*."

"That's right, Tina."

"Dey just kids! What dey gonna pay?"

Cappy fanned himself with the bills and smiled smugly. "Five hundred fat gringo buckaroos."

She snatched them out of his hand, and held them up toward the sun. Mia and Blake joined the little kerfuffle. "Dey counterfeit, I know it!"

"I know a bad bill when I feel it, Tina. That's five hundred slices of American pie."

She gave an ear splitting whistle, and shouted over her shoulder. "Flaco! Flaco! Come to momma, Flaco!" She whistled three more times. The kids held their breath, expecting a muscle-bound minion to come lumbering around the corner of the domicile. But it turned out to be a pretty, pink pig that came trotting up to the deck.

"Come to momma, sweet pig! Here, find me de good ones!" Tina spread the hundred-dollar bills out on the ground. Flaco sniffed the first one, and grunted approvingly.

"That's a good one!" said Cappy. Flaco moved to the next specimen, sniffed it and grunted again. "And another—that's two hundred." The pig approved bills three and four. The fifth C-note elicited deeper grunting, excited nuzzling, and deep inhalation. Flaco raised his head—Benjamin Franklin stuck to his wet snout—and grinned, while making happy little screeches.

"Dat one's got cocaine on it. Dey smugglers!"

"Everything's got coke on it down here, Tina."

"*Kristen Rachel* cost you a thousand!"

"Five," said Blake.

"Nine, and I trow in the scuba gear."

"I've seen your tanks. I'll get my own. Five hundred."

"You runnin' down my gear? Eight fifty, damn you!"

"I don't think we want this boat," Mia countered, sourly. "We'll take our money back. "

"Wait! You scuba certified?"

"Who gives a damn? Tux, kindly rescue Mr. Franklin from that squealing mucus beast."

"I got new tanks in de back. Six hundred, I trow dem in the bargain."

"Deal," said Mia.

***

Mia set the choke and turned the ignition. She was pleasantly surprised when it fired right up and rumbled amiably.

"Watch out for all of the coral heads and reefs," called Cappy, as Blake cleared the moorings, and Mia throttled up.

Tina was overcome with emotion. "You kids bust up my boat, and I'll put de woo-doo on you! All your kids be born wit short tingies!" she shouted. "An' dat go for de boys, too!"

Once clear of the inlet, Mia ran the *Kristen Rachel* full throttle along the coast, past the spectacular Golden Eye Resort, only backing off as they rounded into fisherman's wharf.

"Why do you hate Jamaica so much? It's gorgeous!" said Blake, over the droning engine.

"My brother pulled some stupid crap on me here. Just about got me raped."

Blake didn't reply.

"There's Captain Dumbass," she said, bitterly.

Newly stood on a stout dock, Nebuchadnezzar sitting on a small Styrofoam cooler and a case of bottled water.

"What happened to my aunt?" said Mia, as they collected their guide, and headed back to sea.

"I thought they were gonna let her go, but then the fat fellah said she had to wait for the big cheese to come back from Kingston. She said she'd get a room and call you later. She sure is a great gal. Wind's perfect, we can reach all the way there. Should take about four hours."

"We know how to sail," snipped Mia.

He popped the cap off a bottle of beer and sprawled himself out on the leeward bench. "Well then, point her to forty two degrees and sail on with your bad self, Captain!"

The sails in order, Mia shut off the engine. Midway through the trip, she went to lie down in the forward cabin while Blake took his trick at the wheel. He was so anxious to spot *Tarshish* that his anticipation bordered on irrational exuberance. He breathed it all in. The whole adventure had been grand, he reflected. Worth every bit of the trouble—even if Mia were to dump him next semester. Who among the twerps of Pemberton Academy had spent their winter break turning the Caribbean upside-down? He conversed with Newly about his drifter life, and reaffirmed his own resolution to stay.

"It's hard to keep 'em down on the farm, once they've seen Paree!" Newly agreed.

Two hours later, Marley's Rock, a ragged hump of basalt and palm trees, finally appeared on the horizon. Mia, roused from her reclusive nap by Blake's triumphant shouting, was sure Newly had gotten him tanked up. She returned to the cockpit and took the wheel, so Blake could reconnoiter with the binoculars. He scanned the horizon until Mia called for him to douse the sails and set the anchor. They were a quarter mile off the island.

"Nothing," said Blake. "I think there's sand or something in the focus wheel."

"He may be on the other side of the island," said Newly. "Could have gone on to Navassa. You never know,"

"Navassa? That's almost to freakin' Haiti!" said Mia.

"Aw, he's out there somewhere." Newly shifted on the bench. "Lemme see your spyglass." He blew into the nooks and crannies, and turned the focus wheel. "I think I saw a screw driver in one of those drawers in the galley, when I was hunting a bottle opener. You go look, I'll set the anchor for Anne Bonnie, here."

Blake rummaged through the drawers, listening to Mia shout orders at Newly. The windlass motor stopped paying out chain and she killed the engine—the anchor was set. A distant hum reached Blake's ears from somewhere outside. Through the companionway, he could see Mia shielding her eyes and squinting into the distance. Then she looked to Newly on the bow. Her head jerked back in the direction of the hum, then suddenly she sprang to the helm and cried "Blake! We've got company!"

She started the motor, jammed the throttle forward, and threw the wheel hard to port. The boat jerked savagely against the anchor chain, knocking Newly off balance and sending him stumbling over the side. Blake fell back across a small table behind him. Something battered the hull like hail. Glass exploded from two portholes, and woodwork splintered from the inside out.

The emergency kit burst open and scattered its contents of first aid and signals flares.

"Blake!" Mia dropped to the floor of the cockpit, and grabbed her scuba tank and goggles. Blake could hear the dissonant hum over the rumbling diesel of the *Kristen Rachel*, still dazed by the sudden chaos. A relentless series of thuds rattled across the hull. The diesel choked and died. Now he could hear the crackle of automatic weapons and knew they were taking fire.

Mia's panicked face appeared in the bottom of the companionway. "Blake!"

"Go! Just go! Now!" he yelled.

She looked him in the eye, bit her lip, and then plunged over the side.

The hum grew into the groan of an outboard motor; the shouting of men filled the air. Blake cast about frantically. The door below the stove was hanging open, with one of the propane tanks tilted out. He grabbed it by the handle and yanked it from its rusted bracket. He cut the supply line with his knife, then snatched a signal flare from the floor. The attackers came along side, as Blake retreated into the tight passageway that led to the cabin. He jerked open the door to the lavatory and crouched behind it, igniting the flare. He grasped the tank's nozzle with white knuckles. Feet thudded into the cockpit. One of the boarders tramped across the cabin roof.

The first pirate jumped down into the cabin, his .45 pistol extended at arm's length. "Yahso, mon!" he called to his comrades. The next boarder jumped down. Blake's heart was in his throat, and his palm so sweaty he wasn't sure he'd be able to turn the valve—if it wasn't stuck to begin with. He squeezed hard and twisted. It opened easily. The pirates edged their way forward, scanning every nook and cranny. One sniffed the air, and wondered at the strange hissing sound as they advanced incautiously toward the cabin. The hiss roared into a wall of searing heat and flame. Blake lunged out with a shout, keeping the hellish jet on the thrashing, shrieking pirates. He chucked the tank at them and dove back for the cabin, as the sentry above opened fire through the deck.

The first burst pierced the diesel fuel tank, almost directly below. Blake scrambled through the small hatch in the forward deck, as the second propane cylinder took three rounds and ruptured. He flew off the bow as the fireball blew out the remaining glass in the portholes. It billowed out of the companionway and cabin-top skylight, blinding the sentry and setting his jeans alight. He fell jerking and screaming into the blazing cockpit. The boat sent up a pillar of thick, black smoke. Blake swam under the hull and freed the attacker's Zodiac-style speedboat. He gave it a mighty shove, and swam after it—pushing it a good three hundred feet before he surfaced under its angled bow. He watched helplessly as the *Kristen Rachel* burned. His unused scuba tank, super-heated by the inferno, finally exploded. An ugly mushroom cloud roiled into the sky, as the yacht listed quickly and sank. The column of black smoke drifted away to the southwest and slowly dispersed like a defeated specter. He hoped it would bring help. Blake swam to one side of the inflatable boat, took hold of the hand-line, and hauled himself in. He started the motor, and checked the only fuel tank. It was barely one quarter full. He wondered if that would get them back to Jamaica. Blake revved the motor up and down in a *Shave and a Haircut* rhythm, over and over. After two minutes, Mia surfaced and yelled from behind. He wheeled the boat around and dashed five hundred feet to meet her. "Are you alright?" he said, seizing her hand and helping her over the side.

"I'm Fine," she panted. "What about you?" She pulled off her goggles, shed her tank, and rested heavily against the side. "Uhhh, where is *our* boat?"

"Guess."

"Are you sure you're okay? You look dazed."

"I'm kind of overwhelmed."

She scanned the horizon, then the island. "There's dirt-bag, on the beach. Where's the bird?" She looked up at Blake. He was staring into the distance.

"Hey, Buddy? C'mon." She stood up and put her arms around him. "It's okay. You saved my butt, as usual." She combed slabs of wet hair out of his eyes. "Look at me, Blake." She was still trying to get her breath. Their eyes met, and she smiled. "Thank you."

"Thank God."

"Amen! What is it with you and sinking boats? How many is that, now?"

He looked away, again. "Like, five. And a submarine, and..." He shuddered. With a quivering voice, said, "fifteen men."

"Hey, put it out of your mind, Blake. Remember what you said to me when Lance Hopkins died?"

"I burned them alive," he whispered. "I can hear them screaming." He slowly collapsed onto the rigid floor of the boat. "They're still screaming!" he wailed, sending a chill down Mia's back.

She had really wanted him to be the strong one, this time; this revelation made her feel completely selfish. She cradled him for a solid ten minutes, and let him cry it out. When he stopped trembling, she said, "Where are we, buddy? Talk to me."

He snuffled hard. "Thirty-five miles off Jamaica. In international waters, without our passports. And there's not enough gas to get back home, or anywhere."

"So, up Stinky Creek without a paddle, basically? What're we gonna do?"

"I guess we better pick up Newly."

"Ding! Wrong answer. He's one of them. He was trying to signal the bad guys. Next order, Cap'n?" He didn't reply. "Blake, look at me. You gotta get us back home so you can marry me, right?"

"Yeah. Let's see what's on the other side, then head back," he said. "We'll be in the shipping lane. Somebody will pick us up."

They left Newly standing on the sand, and rounded Marley's rock.

Gentle waves lapped over three bodies along the waterline. Another Zodiac boat, half deflated lolled in the light surf. Two more corpses lay face down in the sand. One appeared to have the Stars and Stripes on his boonie hat.

Mia's stomach churned. "What the *hell* happened here?" she hissed, in disbelief. "Let's go Blake, now."

"There's a tank of gas in that boat. Here, take over."

"No! I'll go."

He maneuvered in behind the other craft. It reeked of gasoline. Mia jumped out in waist-deep water and looked over the edge. There was a white man in a horrid pool of blood covered by a rainbow sheen of gasoline. A bald eagle tattoo spread its wings across his chest and carried a red, white, and blue banner in its talons. The fuel tank looked like a block of Swiss cheese. She retched in the water, then reached in without looking and retrieved the man's Uzi sub-machinegun. She dunked it in the surf, and returned to Blake.

"No good?"

"Tank's all shot up." She popped the magazine out of the gun. Empty. She chucked the whole thing overboard.

A horn sounded faintly out of the north. Still small on the horizon, a ship appeared to be headed for them. Blake rooted around in the bottom of the raft and came up with a pair of small binoculars.

"Definitely headed this way. Mega yacht!"

Blake turned the boat around and gunned the motor. They bounced across the mild sea at twenty-five knots. Soon they could see the spectacular black and red ship clearly. The sun glinted off its three glass-enclosed decks, which soared over the sleek hull. The top level was crowned by spherical radomes and slanting chrome exhaust stacks. The behemoth yacht cut her speed while yet a fair distance away. Blake noticed that it was not black after all, but a gleaming navy blue.

"That thing could eat Wexler's cutter, and still have room for desert," said Mia.

"I'll say it again. Where did the money come from?"

A rectangular panel near the stern of the ship began to open as they approached. It became a docking platform, and a bald black man in a short white steward's jacket strode out onto it. A brigade of attendants followed him, carrying sections of polished guard railing which they seated in sockets in the deck. The steward waved, Mia returned the gesture. Blake backed off the throttle and pulled alongside. Two attendants knelt and caught the hand-lines as Blake killed the motor.

"Oh my, oh my!" said the steward, gesturing with concern. "What have we here? We saw smoke! Are you alright?" He had a distinctive accent, French African Blake guessed. "Please, come aboard!" The attendants assisted Blake and Mia from the craft.

"We were attacked by pirates at Marley's Rock," said Blake. "We left our guide on the island. He was one of them."

"My goodness, but we must notify the authorities!"

"There are bodies all over that island," said Mia. Someone needs to know."

"Sergio, inform the JDF of the situation, of the survivors, and of the castaway on Marley's Rock. Capriccio, load this boat into the starboard bay." One of the men jumped into the Zodiac, started the motor, and zoomed around the stern of the ship.

"Please, come inside." The steward gestured to the interior. They were escorted in to an opulent lounge with a full bar, and seated in a circle of comfy chairs with towels draped over them. A glass coffee table sat in the center.

"Close the bay, and notify Lucien we are clear. Proceed when the dinghy is berthed," said the steward to one of the attendants. The railings were removed; the deck was quickly mopped, and evacuated. Slowly, it rose and fitted itself into the side of the ship, and became a wall.

Mia settled into the thick cushions, and caught her breath. Blake leaned forward, elbows on his knees, and looked pensive.

"Now, what may I do to make you more comfortable? Are you sure you are alright, Mister, eh,"

"Barber. Blake Barber."

"I'm Mia Devlin. I need to let my Aunt know we're okay. And thanks for picking us up."

"We are so glad to have spotted you, Miss Devlin! I must apologize, but we are having trouble with our communications array. We will get word to her, rest assured."

"Can you just take us back to Jamaica?" said Blake.

"Again, I must apologize. We are on a strict schedule for the Cayman Islands." The steward smiled warmly. "We have already deviated significantly from our course. If you will provide me with a phone number for your aunt, we can notify the shore authorities by radio, and have them contact her."

"She's not expecting us until tomorrow," said Mia. "We can call from the Caymans. I'm sorry, but I missed your name, sir?"

"Ngandu. But call me Maurice, please. Allow me to bring you something to drink. A fountain soda?"

"Buddy, a cherry cola would be unbelievable right now," she said.

"Mr. Barber?"

"Root beer?"

"Very good." He called to the barkeeper in another language. The other nodded, and put two glasses and a frosty mug on the counter-top. Ngandu sat down opposite them.

"West African? Maybe Bissa?" said Blake.

"Yes! How do you know Bissa?" Ngandu smiled with delight. Mia thought there might have been a hint of unpleasant surprise mixed in his expression.

"I hear the French influence, so I figured West African. I had to report on language groups in Social Studies last semester. I guessed Bissa."

"You amaze me, Mr. Barber."

"We call him Mr. Professor, back home."

"Indeed!"

The barkeep brought the drinks. Ngandu raised his glass. "To your survival and good health!"

There was a moment of quiet sipping followed by deep, satisfied sighs.

"You have suffered quite a trauma, today. I can empathize. I know a little of pirates myself. I am from Cote d'Ivoire. Ivory Coast. And do you know what we produce in Ivory Coast?"

"Chocolate, isn't it?" said Blake.

"That is correct! On the order of eighty percent of the world's chocolate! Sadly, I must add, harvested and processed most often by slave children."

"I had no idea," said Blake.

"Most do not. But I *would* know. I was rescued by a very kind man. A former Anglican bishop from Congo—though he was educated in Europe. He was like an uncle to me. He brought me to Tobago, and saw to it that I had an education and a future."

"My uncle..." Blake began, but was interrupted when Mia peeled the monogrammed napkin from the bottom of her glass and read it aloud.

"*Mother of Harlots*? Tell me you got these in Las Vegas, and it's not the name of the boat."

"Scandalous, I know!" laughed Ngandu.

"Don't tell me *you* picked that name."

"It is the owner's sense of humor."

"And who is she?"

Mia noticed a trace of hardness surface in Ndangu's cheerful face. "Your host is Nineveh Cotillion." He pronounced it Co-tee-yone. "You have likely never heard of him."

Blake was now sitting up and beginning to relax. Mia suppressed a yawn.

"But you must be exhausted! Come, let us arrange your accommodations so you may rest before dinner. Your clothes will be laundered and returned to you in the meantime."

***

Feral Cain sat in the shadows of his room, and stared down from his window. Fritz lounged placidly under his tree. The pool was deserted. The sun was sinking into the ocean. He regretted the loss of that kid and his cranky girlfriend, and felt it deep in his gut. "All in the line of duty. True Americans, God bless 'em," he mumbled. He dialed a number on his satellite phone.

"Encryption, channel nine-six. Navigo one-two, niner-six, three." Cain waited for the computer to voice-print his request and encrypt his signal. The phone rang on the other end. "Cumulus, this is Radian Five," he said in a somber voice.

"Sounds like a bad day at Black Rock, my friend," replied Cumulus.

"Yeah. Belly up. Whole damned thing. Squad down. Leads cold. Assets gone Elvis without a trace."

"What about Auntie Em?"

"Got her locked up here in the Lizard Lounge. She doesn't know. Swim Team is in the dark."

"Hmm. Tough spot. Who bought it?"

"Passely, Quillian, Rivard, and Chase."

"And the bad guys?"

"Four tangos down. We found one guy in the shallows on the west shoal, roasted alive. The kid's boat is on the bottom. Looks like they took a grenade. Probably blew their propane tank. We cleared out before the Rasta Cops arrived."

Cumulus sighed quietly. He hadn't been happy about involving the kids. But the promise of finally exposing a long sought hard-target made it seem a worthwhile risk. Now it was square one, with four known casualties and two presumed. Two who would be missed in a matter of days.

Cain waited a moment. "What's the status on the luggage, boss?"

"Fortunately, the word is that the CIA lost track of it Tangier. I think we may assume it is safely on its way to Venezuela right now."

"Do the Venezuelans know?"

"Negative."

"Then, U-BOAT is still green?"

"Green," Cumulus affirmed. "Keep Auntie Em under wraps. She can't go back to Kansas. Resume project TOURISM until further notice."

"Understood."

"God Bless America. Cumulus out."

***

Mia was no stranger to luxury, but even in her exhausted drowsy fog the stateroom didn't fail to impress. The steward who attended her pointed out the bathroom, and advised that she would find a robe on the back of the door. She closed it behind herself and in a moment handed out her damp clothes. Mia labored back to the massive bed in her robe, struggling to comprehend the crushing lethargy that made each step feel like slogging through wet cement. She collapsed on the mattress and plunged into a deep and dreamless sleep.

Blake felt strangely at ease, he thought, for what he'd just been through. But, he told himself, people reacted to stress differently, and maybe it would hit him later; come rushing back unexpectedly at some inopportune moment. He showered, put on his robe and went out on deck. A steward stood nearby, and smiled courteously. The sun was setting over the bow. *Heading west,* he thought. He looked down at the froth curling along the hull. *Maybe about thirteen knots. She's never going to let me live this one down.* He stared into the soft blue distance. *Where was Uncle Carson? What happened on that island?* He thought. *What did Newly have to do with it? What had Serena told him? It was a trap. Newly led us into a trap. Now, Why?*

"Señor," said the steward, "Your clothing has been returned. Please dress for dinner."

Blake went back inside. His shorts and tank top lay folded on the bed, and next to them, a white shirt, black pants, shoes and a scarlet tie.

"My dad must be in charge of the wardrobe," he said, donning the shirt. The phone on the night stand rang. He answered "Gunn's Marina, um, I mean, hello?"

Ngandu chuckled on the other end. "Mr. Barber, if you are you ready, the steward outside your door will show you to the private dining room."

"Thank you. Be right there."

Blake hung up and found the steward outside his door.

"The clothing fits well, Monsieur?"

"Yes, thank you. Where did you get it?"

"The steward's wardrobe, Monsieur. This way please."

They made their way down a long hall to a sort of foyer, at the center of which was a glowing spiral staircase. Its steps appeared to be cut from blocks of crystal, lit by blue neon. Blake grinned, and looked up the center of the spectacular vortex. The effect was like one of those dizzying illusions by M.C. Escher, which he loved. The steward led him up through three decks to another foyer, and ushered him through a set of red double doors.

Blake was shown to the dining room. It was surrounded by glass and punctuated, strangely, by displays of ancient artifacts. "Please make yourself at home. Monsieur Cotillion will join you shortly," said the steward, closing the door. Blake took in the whole room; from the shining ebony table—fifteen feet long—and its high backed chairs, to the wine colored horizon. He was simply awestruck.

He passed down the length of the room surveying each item in its elegant acrylic case. He stopped at a slab of black stone carved in bas relief. It featured a chariot leading a procession of slaves, each tethered to the next by a chain and ring in the lower lip. The chariot driver sported a long square beard, and a hat like an upside-down flower pot. The next display was not enclosed. It was a three-foot-tall statue of a demon with four outspread wings, a man's body, and a grotesque lion's head with a sort of Mohawk; its clawed right hand raised as if taking the oath of office. Blake gave it a wide berth, and continued on to a slab of basalt covered in thousands of little wedge-shaped marks, like clusters of golf tees. On the floor, next to the display stand, he noticed a short red feather. The wheels began to turn in his mind.

"Can you decipher it?" came Ngandu's smiling voice.

Blake startled, and turned. The chief steward crossed the room and joined him at the slab. He was no longer wearing the white jacket, but a fine black suit, with a scarlet tie and matching pocket kerchief.

"I don't read cuneiform. Maybe it's a contract."

"Very good! Or perhaps a receipt for slaves. Or an Assyrian death sentence? And tell me, who is this?" Ngandu gestured to the demon.

"Arioch of Ellasar?"

"An excellent guess, but no. This is Pazuzu."

"Are these originals?"

"I assure you! Direct from the Iraqi Museum. Please, let us have a seat. Our dinner will be here shortly." He went to the table and pulled out a chair for Blake.

"They were looted during the war?"

"Au contraire! Saved from certain destruction at the hands of savages. And what is archeology, if not sanctified looting?" Ngandu said amiably, as he pushed the chair in behind Blake.

"Will Mr. Cotillion be joining us?"

"I must apologize, Mr. Barber, for the charade." Ngandu took the seat across the table. "But, in my line of work, one must make new acquaintances with the utmost caution. I am Nineveh Cotillion, and I am delighted to have you aboard."

"Thank you again, for rescuing us, sir."

"Certainly! So, what do you think of my Assyrian collection?"

"Intriguing, to say the least."

"That *is* the word for it—intriguing! To touch the same stone that the scribe etched as the king decreed bloody doom and horrific suffering to the nation that dared defy his authority. To feel that power, to know it was executed! To hear its trembling echoes through the millennia! It is almost mystical." Cotillion spoke in a subdued, wistful tone, his expression seeming as if he were lost in a pleasant daydream. "What do you know of the Assyrians, Blake?"

"They were beyond vicious. Hated. Feared by everyone. Pioneers in terror tactics and extreme torture."

Cotillion exhaled with satisfaction. "Yes."

A young black man entered through the double doors and stood silently at attention. Lank, and finely featured, he struck Blake as a ballet dancer.

"Ah! This is Lucien, my personal assistant. You may serve us!"

Lucien opened both doors, and a small all-male wait staff brought in the meal: Gourmet cheeseburgers, steak fries, and root beer. Lucien stepped out, but returned with a red macaw, which he carried to a corner perch-stand that Blake had not noticed.

"I believe you know Nebuchadnezzar?"

Blake struggled against a sudden tide of panic. "If I may ask, where is Mia, Mr. Cotillion?"

"She is quite safe, I assure you. As a team, you are far too dangerous and resourceful to keep together. Your escape today was brilliant. Not one person in a thousand could have done what you did. You saved your skins, and killed three of my men. What will I do? Do you know how hard it is to find good pirates these days?" he chuckled.

The awful comprehension rolled over Blake like a drowning swell.

"You were observed by the ship's spy drone, Mr. Barber. I watched the entire spectacle, live, in the ship's theater. I have been studying your Facebook page, and the voluminous archives of the Freeman Gazette Online. Do you know, I believe I own a mall, and a frozen custard franchise in Indiana?"

Lucien and the wait staff cleared out. Blake thought he might faint at any moment.

"Breathe, Mr. Barber! Please, have a drink. Have a bite! Take a moment to collect yourself. We have much to discuss."

Blake took a swig of his root beer.

"What if," said Cotillion. "Two very powerful words; the very essence of the mystical future. What if you, Blake Barber, could become the second most powerful man in the Caribbean? What if you had the reins of power, wealth, and control in your hands? What if together we could bring the drug cartels into line, and stop the needless violence, establishing economic stability in hundreds of villages across the Americas? I am a business man, Mr. Barber. I use simple, but almost fool-proof shipping methods. But someone has discovered the secret to my success, and it is cutting into my profits—deeply."

"With all due respect sir, what do Mia and I have to do with that?"

"Indeed," smiled Cotillion. "I had hoped that you could enlighten me. A submarine went down with all hands a few days ago between St. Croix and Vieques. What do you know about it?"

"You mean, like a Navy sub?"

"You tell me. All hands were lost."

Blake remained silent, trying to look puzzled.

"Along with a cargo of narcotics and a squad of Muslim terrorists. Fortunately for both of us, they did not reach the mainland."

"That *is* a good thing."

"However; they were weapons themselves! Diseased with an extremely virulent pathogen. Anyone who came into contact with their bodies is dead or dying. Just two hours ago Puerto Rico declared a state of emergency. The whole island is quarantined."

"How…"

"I have my sources. The submarine, Mr. Barber. Tell me about it."

"I, I signed papers."

"Undoubtedly. What did the sub look like? Were there any unusual markings?"

"I can neither confirm nor deny any knowledge of a submarine."

"Come now, Mr. Barber."

"Why is it important to you? Were those your men?"

"I assure you they were not. I am relieved that they were stopped short of fulfilling their mission. I have a vested interest in the well-being of the United States. Just as you have for the *girl.*" Cotillion smiled, and Blake took his meaning.

"I didn't get a good look. We crested a monster wave. There it was in the trough. We slammed into it."

"The color?"

"Patchy shades of blue. Like camouflage."

"No unusual markings or insignias?"

"Not that I could see. We thought we hit a whale."

"It was a large vessel, then?"

"Twice our length or more. Maybe eighty feet."

Cotillion rubbed his palms together, and offered a business-like smile. "Thank you, Mr. Barber. That is good news. Tell me about your debriefing."

"The Coast Guard. Captain Wexler interviewed us."

"I rather think there was another. On St. Croix, perhaps."

Blake hesitated.

"Think of the girl."

"I'm thinking of my word."

"You may trust my word, Blake. Deal truly with me, and I will deal truly with you. Now, I know that your uncle is out there somewhere in a yacht ostensibly leading ecotours. But no one has seen him for months. There is a ghost ship marauding my convoys. It jams the radio, radar, and GPS of my scouts. The courier boats disappear without a trace. My cargo sleds do not release their beacon-buoys. I have come halfway around the world to unravel this mystery. I wonder; *what if* your uncle and his ship have something to do with it?"

"What if..." Blake stared at his plate, and summoned his courage. "My head explodes and your ass catches fire?"

It took his host a second to comprehend and, for a moment, it appeared this might have been the wrong time for defiance. But then Cotillion burst into uproarious laughter.

"You Americans and your knack for the wonderfully ridiculous retort! May I quote you?" He settled down, and mused, "I am looking for an extraordinary man to be my aide de camp, my right hand. Who would think that I would find it in a teenager from Indiana."

"Who said that you have?"

Cotillion stood. "Look at you—fantastic! Intelligent, fine-looking, spirited, enterprising. What if—I leave you here to think about it, tonight?

Discuss it with Nebuchadnezzar, if you like. And take some time to consider my Assyrian collection, carefully. You will be watched, and the doors will be guarded. "Bon soir, Monsieur Barber." The parrot squawked something that Blake was sure was not 'good night.' Cotillion chuckled as he walked out.

Blake rested his elbows on the gleaming table, put his face in his hands and exhaled. "Lord, what have I done? What can…"

The Macaw flew over and landed near him. It eyed the little cluster of grapes on his plate. Blake looked up and, jerking the plate to himself, scolded "Stoof it in yer pookits, you freakin' traitor!"

"Merde!" shrieked the bird.

"Stoof it in yer pookits!"

"Merde!" Nebuchadnezzar lunged for the grapes.

"Get lost!" Blake nailed him with a grape. The macaw snatched if off the table. "Merci! Zut alors!"

Blake nailed him with another. "Merde! Zut alors! Merci!"

Then it occurred to him. He offered a grape to Nebuchadnezzar. "Stoof it in yer pookits! Say 'Stoof it in yer pookits!'" The bird went on cussing. Blake persisted until he ran out of grapes, then asked the steward outside the door for more. By two a.m., the table was decorated with a white splattered mess, and the Macaw at last uttered his first "stoof it." By six he had the whole phrase.

When the stewards came in to clean up for breakfast, they stopped in their tracks and stared at the table in horror.

"Oh hey," Blake said, from the couch. "Just a tip. Don't ever, I mean *ever,* give that bird grapes unless you're planning to get into the guano business!"

Stacks of Towels, and a couple of gallons of bleach were fetched and the decontamination commenced in earnest.

"Holy cow, can we open a window here?" asked Blake. When the cleaning crew ignored him, he asked loudly in Spanish and pantomimed. He was politely refused.

"Oh, sorry. You're busy. I'll get it myself." He went to the demon statue, and broke it free from its base. The stewards froze in stark terror as Blake hefted it up and chucked it through the glass with a shout of triumph. He smiled at them as he retrieved Nebuchadnezzar and launched him into the friendly skies. The salt air smelled good. It smelled like freedom. He retired to the couch, heart pounding, and managed a few more minutes of edgy sleep.

***

"Daniel! Has your God been able to save you?" said Cotillion grandly, as he strode into the room. He regarded the window with a curious glance and amused expression, as he motioned Blake to his seat at the table. Lucien followed, and stood by his master's chair.

"You stayed up all night teaching Nebuchadnezzar English? And you chucked poor Pazuzu out the window! A rather unorthodox escape plan."

Blake peeled himself off the couch and came to the table. "Got to work with what you've got."

Cotillion chuckled. "Good. The Phobolyn has given you focus, and nerve."

"You've been drugging me?"

"Oh, no-no, Mr. Barber! Miss Devlin was drugged. You have been medicated and carefully monitored for side effects—of which I am happy to report, there are none. Although I must warn you, the withdrawal from this particular anti-anxiety compound is quite unpleasant."

"Where is Mia."

"She has been relocated to more suitable accommodations. Time is growing short, Mr. Barber. The wheels of fate are in motion. What if I let you go? You would return to Indiana, back to building coffins and racing little boats, when there is so much more in your grasp?" He slid smoothly into a chair and drew close. He put his arm across Blake's shoulder and breathed gently in his ear. "Blake, Blake, I can give you everything, if you just tell me what I want to know. So much more than any little girl." Blake quivered as he realized what Cotillion was intimating. He felt filthy. "What if, Blake? What if you don't tell me about the ghost ship?" he whispered as he caressed Blake's neck and cheek. "Let me tell you what will happen to Mia." Tears rolled down Blake's face, and his stomach prepared to offer up its meager portion of acid, mucus, and bile as Cotillion narrated his most inhuman intents. Excruciating tension burned in his head. It felt as if his brain was made of glass, and that it was about to shatter at the speed of light—and he wished that it would as Cotillion concluded, "And you will see, and smell, and hear every moment of it. And the video will make me millions on the black market."

Blake suddenly clutched fistfuls of his hair and wailed, stark raving mad. His whole body shook violently. The air suddenly stank of raw sewage. Cotillion stood back, and smiled with satisfaction. "Quickly, tell me about the ghost ship!"

"*Tarshish*," groaned Blake.

"And?"

"Staysail schooner."

"Masts. How many?"

"Two."

"Her length?"

"One hundred ten at the waterline. One hundred thirty overall."

"Propulsion?"

Blake shook his head. "I hear she's fast."

"For a schooner, she is damn fast. You are doing well, Blake. Crew?"

"Carson Urquart. Barrett Reynolds, Master." Blake began to wail again, then threw up on the table.

"Last known location?"

"Tobago. Headed west for the Dutch…" Blake dry-heaved painfully.

"Antilles. Again, who questioned you after you sank the submarine?"

"Coast guard. Captain Wexler."

"And in St. Croix?"

"Agent Feral Cain."

Cotillion almost swooped to Blake's side. He produced a silk handkerchief, wiping Blake's cheeks, chin, and mouth. "Tell me about this man."

"Short. Stocky. Bald. Face like a lunatic skull."

"How does he speak? Is he brash? Does he use profanity?"

"Soft spoken. In a way that makes you distrustful."

"Which agency? What did he say about your uncle?"

"DEA. He said to forget Carson and go back home before something bad happened to us."

"So, this is my nemesis!" He stood up and stalked away, smiling in delight. When he reached the end of the table he turned on his heel. "Your uncle and his friend are working for this Agent Cain."

"No."

"I am afraid so. They did not return to Puerto Rico as you anticipated. They proceeded to hunt my little squadrons all the way to Barranquilla, Columbia where they narrowly escaped my ambush. I would wager that they met their master in Jamaica, with their hold full of my cocaine."

"My uncle is a veteran and a patriot!"

"Then we must rescue him from the clutches of this Agent Cain and provide him with the opportunity to truly serve his country."

"He will never…"

"What if I told you that the very fate of the United States is in *your* hands?"

"Blake shook his head, and it hurt. "What?" he heaved.

"I need your uncle, and I need his ghost ship. I have discovered that the Suiza Cartel is working with the Venganza de Dios—an Islamic terrorist cabal in Venezuela. They have acquired a nuclear device. Probably Russian. If their plans are successful, thousands of your countrymen will perish. Your President will declare martial law. Your economy will collapse. Anarchy will consume your cities. The borders will close."

"And you will have no buyers. No victims."

"Precisely. You need to rest. Recover your wits. We will speak again in the afternoon." He clapped his hands twice, and a trio of stewards appeared instantly. "Clean this up." To his assistant he said, "Lucien, take Mr. Barber to his cabin. See that he has whatever he needs to be comfortable." Stepping close to him, he whispered "Increase his Phobolyn to 10 milligrams, each day."

***

Blake stood in the shower, inundated by water jets from all directions. Primal anxiety churned in the pit of his stomach, quivered in his low back and spine.

His knees threatened to buckle. He closed his eyes and concentrated on simply taking one steady breath after another.

The slightest thought of his situation sent prickling waves across his skin that felt like his soul was being squeezed out through his pores. After a half hour he turned off the water, barely toweled himself dry and, step by tenuous step, went to the bed. His cargo shorts and tank top were still there. The crossed cannons and faded words *Gunn's Marina* on his shirt brought back memories of the familiar, restored a little reality. There was also a red Guyaberra shirt with white decorative embroidery on its front.

On the night stand there was a note, a bottle of water, and a little paper cup containing a single baby-blue pill. He read *Please take the Phobolyn tablet. Enjoy breakfast in your stateroom. Be ready to tour the ship this afternoon. Your briefing will commence after Dinner. Cotillion.*

He stared at the pill. *Nothing matters but Mia, now,* he thought. He threw it into the back of his mouth, wrenched the cap off the bottle and drank it down. He paused to make sure the water would stay down, then said, "Blessed be Yahweh my strength, which teacheth my hands to war, and my fingers to fight." In three minutes, a wave of calm washed over his body like a refreshing breeze. There was a knock at the door. Blake dressed, leaving the Guyaberra unbuttoned. It was Lucien. He scanned Blake from head to toe with a single contemptuous flick of his eyes. "Breakfast for Monsieur." His voice was soft, and petulant. Another steward wheeled a cart into the room and exited.

"I want to speak to Mia."

"I will return for you in ninety minutes."

"Tell Mr. Cotillion."

"You may ask him in ninety minutes." Lucien's nostrils flared. "That was *Ngandu's* shirt." Lucien and the steward walked away.

"*Was* Ngandu's?" Blake said to himself. "*Was?*" He pondered whether Lucien's pouting declaration was a jealous lament or a veiled warning. The aroma from the breakfast cart hijacked his attention. It was loaded with steak, eggs, and anything else he could have asked for. He ate it all.

20

Mia struggled to consciousness through what felt like a heavy hangover, and groaned. She'd have lain there for another hour if the call of nature hadn't been so insistent.

Something was off. The room wasn't moving, not rocking gently with the ocean swell. *We're in port. Thank God, we're in Grand Cayman, she thought.* Then she realized that the mattress was on the floor. The drapes were open a little. She struggled to her feet and peeked through them, her eyes stinging as they adjusted to the light. Forest. Hillside. Balcony. A very ugly, very muscular brown man with an assault rifle, in the clearing below. He leered at her and curled his upper lip in an evil, lascivious smile. She checked the latch on the glass doors. There was no bar in the floor track. The call of nature was becoming a scream. The room was small, almost like the one at the Azure Haven. The deadbolt on the door was locked from the outside. She was a prisoner.

When the going gets tough, the tough go pee, she thought. The little bathroom was clean, and the doorknob had a working button-lock. She sat down and tried not to hyperventilate. Voices rose outside her room. She finished her business, and looked for something to swing, throw or stab with. *Okay, Tux. Gloves are off. If they want Karate, they get Karate.*

They banged on the door. "Hey! gyal, wake up! You deh home?" called a raucous voice. There was more banging. "Wake up. You got phone call! You wake?"

"She's no wake mon," said another. There was muffled banter that made her think there might be four men outside.

"I comin' in gyal! We all got guns, so you play nice!"

She heard the deadbolt turn, and the door ease open.

"Where you at? You don' want miss dis call!"

"Check deh bawtroom, Robaire."

The first sentry tried to turn the knob and found it locked. "Okay, I slide deh phone unnah deh door."

The phone popped under the door and skidded on the tile. She picked it up. "Hello?"

"Mia? I am so, so sorry! Are you okay?"

"Blake! I'm in some kind of house. Blake, where are you?" she said, trying to stay calm.

"On the ship. Listen to me. As long as I do what Mr. Cotillion wants, you'll be okay. He'll let us go. It'll take a few days. I love you."

"Blake, please get me out of here!"

"I will, or I'll die trying. I promise. Pray, Mia. Pray. And remember, Viking or victim."

"Blake?"

"Miss Devlin, a pleasure to speak with you again!" came Cotillion's voice. "I hope you are finding my little 'guest house' a suitable accommodation. If you need anything, simply let the sentry outside your door know. I apologize for the inconvenience, but I need Mr. Barber's complete obedience and you are the only leverage I possess to guarantee it. With any luck, you will be free in a matter of a week or so. Good day."

The connection ended. "You gimme back, gyal!" said Robaire.

Mia slid it under the door. "Get out."

"We goin'!"

"Wait! There's a scary guy under my window."

"Aw, dat just Macoute!"

"Keep him away from me."

"Don' worry! Deh boss tell him stay 'way!"

The door closed and the deadbolt slid into the metal jamb. It was two hours before she opened the bathroom door.

***

Cotillion slipped the phone back into his jacket. "There. You see she is fine." Blake's tour had concluded on the highest deck on the ship, with the phone call. They stood at the railing, wind blowing in their faces. The *Mother of Harlots* was now making a good twenty knots southeasterly, Blake estimated. There was no land in sight.

"I wonder what you must be thinking. My God, my God! Why hast thou forsaken me? How could you let this happen? Hah! Throw yourself down, Blake! He shall give his angels charge concerning thee: and in their hands they shall bear thee up!"

Blake gave him a quick, side-eyed glance.

"Go ahead. Say it." Cotillion smiled.

"Get thee behind me."

"Finish it. Don't be afraid."

"Satan."

"Yes. Very good! Why do the Muslims call your country The Great Satan?"

"They hate our freedom."

"Or perhaps it is your backing of corrupt and cruel monarchies and exploitation of national oil resources? Or the voluminous export of pornography? Your country has a problem with illegal immigration, isn't that so? Why do you think that is?"

"We're the most prosperous nation in the world. People are looking for a better life, I guess. Democracy and freedom."

"That is the red, white, and blue view from the suburb. Many on the outside see it differently. Perhaps it is connected to your government's long standing habit of overthrowing democratically elected regimes? And let us not overlook the installation of vicious puppet-dictators who guarantee the interests of rapacious American corporations, and ensure U.S. political domination? Civil war inevitably erupts! Civil order vanishes. Death squads terrorize the people, the economy is destroyed. Men sink into the darkest brutality imaginable. Those who can, flee to the U.S.A.—the Promised Land—where they are hated, demonized, and exploited still further."

Blake stared into the distance, red shirt-tail flapping in the breeze.

"Surely you can appreciate the tragic irony? All over the world, men and women must labor to feed the hunger of their families by feeding the addictions of yours. From chocolate to soccer balls to basketball shoes, America thrives on slavery—most often child slavery."

Blake remained pensive for a long moment. Cotillion's assertion brought a damning verse from the Bible ringing into his head. Finally he spoke, "For all nations have drunk of the wine of the wrath of her fornication, and the kings of the earth have committed fornication with her, and the merchants of the earth are waxed rich through the abundance of her delicacies."

"And slaves, and souls of men," Cotillion concluded, with a grimly dramatic tone. "To change these things requires power, Blake. Control, influence, wealth; with these you can make a difference. Improve the lives of tens of thousands. Lift them up, Blake! The widows, the orphans, the oppressed! Leave your mark on the world. Do justice for the defenseless! It is all within your grasp, Blake Barber. Take hold of your destiny! Only submit to me and I will give you all that you need to accomplish it. Or will you go back to building boxes for the dead?"

Blake scowled. "It is written: You shall worship Yahweh your God. Him alone shall you serve."

Cotillion's phone dinged softly in his pocket. He read the text message from Sergio, his chief of intelligence:

Intel confirms disappearance of 3 Suiza fast-boats between Capurganá to Cartagena in the last Eighteen hours. Indicates northeasterly course of Target. Expect Target to Refuel in Curacao.

Cotillion dialed.

"Wonderful news, Sergio! Send Newly, Davis, and Shelton to Willemstad immediately. Set Course for 30 kilometers north of Curacao. Notify Chichiriviche to establish a picket around the islands and the coast. Aruba to Bonaire." He popped the phone back into his pocket. "Your uncle has been busy! He has taken three of Suiza's boats in one night. There will be hell to pay!"

***

Blake ate lunch in the game room, skipped his Phobolyn tablet, and went swimming in the ship's main pool. He sidestroked past Lucien, who stood by with a steward holding a stack of towels, and a robe draped over one arm. It was time to pull it together, and go Viking.

"Is he here to keep an eye on me, or you?" Blake taunted.

"Monsieur asks you to take a nap this afternoon. You will dine with Monsieur at sunset."

"Did Monsieur tell you I'm your replacement? So, what do you think you'll do next, buddy? Looks like I'm in training for your job!"

Lucien sucked it up.

"So, what happened to Ngandu? You do him in, too?"

The steward looked away. But Blake caught the restrained expression of fear and anguish that gripped his face. Lucien swallowed hard. "You will not speak of him."

***

Lucien escorted Blake into the main dining room, followed by the wait staff. Cotillion was already seated.

"I thought we would dine where the view is not obscured by plywood," he said, alluding to Blake's handiwork in the Assyrian Lounge. He gave a triumphant smile. "Good news, Blake. We have located *Tarshish*. Mr. Newly will be aboard by morning."

"So, I guess I'm not going anywhere for a while?"

"It would seem so. Were you able to rest?"

"No. I kept having nightmares. The men I killed."

"Ah, a side effect of the Phobolyn. Very vivid, I understand. Come, enjoy your dinner. Let me tell you about our organization."

Blake sat down and surveyed his steak and lobster. "What's happening with Mia?"

"She is safely sequestered. You may have the opportunity to speak with her, pending events aboard *Tarshish*, tomorrow."

Blake, not wanting to elicit any discussion about Newly, much less Nebuchadnezzar, changed the subject.

Lucien came and stood by his master's seat.

"I haven't seen any women aboard."

"Females are for breeding. Real pleasure is found elsewhere. Their presence is a corrupting influence."

"Vive la corrupcion," said Blake.

"Point taken! I find your defiance refreshing. It is exhilarating; unlike Lucien, here. He had such promise. He is a competent administrator, but he has no ambition. No vision. He is utterly content to be a sycophant. His life's goal is simply to be, as you say in America, my *bitch*. Such a disgusting disappointment when I need a lieutenant. I need a captain! A general! I do not need a *bitch*."

Blake noted Lucien's sly and hateful glance. "Not to mention a jealous one," he ventured. "The worst kind."

"Indeed. Lucien, leave us."

The man stepped smartly to the door. He returned to his cabin, sat down on the edge of his bed, and wept.

"You have not touched your dinner, is it not to your liking?"

"I don't eat shellfish or pork."

"But you are Christian, not Jewish?"

"Some rules never change."

Cotillion clapped his hands and ordered a new entree to be brought.

"I think Lucien is going to make an attempt on my life," said Blake.

Cotillion grinned. "You are very shrewd, Mr. Barber; divide and conquer. But he would not dare. They do not call me the *Assyrian* for nothing, as poor Ngandu discovered. So, what is this all about?" Cotillion gestured broadly, indicating his world. "What does one do when he has everything a man can have?"

"What are you going to do with the nuke. That's what I want to know."

"The options are open. What would *you* do with a nuclear weapon?"

"Ah, well. My grandmother's boyfriend is making my life hell. That's why I'm here, actually. And my English teacher is giving me a rough way to go."

Cotillion laughed hard. "Well played. But surely your vision is broader than that."

"I guess if I could find a way to use it to keep terrorists from attacking my country."

"Yes. I had considered indirectly blackmailing the Saudi's, myself. I would threaten the Kaaba. The Dome of the Rock in Israel, the oil or the Royal House itself. Pressure them to reign in the Wahabists."

"Or the Taliban. Or Al Quaeda. Or the Islamic State."

"All creations of your own government and its close allies in Jerusalem and Riyadh, I am afraid. I have not survived this long, nor amassed this empire by being conspicuous, or impulsive, Mr. Barber. I do not intend to start now. Otherwise I would simply take out the entire Suiza operation in one fell stroke, and then fill the vacuum with my own organization. But that would take years. This is not the only device to be had. I intend to intercept as many as possible, and use them to my full advantage. These are not merely the weapons of the lunatic martyr, Blake. They are weights in the magnificent balance of terror. Are you beginning to see the power I am offering you? The power to shape the world! I have a number of films you will watch. The first is called *Harvest of Empire*."

"Propaganda?"

"I will leave you to decide."

21

Serena turned off the TV. There was nothing but non-stop reporting on the quarantine in Puerto Rico, the exodus of tourists out of the Caribbean, and the heightened degree of alert in the United States.

For almost three days, she'd been stuck in a second floor room with no windows, at the Azure Haven. Nello had explained when he put her on the plane that Newly was a dangerous criminal tied to *extremely* dangerous criminals, and that her current confinement was for her own safety. He said that the kids would be fine, and that Newly would never make his rendezvous with them.

Then he plunked her down in this little room, afforded her carte blanche room service, and waited on her hand and foot. She asked him continually about Blake and Mia, but he would only say that he had no new information from his superior, Agent Cain. She actually liked Nello. A lot. He was a short, good-looking man of about thirty; self-deprecating and bashful in the most adorable way, and thoroughly east coast Italian-American. How he'd ever ended up in the DEA, she thought, was anyone's guess. She thought he would make a nice elementary school teacher.

Cain, on the other hand, she had pegged for a sociopath from the start. He was a man with a plan, and would use anyone in any way necessary to accomplish it. He had used the kids to catch Newly. And he was still using them; and *that*, she was sure, was the only reason she hadn't been reunited with them.

And then there was Abel Newly. From the get go, he'd been pushing for information on Carson, and *Tarshish*. Newly was after Carson, and Cain was after Newly. And they were both bending over backwards to accommodate and encourage Blake in his quest. What was Carson tangled up in?

What's going to happen to all of us when this is all over with? She thought. *The Witness Protection Program? What if these guys are really the bad guys? No, that's only in the movies. Why, why, why didn't I listen to Bunny? Great. Guilt on top of worry. One thing is for sure. It doesn't feel right. If I could just get word out to somebody.*

***

Mia stared at the ceiling fan, and blinked rapidly to make it appear to be standing still. She huffed at the wish that she could blink herself out of this situation, like the character in one of her favorite childhood books. She'd been huffing at that little girl in her soul for a long time.

Fiona came to mind, and the unsent reply laying on her desk. *She'll be climbing the walls wondering where it is. I pity the mailman. And then she'll drive herself nuts over why I'm not returning her calls. And then she'll see it in the news: two American teens disappear in the Caribbean. Dammit, Tux! Why did I ever let you... do anything?*

The new shift of sentries jabbered and laughed up the hall and rapped at the door. They commanded her to stand on the balcony with the glass door closed. Even then, three of them came in, the first two with their AK-47s at the ready. Macoute stood in the clearing below her concrete balcony, and consumed her with his eyes.

"You look like that guy from those Machete movies, you know that? And I don't mean that in a good way," she sniped.

The sentries left a bag of fruit and a roll of toilet paper, and exited.

She went back inside, sat down on the mattress and tried to ignore the heat. *Macoute. This is going to be bad.* She remembered the first time her brother's buddy, Mark Bader touched her. *I was Fiona's age,* she thought. She remembered how he'd teased her until she attacked him, then rough-housed her, pretending it was all good fun. It ended when he pinned her for three minutes of close wrestling that she didn't fully understand, other than it felt very wrong. *Freaking filthy bastard! Nobody listened. Mom was never there. Dad blew it off. Hunter threatened me, like always. Gabriella was afraid of losing her job.*

The words of Father Taylor, the 'Church Rectum,' came to mind. "Do justice for the widow and orphan, and the oppressed," she murmured. "Defend the defenseless. *Thanks*, Jesus. *Wait!* Wait, I didn't mean that. It could always be a lot worse. Bader didn't... he just... I've got shelter, food, and running water. And toilet paper. And a couple of people who need me not to die. So, really—*thank you*, Jesus."

***

It was the usual picture-perfect day on the island of Curacao. Newly smiled grandly as he strolled along the waterfront in Willemstad, Nebuchadnezzar on his shoulder. His ratty ditty bag was stuffed in the acrylic macaw carrier, slung on his back by its carrying strap. The fresh air, the sunshine on the gaily colored Dutch architecture, a snort of orange bitters, and two tall masts just beyond the canopies of the open-air market delighted his very carnal soul.

Surely this would make up for the Jamaica disaster; the loss of an entire team—and the woman. As far as Serena went, failed abductions were common enough in the supply trade. It was like any hunting sport. But he had totally underestimated his quarry, and she turned out to have some very nasty loose ends. He couldn't figure what had happened at Marley's Rock, who those dead Americans were, or what had tipped them off. All he cared about was getting aboard *Tarshish*, doing his recon, and delivering a pleasing report to the boss. Then Davis and Shelton would do the dirty work, and he'd be back cruising a beach somewhere for free drinks and easy marks.

Newly emerged from the cheerful little market and beheld the sleek lines and glossy black hull of the vaunted ghost ship. He noted the cluster of halyards that ran up the main mast, obviously concealing a thick cable, to a large and oddly placed mop of scruffy baggywrinkle. "That's the jammer, right there, Nebby!" he said. "I betcha!"

He'd signed up for the dinner cruise, as the morning scuba tour had been booked almost as soon as it was announced on local social media.

A middle aged man in a Panama hat and monogrammed polo shirt greeted them at the foot of the gangplank. "Newly and Nebuchadnezzar, I presume?"

"That's right!" Newly shook hands with the man.

"I'm Barrett Reynolds, ship's master. That's a fine bird. Gets along with people, does he?"

"Nebby? Oh yeah! Loves people. Gets a little noisy, but that's all your big birds. Nebby here's a real entertainer."

"Does he, uh, make a big mess?"

"Nah, he's potty trained! Unless you give him grapes. Then it's Nelly bar the door!"

"Then we'll lock those up! So, welcome aboard! We're still waiting on the last couple of reservations to show up. Have a drink. Settle in!"

"Now you're talking my language!"

***

Mia pulled at her curls. The boredom was crushing. It was almost worse than the anxiety.

"Breathe Mia! C'mon, listen to Haraguchi. That's what you paid him for. Breathe deep. Let it out slowly. Count. Right now! Breathe. I can't believe I'm talking to myself!" Mia took that deep breath and let it out.

"Oooooh, why not," she said aloud, running her fingers across her scalp and tugging her hair. "Dear Fiona, did I ever tell you about my first solo Kayak ride? I was ten. I had already quit sailing to spite my dad. Hunter's buddies stayed over a lot, back then. I mean, in the summertime, they were always around—day and night. Hopkins was just a big dumb jock, but Bader was a perv, and he took a shine to me. Locking my door didn't help, because it was the kind that you could open with a screwdriver, or a chopstick or whatever."

"Anyway, nobody was looking out for me, so I decided I was going to have to look out for myself. So, I slept in my walk-in closet, because I could push the dresser in front of the door. Then I got up super early, like four in the morning, slipped out of the house, and down to our dock. The lake was so huge and quiet. Lights from the dam, and the freeman waterfront, and the Marina spilled across the water. It was so peaceful. I slid my little blue kayak into the water and slipped away. At first I stayed near the shore between our house and Dad's marina, but then I got my nerve up and paddled to the middle of the Upper Lake. I just drifted, and watched the sun come up. Nobody missed me. So I made it a habit. I stashed a sleeping bag at the sailing club, down on the Lower Lake, and crashed there for like—I kid you not— three summers. Until Blake's slacker uncle got the same idea. Yeah, as long as I was present and accounted for at lunch and dinner, the head housekeeper didn't suspect a thing. That's worse than knowing that someone hates you; knowing someone doesn't care."

"I wanted to hurt them. I wanted them to notice I wasn't there, and be terrified that something happened to me, and shock them into mending their evil ways. But no one did. Damn, did that hurt. Now I'm going to disappear and it's gonna hurt a bunch of people. And knowing *that,* hurts even worse."

She got up to go to the bathroom, and glimpsed Macoute through the window. *I wonder what his story is?* she thought.

***

The buzzy riff of *Spirit in the Sky* drifted across the dark sea. The sails glowed faintly under the waning crescent moon as *Tarshish* clipped through low and easy swells.

Twenty tourists from all corners of the Caribbean, Europe, and North America chatted, drank, and danced on the deck as she made her way back to Willemstad. Newly had managed to stay sober enough to maintain his drifter charm, and conduct his mission inconspicuously. Nebuchadnezzar, excited by the crowd, became unbearably loud and rowdy. He was summarily banished to his tube, and stowed safely in Barrett's cabin.

Newly trod lightly with Carson, who was taking his trick at the wheel, lest he give anything about his nephew away. He had to admit that the family resemblance was striking.

"Steam" Ebeling, the Chief Engineer, came on deck with a bottle of beer, and Newly was right on him, ingratiating himself with thin blather about his own stint in the Navy, and questions about horsepower, max speed, and fuel capacity. Steam obliged him with a string of equally thin lies.

Harry "Monster" Manzer, ship's cook, came on deck bearing another tray heaped with shrimp cocktail, the chrome shaft of his prosthetic leg reflecting the colored lights strung around the deck. Barrett Reynolds followed closely with four pitchers of Margarita.

The *Tarshish* men hated operation TOURISM with a passion. It was supposed to be a way to lay low in plain sight, make a little mad money, and decompress. But after losing three men in the deadly December firefight off Barranquilla, there was no solace. This was like giving pony rides on American Pharaoh at a church fair, right after your best friend's funeral.

Finally, the soaring arch of the Queen Juliana Bridge came into view, and the floating Queen Emma Bridge swung open to admit *Tarshish* to her berth before the venerable old buildings of the Punda Quarter. The crew of *Tarshish* happily debarked their extravagantly tanked compliment of passengers. All but one. Newly had convinced Monster to allow him to help with the clean-up, particularly in the galley and the head.

After all was said and done, the crew and their lingering guest sat around the table in the ship's main saloon, relaxing over a few beers, and laughing at Nebuchadnezzar's vulgar French repertoire. Carson was over it. He could see that Steam, while guffawing heartily at Newly's English translations, wasn't buying the affable beach-comber act. It was time to get rid of this parasite. He gave the old Chief a sly nod, and got up to use the head. Monster had just returned to the table with a cluster of grapes, and tossed one to the macaw. He snapped it out of the air and belted out "Stoof it in yer pookits!" loud and clear. Carson stopped in his tracks.

Newly was earnestly surprised. "Never heard him say that before!"

Carson took a moment to collect himself. He took a deep breath, forced a smile, then turned around and went to the table.

"That don't sound French to me!" he laughed. He took a grape from Monster's hand and tossed it to Nebby, who repeated the phrase.

Carson seized Newly by the shirt, dragged him over the table and slammed him on the floor. Nebby screeched and flew for cover.

"Get that bird!" Steam shouted.

Monster leapt up to block the companionway. Carson got right in Newly's face and growled "I only know two people in the whole world who say that! Which one do you know?"

"I never heard…"

"Spill it! Or so help me I'll gig you all over and dangle you in the water for shark bait!"

"What the hell, Car?" said Barrett.

"Barry, we've been compromised!"

Barrett wasted no time. "Steam, get us out of here. Monster, secure the bird and help me cast off."

"Somebody gimme some duck tape!" shouted Carson.

"Comin' right up!" replied Monster. He sweet-talked the macaw onto his arm, then took him to Barrett's cabin and placed him in his carrier. He grabbed a roll of black tape from a drawer in the galley as he ran for the companionway, and tossed it to Carson as he passed by. Newly quickly found himself hogtied with sturdy tape. The big engine turned over, and *Tarshish* started away from the seawall. Steam blew the ship's horn three times, jolting the Queen Emma Bridge operator into action. *Tarshish* already lay with her bow toward the ocean, and Steam drove her expertly through the slowly widening gap between the end of the bridge and the Punda seawall, with barely three feet to spare on either side. He throttled all the way up. "Goin' dark!" he cried, opening a keyed panel next to the throttle and pressing several buttons.

Newly's co-conspirators sprang to the window of their hotel on the Otrabanda side of the narrow bay, as *Tarshish* charged in to the night. Shelton grabbed his cell phone which, to his surprise, had no service. In fact, no one had cell service for miles, nor Wi-Fi, radar, GPS, TV, nor radio; and half-dozen private drones fell out of the sky.

Barrett ran to the companionway and yelled to the helmsman as he went below. "Steam, stay dark. Evasion plan B. I'm calling in!"

As soon as they were in open water, Steam turned *Tarshish* southeast. Barrett headed for the radio room, and heard Carson pressing Newly.

"Car, we need him alive!" he shouted, as he unlocked the radio room. He seated himself in front of a large laptop mounted on the wall, changed several settings on the screen to allow his signal to get out, and dialed his satellite phone. "Encryption request, channel nine-six. Key niner-five-three zero, six. Radian Five, This is Tenderfoot. Swim team is diving, Plan B. Suspect in custody. And his bird."

"Copy Tenderfoot," came the reply. "Did you say *bird?*"

22

Blake was roused early from a fitful sleep. It was two-thirty in the morning. Lucien was banging on the door. "Monsieur Cotillion will see you immediately! Get dressed!"

Blake mopped cold sweat from his face and chest, then pulled on his shorts and the red shirt. Lucien and two stewards escorted him to the Assyrian lounge and ushered him in. The escorts waited outside the door. He could hear a jet engine whining somewhere outside. Cotillion was by the window at the far end of the room, looking down over the bow of the ship. "Good morning, Mr. Barber. Come!"

Blake joined him. A sleek executive helicopter was warming up on the landing pad below. "I am highly annoyed with you, young man, but; fortunately for you, also quite amazed. Your ingenuity has complicated my plans."

Blake's head was still half fogged, half on edge, and a missed dosage wasn't helping. He thought better of attempting any sarcasm.

"You are full of promise, Mr. Barber. But you need a mentor. Someone to groom and shape you for success."

"I have mentors back home," Blake replied. "Honorable men. And I will do everything I can, not to disgrace them. But Mia doesn't deserve this. I will do anything necessary to save her."

"This mission is your only chance to do so. Tell me: would you break the law for her?"

"There is no law out here."

"The laws of your god, then?"

"Tell me which ones apply."

"Would you kill for her?"

Blake held his tongue, and scowled to himself. He remembered the moment from that crazy summer when he was poised to kill Hunter Devlin with a sod fork; and would have, had Carson not intervened. He looked Cotillion in the eye and said coldly, "Yes."

"Even... the innocent?" Cotillion smiled in the long silence that followed.

"Just tell me what I have to do."

Cotillion called to Lucien, who brought a waterproof hard-shell travel case. Lucien opened it and held it up. Cotillion reviewed its contents.

"I will put you in the path of *Tarshish*. You will deliver the message recorded on this tablet to Feral Cain. You see there are three rocket flares, two bottles of water and a protein bar in case, somehow, they miss you. A waterproof tube of your medication. Ah, lest I forget! I must reveal that your Phobolyn also contains a toxic chemical agent. You will need to return to me to obtain the antidote prior to your release. When the medicine runs out, you have but forty-eight hours to live. I suggest you wear it around your neck." He held up what appeared to be a narrow neon-green cell phone on a lanyard. "This is a personal satellite locater beacon. If possible, keep it hidden under the foam insert of the case. Here is the operation manual. Leave it on the helicopter. And this... This is a reminder for you. It is also the password for your tablet."

Cotillion handed him a black leather wallet embossed with fancy lettering. Blake read it. "Ngandu. Ngandu's wallet?" Beyond the practical aspect of the password, he couldn't grasp its significance. He noticed Lucien looked away.

"Once the device is aboard, your options will become obvious. Activate the tracker once you have done what needs to be done."

"What if they take it away?"

"As I said; your options will become obvious. You may also get word to me via P.K.'s Dance Club in Port of Spain Trinidad. Now, good luck!" Lucien and his stewards escorted Blake out. On the elevator down to the Flight Deck,

Blake took one last opportunity to goad his enemy. "Wow. Ngandu's wallet. I guess I rate, now!" The utter heartbreak and hatred in Lucien's expression was plain to see, as they exited through the forward lounge. The sleek copter sat in a ring of pulsating red lights, its rotors swinging with ominous impatience. As Blake boarded, Lucien smiled wickedly and sneered "You little fool! The wallet does not belong *to* Ngandu. The wallet *is* Ngandu!" He savored the look of horror on Blake's face for a moment, then evacuated the helipad.

***

The interior of the helicopter was like a luxury boardroom. Blake strapped himself into one of the big leather seats as the motor whined higher, and the helicopter lifted into the air and swooped away.

The copilot, a young African man, came back to the cabin.

"How ya doin'? Okay, I got ya PFD and ya raft, here." He pulled a bright yellow valise the size of a gym bag from a storage panel. "When we get to the drop, we'll chuck it out and pull the cord so she blows up. Then out you go! Be about thirty minutes. Let me show ya how to use the locater."

Blake handed him the green gadget. He was amazed at the courtesy and good humor of the man, and wondered if he knew what he was tangled up with.

"Okay, any questions?" grinned the copilot.

"How much did this helicopter cost?"

"About fifteen million! Brand new Bell 525 Relentless. It was a gift from the Saudi's. Not bad, eh?"

"Mr. Cotillion sure gets around," said Blake.

"You know it! I was back home with my girl in Tanzania, just last week!"

"My girlfriend is doing some work for Mr. Cotillion around Grand Cayman."

"Oh, yeah. His little island up by Cuba."

"Yes! But, I can't remember the name."

Jonas was about to answer when the pilot called over the intercom, "Jonas, get up here and start scanning!"

"Okay, won't be long now," said Jonas, as he got up.

"How can you find a cloaked ship?" said Blake.

"Fly around until the GPS link dies. Then scan with the FLIR camera. Don't worry, we'll find him."

It only took another ten minutes. The pilot had guessed well, and headed southeast. When the radio chatter from the Chichiriviche picket boats died, he knew they were almost on top of their target.

"There she is," said Jonas pointing to a display screen in front of him. "Come to eighty-five degrees. She's eight kilometers out"

"We'll make for Klein Curacao," said the pilot. "Then get out ahead of him."

They buzzed low over the little island, switching out the cabin lights and anti-collision lights, then flew ahead at a leisurely hundred knots to a point five miles ahead of *Tarshish*.

Jonas returned to the cabin, grinning. "Okay, my friend, this is your stop!"

He unzipped the valise, peeled it off the raft and handed Blake the towline. Blake tied it to the handle of his case with a bowline knot, and put on his life jacket.

"Seems like a damn waste, throwing a perfectly good white-boy out of the plane; but I got my orders ya see!" Jonas slid the side door open. Salt air and an amazing level of noise from the engine and rotors filled the cabin. He knelt on one knee, wrapped the inflation lanyard around his hand one time, and shoved the block of vinyl out the door. He gave the lanyard a hard jerk as it went and suddenly a happy yellow raft exploded into existence ten feet below, its water-activated strobe beacon blitzing the copter in harsh bursts. He scooted aside, and Blake took his place at the door.

"They'll be here in fifteen minutes. Happy New Year!"

The towline drew taught, and Blake jumped. No sooner had he hit the water than the Bell 525 rose a hundred feet and swooped away. Blake pulled himself to the raft, chucked his case in, and clambered aboard.

"Well, mark that one off the bucket list," he mused. The helicopter was already ten miles distant when they turned the lights back on. Blake opened his case, pulled out a rocket flare, and fired it into the black sky. He cut the line off the raft and tied it around his waist.

***

"We got a strobe and a flare to port!" cried Monster, securing a big Browning M2 50 caliber machine gun in its mount on the gunwale, and donning FLIR night-vision goggles.

Barrett ran forward adjusting his own goggles. "Can't tell what it is, yet. Looks like there's a bogey coming in from the south to meet it."

Monster switched his goggles to thermal imaging, and adjusted the gain on the scope. Suddenly night became black and white day. "It's a pick up. Let's get the other gun on the rail," said Monster.

"Could just be rendering assistance. But I'll get another fitty. Carson! Intercept course!"

Carson was at the wheel, Steam having retired to the engine room to baby-sit the roaring beast that was driving them at almost twenty knots. Barrett mounted another gun in the middle of the starboard gunwale. He threaded its ammunition belt through the feed tray, with the lid down, pulled the charge lever three times, and grabbed the first belt link as it came out of the other side of the weapon.

"Bogey is a Scarab-type fast boat," said Monster. No lights,"

"You win again!"

"Gonna get there just before we do. Can't see who's in the raft."

"Carson! Battle stations!" called Barrett. "Get Steam up here, and mount your fitty, starboard side!"

Carson paged the engine room on the ship's intercom. Steam was at the wheel in thirty seconds flat. Carson pulled another machine gun from the locker, donned his night vision gear, and mounted the weapon on the starboard side.

"Second bogey coming in from the north!" said Barrett. They were now within a half mile of the raft. "Steam, ten degrees starboard!"

"Aye Aye!" Steam adjusted their course to bring the bogeys into their field of fire. The approaching Scarab heeled over and swung in a wide arc to inspect her prize.

"Bogey 1 is on site, looks like nobody in the raft. I see AK's!"

The castaway popped up and fired a flare into the marauder's cockpit, then dove over the side of the raft. The Scarab crew danced madly trying to stamp out the burning chunks of phosphor. The second, smaller boat opened fire on the raft.

"Whoa! Not good guys!" yelled Barrett. "Light 'em up!"

Monster took aim ahead of the burning glow in the cockpit of the first boat, and pulled the trigger. The flash hider on the muzzle reduced the signature chunk-chunk-chunk of the Browning heavy machine gun to a quiet thip-thip-thip, followed by the cracking echo of bullets ripping through the air at twice the speed of sound. He expertly guided the stream of streaking tracers into the Scarab's path.

Barrett opened up on the smaller boat, zeroing in on the muzzle flashes from its crew. "Steam, gimme flares!"

Steam fired two rocket flares out over the field of fire as the Scarab's hull shattered under the hail of lead. Barrett's target swerved away and ran tight circles, what was left of the driver slumped over the wheel. He compensated his aim, and let another fifty rounds fly into the belly of the boat as it banked sharply. The motor stopped, the craft settled and quickly sank.

"Carson!" called Barrett, heart pounding.

"Clear to starboard!"

"Everybody scan for life forms. Steam, fetch up to that raft."

Steam throttled well back, and steered for the raft.

Carson drew his Smith and Wesson M&P 45, went to the port rail, putting his laser sight on a lump in the middle of the yellow octagon, now a mere twenty-five feet away. A life jacket floated nearby.

"There ain't a mark on it!" marveled Monster.

"You! Under the raft! Identify yourself!" shouted Carson.

The muffled voice of a young man replied, "Uncle Carson! Don't shoot!"

All eyes suddenly shifted to Carson, who tensed visibly and kept his laser-dot on the lump, as the raft drifted up alongside.

"You're not really gonna shoot your nephew are you, Car?" said Barrett. Carson didn't answer. "Urquart! Stand down."

"Shut up Barry!"

"That's an order!"

Carson sucked in a deep breath and holstered his pistol.

"Alright kid, the coast is clear," said Barrett. "Steam, get a ladder over the side. Monster, keep us covered."

Blake pushed the raft away, and looked up the black side of the schooner to see three insect-headed aliens staring back at him, in the blinding white flashes of the strobe beacon.

"Gort, Klaatu barada nikto?" said Blake, tentatively.

Carson stalked back to his machine gun on the starboard side, pulled the charge handle and raked the empty distance with gunfire. Steam rigged the rope and plank boarding ladder and tossed it over.

"I said stand down! Now knock it off!" shouted Barrett. "Kid, get your butt up that ladder, we gotta get movin!"

Blake got hold of his floating case, and struggled up to the rail were he was seized and hauled aboard.

"Steam, get us under way. Chichiriviche."

"Um, that wouldn't be my first choice," said Blake.

"Oh, really?" retorted Barrett, pulling off his goggles.

"There's a picket line of fast-boats from Chichiriviche to Bonaire. We're hemmed in. I have to see agent Cain. Is he aboard?"

"Agent Cain, my ass! Steam, make for Bonaire. Monster, take him below. Carson, you're on watch!"

Below deck, Monster gave Blake a couple of towels and seated him in the saloon. "I guess someone should ask you if you're okay," he said.

"I'm good. Thanks."

"How old *are* you, kid?"

"Fifteen-and-a-half."

"And already had your first firefight. Pretty impressive."

"Fourth, actually. I killed three pirates, and sank a boat, a few days ago. Well, and then I sank the *Covenant* two years ago, back home. And *Plague X.* And *Tantrum II.* But, *that* wasn't technically a firefight. So, three."

"No kidding?" said Monster, a little incredulous. I'm Harry Manzer. Ship's cook. Everyone calls me Monster." Blake could see why. He was tall and bulky, with an ample gut, round nose, and a short black Mohawk. Garish tattoos of psycho zombie-clowns covered his arms. A trim, jutting beard with no mustache, and a chrome leg from the left knee down, added to the effect. All he needed, Blake thought, was a stove-pipe hat and a harpoon to complete the Queequeg ensemble.

"I'm Blake Barber. Carson's my uncle. People call me Tux."

"You want a coke or a beer?"

"Root beer?"

"Coming up!"

Barrett entered the saloon. "Monster, is the kid okay?"

"According to him."

"I better check on our guest before the boss arrives." He passed through the galley door, and went on forward to the crew quarters.

He returned a few minutes later, looking a little rattled.

"What's wrong?" said Monster.

Barrett went to the intercom. "Steam, send Carson down to the saloon." Carson appeared in the doorway thirty seconds later. He tried to ignore Blake's presence.

"Was the bird-man alive when you left him in the cabin?" said Barrett.

"Hell yes, he was alive!"

"You sure?"

"What are you sayin', Barry? That I killed him? I hog tied him, and when he wouldn't talk, I put tape over his mouth and dragged him up to the cabin. He was snorting and grunting when I shut the door, but he was definitely alive."

"Well, he isn't now," said Barrett.

"You're not talking about," Blake interrupted.

"Shut up!" Carson shouted.

"Nice to see you, too!"

"Cool it! Both of you!" commanded Barrett. "Talking about what, kid?"

"Name's Blake," said Monster. Barrett shot him a stern look.

"Abel Newly? Had a macaw with a message from me?"

There was stunned silence among the men.

"Yeah, that's him. He's dead," said Barrett.

Blake smacked the palm of one hand against his forehead and uttered a choice word.

"Since when do *you* talk like that?" sneered Carson.

"Since you freaking killed the only guy who could tell me where they've got Mia."

"Now just wait a damn minute! I did *not* kill anybody!"

"Whoa, everyone, time out!" shouted Barrett. "I found an inhaler in the bird-man's pocket when I was checking him over. He was blue in the face."

"There!" chided Carson.

"Okay, yes, he had Asthma! I saw him use the inhaler in St. Croix," Blake affirmed.

"Start at the beginning," said Barrett.

"Mia's Aunt Serena wanted to take us to Puerto Rico for Christmas break. Serena met Newly as we were casting off. Mia and I sailed to Vieques. We were all going to meet in St. Croix for the Carnaval. I started asking around about Uncle Carson because we hadn't heard from him in months."

"You people been belly-achin' at me to do something with my life forever! Why can't you leave me alone and let me do it?"

"Because Nana's got a boyfriend who's cleaning her out. He's wearing your dad's hat and smoking your dad's pipes, and generally making my life a living hell. I hoped you could get rid of him."

"So you start snoopin' around and burn an entire covert team, so I can come chase off Grandpa Jones? I finally start doing something that matters,"

"I guess if what matters includes murdering dirt-poor fishermen." Blake never saw the flying back-hand—only an explosion of sparks. He felt his brain jar against the inside of his skull as he hit the floor. Barrett leapt to restrain Carson, but was shoved back.

Carson leaned over his nephew and yelled: "You think those *dirt-poor* fishermen feel the slightest bit of remorse? They are delivering death by the boatload to our doorstep, and making a good living at it!"

Barrett helped Blake sit up. The little sparks were still swimming in his eyeballs.

"Damn, Car!"

"Shut up, Barry! Oh, by the way, your *dirt-poor* friends were the ones shooting at you tonight, in case you were wondering. Not to mention we lost three men—three friends—to your *dirt-poor* fishing buddies last month. Who do you think got to scrape their guts off the main mast? Who do you think swabbed their brains and blood off the deck? And here you are spoutin' off like little Karl Marx!"

Steam's voice came over the intercom. "Dutch Coast Guard on intercept. Probably the Boss."

"Alright, everybody topside!" commanded Barrett.

Blake was last on deck, head still swimming.

Barrett barked orders to Steam: "Stand down ECM, running lights on, ready to heave-to," he announced.

"Aye, Aye. ECM going standby."

Barrett helped Monster put the boarding ladder over the side. Carson readied a heaving-line. Blake stood by Steam and observed the control panel mounted by the wheel. He could see the lights of the approaching cutter, still a mile off.

Barrett's phone rang. "That you, boss? Ladder's port side. See you in a few. Steam! Heave to!"

Steam reversed the engine and dropped their speed to zero. "Lots of blinky doo-dads, eh?" His voice drawled up out of the Deep South.

"The satellite display is really cool. I'm Blake, by the way."

"Steam Ebeling. Pleased to meet you." Steam was a good old boy with no teeth and a conspicuous Confederate flag belt buckle. "I sailed with your uncle in Desert Shield, way back in ninety."

"He told me about that. So, what's this keypad?"

"Ohhh, that's secret!"

"The cloaking device," Blake mused out loud, rubbing his stinging cheek. Steam shot him a wary look.

Police lights flashed atop a large, inflatable Navy pursuit boat as it zoomed across the dark and gentle sea. It pulled alongside, and two men climbed up the boarding ladder. Cain was first over the rail, followed by the smiling face of Jayce Mitchell. The Dutch boat sped away.

"Alright, what's our status?" said Cain, addressing Barrett. Then he caught sight of Blake, standing by the helm. "Holy… I don't believe it!" He strode straight past Barrett and Carson. "Buddy, you are a sight for sore eyes!" He took Blake by the shoulders, and beamed. "How the hell did…? Where is your girlfriend?"

"Being held hostage. Where is Serena?"

"We've got her in a safe place."

"I have a critical message for you. It's 'eyes only,' as they say in the business."

"Then let's go below, buddy. Mr. Barrett! Keep station and hold my calls. I have a meeting with Agent Barber, here."

Again, the crew of *Tarshish* found themselves dumbfounded and looking at Carson in amazement.

"Where's the twerp with the bird?" said Cain, as they made their way to the saloon.

"Died about an hour ago. Asthma attack." Blake retrieved the tablet from the case and tapped in the password. A video appeared: Cotillion at the table in the Assyrian lounge.

Cain took the tablet and tapped the play button.

"Agent Feral Cain, allow me to introduce myself. My name is Nineveh Cotillion. As Blake has surely apprised you of the generalities concerning me, I will be direct. You and I are seeking the same prize from a common enemy. We have inflicted considerable losses upon one another in the past few weeks. This pointless slaughter must stop if we are to keep the weapon from reaching the United States. You possess the assets needed to successfully acquire the device: advanced electronic countermeasures, and a Special Forces team. But you lack critical intelligence—the whereabouts, timetables; the eyeballs on the target, as you say. These are the things which I bring to the bargaining table. Along with the lives of Mr. Barber and Miss Devlin.

The weapon is being held inland, and will be loaded onto a submarine somewhere in the Orinoco Delta. I suggest a two pronged approach. *Tarshish* will deliver a small recon team and divers to the inlet. My people in country will attack the holding center, forcing the Suiza cartel to move the device to the submarine ahead of schedule. You will sink the sub and retrieve the weapon.

We may concern ourselves with the details of the exchange after we have obtained the device.

I would advise that you move *Tarshish* at top speed to Chaguaramas, Trinidad. There, put Mister Barber ashore to receive final instructions from his contact. You may also deactivate the Electronic Counter Measures. You are now under direct surveillance by a multitude of small craft which you cannot possibly outrun.

Please consider Mr. Barber as my representative.

Good luck, and Adieu."

Cain stared at the image for a moment, then went to the intercom by the door and pressed a button. "Mr. Steam, please set course for Chaguaramas, top speed."

***

On deck, Monster fetched a spare anchor from the dinghy and secured it to Newly's corpse. He said a short prayer, and heaved it over the side. The rest of the crew had gathered around the u-shaped table between the helm and the deckhouse.

Blake recounted the incident at Marley's Rock, and was about to mention the dead Americans when Cain interrupted and asked who had picked the two of them up. Blake took the cue, and resumed his narrative with the rescue, leaving out all detail about the *Mother of Harlots,* itself. "We were making maybe ten knots through the night. Probably not to raise suspicion. Heading west. Then they took Mia off and we turned south. Close to sunrise I think we headed more southeast."

"Barranquilla," suggested Steam, from the wheel.

"Like as not," replied Carson.

"When did you let the parrot go?" said Jayce.

"Just before sunrise."

"What're you thinking, Jaybird?" said Cain.

"It's clear they cruised all the way around Jamaica. She's somewhere around there. Cuba. Grand Cayman. I say tag the bird with a tracker, take it to Cayman Brac and let it go."

"We're a little short on personnel, if you hadn't noticed," objected Carson. "Hell, that girl is half-way to some whorehouse in Bangkok, by now."

Something twinged in Blake's chest.

"Send me!" said Jayce, in an eager tone that really meant *you bunch of wussies!* "Drop me on Gran Roque, I'll get a puddle jumper back to Bonaire. Have Flint meet me and fly me up there. I'll find Mia."

Blake was a little suspicious of his enthusiasm.

"We can't go after the girl just yet. He'll keep her alive until he has what he wants. We'll integrate a rescue op into the final phase of our mission. Bartering the weapon for Mia is *not* out of the question, Blake."

"I thought our mission was interdiction, Chief?" said Monster.

Cain looked his team over. "To this point it has been. We've been hitting the commerce of a small-time operator. It's been easy pickings."

"Three dead is easy pickings?" said Carson.

"Our vision comes with a price, Urquart. Thanks to the intelligence provided by your nephew, we now know that our small-time operator isn't small, and he's after the same thing we are."

"Which *is?*" said Monster, realizing that he and his mates had been kept in the dark.

"Mr. Barber, being as you are now a vital player on our team, would you brief your new shipmates?"

The angry eyes of the *Tarshish* men locked on him.

"Several days ago, Mia and I were sailing from Vieques to St. Croix. We got caught in a squall, and collided with a narco-sub carrying a team of terrorists."

"That plague sub?" said Steam.

"I should have known," sneered Carson, in disbelief.

"The short story is that the terrorists were part of an Islamic cell in Venezuela called Venganza de Dios, which has forged an alliance with one of the Columbian Cartels. Together, they've acquired a tactical nuclear device."

"Does he always talk like that?" smiled Jayce.

"Wait, how long has this *been* our mission?" said Monster.

"Since Blake filled us in," answered Cain, resolutely.

"You said final phase of our mission. Like it was…"

"Some things are on a need-to-know-basis, Harry. You know that."

"Did *you* know?" Monster pointed at Jayce, who shrugged slightly and smiled.

"We have a helluva gambit to plan and execute," Cain interrupted. "And a hostage situation to resolve. What I can tell you now is that there will be a diversionary attack on the terrorist base by what's left of our original target's force, while we intercept the device."

"We're teaming up with these bastards?" said Carson.

"Like you said, we're short on manpower. Anything could spook 'em into moving early. Then the nuke makes it to the mainland for sure. By forcing Venganza's hand, we put 'em on our timetable, and *we* get the bomb."

"Godammit!" shouted Carson, stalking away, then returning. "And this sonofabitch is just doing this out of the goodness of his heart?" There was general assent. "We're bein' played!"

"Cotillion doesn't want the bomb to reach the mainland, either," said Blake. "His business depends on it."

"I oughta snap your neck, you little traitor."

"Belay that, Urquart!" ordered Cain. "If it hadn't been for that kid, there'd be ten thousand Americans dead already, and martial law! He discovered our kingpin! He'll get the coordinates to the embarkation site! I like that kid. I've never seen a better kid than that!"

"This is a CIA job, anyway."

"CIA dropped the ball, Urquart. Time's run out. Now it's down to us."

"Who gets the bomb when we're done?" said Steam.

"What do you mean *who*?" retorted Cain.

"What are we gonna do with it once we have it?" added Carson. "Or is that on a need-to-know-basis, too?"

"You got a problem with that?" snapped Cain. "You were chosen for this mission because you are patriots, not mercenaries. We'll get more detail in Trinidad. Steam, we're detouring through Gran Roque. Jaybird, call ahead and get a plane back to Bonaire. Monster, get Blake set up in the aft port-side cabin. Son, wash up and some get sleep."

Cain dismissed the crew and went back on deck. He dialed his satellite phone and went through the routine encryption protocol.

"Cumulus, Radian five. As Stonewall Jackson said: *God has been very kind to us, today…*"

***

Blake lay bare as his thoughts on the comfy double bed, his damp clothes drying in the rigging above deck. *Newly is dead,* he thought. *Just like that. He was a bad guy. But, he is…dead.* And then Newly was there, in the saloon, waving his arms above his head, and Nebuchadnezzar was flying wildly around him shouting obscenities in English. Blake was shooting at him with his Beretta 9 mm, but kept hitting the drifter, who flinched and giggled with each slug. Then, in anger, Blake gnashed his teeth and squeezed the trigger hard, and flame billowed out of the gun, roasting Newly, and the macaw. Their screams grew louder and louder until Blake was wakened by the sound of his own cries, and an insistent knocking on his cabin door.

He pulled the sheet around him and opened the door, heart still pounding. It was Cain.

"You alright, buddy?"

"Yeah. It's my meds. Vivid nightmares are a common side effect."

"Is it worth it?"

"All things considered. I wouldn't have made it this far without the stuff. Cotillion gave it to me. I think I'm hooked on it. What time is it?"

"About nine. We dropped Jayce off. We're bound for Trinidad. We'll see Isla Margarita in about ten hours. Not exactly how you planned to spend your Christmas break, huh?"

"I need to call Serena."

"We'll see what we can arrange. I'll get your clothes. Monster made you breakfast. We gotta talk turkey, ASAP."

Blake noticed that the name plate on the door across the hall read Radio Room: Danger High Voltage.

"Be there in a minute. May I eat on deck?"

"Enjoy it!"

While Cain retrieved his clothes, Blake got the satellite beacon out of his case and hid it in the cabinet under the bathroom sink. He sat down on the can and began to work out a watertight narrative that omitted anything about the true size and name of the *Mother of Harlots* or her likely whereabouts. It was the first time since Jamaica he'd really been able to relax and think things through: Newly had set them up. The pirates had been waiting for them. Cain had denied he had heard of Carson, or Tarshish. They took Serena. They were after Newly. The dead Americans on the island…were waiting for the pirates. They were Cain's men. *Bait! He used Mia and me for bait!* His head was swimming. He buried his face in his palms and groaned, "I am going to get Mia out of this, go home, and never leave Gunn's Marina again." He took up the chrome vial around his neck. "I gotta get off this stuff," he said as he unscrewed the lid.

***

Blake started up the companionway with a plate piled high with omelet and hash browns drenched in hot-sauce. He met Carson's angry glare from the wheel, and went back below. Wedged in beside the steps was the small door to the engine room. He found it unlocked, and peered in. The space was wide open, with the roaring white diesel beast set into steel deck plates. Steam caught sight of him, and waved him over. "C'mon! Set your food down on this tool cabinet, right here. I'll tell you all about it." He had to yell to be heard above the noise of the engine.

As much as Blake hated lectures, anything that would divert his thoughts from the nightmares—from this entire nightmare—was welcomed.

"I'm Bryce Ebeling, but they call me Steam." He spoke slowly and deliberately. The gray stubble on his sallow cheeks and the absence of teeth made him seem like some amiable old papaw in the nursing home, back in Indiana. "So you're Car's nephew, huh?"

"I'm not sure he claims me, anymore."

"Well, I don't know what you got yourself tangled up in, but let me show you around." Steam proceeded to point out the watermaker, three generators, the batteries, and the watertight bulkheads, and beamed with pride over the great 600 horsepower diesel engine, which he referred to as the *Kraken*.

"What about these tanks?" Blake said, motioning to a series of tall metal cylinders mounted along the wall.

"Oh, that's the secret to our success, there!"

"Nitrous oxide? So, you're supercharging the engine! But what's the max hull speed? We must be making twenty knots. How is that possible?"

Steam grinned with delight, as if he could barely stand to keep that secret. "You're pretty smart!"

"I work in a boatyard. Seriously, tell me."

"Well, you tell me!"

Blake observed the other tanks more closely. One was propane, the other a small tank of liquid nitrogen. They were connected to a strange, boxy apparatus which itself was fed by the watermaker. A pipe ran from the box to a pump, then through the bulkhead. "You're heating water, then super chilling the steam, and pumping it forward?"

"Yeeup! Now why?"

Blake thought long and hard. "You're pumping micro-bubbles out of a vent in the bow to reduce drag on the hull! And that's why they call you Steam?"

"Hot dog!" laughed the old engineer. "Now how'd you figure all that out?"

"I write all my school papers about sailing technology. I saw an article on Russian torpedoes that used the same idea."

"We use a high-tech paint that reduces drag, and the hull shape is special, too."

Blake returned to his breakfast at the cabinet, and began to wolf it down.

"Must've been a big jolt when you hit that sub."

"You could say that. I'm not actually supposed to discuss it."

"I gotcha," Steam said, with a nod.

"So how did you end up on this crew?"

"I got sick of seein' how drugs was destroying my Georgia. My country. Figured I could spend the rest of my days rottin' in the VA home, or do something about it. Got involved with my local patriot network, eventually met Cain. And here I am."

The intercom crackled and someone made an announcement which Blake couldn't understand over the droning machine.

"Uh oh! Busted!" grinned Steam. "You're wanted in the saloon. Monster must'a counted the silverware!"

Blake grabbed his plate, shook hands with him, and went back through the small door.

Cain was waiting for him in the saloon. "Where you been?"

"Sorry, I was in the engine room talking to Steam."

"Pretty impressive, huh? Look, now that you've got some sleep under your belt, I need you to fill me in on your adventure, so far. Let's go back to my office." By office, he meant the master guest cabin.

***

Cain's cabin was orderly, and fresh. A King James Bible lay squarely on the night stand, and a half model of *Tarshish* graced the wall above the queen-sized bed. He seated Blake in a wooden captain's chair, then perched himself on the edge of the bed and listened intently with his chin on his fists.

Blake told his revised tale, and it seemed good to Cain.

"Okay, that fills in the blanks. Here's the deal, Blake. I need you to be careful around the guys. Watch what you say. Do not—I cannot emphasize strongly enough—do not talk about Marley's Rock. Period. Morale is lower than whale crap, right now. We lost three men back in December. The guys are pretty twitchy about the new assignment, as it is. If they hear another four of their brothers died, well… just don't say anything. I told them they were needed elsewhere, and reassigned."

"I understand. I also understand that you used us as bait. You lied to me about Carson. You played me."

"Deceiving someone who is not entitled to the information is not lying. It was a 'need to know' situation."

"With all due respect, that's horsecrap, sir. I need to know how we're going to get Mia back. I need to know how I'm going to get off this stuff, alive." He held up the vial of Phobolyn. "There's a chemical in it that will kill me when I stop taking it. I have to get the antidote from Cotillion."

"We'll send one in for analysis as soon as we hit Trinidad. What do you think of this guy Cotillion?"

"Absolute evil. But, so far he hasn't lied to me. He's kept his word."

"You know he plans to deep-six all of us after he gets what he wants, right?"

"He doesn't just want the bomb. He wants me. And if he's going to get me, he has to let Mia go."

"You'd do that for her?"

"That's the *least* I will do for her."

Cain seemed sincerely moved. "Whoa, I never thought… You are a true American Hero."

"It's not heroic. It's just what's right."

"We'll see what Jaybird has for us when we get to Trinidad. Could be a game changer, so don't give up hope."

"That's all I have to go on right now."

"Listen, I know about grief and loss, okay?" Cain said, sounding a little offended. "I was a squad leader in Afghanistan. I've lost seven men under my watch in the last four weeks. But, I still have a job to do. An *important* job. I cannot allow obsessive feelings of guilt or anxiety to debilitate me. I have to keep busy and focused on things that move the mission forward, and prepare to complete its goals. Doesn't mean I love my friends any less. There is just nothing I can do for them right now. I have to put it aside and see to the mission. I'll grieve later. You understand? We can't save Mia by dwelling on our failures. Right now, the best you can do is pray for her, and keep yourself fit, sane, and ready."

Blake only nodded.

"What did I say? What are you gonna do, soldier?"

"Stay fit, sane, and ready. And pray."

"That's right. To that end, Monster has worked us into the crew rotation. You'll relieve your uncle and take your trick at the wheel from ten until fourteen hundred; that's, uh, two o'clock,"

"I know."

"Then you're with Monster serving dinner. After which I have KP, and you take another trick at the wheel, followed by me. That'll give the guys a little time to relax, and something to keep your mind busy."

"Sounds good," said Blake.

***

Blake was able to put Cain's advice into practice at the helm, focusing on the instruments, and making minute adjustments to the wheel. Gradually, the realization that he was steering a big schooner across the sunny Caribbean began to set in and, to his great annoyance, he began to enjoy himself in short bursts.

Assisting Monster in the galley was a different matter altogether. Where the helm afforded a measure of solitude on the wide-open sea, the galley did anything but. It was small and Monster was big, garrulous, and picky. He tended to micromanage, even down to the drying of dishes.

"You probably want to know how I lost my leg," he said. "S'alright. Everybody does. It was my second tour in Afghanistan. Feral Cain was my squad leader. I was a demolitions expert. We were raiding a mud-walled compound in the middle of a poppy field in Baramcha. Didn't go so good."

"To say the least."

"Ironically, it wasn't even the Taliban we were fighting," Monster continued. "They flat out outlawed opium production, when they were in power. It was Dubya's administration that put the anti-Taliban drug lords back in the saddle, after 9/11. How many billion dollars on that war? Like eight hundred, I heard? And what, a hundred fifty thousand US troops? We spent eight billion to wipe out poppy production, yet drugs still count for something like fifty percent or better of the whole country's GDP; and now we have ISIS! Can you believe that? Anyway, that's when Feral got involved with the DEA."

Blake began to contemplate Cotillion's potential involvement. Hanging around that part of the world would explain the artifacts, and the Saudis, and the money.

"You know how they cured my phantom pain?"

Blake was getting fidgety and thinking of another cure—the one hanging around his neck. "You mean from losing your leg? How?"

"Mirror. Can you believe that? Stuck a mirror between my legs so it looked like I had two whole ones again, and told me to wiggle the toes on both feet. All the sudden the phantom leg went away. Haven't had any pain since!"

"We are fearfully and wonderfully made!" said Blake.

"Is that Shakespeare?"

"No, uh, King David. As in the Bible."

***

Sky's the Limit taxied into a parking space at the Charles Kirkconnell International Airport. A fuel truck rolled up and parked alongside. Jayce coaxed the macaw out of the carrier, and spoke to him soothingly as he spread the plumage on his back. He glued the little black transponder to the shaft of one of the longer feathers.

"Alright, make it quick, Mitch!" called Flint. "Zero loiter. Chief wants us back ASAP." Flint was a bad tempered, gray-haired man who'd flown in the last years of Viet Nam. He'd been a bush pilot on numerous black ops since.

Jayce carried Nebuchadnezzar to the tarmac, and thrust him into the air. He circled around the plane in three widening laps, then headed northeast toward the far end of the island. Jayce smiled and walked to the terminal building, pretending not to hear Flint yelling from the cockpit. Flint caught up to him in the restroom. Jayce was barricaded in a stall.

"Hey, what the hell? Did you hear me? This ain't no boondoggle pleasure trip," said the pilot.

"Aw c'mon, Flint! Can a guy take a dump?"

"You forget there's a can on the plane?"

"You know you hate people using the 'Bird Turd.' I came in for a candy bar, and had the urge to purge. Get over it!"

Flint left, grumbling curses. Jayce watched the blip cross the map on his smartphone, already eight miles over the ocean and still headed northeast, toward the Jardines de la Reina Archipelago. "Not Cuba, dude!"

The restroom door opened again. "You gonna be done anytime soon?"

"First load in three days. Been savin' up."

"I'm going for coffee." The door closed.

"Try decaff! Just sayin'. 'Cuz I care. Not really." Jayce grinned, and zoomed in on the map a little. Nebuchadnezzar made eighteen miles before Flint ordered Jayce to return to the plane. *Definitely knows where he's going,* he thought. *Wonder where Wexler is?*

***

They had just activated the auto-pilot and served dinner on deck when *Tarshish* suddenly slowed down. When the slight vibration in the deck boards faded, and the faint hum of the Kraken ceased, the ship settled in earnest. Looks of apprehension were exchanged, and Steam appeared from the deck hatch behind the helm station.

"What happened?" said Barrett, standing up.

"Just what I said would happen!" Steam was wearing a ball cap now, and had his teeth in. Blake was surprised at how it changed his appearance. He no longer looked like an easy-going hillbilly. There was an edge, a fierceness in his expression. He spoke decisively through tight lips, as if he were holding his dentures in with them.

"Thermal stress! I been gripin' about it since Thanksgiving. We lost two pistons, at least."

"We can still run on that," said Cain.

"Go ahead. The others can't be far behind."

"Margarita is just over the horizon. We'll pick up parts there."

"Not for this beast! Chaguaramas is the only place in the Caribbean we'll get what we need," contested Steam.

"Mr. Barrett, I appeal to you," said Cain.

"Steam, I say we get into port under power. Then start breaking down the engine. I'll call ahead and see if I can get parts ashore. If not we'll have to sail to Chaguaramas."

"If you say so. Goin' into hostile territory is no time to be runnin' in new pistons and rings. I'll go ahead and fire it up." Steam went to the helm and started the engine, re-engaged the auto-pilot, and descended back into the engine room.

Cain excused himself. "Gotta call Flint. Blake, come with me."

Blake didn't miss the bitter glance from his uncle.

The men were quiet until the back of Blake's head vanished down the companionway.

"Pretty nice kid," said Monster "Good worker. Looks like you, Urquart."

Sensing his friend's rising blood pressure, Barrett was more circumspect. "Car, if he can handle the wheel under sail, you can sleep in tomorrow."

"He knows what he's doing. Just what he's gotten us into is anyone's guess."

"Or what Cain is using him for," added Monster.

"Exactly. I want answers," said Carson.

"It'll be easier to get them, if you don't kill him," said Barrett.

Carson took a long swig of beer.

Barrett went on. "You have to admit, he's uncovered something huge, and given us an opportunity to stop it."

"And," Monster added, "he called the chief's bluff. I'm sorry, but Cain's changed. He's not the same man I served with. I don't trust him anymore. The whole game has changed on us. If it weren't for this nuke thing, I'm tellin' ya, I'd hang it up."

Carson looked at his plate, idly stirring his Spanish rice with his fork.

"Roger that," said Barrett, leaning forward. "The bad guys found us, Car. The bird-man was a forward observer. There had to be a strike team right behind him. But that kid programmed a *freaking parrot* with a coded message only *you* could understand, right under his kidnapper's nose. It was life or death on a lee shore, and he saved our mangy hides. You think you could give him a little credit, instead of your foot up his butt?"

Carson turned away, and gazed out over the waves. "He's my sister's kid. She's... I can't lose my sister's kid. I can't be responsible..."

"He isn't Becky Lynn, Car. And he seems to be pretty responsible for himself."

***

Cain dialed Trinidad and Tobago Directory Assistance, and got the number for P.K.'s night club. He handed Blake the satellite phone.

A man answered, and Blake asked for P.K.

"Don't know any Blake Barber," he contested.

"She's expecting my call."

"Dot's what dey all say. We open at five." The line went dead.

Blake redialed, and the man answered again.

"Tell P.K. that Abel Newly is on the phone." There was silence. Cain smiled. Blake re-emphasized "Abel. Newly."

"Just one moment, sir."

A moment later, a woman picked up. "Mr. Newly, where have you been?"

"Is this P.K.?"

"Not if this isn't Newly," she replied, smartly.

"Tell Cotillion that Newly is dead. *Tarshish* is having engine trouble. We are proceeding under reduced power, so it'll be a couple of days before we arrive…" Cain mouthed the word 'Friday.' "Friday, most likely."

"I'm sure I don't know what you are talking about, but if I did, I would certainly pass the word on." The line went dead again.

"She said she would pass the word on. I want to call Serena."

"Well, I need to call Flint. You get back on deck and remember, watch what you say around the guys."

Blake didn't push the matter. When he rejoined the crew, Monster ordered him to bus the table. Steam and Barrett were conferring, and Carson was at the wheel. Venezuela was rising from the fiery orange horizon to meet the setting sun. Blake could hear that Steam's prophecy had been true—there were no parts for the Kraken in Isla Margarita.

"Land ho! Margarita dead ahead, boys. What are we gonna do?" said Carson.

"I think the Chief wanted to put in for the night," said Barrett.

"I'd sooner heave to in Detroit than Porlamar!" Steam retorted with contempt. "We're making eleven knots on sixty percent power. We can do almost as good under sail, and I can get started tearing her down."

Barrett went to the intercom and called down to Cain, who assented. "Chief says we're good. Make sail!"

Blake filled the bus tub with dinnerware and returned to the galley, where Cain was energetically scrubbing pots.

"Get hold of Flint?"

"Yeah. This gives him time to pick up some things for the mission."

"What about the bird?" said Blake, nervously.

"Flew to a little island off Cuba." Cain didn't even look over his shoulder. "I'm sorry, Blake. Nothing we can do at the moment. Tracker's still hot, though. 'Bout time for your trick, isn't it?"

"Aye, sir," Blake affirmed. *Do you really think I don't know you're blowing me off?*

On deck, Monster and Barrett had gotten the mainsail set, and were working on hoisting the jib and staysails. "Come to relieve me?" said Carson.

"If I may."

"You may. I got a couple things to say to you."

"Don't let me stop you," said Blake, full of sour snark.

"You saved our asses, and I'm grateful." Blake felt a lump forming in his throat, and tears welled in his eyes. At last a friendly, familiar voice. "This ain't your fault. We're all in a spot here. I think you already have a feeling about Agent Cain."

"He won't let me talk to Serena. I think he's lying to me about Mia. About trading the bomb for her."

"You're in good company. But we need you to play along with him, for the time being—like you're on his side. The rest of us are gonna be a little adversarial when he's around, so don't take it personal. Hand some back."

The tears streamed, and Blake bit his lower lip. Carson threw an arm around him and drew him close. "I know, kid. Hold it together. C'mon, I know. How's the old man?"

Blake took a deep breath. "Getting older. The Pagáns take good care of him. Sylvana moved into your room."

"Who's this booger at Mom's?"

"Brett Turlow. Gold digging son of a…"

"Staysails set, Carson!" called Barrett. "Put her on the wind!"

"Take the wheel kid. Throttle up a little, put us on a close reach." Blake complied, and the great sails filled, the schooner heeled and began to make way. Carson killed the engine. "I'm gonna go help Steam. East southeast.

Mind the Garmin and the Simrad. Sail by the luff of your main. Steer one pin at a time. Holler to Monster if you need anything, he has watch." Carson gave him a pat on the back, and went below.

"Aye aye, Uncle Arctica," Blake said quietly.

23

Blake appeared on deck as the sun crawled out of the dark ocean ahead, setting golden fire to the hazy horizon, and turning the opal gray sky a pale baby blue. High, thick cirrus clouds in the east were the only hint of brewing weather.

"Morning, Mr. Barber," said Barrett, from the helm.

"You are relieved, Mr. Reynolds," Blake replied, taking the ship's wheel.

"Boy, you never get tired of that sunrise."

"You know, my uncle named a boat after your sister?"

"Oh, yeah?"

"My boat, actually. He commandeered her, repainted her with this horrible camo scheme, and renamed her Becky Lynn. Then he used her to start a one-man war on drugs on Highland Creek Reservoir."

Barrett looked back to the sunrise, and remained silent for a moment. "We lived right behind the Urquarts. Carson and I were like brothers. There was one time, Becky Lynn, she was madder than hell at him, and..." he smiled, fondly.

"I'm sorry. I shouldn't pry."

"S'alright. Carson's always blamed himself." Barrett went to the windward rail and gazed down at the water rushing by. "Dad worked third shift, so we didn't see him too much. A little girl needs to know her daddy loves her. Needs that attention."

"And she'll do anything to get it," added Blake. "That was my girlfriend."

"Yeah, well. Becky Lynn… I guess Dad just didn't know how to connect with her. Anyway, she made it a point to get his attention by running with the wrong crowd. Started partying pretty early on. Carson loved her. He'd have done anything for her. And he tried. She couldn't see it. Wouldn't see it. Wouldn't have it."

"What happened?"

"Whiskey and the wrong pills. The wrong boyfriend. Head injury. We never learned what really happened. The psycho she was shacking with died under suspicious circumstances a week later."

"Carson?"

Barrett stretched and headed down the companionway. "Time to get Steam on deck for his watch. Cain's cooking breakfast. God have mercy on our souls!"

Blake realized he was alone on deck with the lives of five men below, and the welfare of this beautiful ship in his hands. He said a prayer for Mia, and felt guilty about forcing her out of his mind so that he could focus on his duty. "Blake Barber. Fit, sane, and ready—my Butt!"

***

He was assigned KP for lunch, assisting Monster again. Cain passed through the galley with suspicious regularity, so Monster spouted verbal abuse at Blake, who made a good show of slamming drawers, dropping utensils, and looking petulant.

When they served the men at the table on deck, Blake dropped Carson's plate in front of him.

"You got a problem?" his uncle snapped.

"Somebody's been into my stuff!"

"You don't *have* any stuff!"

"My case! Somebody pulled the foam insert out, and put it back the wrong way. And my tablet's been turned on. It was still warm."

Cain looked perplexed, and slightly pleased. "You two, knock it off. That's and order."

"Tell him to stay out of my damned cabin!"

"I wasn't *in* your damned cabin!"

"You did this all the time back home! He used to do it all the time!"

"I said knock it off! That was an order!" shouted Cain. "Blake, take your meal in the saloon."

Blake huffed back down the companionway, proud of his performance.

"Which one of you was it?" Cain demanded.

"That kid's gonna be trouble," said Steam.

"I said, which one of you?" Cain shouted.

"Needed to be done," said Carson. "We forgot to check the case the first night."

"What was in it?"

"Tablet. Foam insert. Like he said," Carson guessed, hoping to heaven that Cain hadn't seen inside the case. "Of course he could've unpacked. Probably *should* search his cabin."

"Nobody goes in his cabin, but me. Is that clear?"

"Whatever you say, Boss."

***

Mia paced the bare wooden floor, running scenarios through her head. A dummy on the mattress, hide in the bathroom. Flying kick. She went to the door.

"Hey, in the hall!"

"What ya want gyal?"

"A couple of pillows and a bed sheet."

"Boss say no pillows, no sheets. Ya get fruit, jerky, water and some roll paper for ya bum."

"Well, it's the little things in life, right?" she said to herself.

Mia went back to the mattress and sat with her back against the wall, trying to keep a handle on her anxiety. She remembered Blake's words. Viking or Victim. Remember to pray. *Pray. Me?* she thought. *No atheists in foxholes, right?* "Yahweh, God of Abraham, Isaac, and Blake Barber..." The tears began to roll. "I am so afraid. I don't know whether I'm going to live or die, or which is worse. I don't know what to say except please help me. Help Blake.

I treat him so badly and he loves me so much, and I… I just don't know what to do," she sobbed. She heard Macoute say something below her window. He laughed mockingly and offered to come up and comfort her.

"Shut the hell up!" she shouted. "You look like you had a fire on your face, and your dad put it out with a golf shoe!" She knew it would be tonight. He would come to her room. Viking or victim. He was easily more than twice her weight, and built like Vin Diesel. *My best flying kick right between the eyes, and he might be stunned long enough to…what? If he gets a hold of me, or lands a blow, he'll pin me and it's game over.* She rubbed her eyes, dried her cheeks and scanned the bare room again. Staring at the front door it struck her— *Hinges on the inside?* "Hinges on the inside!" she whispered. "But I need something to knock the pins out with." She drowsed, and gave herself over to it.

A raucous squawk and ear piercing wolf-whistle from the balcony shredded her uneasy sleep. She screamed, as she flipped over and clutched the mattress. A big red, blue, and yellow macaw perched on the balcony railing.

"Zut Alors! Merde! Voulez-vous couchez avec moi?"

She gave heaven a wry smile. "*Really?*"

An egg-sized rock ricocheted off the glass door, and Macoute yelled an obscenity. "OMG! Nebby! Come to mama, baby!" She grabbed a handful of fruit as she got to her feet, and held it out. Nebuchadnezzar wasted no time, as another rock spanged off the iron railing, and Macoute bellowed. Mia offered her arm as a perch and the bird hastily accepted. She closed the sliding glass door.

"Where have you been, huh?" She fed him a grape.

Nebby obliged with a hearty "Stoof it in yer pookits!"

Mia's heart leapt, and for a second she felt as if she'd faint. "What did you say?" she fed him another grape.

Nebby repeated himself. "Stoof it in yer pookits!"

"Oh, God! Oh, God! Oh, God!" she cried. "Thank you! Thank you! Best parrot ever!" she laughed. She took a deep breath, barely holding her emotions in check. "Okay, no more grapes. Let's have some banana. As she stroked his plumage, he craned his neck around and dug at a spot in the middle of his back. "Something gotcha there, buddy?" As she scratched the spot, her finger passed across something hard and strange. "What's this? Lemme see." She distracted him with another piece of banana, and gently spread the plumage apart until she came across a small black cylinder glued to the shaft of one feather.

"What have we here?" She pried it free with her fingernail, and held it up. "Is that really what I think it is? Oh hell… I mean, *Heavens* yes!"

She got up, opened the glass door, and yelled at Macoute. "My boyfriend knows where I am, and he is gonna kick your ass!" She slammed the door so hard it nearly came off the track. Mia took Nebby and the fruit to the bathroom and perched him on the edge of the bathtub. "Now, what is there to work with in here? She stared at the toilet. "The jerks even took the tank cover." She looked into the tank. It had the old-fashioned float-ball on a flexible metal arm. "Okay! Okay! Here we go! Why didn't I see this before? Because I was thinking of it as a toilet and not a weapons factory! Oooh, and a metal arm on the handle!" she set about disassembling it, and unscrewed the float-arm from the shut-off lever. A sliver of banana stem wedged under the shut-off kept the water from running. She took the flat metal arm from the flush handle, and carefully bent it into a U shape wide enough to fit comfortably around her middle two fingers, with the "legs" of the U protruding a good three inches out of her fist. She did the same with the float arm, giving the float-ball to Nebuchadnezzar to play with.

Macoute stood up when the glass door slid open. He could barely see the top of her head, as she squatted in the door frame. A scraping sound echoed from the concrete balcony, setting his rotten teeth on edge, and grating his nerves. It went on for two hours, and no amount of bellowing could stop it. When the rock throwing commenced, Mia pulled her mattress onto the balcony and continued her work under its shelter. At last, she slipped the sharpened spikes between her fingers, and balled her fists. "Whatta ya know? Homemade Black Cats right out of the litter box!"

She latched the glass door. Macoute's watch had ended, and now two lanky teenagers stood with assault rifles in the clearing, twenty feet below. She dragged the mattress to the corner just outside the bathroom, out of the line of sight for anyone entering from the hall. She jimmied the shut-off valve on the toilet so it would run a little, turned on the bathroom light, then locked the door and closed it from the outside. "Let's get a little shut eye. It's gonna be a long night." She settled on the mattress, the macaw snuggling up to her and resting his head on her arm.

***

Blake poured the pills from the silver vial into his palm, and counted them. *I can do two a day. Five days left.* It felt so good to know that the crew was behind him; at least to *believe* that they were for the time being. But what if they turned on Cain and abandoned the mission? What if they got the nuke without him? They wouldn't trade it for Mia—he was certain of that.

He contemplated Cotillion's words: *your options will become obvious. Activate the tracker once you have done what needs to be done.*

At minimum, that meant disabling the ECM cloak; which also meant getting into the radio room. But doing what must be done—the options were unthinkable. They were wrapped in a black shroud, and loomed at the edge of his imagination like the shadow of death. Had Carson done what needed to be done to avenge Becky Lynn? Is that what haunted him? Blake imagined the worst—failure. Never knowing what would become of Mia, or worse, finding out. *knowing or not knowing,* he thought, *it would kill me. So, I will die trying. What I do can only haunt me as long as I am alive. As long as Mia is safe, it doesn't matter what happens to me, or anyone else.*

Blake swallowed a tablet.

***

It had been a long day. The novelty of schooner life had given way to tedium very early—cleaning toilets, peeling vegetables, scrubbing Cain's scorched pots under Monster's meticulous eye. Even taking his trick at the wheel had lost its thrill. Playing the part of whipping boy was especially stressful—it was a lot like life in his father's house. Although, there was something satisfying about telling his uncle to kiss off on a semi-regular basis.

He lay in bed contemplating how he could get the key to the radio room, and how to deal with it if he couldn't. He walked through *Tarshish* in his mind. There was a small sledge hammer in the engine room. There was an axe mounted by the fire extinguisher in the passageway, but not much room to swing it. *But if I could get a gun from the ammo locker on the other side of the galley… how will I deal with the confrontation? They'll shoot me if they have to. Cain might give me a gun, if I play my cards right. How can I do this to the guys?* He pressed his fists against his eyes and groaned, "God, how? What am I supposed to do? We are *all* bad guys! There is none righteous, no not one!"

"You can bet your lunch on that!" said Cain, strolling down the passageway. He stopped outside Blake's door. "You alright pal? The guys were kinda hard on you today."

"I hate those jerks!"

"All things work together for good to them that love God, to them who are the called according to his purpose, son. Remember that. I believe you've been brought to the Kingdom for such a time as this, Buddy. Can I get you anything?"

As if having the Antichrist quoting scripture through my door isn't enough? Blake thought. "Get me an exorcist."

"Lot of demons on this boat, for sure. Resist the devil, and he'll flee from you, Blake! God bless America and Good night, pal!"

He understood Cain to mean the things that drove his men to this vocation. Was it patriotic service in the war on drugs, or just a thinly justified vigilante crusade under a spread of canvas? Were the sailors of *Tarshish* lauded patriots, or sanctified pirates? Blake buried his face in his hands. *We all think we're King David, or Gideon when we're really just Jonah, or Captain Ahab. Cotillion is the only one who really knows who he is.* Blake stewed for a minute, on that thought. "Where did I go wrong, Father in Heaven?" he whispered. "Where did I get off track? I used to read my Bible. I used to pray. I tried to do right by people. Then Turlow came along. I started worrying, and being afraid, and hating. And now Mia… what am I about to do? What *should* I do?"

He pulled the sheet over his face.

"No matter what happens to me, Lord, save Mia. Save Mia."

***

Macoute returned to the guest house at 3:00 AM, with two bottles of dark rum and a handful of joints. Mia heard him cajoling the boys in the clearing. Two older sentries joined them. "Once that door opens, it's every critter for himself," she whispered to Nebby. She crept to the door and listened, Black Cats at the ready. Macoute tromped up the stairs, joint blazing between his lips, humming tunelessly. The sentries laughed joyously when they saw him bearing gifts. Mia could smell the pungent marijuana smoke seeping under the door. There was some apprehension on their part when Macoute relieved them of their duties. But, when he looked offended, they quickly took the bottle and reefer, and ambled down the hall praising his generosity.

The time she dreaded had finally come. The deadbolt slowly scraped across the striker plate in the door jamb. She retreated around the corner, plastered herself against the wall, and hoped to heaven that Nebby would sense the gravity of the situation and stay quiet. She held her breath as the door creaked open, and kept her spiked fists at the ready. Macoute entered and relocked the deadbolt, his attention immediately drawn to the light leaking from under the bathroom door. He heard the toilet filling. *Too easy*, he grinned to himself. He unbuttoned his fatigues, dropped his fly, and kicked the bathroom door off its hinges. Nebby shrieked and took flight. Macoute, eyes dilated from the darkness and the weed, was temporarily blinded by the sudden flood of brightness, and startled by the bird. Realizing the bathroom was empty, he turned toward the room. Sudden, searing pain exploded in his eyes and everything went black. His screaming drowned out the bird's, as he staggered toward the open sliding door. Mia could hear the sentries shouting and running up the hall. Then something happened that she hadn't anticipated. Macoute pulled his pistol and started firing wildly. She hit the deck and scuttled on her belly toward his feet. She heard a body hit the floor in the hall, then another. His magazine empty, Macoute continued to stagger and howl, jerking the crude weapon out of his eyeballs. Nebby was still screeching hysterically. Mia leapt up, darted to the hall door to get a running start, and landed a flying kick with both feet square in his chest. Macoute went out the glass door and over the balcony railing, Nebuchadnezzar close behind.

The remaining four sentries, drunk and stoned, rushed up the steps and stopped cold. "Oh, dis some obeah, mon!" said one of the juniors. They picked their way between their fallen comrades. "Macoute? Macoute, Wah gwaan?" called the most senior, as they cautiously entered the room. "Awww ma gawd!" he groaned as he looked into the bathroom and saw Mia's body draped limply over the toilet. "We all dead now, mon!" There was general assent, as they continued toward the balcony to see what had become of Macoute.

They didn't hear the door shut, nor the bolt slide. Mia flew up the dirt road, cursing herself for not grabbing one of the dead men's rifles or flashlights on her way out. The waning crescent moon offered little help, filtering through occasional thin spots in the deciduous canopy. The road forked and she followed the right branch. It was slow and treacherous going.

***

Lucien brought Cotillion his phone. "It is the warden. Trouble at the guest house, Monsieur."

Cotillion was all business. "What has happened, warden?"

"Monsieur, we have a situation," he said, nervously. "I will allow Robaire to explain. He was there." The warden handed his phone over to the trembling thug.

"It's Macoute, sah. He gwaan do sumting chupid, Sah."

"The girl?"

"She jock him up real bod, sah. Real bod."

"Is *she* alright?"

"She gouge Macoute in deh eye, and chuck him out deh window. We thought she dead, sah. But..."

"But while you were all looking over the balcony, she locked you in the room?"

"She obeah gyal, sah. Ya bird come talk to her. Then she kill Macoute, an jus' disappear."

"I will speak with the warden." Robaire gladly handed the phone back. "You will find the girl and take her to the hostel. And you will Capture Nebuchadnezzar. But first, this is what you will do with Macoute..."

***

As soon as it was light enough, Mia started running. The road narrowed to a trail, which started to go uphill. The temperature and humidity were pushing higher, and it was getting hard to keep her exhausted body going. She jogged into a clearing and dropped to her knees. Salty sweat dripped from her brow and stung her eyes. A gigantic rusted gear stood out of the undergrowth not far from a crumbling stone arch and chimney. Everywhere there were low mounds where the earth had been turned over. A lot of digging had been going on here for a long time. Something under a bush caught her eye. It was grubby gray and very round, like a giant egg. She crossed the clearing and knelt before the bush. Mia recognized the squiggly cracks that divided the object's surface into symmetrical plates. It was a human skull. She looked back at the mounds, got up and slogged into the forest. "Blake is coming. Just got to hide and wait," she said. She noticed that she was slurring her words. "And find some water." Something in the distance clacked, then rattled indistinctly.

She staggered up a low ridge and dropped just short of its summit. It overlooked a large clearing with some kind of compound in its center. A twelve-foot chain-link fence topped with barbed wire surrounded a square courtyard and a wretched single-level cinder-block building. An armed sentry was posted outside two opposing corners of the fence.

She was about to slip away when a chorus of distinctly mechanical clicks announced the armed party behind her.

24

The chain-link gate jingled closed behind her. The sentry dialed his smart phone and waited. Mia stared at the squalid prison. A Hispanic woman's face appeared briefly behind one of the filthy window panes, and glared bitterly. The sentry whistled for Mia's attention, and handed the phone in to her.

"Hello?"

"Miss Devlin, I understand you had an eventful evening? I must apologize for Macoute. I trust you are unhurt?"

"I want to talk to Blake."

"I am sorry, but the amazing Mr. Barber is presently on an errand with his uncle. Since you did not approve of the company at my guest house, I have made arrangements for you at the ladies hostel. And do not concern yourself about the sentries. Each of them now carries one of Macoute's fingers to remind him not to touch what is mine."

"You're an animal!"

"Oh, Miss Devlin, you underestimate me! I am not an animal. I am a *monster*. You will do well to remember that. As always, tell the sentry if you need anything. Oh, and any more unauthorized excursions will be punished most severely. Adieu, Miss Devlin."

"Wait!"

"Yes?"

"My father is very wealthy. He…"

"I know! But, your father's entire net-worth would barely pay two weeks operating expenses for the *Mother of Harlots*. As I said, it is Blake's complete obedience I require. Make no mistake, Miss Devlin; your life is in his hands. Good day."

She handed the phone back through the gap in the gate, hating herself for having groveled. The sun was now beating down into the clearing. Her legs were beginning to feel like lead, and she nearly staggered as she approached the rusting front door of the building. Mia stopped short of the portal, head swimming. She knew she had to get out of the sun, and hoped to Heaven that there might be water inside. She took a trembling step through the door. It was dim and stuffy, and stank like a neglected women's room in August. Her stomach did a somersault.

Mia's eyes adjusted and she could see ratty mattresses around the perimeter of the room, and half a dozen women occupying them in varying states of consciousness. The room appeared to be about twenty by thirty feet. Paint peeled from the block walls. One mattress lay in a corner away from the others. On it was a small, motionless body—face up. The crumpled plastic wrapper of what looked like a case of bottled water rested near the only woman who was sitting up. *That's what I need,* she thought. She took a couple of steps forward.

"May I have a bottle of water, please?" she asked, in Spanish.

"Try and get some, puta! I'll kill you," hissed the other, sweat rolling down her face.

She noticed a discarded hypodermic needle by the next woman, then small dark splatters on the walls. She went to the lone mattress. The dirty body that lay upon it was a young girl. *Maybe thirteen*, she said to herself. Mia saw that she wasn't sweating, and her breathing was shallow. Mia knelt down and checked her pulse. Rapid. She was very hot. The girl opened her eyes. Mia smiled at her.

The girl whispered. Her dialect was difficult, but Mia caught enough to understand "Mama, the angels are white!"

"Shhh, I'll be right back." Mia got to her feet, putting one hand on the wall to steady herself, and went to get a bottle of water. The woman who'd threatened her started to get up. "Don't do it, chica!" Mia said, sternly as she fished out a bottle. The woman swung at her. Mia caught her wrist easily, and shoved her back down on the mattress. She noted that there were no needle tracks on her arm.

"I just want to help the girl."

"She's good as dead. What do you care, puta? We're all worse than dead."

"I care, because I care." She returned to the girl and opened the bottle. "My name is Mia. What's your name?" she said, sweetly.

"I tell you she's dead. Don't waste the water!"

Mia poured a little in her hand and patted the girl's forehead, and face.

The woman got to her feet again and piped up. "She is from Peru. I can tell you that."

"Then I'll call you Inca." She poured some water into the bottle cap, lifted the girl's head and pressed it to her lips. The girl revived a little. Mia did it again, and again. She heard the woman approaching, and stood up. As she turned around, she caught a fist square in the eye. Mia fell across Inca, and took a solid kick in the ribs.

"Puta blanquita!" screamed her attacker.

A couple of the other women stirred from their mattresses. Mia rolled against the wall on the other side of Inca and compressed herself into the corner. As the woman bent over to pick up the bottle, Mia pivoted and kicked her hard in the shoulder. She went down, and rolled with a cry. Mia struggled to her feet and stood over her. "I am not your enemy! I want to help you! I am Mia, what is your name?" The woman spat at her. The other three who had gotten up kept their shuffling zombie distance. A whistle came from the gate outside, and they made for the door, the other two rose and followed after them.

"What's your name? Come on, or it's gonna be Loquita." The supine woman looked away. "Okay, you wanna be 'crazy girl,' then Loquita it is." Mia got herself a bottle of water and guzzled it down. "You want some more water, I can get it. Maybe a few other things, too." She returned to Inca, and resumed her hydration.

The other women returned, and Mia watched in revulsion as they squatted on their grubby pallets and performed the grotesque ritual of candle, tourniquet, and needle.

At last, Inca was able to take small sips from the bottle. She called Mia "Angelita."

***

Twenty-four hours to Chaguaramas, Cain had said. The name that had started it all in Serena's living room. Blake's trick was nearly over when the dissonant whine of jet engines rose in his ears. He looked all around, then checked the GPS to make sure he hadn't strayed out of international waters. Cain and Carson came on deck as *Sky's the Limit* screamed past at three hundred fifty knots, rocking her wings.

"This ain't Reno, Flint!" Cain cried, lifting his carrot-juice cocktail in salute.

Carson relieved his nephew at the helm as Steam emerged from the companionway. Blake couldn't believe his luck, and intentionally tripped himself over the engineer's foot. He took a controlled tumble down the stairs, and commenced to shouting immediately.

"You freakin' people have been trying to kill me since I came on board!"

"Why, Grace, you fall down like Cooter Brown!" sneered Steam.

Cain pushed past Steam and dashed down the steps to Blake's aid. Steam ambled on, tossing Carson a knowing look.

Blake pulled himself up with the handrail, and limped into the passageway.

"C'mon in here," said Cain, opening his cabin door. "You okay?"

"Just barked my shins. Lucky, I guess." He sat down in the padded leather captain's chair. Cain sat on the edge of his bed.

"We're in a tight spot here, Blake my boy. I overheard the men talking. They think I've double crossed them. It's just a matter of time before they round on us. We gotta be ready."

"I agree. I'd feel safer if I were packing."

"You know how to handle a gun?"

"Yes sir. Proud member of the NRA. I can field strip a Glock in the dark."

"You'll have to make do with Smith and Wesson in this man's navy. But first, I *gotta* know that you're on board with me Blake."

"What are we going to do with the nuke?"

"Keep it out of the wrong hands."

"Could you be more specific?"

"Your buddies on deck—they're good guys, Blake. Patriots. Heroes to the last man. But they're playing for the wrong team. Tangled up with a dangerous, anti-government group. They have well-placed people in positions of command. They intend to take America back. And I mean back to 1955. Their superiors take all the drugs they seize on these missions straight to the street. That's how the network funds itself."

"The guys didn't seem to know about the nuke."

"They put up a good front. I had to tip my hand a little, and play the bully to cover for you that first night. You're uncle looked like he was ready to kill you right there. We were about to put a stop to this, when you turned up. We're in this together 'til the end, Blake. Are you with me?"

Blake mustered the most boyish sincerity he could and declared: "Yes, sir! I *am* with you!"

"Good man! I knew I could count on you the first time I saw you. I know you're worried about Mia. I'll do everything I can. But you have to understand the sacrifice we're all making to save our country."

"What about the other guys?"

"Nello, and Flint are with us. Jayce is a wild-card. I'll have some heat for you by your watch tonight, but you can't take it ashore."

"Thank you, sir. Could I, uh, borrow your Bible?"

"You bet, kid! Comfort for the soul. Strength for the battle."

Blake took the book from him. "I've got some time before KP. May I just stay in my cabin for a while?"

"Why don't you? Tomorrow, things get interesting," Cain smiled. "So what's your favorite scripture?"

"No greater love has a man than this. That he lay down his life for his brethren," Blake replied, as he got up.

"Perfect love casts out all fear! A-men, little brother!"

But Blake was really thinking of one of the Psalms: 'I said in my alarm, all men are liars!' He returned to his cabin and looked it up. He read aloud, exchanging, as was his habit, the title 'Lord' with Yahweh.

"I love Yahweh, because he hath heard my voice and my supplications.

Because he hath inclined his ear unto me, therefore will I call upon him as long as I live.

The sorrows of death compassed me, and the pains of hell got hold upon me: I found trouble and

sorrow.

Then called I upon the name of Yahweh; O Yahweh, I beseech thee, deliver my soul.

Gracious is Yahweh, and righteous; yea, our God is merciful.

Yahweh preserveth the simple: I was brought low, and he helped me.

Return unto thy rest, O my soul; for Yahweh hath dealt bountifully with thee.

For thou hast delivered my soul from death, mine eyes from tears, and my feet from falling.

I will walk before Yahweh in the land of the living.

I believed, therefore have I spoken: I was greatly afflicted:

I said in my haste, all men are liars.

What shall I render unto Yahweh for all his benefits toward me?

I will take the cup of salvation, and call upon the name of Yahweh.

I will pay my vows unto Yahweh now in the presence of all his people.

Precious in the sight of Yahweh is the death of his saints.

O Yahweh, truly I am thy servant; I am thy servant, and the son of thine handmaid: thou hast loosed my bonds.

I will offer to thee the sacrifice of thanksgiving, and will call upon the name of Yahweh.

I will pay my vows unto Yahweh now in the presence of all his people.

In the courts of Yahweh's house, in the midst of thee, O Jerusalem. Praise ye Yahweh."

"That's a good start," he said to himself, closing the book.

***

Mia approached the gate. "Hey, dirtbag! Get the skipper on the phone." He didn't understand a word she said. She pantomimed a telephone at one ear. "Ringy, ringy? El Jefe? Le Monsieur?"

The sentry nodded, and dialed. It took a minute, but finally he slipped the phone through the gap. Loquita watched from the window. Mia saw, and pointed at the phone.

"Mr. Ngandu?"

"How may I be of service, Miss Devlin?"

"We need some hygiene down here. Water. Feminine products. Lights would be nice."

"Hygiene is of little concern to the heroin addict. The drug produces a deep apathy. Do not worry. We will hose them off before delivery."

"This little girl needs medical attention."

"And what would you be saving her for? Surely you realize that she is better off dead."

"Then give her to me. Whatever it is, Blake will come through for you. It's the least you could do in return."

There was a brief silence. Cotillion chuckled. "Very well, then! If Mr. Barber can save you, and you can save the girl, she is yours. And what would you prescribe, Dr. Devlin?"

"Antibiotics. Ibuprofen. More water and some ice. Some of that fizzy vitamin stuff would be good. And feminine products, for the love of Pete."

"You will have the water and medications by mid-day. The others will take some time."

"Thank. You."

The line went dead. She slipped the phone back to the sentry.

She could hardly bring herself to go back inside. Instead, she walked around the building. On the other side, against the wall, were several reeking, fly ridden five gallon "buckets full of shhh…I don't wanna think about it," she said out loud. She took a deep breath, returned to Inca, and coaxed her into drinking a little more. "Hey, Loquita. We'll have more water by noon."

"You must be real special! Maybe they're going to put you in one of their fancy movies. You know, the kind where they cut your throat while they're…"

Mia flinched. "Why are you so hateful? We're in the same trouble here! I think we should be helping each other."

"We're all going to die drug-addicted whores."

"*You're* not taking the drugs. You're a fighter. You must still have hope?"

"Shut up, puta! You don't talk about me! I'll kill you!"

She looked back at Inca. "How are we gonna sleep, huh?"

"I heard you! I'll kill you when you're asleep!"

***

A quad-ATV rolled up to the fence three hours later. The sentry set a Styrofoam cooler inside the gate, stacked a case of bottled water on top of it, and a cardboard box on that. He closed the gate and whistled. Mia lugged the items back to her corner. "You see that, Loquita? One phone call, and I got all that. One phone call, and you're dead! Dead!" she started shouting in Spanish. "You hear me? One damned phone call! Anything happens to me, and you're done! Finito! You want hard-ass? You got hard-ass! Comprende?" There were packets of trail mix in the box along with the medications. "Here!" she pitched one to Loquita. "Thanks Mia!" she mocked. "You're welcome, Loquita!"

She took some ice from the cooler and rolled it up in Inca's filthy shirt.

"By the way," she said, taking her two empty water bottles and heading for the door, "I killed Macoute. Ask the sentry if you don't believe me."

She went out to the gate. "Cut the tops off these." She pantomimed with the bottles, then thrust them through the fence. The sentry pulled a knife from his boot, and sawed away. "I want the tops, too." He pushed them back through to her.

Back inside she found the supplies undisturbed. She filled one improvised glass with ice and approached Loquita, who stared at it with obvious desire. "This is for you. If you throw this away, I will kick your puta head through that puta wall. Don't think I can't do it." She set it on the floor. "It ain't a red Solo cup, but it'll do." Mia returned to Inca, filled her own cup, and rested it on the girl's forehead for a moment. She used the top of one of the bottles to scoop up a few chunks of ice, and fed them to her.

Loquita slowly reached for the ice. She clutched it to her chest as she leaned back against the wall, and breathed heavily. She pressed it to her cheek.

An anguished grimace twisted her features, and she began to cry. Mia kept a wary eye on her, and gave Inca a dose of liquid antibiotics.

***

Mia carefully lugged the least full bucket of muck to the gate, commanding the sentry to "Dump it!"

The sentry laughed and refused. She pointed to the back of the hostel. "Dump it, or I will dump one at every corner of this fence!" She pointed and pantomimed, then returned to the doorway. He called his partner on watch, and commanded him to retrieve the bucket while he kept his gun on the prisoner. The task completed, Mia returned with a bottle of water, rinsed the bucket, and went back inside. She helped Inca perch on the edge and relieve herself.

Mia got her back to bed, and checked her vitals. "Still hot and weak, but at least you're peeing. That's a good thing, sweetheart."

Loquita spoke up. "You speak Spanish pretty good, puta. You sound Mexican."

"Thanks, pendeja. I'm from the Unites States. You know, this is actually the second time I've been kidnapped? First time was my fault. I blame my boyfriend and my aunt for this mess."

"You really killed Macoute?"

"Really and truly."

"How did you do it?" she said, grimly. "I would like to have seen that. He used to guard us. I was his favorite because I would fight back. Until he heard about you. So, I should thank you for that much."

"Wow. Well, you're welcome. Very welcome," Mia said, hopeful that she'd finally gained some ground and made an ally.

***

After his evening trick, Blake sought out his uncle in the forward crew quarters. He found him drowsing on his bunk.

"Uncle Carson?" Blake said quietly. "Uncle Carson, I need your keys. I locked myself out of my cabin."

He unclipped the key-ring from a belt loop and tossed it to his nephew, without opening his eyes. "Just gettin' a little shut-eye before my watch. That gold one's the master key."

"Thanks!"

Blake returned to his cabin, which he had intentionally locked, and used the master key. Then he listened at the radio room door across the passageway. He tried the key. No good. The next one turned, and he slipped in. It was cramped but cool, and smelled of electricity. He scrutinized the large laptop fixed to the bulkhead, trying to comprehend the bar graphs and performance curves. He took note of the on/off buttons on its screen. He inspected the equipment racks, and the thick cable bundle that went up the mast and through the deck. *Axe—right there,* He thought. *They won't fix that with duct tape.* He barely heard Cain's cheerful whistling in the hallway over the hum of transformers, cooling fans, and the AC unit. He wedged himself behind the big transmitter cabinet, and strained to hear over the din of the equipment.

Cain entered and sat down at the laptop. He made several adjustments to the parameters, then dialed away on what looked like a heavy-duty cell phone with an antenna the size of a hotdog.

"Flint? Everything's green light on U-BOAT. Yeah. We should get in about noon tomorrow. I know. I have the same concerns. Cain out."

Cain made another call.

"Encrypt, secure channel niner-six. Bravo hotel eight six seven nine." There was a long pause. "Cumulus, how goes it on your end? It's all ducks-in-a-row here, barring the engine. Could be a problem. Steam'll have it running in no time. With any luck, in a couple of days, we'll have ourselves a one-way ticket to D.C. for a little congressional oversight. Oh yeah. Will the pharaoh-in-chief be there? Fantastic. Hold on, there was a glitch there. You say we're going forward with HEADLINE?" Cain paused. Blake thought there was trepidation in his voice. "Understood. Affirmative. God Bless America, brother! Over and out."

The combination of claustrophobia and panic at Cain's words exerted a powerful influence on Blake's bladder. He bit his lip and considered the drawbacks of peeing into the back of a multi-thousand-watt transmitter rig. *Did I miss my pill, or what?* he thought.

Cain placed a third call. "Nello, Slight change of plans. We're gonna have to go ahead with HEADLINE. Yeah, lost with all hands. It's a shame. Patriots one and all. And I really like that kid. Make a hell of an agent. EZ-BAKE goes green as soon as her keel hits the rocky bottom. How's Auntie Em? Great gal, I know. Make it painless. Accidental overdose, or something—but not until HEADLINE runs. All for the greater good. God Bless America, brother! Cain out."

Blake heard the door close. He dislodged himself and peeled the sweat-soaked shirt from his back and chest. He slipped into the passageway, shielded by the other half of the mast. He could hear banging from aft. He darted into the engineering space, and around the big engine. He found Steam in the shop bay, hammering the daylights out of something on an anvil vise.

"Hey, thought you was s'posed to be peelin' potatoes for Monster?" Blake was panting. "Uh oh. What'd you say to your uncle?"

"We're screwed, Steam. Totally screwed. It's a double-cross."

Steam frowned impatiently. "We'll don't keep me waiting, boy!"

"Cain. He's gonna kill us all. I was in the radio room. I overheard…"

"What in the name of… how…"

"My uncle's key. We were right about Cain. He was talking to somebody high up. As soon as they have the bomb, we're all deep six. And my girlfriend, and her aunt. Captain Flint and Nello are in on it. They're going to nuke the Congress and the President."

Steam seemed to shy away from him, then slammed the hammer down and howled at the top of his lungs. "Get back to your potatoes, boy! And tell Monster to bring me some ice. I done smashed my hand. Tell *him* to bring it. Gimme them keys and git!"

Blake ran to the galley. Monster fetched the ice and, cursing Steam's clumsiness, left Blake to tend the spuds.

By the time Blake took his watch on deck, word had passed between the men. Blake scanned the horizon with FLIR goggles, a Smith & Wesson 9mm semi-automatic pistol in a shoulder holster.

Cain ordered everyone to carry their side arms, citing possible trouble as they neared the coast of Venezuela.

Carson emerged from the forward hatch to relieve him.

"You look halfway between Star Trek and Miami Vice! Anything out there?"

"Nothing." Blake handed the goggles to him.

"We'll be in the Bocas del Dragon Straits by late morning."

"Mouths of the Dragon? As if one weren't enough."

"You can say that again. Plan is, you keep playin' up to Cain. We'll come up with something while you two are ashore."

"He said Jayce is a wild-card. Can we trust him?"

"Time will tell."

"There's something else you need to know. But, I'm afraid…"

"Tell me."

"Promise you won't kill Cain until after we have the bomb."

Carson looked grim. "I promise."

"Cain's been taking all the stuff you've been seizing, and selling it. That's how he's been funding this whole operation. And…"

"Go ahead."

"The rest of your team… Cain set a trap at Marley's Rock. Mia and I were the bait. The bad guys won. That's how I ended up here. I'm sorry."

Carson went to the windward rail, and donned the goggles. "Play your part, tomorrow. Play it well. Our lives depend on it."

"I'm sorry."

"Go to bed."

Blake returned to the companionway. Steam was at the wheel. "How's that storm look, Mr. Ebeling?"

"She's a brewin'! They'll give 'er a name soon."

25

Mia spent the morning trying to talk to the other women, offering them water and a little trail mix. Two were hostile, the other three catatonic. She decided that one irrationally angry woman was enough, and returned to Inca. She felt her forehead.

"I think the fever's broken, Inca!" Mia smiled. "You want to try some dried fruit?" Inca nodded a little, and smiled. Mia nearly burst into tears.

She fed her a little chunk of sugary papaya from the trail mix bag. Inca took a deep breath and puckered her mouth in delight. "Good, huh? So, what does your mama call you?"

"Perla," said Loquita.

Mia looked over her shoulder "Sorry?"

"My name is Perla."

"That's really pretty."

"Might as well be Mierda, now."

"I'm Mia. Where are you from?"

"El Salvador. It's bad there, you know. So bad."

"How did you wind up here?"

"I just wanted to escape. My brother-in-law said for $1000 he could get me to the USA. Get me a job cleaning. I begged. I worked. I laid on my back. Just to get $200. He said I could work the rest off in the United States. He put me on a truck with some other women and two men with guns. We drove all night. Then they tied me up, put me on a boat, and here I am."

Mia was truly at a loss. "I can't tell you how sorry I am."

"Try," Perla said, bitterly.

"I have to hope my boyfriend will find us."

"Ha! Crap in one hand and hope in the other, then see what you've got."

"He doesn't give up. He'll find us or he'll send help. We just have to survive until then."

"How do you know?"

Mia patted the little tracker in her pocket, to reassure herself. "I just know."

"Mama Angelita?" cooed Inca. "More sugar!"

Mia obliged with another chunk of papaya. "That's Tia Angelita, to you. What's you're name?"

"Inca."

"No, your mama gave you a name. What is it?"

"You are my mama!" She managed an impish smile. "Inca."

"See, you are feeling better, funny girl!"

The ATV came growling down to the gate with another delivery.

Mia retrieved the box, more water, and ice. She tossed a pink, plastic wrapped cube to Perla. "Check *that* out! Holy cow, look at this—a set of bed sheets! She pitched one to Perla. "And some garbage bags for the bucket! What else? Fizzy stuff, and a sponge! I should have asked for a fifty-five gallon drum of air freshener." She opened a packet of the vitamin powder and carefully poured it into one of the homemade plastic cups, added ice and water and offered it to Perla.

"Why?"

"Why what?"

"I hate you, but you are kind to me. Why?"

"I don't know. Something in here wants to," she said, touching her chest. "Which is a total surprise to me because I'm usually a totally selfish, hard-hearted pendeja. I guess it's just the stress."

"That's what you tell yourself."

"Here. You'll like this."

Perla leaned forward and took the cup. She tasted it. "Madre de Dios, that *is* good."

Mia undressed Inca, covered her with the sheet, and washed her ragged blouse and skirt in the water that remained in yesterday's cooler. She hung them to dry on the fence. For a moment she caught herself thinking that she should call and thank Cotillion, and apprise him of Inca's progress. "Damn you, Stockholm syndrome!" she said aloud.

She gave Inca a sponge bath, then put the clean sheet under her. Inca drank half a bottle of water, and tore into the trail mix.

"Now, take a nap, piglet!" Mia teased. She told her a story about a rotten little girl named Fiona, who lived in the snowy north, and had been very sick once upon a time. Inca took that nap. Mia went outside and walked laps around the compound, trying to figure out what was going on in her head.

***

Blake swallowed another Phobolyn and took his trick at the wheel, under Monster's watchful eye. He bellowed his orders to tack with a confidence that surprised the veteran.

Tarshish passed through the east-most strait of Bocas del Dragon under sail, between Monos Island and Trinidad's mountainous northwestern peninsula. The wind and seas had risen ahead of the approaching storm, and Blake was glad to be on the sheltered side of the island. They rounded the last headland, and turned east-southeast.

"Take us around Little Gasparee on the outside. Call down, see if Steam is ready to pilot," said Monster.

"Aye aye sir! Ease for a reach, ye lubbers!" Blake shouted, in his best Scots brogue. Monster smiled. "You might want to tone that down," he said, going forward to ease the main sail. "Get Steam on deck to take us in."

Barrett eased the staysails, then the jib. Blake keyed the mic on the intercom, and spoke normally. "Mr. Ebeling, Monster's compliments, sir. We're rounding Little Gasparee. Request harbor pilot on deck."

"I'll be there D-G-and-R," was the simple reply.

Blake reverted to his Scots, and shouted "Mr. Monster! Mr. Steam will be topside when he's damn good and ready!"

Five gray cutters of the Trinidad & Tobago Coast Guard Station lay along twin piers that angled like hockey sticks. *Big boats,* Blake thought. *Still only half the size of the Mother of Harlots.* He had told no one about Cotillion's ship. Not the truth anyway. If anyone attacked, Mia would be doomed.

It wasn't long before *Tarshish* was passing Little Gasparee Island on the outside. Monster bellowed back in his own affected English accent. "Steady on! All clear to starboard. Mind those boats to port, if you please Mr. Barber! Ready to head up!"

Blake switched the intercom to 'all,' and announced "All hands on deck to strike sail!" Carson popped out of the companionway, and jogged forward to help with the sails. Cain, with shoulder bag and backwards flat-cap, came on deck and joined Blake at the wheel.

"You ready for the big adventure, Agent Barber?"

"Fly the Q flag, Mr. Monster!" Blake shouted. "We're coming into port, for heaven's sake!" He looked at Cain. "Yes, sir. What are we going to do about my passport?"

"Already taken care of."

"I'm worried about the storm."

"May work to our advantage. Still two days out."

"Come head to wind, Mr. Barber! Put her in irons!" called Monster.

"Aye aye!" Blake turned the wheel one pin at a time, carefully bringing *Tarshish* into the wind. Her sails began to flutter, then rattled and shook thunderously.

Steam came to the helm. "Alright, boy, drop the hook."

"Strike jib and staysails!" Blake shouted.

As the canvas came down, he flipped a switch on the control panel and 300 lbs of anchor plunged into the sea from beneath the bow. "Seven fathoms beneath the keel, if you please, Mr. Steam."

"Give 'er three hundred fifty feet of chain," Steam replied.

Blake watched the numbers tick away on the controller, and stopped it at 350, on the nose.

Cain slapped a hand on his shoulder and said, "Alright Jim Hawkins, let's get the long boat and check in with Mr. Tally Man."

"I'll be right there. I need my case." Blake went below and retrieved it, checking to make sure his satellite beacon was still hidden safely under the sink in his cabin. By the time he returned to Cain, the longboat was suspended over the side by the davits.

They were joined by Steam, who had a parts list a mile long and trusted no one with it. The longboat was lowered. Steam started the outboard and steered them toward a small red and white striped lighthouse. The normally clear blue sky was increasingly crowded with billowing cumulus clouds and the wind was making hard shifts to the east. They tied up, and entered the Customs office. A man at the counter smiled.

"Mister Cain, welcome back!"

"Nicholas! How's the family?" Cain pulled a sheaf of completed forms out of his bag and handed them to the Customs agent, along with his passport.

"Very good! Getting bigger! Let's see..." He thumbed through the documents. "Everything is in order as always, sir. Your passport, Mr. Barber. Fresh from the U.S. Embassy." He handed Blake the new booklet.

Steam presented his passport. "Nothin' to declare. All my forms are in there," he said, indicating Cain's submission. Nicholas stamped his passport and handed it back. "I'm goin' shoppin'. See you fellahs back aboard." He went his way.

"So," Nicholas said, "You're coming in, everyone else is going out."

"We heard it's gonna be a doozey. Say, where the devil is this place they call P.K.'s?"

The man frowned, and side-eyed him. "You mean P.K.'s, the dance club? Down near Queen's Park Savannah. You didn't come in just to dance in the middle of a hurricane?"

"Official business. What kind of place is it?"

"Nightclub. Trendy, but shady. There's talk."

"Always is."

"Be careful in there. He looks too young."

"Passport says he's eighteen, right?"

Blake checked. "Um, yeah, eighteen. That's right."

"Stay out of trouble. Both of you," said Nicholas, with a skeptical smirk.

"Kiss the wife and kids," said Cain, as they headed for the door. Outside, he dialed his phone, called for a taxi, then dialed again. "Flint? The Q is down and the boys are back in town. Any trouble? Good. Got an errand. We'll be back aboard in a few hours. Hey, how would you feel about violating Venezuelan airspace? Think about it. Anything new on the bird? Alright, see you on the boat tonight."

"Any news?" said Blake.

"Still on the island. Was all over the place, then it stopped. Moved about a mile overnight. Stationary now. Looks like somebody got it. Good chance it was Mia. Let's get a bite before we call your boss. How about KFC?"

***

The cloud cover blotted out the sunset, and it seemed to get dark very quickly. People were streaming into the palatial, rosy facade of P.K.'s. The bouncer stopped Cain and Blake. He looked like he could stop King Kong. "Sorry, gentlemen. Dere is a dress code."

"We're expected," said Cain, flashing his badge, confidently.

"Pretty. How long you spend shining dat?"

Blake looked the man straight in the eye and gave him Mia's best hard stare. "You will tell P.K. that Mr. Barber is here. Do it. *Now*."

The bouncer, more amused than impressed by Blake's chutzpah, touched the wireless transceiver in his ear, and mumbled something.

"Go on in, young Jedi. P.K.'s at the bar."

The place was packed. Pink lasers sliced through the air to the beat of unbelievably loud dance music. It was an assault on the ears of those accustomed only to the rush of wind and splash of waves. Fog machines chugged away and strobes flickered. Blake pulled the wallet from his case as they skirted the dance floor and made themselves conspicuous at the end of the long, neon-trimmed bar.

A very short black woman of about thirty-five met them at the end of the bar. Her purple eye-shadow matched the lipstick on her pouty mouth. Her crew-cut was brilliant red, and styled such that she looked like a walking ember. She regarded them with bored contempt.

"Health inspector was here, last week."

"Are you P.K.?" said Blake.

"You look awfully young, to me. You got some ID?"

Blake held the wallet up so she could read it. He was surprised by the sudden, raw hatred that welled up in him, and spoke like he meant business. "Yeah. I'm Maurice Ngandu. I'm Lucien's replacement."

Cain caught the slightest tremor of fear course through her whole body, though the casual observer would not have seen it. *This little vixen is one cool customer,* he thought.

"Come with me. Your CIA friend stays here."

"DEA, actually, but he's off duty." Blake put the wallet back in his case, and followed the woman along the back wall of the bar, then down a narrow passageway. They entered a spacious room filled with corpulent leather furniture. She plopped down in a chair, threw one leg over its arm, and produced a cell phone. She touched the screen and rolled her eyes hard at the ceiling while she waited. "Monsieur, your guest has arrived. I expected someone taller. Yes, the G-man is at the bar." She held the phone out with a languid expression. "Here."

"Monsieur?"

"Mr. Barber, how good and how pleasant it is! What is your present situation?"

"What is Mia's present situation?"

"Miss Devlin is safe, and proving herself a force in her own right. She has already killed one of my most brutal soldiers, and negotiated for better living conditions for my other guests. I was wise to separate the two of you. Now, to business. What is your situation?"

"We lost two cylinders on the engine. If we can get parts today, then we can start breaking them in overnight. Probably be dependable in forty eight hours."

"That is cutting it close. Please, continue."

"Cain intends to use the device against our own government. His orders are to kill us all, after we have it. I alerted the crew. They're coming up with plan B right now."

P.K.'s eyebrows went up like two scimitars.

"And they know how much?"

"They know you want to prevent it from being used against the United States. But I'm sure they'll die before they let you have it."

"Undoubtedly! You are in quite a predicament, Mr. Barber. How is the Phobolyn holding out?"

"I have a couple of days left, taking two a day."

"P.K. will give you three more days' worth. Also, will you please give her your tablet?"

Blake handed her the tablet. She unlocked it, and enabled the Wi-Fi connection.

"Your tactical information will be downloaded to your documents folder. Coordinates, timetables, satellite photographs, and such."

The download seemed to take forever. Blake forgot himself during the momentary lull in the conversation, and absent-mindedly asked "So, how's it going with you?"

"Oh, very well, thank you for asking! The weather could be better, I am afraid. Very unusual for this time of year."

P.K. held the tablet out. "You're done."

"P.K. says we're good, hold on," He took the tablet, and picked a file in the middle of the list. "Only eight files?"

"No, fourteen!"

"Last one is Map3.jpg," said Blake, beginning to pace.

"Let me resend them."

"You got any games on this thing?" Blake's heart pounded as he swiped to the desktop, launched the Internet browser, and logged into his email account. He couldn't believe it. His hands were trembling, and his mouth was suddenly parched.

"I must apologize. Only the essentials."

His fingers danced around the screen and his heart began to pound. *Compose… To… My Contacts…Directory…Select All contacts…Subject: Serena hostage Azure Haven Croix SOS…Send!* He cleared the browser cache, and closed it. "Okay, I've got them."

"Very good. May I ask if you have a plan of action?"

"I do."

"Will you be able to carry it out?"

"I would kill everyone on the planet to get Mia back."

"Are you *afraid?*"

"If the cause is just, we need not fear."

"Then, I wish you the best of luck, Mr. Barber. I look forward to seeing you back aboard. P.K. will show you out."

"Okay, take care." *Take care? What the heck is wrong with me?* he thought. P.K. reclaimed the phone.

"Disable the Wi-Fi, big guy. Let's go."

***

Carson picked them up at the Custom's Dock, and returned to *Tarshish* in the dark. Jayce and Flint were alongside in the ship's large, inflatable launch, sending oblong crates up by way of the davits. Once aboard, Blake and Cain helped move and stow the black pine boxes in the aft hold, behind the engine room and work bay. To Blake's surprise, Nello and two new men were down in the hold, receiving the cargo.

"Dare I ask?" Blake said.

"The latest and greatest in pyrotechnics!" Cain winked. "Heads up, people! Preliminary mission briefing in the saloon at twenty one hundred hours." They handed their box down into the hold. "Alright Blake, let's go see what we've got."

***

Everyone but Steam and one of the new men, Pinnock, assembled in the saloon. Steam was working at a furious pace on the engine; Pinnock was standing watch on deck.

There was much chatter over seemingly endless buckets of KFC. Jayce caught up to Blake in the galley. "Just the guy I wanted to see!" said the Marine.

"Feeling's mutual. Has the tracker moved?"

"Nope. No change. Listen," Jayce looked over his shoulder and leaned on the island counter between them. "It took three proxy servers, and an anonymous 'tell a friend' email-form on a bed-wetting website, but I sent the transponder frequency and a little note to Captain Wexler. He's a lot closer than we are."

Blake closed his eyes, and inhaled deeply, then let it go all at once. "Thank you so much, Jayce."

"Can't let the bad guys get a girl that pretty!" he smiled.

"What about Serena."

"She's safe. There's a new guy watching her. Think she about had Nello wrapped around her little finger."

"I shouldn't ask you this, but… are you in on operation HEADLINE?"

Jayce shook his head slowly and looked puzzled. "Nooo? What's that?"

"Well, you know, there's TOURISM, U-BOAT, EZ-BAKE, and HEADLINE."

Jayce looked nervous and glanced over his shoulder, again. "I know about TOURISM, I'm in on U-BOAT. What are the other two?"

"EZ-BAKE and HEADLINE. And, by the way—Cain trusts Nello, but says you're a wild-card. Which is why I'm risking everything and telling you this. As a wild-card, you're probably part of HEADLINE. Like the rest of us *expendables*."

"Go on. I'm listening."

***

"Okay folks, show time!" Cain declared, over the dinnertime chatter. He activated a 48 inch flat-screen TV on the wall, controlled by his tablet. He pulled up a weather satellite display. "Today is three January, twenty one hundred hours. We have a depression moving in, which will probably make tropical storm status with buckets of rain, and sustained winds of forty knots, but not much more than that."

He swiped his tablet, and a satellite photo of Venezuela's Orinoco Delta appeared.

"Intel reports that our objective arrived in Guayana City, way the hell up the Orinoco River aboard a Moroccan freighter. From there it was transported by truck to Piacoa, then humped through the jungle eighty clicks—that's fifty miles—to a compound near this crappy little river village called Curiapo. As you can see, the compound is on a large island which is itself carved up by little streams." He zoomed in on the island, drawing a red digital circle around a blue cigar shape, barely visible through the forest canopy. "Our objective is this submarine. It is moored in a tributary which opens into a large cove, which in turn communicates with the Rio Grande distributary. Once they're clear of the island, it's another thirty clicks to the coast in a channel a mile wide. We can expect that an escort will accompany the sub to the ocean."

"Approximately twenty one hundred hours on four January, *Tarshish* will arrive on station just outside the twelve-mile-limit. Omega Team—consisting of Reynolds, Urquart, and Manzer—will take the big Zodiac we acquired up the Rio Grande distributary to Curiapo, where they will prepare the dive sled and recon the cove and islands. Alpha and Beta Teams will move in under cover of darkness, at zero hours—that's five January. Our strike teams will deploy on this small island, which gives us commanding fire over the cove."

"Fun and games begin at four hundred hours of five January, when our allies will launch a harassing attack on this side of the compound, supported by a close fly-over by Captain Flint. Simultaneously we will fire AT4's at the enemy picket boats, giving the impression of an air strike. We expect that this will spur the terrorists to load the device on the sub, if they haven't already, and embark ahead of schedule. The allied strike team will break engagement within a few minutes—then we're on our own. During this time, Urquart and Reynolds will use limpet mines or det-cord to sink the sub, before it enters the cove. Once they have possession of the device, we will disengage the enemy and pull out ASAP. Omega team will rendezvous with Alpha team on the river during egress, locating us via our infrared beacons. Should be plenty of rain and dark to cover us."

"What if they don't bite?" said Carson.

"We're not leaving without it."

"Assault? That's suicide!" said Monster.

"We have superior training. Superior equipment. Superior motivation.

We *will* succeed. *Tarshish* will move in to extract all teams, then we go full ECM and run down the coast to clear weather."

Cain went on to review the contingency assault plans in case the bomb was not aboard the submarine. "Remaining team assignments are as follows: Alpha team will be Myself, Nello, and Graffley. Beta Team: Mitchell and Pinnock. Gentlemen, I don't need to tell you how important this mission is. We are the last line of defense. If we fail, this bomb makes it home and it's good-bye baseball, Mom, and apple pie. Many are called, but *you* have been chosen. You are God's chosen instruments in defeating the infidel in this battle. You are true American heroes. I believe in you, and I salute you. Get a good night's rest. There will be an update briefing in the morning at ten hundred hours, with Q & A. Dismissed."

A general murmur arose among the men as Cain exited the crowded saloon. He went to the companionway, and squeezed through the engine room door. Steam was hovering near the rumbling engine, throwing skeptical glances at various gauges; flicking or tapping them testily with a grimy finger.

"Sounds good!" said Cain.

"Only got six hours of break in," replied Steam. "She needs six more, then a day of runnin' in."

"We have to be on station twenty-four hours from now. We have close to a hundred sixty miles to cover."

"The hell you say!"

"Get 'er online, and get us moving. We'll break in or run in, or whatever on the way."

"We'll break down is what we'll do!"

"I have faith in you, Steam!" Cain said, as he ascended the ladder and exited through the deck hatch.

Carson stuck his head in the door. "You ready?"

"Come on!" Steam shut down the Kraken.

Carson entered, along with Monster and Barrett. Monster closed the door and the deck hatch.

"Get them deck plates up. Carson, I got new couplings and the works."

The work was done in an hour's time, and a new plan hatched. The men dispersed. Steam reported to the helm, and started the engine.

"If we're taking that piss-pot, someone better bring it aboard!"

Carson and Barrett returned Flint to shore, then brought the large Zodiac aboard, christening it *Grendel's Mother.*

Steam weighed anchor and showed Blake how to turn the ship around with the bow thrusters. *Tarshish* set out across the Gulf of Paria. "Alright, take the helm while I start up the bubbler."

Pinnock, with his peach-fuzz crew-cut and gaunt features, appeared from the other side of the deck house as he made his rounds. He regarded Blake with beady-eyed suspicion as he passed the helm. Blake was glad he was wearing his pistol. He mused over Pinnock's olive drab jacket, which was covered with a variety of military insignia patches. *I wonder if his mom sewed those on for him?* he thought. Pinnock reached the stern and headed back up the starboard side toward the bow. He gave Blake the same creepy stare.

"How was the flight down?" said Blake. The man's expression didn't change as he strode on. *First time on a boat?* Blake's brain was suddenly bursting with sarcasm which he could hardly contain. *The pointy end goes first! That's the starboard side you're on, in case you were wondering. Been off meth long?* Blake shook his head. "Talk about being on something! Must be another side effect."

Jayce Mitchell came up the companionway, and relieved Pinnock of his watch as he returned down the port side. "Man, it got cool out here!"

"Seventy degrees, with an east wind 25 knots. Wish I had a jacket."

Jayce looked around, warily. "So what's up?"

"I don't know yet. Probably won't find out until Cain sends everyone up the river." Blake smirked.

"So to speak. Let me know?"

"You bet."

***

Serena lay on her bed in a windowless room on St. Croix, staring at the little bouquet Nello had brought her. Its wilted blossoms were a bitter reminder of lost hope, and not just that of escape. Confinement had become unbearable.

Her new warden was not nice. He didn't look nice, didn't sound nice, and had none of the nice emotional weaknesses that had nearly been Nello's undoing. She couldn't stop thinking about the kids. Or about Nello. She had gotten him to admit that they were tangled up in a matter of national security, and that they'd all wind up in the witness protection program when it was resolved. She wanted to believe him. She wanted to trust him. But just before his departure, she had detected something in his bashful charm—something in his eyes, something weak in his voice—the slightest hint of sadness. Perhaps it was disappointment. Her intuition told her that it was remorse, and *that* made her very uneasy. It imbued her own pangs of guilt and anxiety with added bitterness. She went to sleep with the lights on.

***

The Azure Haven's Maitre D' checked his watch—it was precisely nine o'clock—then froze in his tracks as mob of more than a dozen men and women surged into the hotel lobby. Three of them swept him back into the dining room, and sat him down hard on the nearest table. The dozy concierge suddenly found himself confronted by a stern-looking woman in a black jacket, and two minions with their Glock 19s pointed straight at him. The mob, he noticed, bore small shields along with their pistols, as they dispersed up the stairs, and down the halls.

"What is the meaning of this?" he stammered, glancing down nervously at three small security monitors embedded in his desk. There were similar squads at the ready on every corner outside the building.

She opened her jacket to reveal a gleaming gold badge. "Flash Mob. DEA. You didn't get the text?"

Serena's door came off its hinges with a bang like a car wreck, and her eyes filled with painfully bright light, her ears throbbed with startling shouts. She heard the words "We have secured the hostage."

"Miss Krakow?" said someone behind the light.

"That's me, hunny," she replied. "You're late."

26

It was a tough night for the new guys. Even the relatively sheltered Gulf of Paria had been sufficiently choppy to offend their lubberly equilibrium; their grease-gorged bellies reacting accordingly. Even Jayce and Nello were turning green as *Tarshish* rounded Icacos Point and passed into the Serpent's Mouth—the strait between Trinidad and the Venezuelan coast. Once fully out of the lee of Trinidad, seas were running eight feet, and the wind rose to thirty knots. By 2:00 A.M., Dramamine patches had become a fashion statement among Cain's men.

Rain set in just after Blake's watch. He had gone below via the engine room hatch hoping to get the scuttlebutt from Steam, and was not disappointed.

Steam took him into the work bay. "Here's the short of it," Steam said. "We dupe the traitors into attacking the compound while Carson and Barry sink the sub. We get the nuke, pick up the divers, and sail away. We'll have radio contact with the whole team. If they don't find the bomb, Carson will mention dead piranhas. Otherwise, he'll say 'zero target', and 'stem to stern'. We pick 'em up and vamoose, in any case."

"What happens after that?"

"We hope and pray the Venezuelan navy don't come after us. Say, that gives me an idea… Now, you better turn in."

Blake slipped into his cabin. Someone spoke. He yelled and spun around, plastering himself against the door.

Jayce sat in a captain's chair in the corner. "Good thing you're not used to using that pistol!"

"Huh? Oh." Blake put a hand on the holster. "How did you get in here?"

"You left it unlocked."

"I did not!" Blake went to the head, and checked under the sink. The neon-green beacon was still there.

"Tracker's moving around in a really small area. Maybe fifty by fifty meters. So, any news?"

"Not a lot. But my guess is that you guys will have to attack the compound. And I *strongly* suspect that *you* will probably get shot crossing from the small island, fall out of the boat, and disappear. Probably turn up in a bar in Guayana City a week later. Maybe, Tierra del Fuego? Sole survivor. Just a wild guess."

Jayce grinned that perfect grin. "I'll send you a postcard. I hope you get your girl back."

"Thanks. I, uh,"

"Nothing more to say, dude. She's all that." He got up and went to the door. "Thanks for the update. Know any good bars in Guyana City?"

"Have to ask my uncle on that one."

***

It had been a long night for Mia, as well, and her precious little friend. Inca had awakened in the middle of the night drenched in sweat, and vomited. Her fever had come back with a vengeance, and she couldn't even keep water down. By sunrise she was delirious. Mia called Cotillion to beg for help, but Lucien said he could not be reached, and stopped answering her calls.

Nearly frantic with worry, she sponged Inca with water from the cooler, sang trembling little songs, and pelted heaven with faltering prayers.

Then the big truck came. Perla ran to the window and cried out. The other women cowered together.

"What's happening?" yelled Mia.

Six armed thugs jumped out of the back of the truck, and stopped to talk to the guard at the gate.

"We're all going to Hell, that's what's happening. We are going to die!"

Mia ran back to Inca, trying to think of what she should do.

Perla shouted "They won't take me. I'll make them shoot me, first."

The men approached the building, AK 47's at the ready, and shouted in Spanish for the white girl to come outside. Mia swallowed hard. Perla gave her a fearful look. Then it hit her.

"Here!" Mia fished the tracker out of her pocket and went to Perla. "As long as you have this, my boyfriend can find you. Swallow it, if you have to." Mia pressed it between the astonished woman's lips, then went outside.

Two men motioned her to the fence, following at a safe distance. "The little girl stays with me! You hear me?" The men said nothing. They called the other women out. Perla was last. They bound their hands with tie-wraps, and marched them to the truck.

"Via con Dios, puta!" called Perla, with a slight bulge in her cheek.

"Same to you, pendeja!" Mia's heart wrenched with sorrow. Tears streamed down her cheeks as the women were herded like cattle into the back of the truck.

The armed men climbed aboard, the gate jingled shut, and the truck rumbled off into the jungle.

***

Tarshish tore bravely through the foam-streaked silver sea, under a lowering gray heaven that poured down rain all day.

"Does anyone know where the love of God goes," Carson crooned from the ship's wheel, "when the waves turn the minutes to hours?" For Cain's men, the eighteen heaving, churning, rocking hours to the south end of the Orinoco Delta had passed minute by tortuously queasy minute. Pinnock and Graffley passed their watch cowering in the deck house with a large plastic bucket. Carson was singing *Wreck of the Edmond Fitzgerald* for their sake, delivering the line about "Fellahs, it's been good to know ya!" with extra gusto. "You boys must be from I-dee-ho!" he cackled, as the wind whistled in the rigging.

"North Dakota, you bastard," groaned Graffley.

"How long's your buddy been off meth?"

Pinnock tried to shoot him a vicious look, but it came off more like the agonized grimace of a teenager's first hangover.

"Where'd you boys serve?"

"James River Correctional."

"No, I mean your tour of duty!"

"They didn't have X-Box, a-hole! It was a prison!"

"Not *Call of Duty*, stupid! I mean the military. The army?"

"We're in the militia!"

"Ahhhh. Gotcha! Well, the ride'll settle out once you get up the river a ways. Of course, that's when they start shootin' at ya. Ever been shot at? Other than by a liquor store owner, I mean."

"You ever shut up?" shouted Graffley.

"Hardly ever!"

The door opened at the bottom of the companionway, and Blake, clad head to toe in foul weather gear, popped out. "'Excuse me, guys!" he said cheerfully, gripping the hand rail and making his way up the steps. "This is awesome, isn't it? Nothing but the raw power of nature. We're in the Atlantic, now, did you know that?" He pushed past the pukey militia men, and went to the helm. "You're relieved, Uncle Carson."

"Relieve yourself! I ain't handin' this ship over to no bed-wetting middle-schooler in this weather!"

"Technically it's high school, and I won't dump 'er this time, I promise!"

Pinnock and Graffley exchanged worried glances. Blake took the wheel, and Carson headed down the companionway.

"That's my nephew, boys. Good kid, but he don't know his butt from a hole in the ground when it comes to keepin' a boat right side up!"

Blake picked right up where his uncle had left off. "They tell you guys I lost a boat in a storm like this just off St. Croix? Ten days ago!" Blake shouted gleefully over the weather. "But it was just a thirty-five footer, and the waves were like forty feet. Seriously, forty feet! My first squall at sea. Didn't do too badly. Lost the boat, but hey, I'm still alive, right? So, aren't you guys supposed to be patrolling the deck or something?"

Jayce came up the companionway. "I'll take over. You guys are relieved!"

Pinnock and Graffley slithered down the steps on their behinds, and staggered through the door.

"I've got news! I couldn't get away to check my phone, earlier, or I would've told you. The tracker moved. Look at this." He produced his phone, and launched the tracking app. "It was doing sixty miles an hour toward Jamaica, then turned toward Haiti. All of a sudden it stopped, then started again doing twenty-five, on around the island. Looks like they're heading for St. Croix."

"Wexler?"

"I'd bet on it. How are we doing?"

"We'll be on station by sunset," Blake advised.

"Cool. I wouldn't steal her, you know. Not from you."

"Why not?"

"You've got a gun!" Jayce smiled. "Just kidding."

"About the shooting or the stealing?"

"I see what you're made of, man. You kick ass. I respect that." Jayce made his way toward the bow, making sure the inflatable boats were secure.

***

Mia dipped the sponge in the cooler, and wrung it out. She turned back to Inca. Her mouth was open. The color was draining from her lips. The tip of her tongue was turning gray. Her eyelids parted slowly. Mia felt as if the room were moving away from her, space expanding in all directions. She carried Inca's body over to Perla's clean sheet, brushed the hair out of the little girl's face, and stared for a long time. Mia removed the shell necklace Blake had bought her, and fastened it around Inca's neck. Then she wrapped her tenderly in the white cloth.

"I love you so much, Inca. Mama Angelita loves you."

The sentry at the gate quivered slightly at the heart rending cries that echoed out of the concrete building. He rubbed the goose bumps on his arms. What Robaire had told him was true, he thought. She was obeah for sure, this white girl.

Mia emerged an hour later, and sat against the fence in the far corner of the dirt yard.

The sun was high overhead when the truck returned. They bound her hand and foot at gunpoint, and put her in the back. She didn't resist. Soon the truck rolled out onto a tarmac runway, and she was placed aboard a small, twin-engine plane. She watched the ground fall away and quickly become a scabby brown flake on the blue Caribbean. She had never felt such loss. Such utter devastation. Such empty, heart-rending anguish beyond anything she had ever imagined possible. Her clothes stank. She was utterly exhausted.

The gentle jarring of the landing gear on a runway and sudden deceleration brought her out of a deep sleep. It was late afternoon. The plane pulled up to a waiting helicopter. The tie-wraps were cut from her ankles, and she was transferred to the other aircraft.

A cheerful African man strapped her into a big leather seat. He spoke the first English she'd heard in days. "Hey, ya know, I think I met ya boyfriend?"

Mia's mind cleared almost instantly. "Where is he?"

"Dunno. I threw him out the door in the middle of the ocean! Real nice kid,

though!"

When he saw the look on her face, he laughed and added "With a raft, Miss! With a raft and a flotation jacket."

"How long ago?"

"That was New Year's Eve. 'Bout three in the morning. Almost five days ago, I guess. Real nice boy. Hey, we got a big storm coming in, so I better get back to work."

In ninety minutes they landed on the *Mother of Harlots*. Jonas helped her down to the deck as Lucien and four sentries met them. They escorted her directly to her stateroom.

"Your little pet did not make it?" said Lucien, with a smirk.

The hatred that welled up in her made her dizzy. *I will sink this ship with everyone on it, if it is the last thing I do*, she thought.

Lucien opened her door. One sentry cut the restraints on her wrists while three covered her with their pistols. She entered, and kicked the door shut without looking back. Mia stood and stared. Color. Fabric. Polished wood. Art. Lights. Glass. Carpeting. Air conditioning. Not a hard gray surface in sight. Not a speck of dirt nor hint of disorder, discomfort, or death. Yet the fecal stench still permeated her sense of smell, and tinged her dry mouth with nauseous disgust.

Finding a plastic laundry bag in the bathroom, she tied her clothes up, then surveyed herself in the full length mirror. Naked. Dirty. Cheek still faintly yellow, ribs still bruised from Perla's blows. And those ribs stood out, along with her hips, collarbone, and cheek bones.

This is all I am in this world, she thought. *This is all I am! A pathetic, starving animal. A thing to be bought and sold. A thing to be used and thrown away. Just because I have these.* She put one arm across her breasts, one hand on her pelvis, like a battered Botticelli's Venus.

She remembered washing Inca—that innocent little body. She remembered her own mother squeezing suds from a sponge over her head and back. She remembered reading to Fiona in her perfumed mountain of bath bubbles. Then she thought of Bader. She stepped wearily into the stall and took a very long shower, using an entire bottle of shampoo.

Mia wrapped herself in a vast terry cloth robe, and lay down on the bed. The cool mattress received her gently, drew her in. It felt so good. She closed her eyes and wept at the comfort.

An hour later the phone rang. "Mr. Ngandu, I presume?"

"You may call me Mr. Cotillion, now, Miss Devlin. May I send you something to eat?"

"Where will I wake up, this time?"

"Touché. But you will remain aboard until Mr. Barber has successfully completed his mission. There will be no more need for sedatives, unless you become unreasonable."

"I don't want ballet boy near my food."

"Ah, yes. Mr. Barber took to taunting poor Lucien. He is still a little petulant."

"I called you five times. I begged to talk to you. He said you weren't available. The little girl died."

"Oh? But I am sorry, Miss Devlin. This was not my doing. I will confine him to quarters. He will have no communication with the rest of the crew for the duration of your stay."

Not my doing? she thought. *You kidnapped her, you bastard!*

"I am sorry for your loss. Septicemia, undoubtedly. There was nothing either of us could have done. Then again, it could have been Refeeding Syndrome. You would make a good doctor, I think. Commanding. Determined. Dedicated. Oh, and I spoke with Mr. Barber yesterday. He is well, and sends his love. It is not my place to say, Miss Devlin, but I do not think he is a good match for you. He has the wanderer in him. And he seems to be looking for his father, I think, but he will never find him."

"How long is this going to take?"

"I should think less than forty eight hours."

"Send the food and a Dramamine patch. I'm taking a nap." She hung up. The ship rolled a little harder. Weather was definitely moving in.

Cotillion dialed Lucien. "Lucien, have a meal prepared for Miss Devlin. Then join me in the Assyrian Lounge in twenty minutes for dinner." He dialed the galley. "Chef Rameses? Lucien will order a meal for our new guest. When it is done, you will have the man who prepared it serve it to *him* in the Assyrian Lounge. Mix a Charlotte Corday for Lucien. I will try the veal."

There was a knock at the door. "Come!"

Sergio entered and approached the table. "Your orders, Monsieur?"

Cotillion activated a flat-panel monitor on the wall at the end of the table, and called up a map of the Orinoco Delta using his phone.

"I believe we should station ourselves fifty kilometers northeast of Isla Cangrejo, here. What is your opinion?"

"You anticipate that they will run for the storm? Not back to Trinidad?"

"You do not know this boy like I do. If he does not compel his associates to drive straight into the storm, they will run along the coast for better weather to the southeast. If so, we will cut them off. Otherwise, we chase them into the tempest. They will not be able to outrun us in the storm. It is almost certain that the attempt will cause another mechanical failure."

"What if that is what they are counting on?"

"Now you are thinking like Mr. Barber, Sergio."

"You will give him the girl?"

"If he hands me the device, but of course!"

"There will be no… later repercussions?"

"It is to be hoped! He is a work in progress, Sergio. He has thus far, and very cleverly, avoided the full plunge into his dark side. This final test will force him in to it, and it will scar him forever. I am sure I will encounter him again, and then I will turn him."

"Very good sir. Fifty kilometers northeast of Isla Congrejo."

Sergio returned to the bridge. Cotillion flipped through various satellite views and weather reports until Lucien entered.

"Ah, Lucien. How is our guest?"

"Arrogant. Entitled. Like all Americans."

"Still, you must admire them, these two."

"You *know* how I feel about them, Monsieur. Monsieur was very cruel to me."

"Oh but, Lucien, surely you must see that it was necessary? We were all playing our roles to test the boy."

The rotisseur, a line cook, entered and served them dinner.

"Ah, Merci. But you will wait. Bon appétit, Lucien."

Lucien saw the look on the rotisseur's face.

"What is wrong Lucien?"

"The fool has brought me the girl's meal."

"Oh, then enjoy it! I will have Rameses prepare another."

"The meat is… too rare, Monsieur."

"Then please, have your friend sit and enjoy it with us." Cotillion smiled with deep, diabolic satisfaction.

"But Monsieur! I," stammered the rotisseur.

"You what? Refuse my invitation? Sit down and eat, please! I *insist.*"

The trembling rotisseur slipped into the chair next to Lucien, who pushed the plate in front of him. Small beads of sweat broke out in rows on Lucien's brow. The rotisseur cut a piece of meat, and brought it to his lips. Cotillion settled back in his chair and glared.

"Monsieur! I only did as Lucien directed me! I thought it was your wish. I do not ask questions. I just cook what I am told!"

"Damn you!" said Lucien, quietly.

"Go on, enjoy it, chef."

He raised the fork haltingly, stared at it, then plunged it into his mouth. Hastily, he cut and swallowed another piece, and another.

"How is it?" smiled Cotillion.

"There are worse things on this ship."

"*Indeed.* But, not much worse."

The man screamed, arched his back and fell to the floor, rigid arms flung behind him. Cotillion came around and seated himself on the table to watch. Lucien stared straight forward. The hapless rotisseur shook violently, and coughed torrents of blood through strangled convulsions. After three minutes, he made a popping sound in his throat, and stopped moving.

"Bravo, Lucien! Very dramatic! Highly entertaining!" Declared Cotillion. He clapped twice, and called for the stewards. Throw this over, and clean the carpet! Lucien, dear Lucien; let us put this behind us. Soon we will have the device, and we may return to more civilized waters." He raised his wine glass. "Let us drink to it!"

Lucien raised his glass to his master, and drank.

He awoke, and blinked his vision clear. Bright light shimmered off stainless steel walls. His heart nearly stopped when he realized where he was— strapped to a cold, steel table. An assortment of scalpels and skinning knives gleamed on a surgical tray next to him. He was alone.

***

By eight o'clock the wind had increased to thirty-four knots, making the tropical depression an official storm. Blake named it Agatha. The Weather Service chose Angelica.

Even Cain could see that getting *Grendel's Mother* over the side and loaded with the sled and diving gear would be no easy feat. He ordered Steam to assist Blake at the helm, and take them clear into Boca Grande Bay to shelter under Isla Cangrejo. He hoped that if anyone noticed them, they'd be regarded as tourists seeking a storm hole. They dropped anchor, and let out plenty of chain.

Everyone assisted in getting the Alpha and Beta Team's boats inflated, in the water, and secured alongside. The fifteen foot rigid-bottomed inflatable speedboat was rigged to the davits and hoisted off the deck.

There was a lump in Blake's throat as he helped to heave it out over the rough water. *Grendel's Mother* splashed down, and was secured to *Tarshish*. Monster and Barrett boarded her, and received the dive sled as it was lowered. It looked like a seven-foot-long torpedo with the top cut off. Carson sent the rebreather gear down, and then the demolition box. He, like his comrades, was wearing ghost-face camo paint and a boonie hat. Cain gave the order to shove off. Blake desperately wanted to say something important or familial, but the words wouldn't come. He looked at his uncle's blackened face, his features nearly indistinguishable in the dark and rain. Carson offered his hand. Blake shook it, sensing in his uncle's grip the manly acknowledgment of a brother going into combat.

"Come back," said Blake.

"I intend to." Carson mussed Blake's hair, then climbed over the side. *Grendel's Mother* slipped her moorings, and roared into the night.

In the three hours before the remaining departures, Blake and Steam kept watch on deck. Cain briefed his teams in the saloon. The seasoned vets couldn't help but notice that Pinnock and Graffley looked increasingly anxious. Having been exposed to Steam and Blake's dinnertime conversation on the hazards of Orinoco wildlife—piranhas, electric eels, giant caimans, vampire fish, and the tiny candiru, that urine-seeking catfish that can swim up and lodge itself in your... had all but completely eroded any intestinal fortitude that might have been left by Angelica's stormy embrace.

At a quarter of midnight, Barrett radioed in. They were upstream from the island, in a small tributary. The sled was in the water, and they were moving in to reconnoiter the island. Flint called in, crankier than usual. He was going to have to take off without clearance, and would have to make for the Dutch Antilles after his run. Returning to Trinidad and trying to land the little jet in a forty knot crosswind, rain and violent downdrafts was not his idea of survivable.

At last the grease-painted men climbed down into their boats, and cast off. Cain donned his night-vision goggles and waved as Nello gunned the motor. Blake adjusted his own goggles and earphone.

***

The top of Carson's head, and the long lens of the night-scope—which was integrated into left side of his full-face dive mask—were all that broke the surface of the murky river. On that night, it could have been easily mistaken for a river dolphin or a caiman. Carson radioed the group, reporting three or four sentries on the small island, and sandbagged gun nests along the shoreline of the target island. In a few minutes he advised that there was a large fishing boat, along with three large ski boats tied up around the perimeter of the cove.

"Omega 1 to team. We picked the right night, this river's gonna come up fast, and that island's gonna be underwater," said Carson.

"Roger, Omega 1," answered Cain. "Alpha and Beta ETA fifteen minutes. Neutralize tangos in the landing zone."

"Affirmative."

Carson brought his assault rifle above the surface, switched on the infrared laser-sight and waited for the men he had seen to return.

Blake paced in breathless anticipation. Sixty seconds later, his uncle's voice calmly and quietly announced, "tango down." Another Two minutes of radio silence passed and again came the cold, "tango down." A tear squeezed out of the corner of Blake's right eye, as the realization set in. His uncle had just killed two men.

It was another five minutes before the third kill was confirmed.

Blake put his hand on his chest. The satellite beacon and his tube of Phobolyn were there, under his monogrammed Gortex rain gear.

"Alpha, I was sure there were four. No contact," said Carson.

"Affirmative. Proceed to phase two," replied Cain.

"Beta 1, land your man at the north end of the LZ. Clear the island."

"Affirmative," replied Jayce. "Hey, Pinnock, what did you sign up for?"

"To kill terrorists!"

"Well, get ready. There's one left on our little slice of paradise, and the boss wants you to get him. I'm gonna run in and drop you in about three feet of water. When you bag him, come back to the LZ and signal."

"With what?"

"Your hands!" Jayce could see this guy had a better chance of shooting himself.

"When you get your man, make the throat-cut sign, like this," he pantomimed. "If you can't find him, raise your hands and shrug your shoulders."

"How come I didn't get no goggles? Graffley got goggles!"

"Short of gear. Government cutbacks."

"That stupid kid got one!"

"You want that stupid kid to be able see to pick you out of the water, right? Now, here we go!" Jayce gunned the outboard and buzzed into the shallows. He shoved the shivering Pinnock out, and dashed away. Pinnock slogged into the muddy underbrush, and crouched, AR 15 at the ready. He couldn't hear anything over the wind, or his fear. Finally, he crept ashore in a sort of awkward squat. Pinnock stumbled, his hand landing on something warm and oozing—Carson's handiwork. He retched, and rolled on his back. Out of the darkness came his quarry. Both men startled and, had Pinnock's hand not already been wrapped white-knuckled around the grip of his weapon, he would have died on the spot.

Three minutes after the bladder spasms stopped, he appeared in the landing zone, making the kill sign like the triumphant warrior he wasn't.

Jayce called, "Tango down. All clear." The teams landed their boats and took up positions.

"Omega Team reporting," called Carson.

"Alpha 1 here. Go ahead Omega 1."

"We found the sub. Fiberglass. Maybe thirty meters. Twin screws. Plenty of loading activity. They're in a hurry."

"Copy, Omega. T minus ninety minutes. Alfa to Flint. Get the bird in the air."

"Affirmative!" Flint cursed.

***

Blake completed a slow scan of the river and returned to the helm.

"It's time for our famous Plan B, son," said Steam. "It's howlin' forty five now! Start 'er up. Ease her forward. Weigh anchor."

Blake pushed the throttle forward, and started the anchor winch. "Anchor's aweigh, Mr. Ebeling."

"Give 'er more throttle and use your bow thrusters like I showed you. Now, hard to starboard."

Tarshish labored forward against the blast, turning toward the muddy outflow of the Rio Grande. "You go up to the bow, and guide me in," Bellowed Steam. "Channel's only a mile wide. Think we can hit it?"

They ventured fifteen miles up the river, where they stopped and held station without dropping anchor.

***

"Omega 1 to Alpha."

"Go ahead."

"Permission to set charges."

"What's the plan?"

"String det-cord between the dive planes on the stern. We'll be under the sub the whole time."

"Why not the forward planes, too?"

"Too close to the hold. We have exposed skin, Alpha. Can't be swimming into a ninety percent cocaine solution."

"Roger that. Proceed, Omega 1," said Cain.

Carson pulled a spool of thin black detonation cord from his dive bag. He carefully wrapped the free end around the shaft of the large horizontal fin and tied it off, then made his way to the other side. He pulled the cord tight against the hull of the sub like a thin black smile, tied it off, and attached a remote firing module to the end. "One thing's for sure," Carson said, switching it on. "We're gonna have a lot of happy fish, down here."

"Roger that!" Barrett agreed.

They followed a hand-line back to the dive sled, and moved down the channel fifty meters.

"Alpha 1 to all teams. Zero hour is T minus fifteen minutes. Archangel, what's your twenty?"

"Loitering in heavy turbulence off the delta."

"Standby for your run."

"Roger Alpha. Sooner the better."

At 4:00 A.M. Cotillion's men assaulted the island from upriver. The booms of rocket propelled grenades and crackle of gunfire echoed above the wind and rain.

"Alpha 1 to Archangel! Start your run!"

"Omega 1 to team, its pure chaos down here! They're loadin' like mad."

"Roger. Alpha and Beta, ready to engage with AT4's on my command. Archangel, ETA?"

"Two minutes."

"Copy, watch for the IR beacon," said Cain. He turned to Graffley. "Go to the LZ and activate this beacon, and wave it. When Flint passes, deactivate it. He'll make two or three passes. Wave him in each time. You have sixty seconds. Go!"

Graffley gave a nervous "Yes sir," and stumbled into the underbrush.

Flint dropped to two hundred feet and accelerated *Sky's the Limit* to two hundred twenty knots. "Alpha 1 I have your beacon. ETA thirty seconds."

"Roger. All teams, leave that boat on the right shore alone."

Sky's the Limit screeched over head. Cain called "Fire!" and three AT4 shoulder-launched rockets streaked across the cove. Two motor boats and the fishing trawler exploded.

"Watch where you boys are pointin' those things!" said Carson.

"Omega 1 report?"

"Everyone's clearing away. Just the crew left. They're waiting for something. They just started the sub's diesel. Guy on the radio, shakin' his head." Flint made another screaming pass overhead.

"Crew is boarding! Crew is boarding! Omega Team falling back."

They zoomed the sled into the cove, and poked their heads out of the water. In their night-vision scopes, the dim glow of the submarine pilot's instrument displays shone like Coleman lanterns through the conning tower view-port. "Here they come," said Carson. The switch is hot! Alpha 1, I need you to knock that window out!"

"Roger! Alpha 2 give that guy some air!"

Nello trained his sights on the conning tower and gave it three bursts.

"Looks good Omega!" said Cain.

"Fire in the hole!" Carson squeezed the button on the detonator. A plume of water and fire shot a hundred feet into the gloomy night and was carried away by the gale.

The submarine crew, stunned by the shock wave, found themselves instantly enveloped in darkness and water.

"She's on the bottom," announced Carson. "Omega team proceeding with retrieval."

Aboard *Tarshish*, Blake and Steam fidgeted with anticipation. Monster moved *Grendel's Mother* onto the river.

"Omega team, status?" said Cain. "Omega, be advised that the allied team has ceased fire, and Archangel has flown home," reported Cain.

"Conning tower hatch open," Replied Carson. "Going in. Real mess in here. Visibility about thirty percent. Barry, get this guy outside before we have company. Conning tower, no joy."

"Concur," said Barrett, a minute later.

"Radio room, negative," said Carson.

"Forward hold… a lot to dig through here," said Barrett.

"Crew quarters…Negative. Crapper… negative. Engine room…hold on, a lot of damage here. Big Yamaha diesels. Lots of nooks and crannies…Negative. Omega 2?"

"Hold is negative," said Barrett. "Repeat, hold is negative."

Back on *Tarshish*, Blake was breathing hard, and gripping the rail.

Then Carson's voice broke in.

"Alpha, we've got five floating tangos, but zero target. Repeat, zero target. Boat has been searched stem to stern. We got nada."

Blake jumped off the deck and did a double fist pump.

"Get aft, boy! Keep a look out." Steam throttled down to let the raging wind drive them farther up the river.

"All teams to your boats. Omega team, Stay amphibious. Advance as far as possible before coming ashore. Omega 3, stand by to extract all personnel." All teams responded affirmatively. "Beta, swing wide on the north side, and land. Alpha we're going in on the south. Now, go!"

Jayce led Pinnock back to their boat, arriving in tandem with Alpha Team. "Okay, get ready to fire at anything that moves."

"How am I supposed to see what I'm shooting at?"

"Easy, follow their tracers!"

"You guys are a bunch of a-holes, you know that?"

"That's what my mom says!" Jayce grinned.

They zoomed around the little island, Jayce steering in a wide arc before heading toward their target. Pinnock crouched low in the bow. "Put some fire in there, dude!" Pinnock twisted around, tried to steady his rifle on the bouncing bow, and opened fire. A couple of muzzle flashes blossomed a hundred yards ahead. Jayce cried out with a dramatic full-bodied convulsion, and rolled over the side. The militia man scrambled to the tiller, veering away from the gunfire, and ran the boat full throttle into the darkness.

Cain landed his men and laid down a blanket of suppressing fire. They advanced in a line, Graffley trailing warily. After ten minutes of creeping unopposed toward the center of the island, shouting and motor sounds became audible over the wind and creaking trees. Cain waved everyone down and sent Nello forward. He radioed back. "Alpha 1, compound in sight. Sandbag wall. Tent HQ. Looks like they're moving stuff on ATV's. Coke bundles. Maybe thirty tangos bugging out."

"Beta, status... Beta, report!" There was no reply. "Omega, Status?"

"Taking fire! Pinned down!" replied Carson. Which was completely untrue; he and Barrett were already in the channel watching for Monster's beacon.

"Alpha 2, stand by." They moved up to Nello's position. "Alright guys, it's down to us. Graffley, you and I will move down this wall, and engage the tangos as they go into the forest. Nello, you get in and search the HQ. We'll move down the trail and take out the transport. Got it? Now go!"

The initial assault had rattled the enemy effectively. The chaotic evacuation and the darkness made it easy to pick off the sentries, unnoticed. Cain and Graffley cleared the narrow track down to a wide, marshy area at the edge of the island where two large motorboats were being loaded. Men were wading out in chest-deep water with bales of product on their heads.

"Alpha 1, HQ is negative."

Cain was about to answer, when Steam broke in. "Alpha 1, Home Base under fire! We are taking fire!"

"Home Base, get out of there!"

Cain heard Blake yell "Steam, two cutters from Trinidad!"

"Alpha, we gotta heave-to!"

"Negative!"

"They just put a shot over the bow! Dammit boy! Git down a'fore you git your head blowed off!"

Nello arrived at the marsh. "We gotta finish this up, Skipper," he said.

"Affirmative! Nello, take the right, Graffley, you're the middle. Get the guys in the water, Nello and I will take out the boat crews. Graffley, be careful, one of those boats is your ticket home!"

"Mr. Ebeling!" cried Blake. "Here they come!" He rushed to the port side and put the boarding ladder over. *Grendel's Mother* and her crew boarded, post-haste, Barrett casting the inflatable boat adrift. Blake helped each man over the rail. Carson had a long case strapped across his back. It was three feet long, by a foot-and-a-half wide, and a foot thick. "Mr. Ebeling," shouted Blake. "Omega team present and accounted for!"

Steam put the throttle full ahead, and *Tarshish* pushed into the relentless gale. "Git back to your watch station, boy!" Blake could hardly contain himself, he was so anxious to see their prize.

***

The battle in the marsh took longer than expected. One of the boats escaped. The other had taken several rounds below the waterline, and was slowly sinking. A hasty search was made, which turned up nothing but narcotics. "Cain," said Graffley. "There's that other boat back in the cove!"

"Good man, let's hope the keys are in it!"

"Don't matter. I was locked up for grand theft auto. I can hot-wire anything!"

They were thirty minutes up the river in pursuit of the escaped boat, when it dawned on Cain. "Nello, did I hear the kid say cutters from *Trinidad*?"

"Affirmative. That's what I heard."

"Two hundred miles from Trinidad, in Venezuelan waters?"

"He was under fire. Probably the first thing he could think of."

"No! He sounded too sure. I know that kid, we've been had. Turn this bucket around!"

***

At last, *Tarshish* plodded into Boca Grande Bay. Blake, relieved of duty by Monster, rushed to the saloon—it was empty. So were the galley and the crew quarters. He staggered back down the rolling passageway to the engine room. Carson and Barrett stood straddle-legged at Steam's workbench, admiring their catch. Blake joined them. The case was a drab tan color, with six latches around the perimeter. Snug in its black foam lining was a long, thick, chrome cylinder that occupied two-thirds of the case. At the right end was a rectangular control panel, sporting two keys, an LED timer display, a switch under a red safety cowl, and a couple of knobs.

"It's not at all how I imagined it," said Blake.

"You read Russian, kid?" Carson replied.

"It's on my bucket list."

"Well," said Barrett, "this knob looks like the yield select."

"Is that five kilotons, or megatons?" said Blake.

"So, maybe you turn the keys, set the timer, and throw the switch?" posited Carson.

"Unless that's the manual override," suggested Barrett.

"There's a thought."

Steam called down on the intercom. "Comin' up on open water. Which way do we go, George?"

"Let's head for better weather," said Barrett. "Take us down the coast, Steam. Wait a minute, where's your boss, kid?"

"He's out there somewhere. Don't worry, he'll find us."

"The hell you say!" retorted Carson. "Now what are your final instructions?"

"We have to get her back!"

"Jayce told me the tracker was intercepted, and it went straight to St. Croix. Wexler found her."

"What if he didn't? I have to make contact with Cotillion."

"Steam, what's on the Auto ship ID?"

"A couple of freighters a ways out. And a small fisherman thirty miles northeast, just moving right along. Don't look right, to me."

"That's him. Moving in to cut us off, either way," said Carson.

"ECM, on max!" ordered Barrett.

"Not yet!" countered Blake. "Run down the coast until he starts to follow. Then use the ECM and turn into the storm."

"What are we up against?" said Barrett. "What's out there waiting for us, Blake?"

"The *Mother of Harlots*. A mega yacht."

"How 'mega' is 'mega?'" snarled Carson.

"About three of those cutters we saw in Trinidad. She can do twenty knots, maybe twenty-five."

Carson glared, and got that murderous look in his eye.

"It was *need-to-know*," protested Blake, smugly.

Barrett clicked the intercom. "Steam, belay the ECM. Head down the coast until the fisherman starts a pursuit curve. *Then* cloak, and circle wide until we're north northeast into the storm."

"Aye aye, Captain Reynolds," Steam replied.

"That'll give us time to figure out this Russian surprise and come up with a rescue plan, anyway," said Barrett.

Blake walked away in a huff.

"Where are you goin'?" said Carson

"The head. You mind?"

Blake stumbled into his dark cabin, and flipped on the light. His pillow, carry case, Cain's Bible and his chair were sliding around the floor. He sat down on the toilet and braced his feet against both sides of the door frame. He popped a Phobolyn tablet and realized that P.K. had not given him any more.

"I have come this far, and now I know what my options are," he said resolutely. "Time to do what must be done." He got up and retrieved the Bible, dumped the wallet and foam liner out of the case, then placed the Bible in it. "My God, My God, why have I forsaken thee?"

Being in the closed space made the mounting queasiness exponentially worse, so he put his hood up, and went up to the deck house. Being able to catch glimpses of the dim gray horizon in the faint dawn helped. He ran scenarios through his head, and then it struck him. "Steam! How far until we're off the continental shelf?" he shouted.

"'Bout a hundred mile, northeast!" Steam bellowed back, at the top of his lungs.

"And then we set the timer, and chuck the nuke over with an anchor?"

"That's what I've been led to believe. Now you stay in that deck house, or go below!"

"Aye aye!" Blake clenched his teeth so hard he thought they'd shatter. *I knew it!* he thought.

Twenty minutes passed. Steam keyed the intercom and called below, "Barry, we have a definite pursuit curve on the radar track."

The reply came instantly. "Engage ECM, continue three miles and start your turn."

***

Cotillion sat placidly in the large leather command chair on the bridge, sipping hot cocoa. Sergio watched the instruments and the helmsman like a hawk.

"Monsieur, *Tarshish* has disappeared!"

Cotillion laughed. "Did I not tell you, my friend? Maintain your course for another eight kilometers, then turn northeast full ahead. Have Capriccio bind the girl and move her to the Assyrian Lounge."

Mia was marched briskly to the elevator, and delivered to the lounge. It was two levels up, which made the ship's rolling that much more dramatic. Capriccio seated her in a comfy chair by the windows. Plastic tie-wraps bound her wrists. He belted her into the seat. Even with the Dramamine patch, the nausea was approaching a new level of unbearable. Capriccio closed the door behind himself. From the opposite corner someone cried, "Zut alors!"

"Nebby! Baby! Where are you? Come to Mama!" cried Mia. The macaw flew from his perch and landed on her lap. She fawned over him, and scratched his belly as best she could. Nebuchadnezzar took notice of the tie-wraps and, recognizing them as something unnatural, began to chew on them.

***

Barrett came on deck and relieved Steam at the helm. It had been three and a half hours, and they'd barley covered thirty miles. The wind was wailing at thirty-five knots, and everyone was puking. The men shouted to each other, but the gale ripped the voices from their throats. *You can hear everything but what you want to hear,* Blake thought as he watched Carson and Monster struggle to move a large white drum across the pitching deck to the davits. It was the capsule containing the survival raft. Blake gathered his courage and went below. Barrett saw the look on his face, and shouted to Carson.

The ship's violent heaving made it nearly impossible to swing the axe effectively, but Blake was determined to get the door to the radio room open. The companionway door burst open, and Carson lunged in. "What the hell are you doing!" he raged, seizing the axe handle, mid swing.

"You're gonna dump the bomb and run! Steam told me!"

Carson jerked the axe back as the bow pitched up, and they both fell against the companionway door.

Carson shoved Blake away as the ship plunged downward again, breaking his nephew's grip. "We've got a plan, dammit!"

Blake skidded backwards, steadied himself, and drew his pistol. "So do I. Get back!"

"You wouldn't."

"Get! Back!" Blake took hold of the beacon with his free hand.

"Take her easy, pardner," said Carson, as he eased away, still ready to swing. "You've done a hell of a job, kid. I can't tell you how proud I am of you."

"Try!" Blake shouted, as he edged forward.

"We've all made big sacrifices, Blake, every one of us. We're all tryin' to do what we believe is right. We *cannot* let that bomb fall into the wrong hands again! That goes for Uncle Sam, too."

Blake was now back in front of the Radio Room door. "Some sacrifices are too great." He pointed the gun at the door and emptied the magazine into it. Immediately the intercom crackled.

"Carson, ECM is down!"

Carson started forward, but Blake turned the gun on him. "I'm pretty sure I counted eight, kid."

"*Maybe.*" Blake ground his thumb into the beacon's activation button.

Carson shifted his grip on the axe and started toward Blake, burning with anger. Blake pulled the trigger. The click of the hammer stopped Carson in his tracks. Blake turned and ran, his uncle hot on his heels. Blake anticipated the roll of the ship as he darted into the saloon, and kept his footing as he plowed on into the galley. Carson fell and rolled, but was back on his feet in an instant. He reversed course and careened toward the companionway.

***

On the bridge of the *Mother of Harlots*, Sergio turned to Cotillion and exclaimed "There she is!"

"Yes!" Cotillion cried in elation. "Ha-ha! I knew he could do it! Now, after them!"

Sergio ordered the helmsman, "All Ahead Full."

***

Carson dashed up the companionway stairs, and found Blake before the helm, gun leveled at Barrett. "Barry, its empty!" he yelled.

Barrett threw the wheel, rolling the boat hard. Blake fell, skidding down to the leeward rail. His uncle landed on top of him as a wave broke over the side and washed them clear to the stern. Barrett righted the boat. At that moment the ship slowed suddenly, as it had a few days before. Monster staggered aft from the bow, and promptly tied Blake up.

Steam called on the intercom. "That's two more cylinders down! Keep it up, boys!"

"Bogey changed course! They see us!" Barrett announced. "They'll have us in ten minutes!"

"Tell Steam to bring it up here," Carson barked. "Monster, blow the raft!"

Monster hoisted the capsule off the deck, and swung it over the side. He pulled all the slack out of the lanyard, which amounted to a good hundred feet worth, and jerked hard. There was a boom, and the two halves of the capsule fell away revealing a black and orange vinyl blob. Monster and Carson struggled desperately to secure it to the railing as it began to expand and thrash violently in the wind. In minutes it became a huge octagonal raft with a tent roof.

Steam came on deck with the oblong tan case. Carson fought to hold the raft steady while Monster untied Blake, lugged him forcibly to the rail, and chucked him into the portal.

Steam heaved the case in on top of him and shouted "you better fix yourself a sea anchor! There's one in the kit!"

Blake sat up in time to look his uncle in the face. "I'm sorry I didn't trust you!"

"Tell your mother I love her," Carson replied angrily, freeing the raft's lines from the railing and jerking the hoist halyard out of its cleat. The raft plummeted ten feet into the churning sea and was swept away.

"Steam, take the wheel!" Commanded Barrett. "Carson, help me with the long boat. Monster, get the other raft ready."

"Go on! I ain't leavin!" shouted Steam. "I'll make it through."

"Me neither!" replied Monster. "Cain'll be back. You need a gunner."

"Then help us with the long boat!" Barrett barked.

Blake watched *Tarshish* labor over the mountainous waves and disappear into the downpour. Rain was blowing into the raft in stinging sheets. He gathered the inflation lanyard, which also served as the raft's towline, and zipped the portal closed. Suddenly, he realized what it was that had hit him when Monster pitched him in. It was the bomb—or at least the case. There was also an orange canvas valise stenciled with the words: *survival kit.* He popped the latches on the tan case, and opened it.

***

The windshield wipers were working overtime on the bridge of the *Mother of Harlots.* Sergio stood by the helmsman, monitoring the GPS, and radar tracks.

"Monsieur, the beacon is coming toward us, but *Tarshish* maintains her course. Her speed has dropped considerably."

Cotillion unbuckled his seatbelt and went to the window. "There! A strobe! They have put him off!"

"Or they have armed the device and set it adrift."

Cotillion gave a wry smile. "Or both! Helmsman, bring the raft alongside. Within fifty feet, and slow down. Tell Capriccio to launch a chase boat."

"Monsieur, it will be very dangerous to open the bay," said Sergio.

"I am aware of the risk. Do it. Sergio, bring me the girl."

Nebuchadnezzar had made it halfway through the last tie-wrap, when Sergio and two sentries entered. One shooed the macaw away and held a pistol on Mia, while the other unstrapped the belt. Mia bent double and groaned as she rose, dropping the broken tie-wraps between her knees. "Bye-bye Nebby! I love you, baby!"

They manhandled her out the elevator door and onto the bridge, where Cotillion greeted her warmly.

"Miss Devlin! Our little drama draws to a close; come, let us greet your hero." He gestured to the blinking strobe, just ahead.

"Blow *Shave and a Hair Cut* on the horn. That's our private signal."

"Sergio, do you know this tune?"

"You *know*," droned Mia. "Dut dutta dut-dut, dut dut?"

"Sergio, allow her the honor."

"It is this blue button," said Sergio.

"Oh, you mean the one with the big *horn* on it?" She put her hands on the large button, and leaned toward the window, hoping they wouldn't see the ragged spots on her remaining restraint. She gave the signal, twice.

Blake's hope revived when he heard the blasts. He pulled a collapsible paddle from the survival kit and extended it, then unzipped the portal. The boarding ramp made it difficult to paddle, but slowly, he managed to turn the raft. *Mother of Harlots* was bearing down on him like a cosmic leviathan. He pulled the tan case close.

"Very good, Miss Devlin. Helmsman, reduce speed," said Cotillion, putting on a rain jacket. "To the main deck!" They boarded the elevator, and emerged in the forward lounge. The sentries struggled to push the doors open. Cotillion clamped his hand on Mia's right arm and took a pistol from one of the sentries, as the group made their way across the rolling deck to the railing. The little raft passed the bow of the giant yacht. Blake looped the beacon around the handle of the case with a ring hitch, and heaved it onto the boarding ramp. He pushed his body as far out of the portal as he dared.

Cotillion, eyes wide in stark anticipation shouted, "Blake! Do not let go! Pull it back in! Where is that damned chase boat?" The next wave surged under the raft and twisted it violently. Blake lost his grip on the case and it was swiftly borne away by the angry sea.

"Don't let it get away, damn you!" He put the gun to Mia's head. "So close, Mr. Barber, and now this!"

Thunder and a wave of searing heat burst across the bow, jolting the deck beneath their feet. Glass and debris rained down everywhere. All eyes turned to the hellish fireball billowing out of the bridge. Cotillion's grip relaxed for a moment and Mia twisted free. She bellied hard over the railing, plunging into the waves twenty-five feet below. The force of the impact snapped the last fetter, and she swam for her life. The sentries grabbed Cotillion by the arms, and dashed for safety.

"No, let me go! I will make them pay for this!"

Mia surfaced, and started shouting for Blake. She crested a wave and could see him swimming in the trough. Swiftly, she found herself sliding into that trough, as he ascended to the crest of the next wave. She stroked like mad as the sea rose and fell beneath her. The stern of the *Mother of Harlots* passed. She could hear Blake yelling, and then something tangled in her hair and jerked her head out of the water. An arm wrapped tight around her chest. "Gotcha!"

"Oh my god! Blake!" she craned her neck to see over her shoulder. Blake!"

"I've gotcha!"

"What is happening? Where is the raft? You left the raft!" she cried, in almost total panic.

"I've got your raft right here!" He held up the towline, which was securely tied around his waist and one shoulder. "Hold on while I do my life jacket."

"Don't let go! No, Blake!" she clung to his arm with a ferocious grip. He pulled a cord on his vest, and it inflated instantly. He hugged her close again. "Wow, this really turned out better than I anticipated!"

Another explosion roared across the water. A ball of bright orange flame and black smoke blossomed out of the hull, near the waterline. Blake glimpsed the white longboat from *Tarshish* cutting over the combing swell. Cotillion's Men were at the railing, firing automatic weapons at the diminutive attacker. A streak of light flashed from the little craft. Another tongue of flame erupted from the *Mother of Harlots*. The missile had struck the yacht as she rolled away, breaching her hull well below the waterline.

"Sink!" screamed Mia. "Sink, you son of a bitch!"

The longboat steered in for the stern. The man in the bow threw a grappling hook at the railing on the ship's low after-deck, and managed to board.

Mother of Harlots was already listing to port. The pilot of the longboat tried to steer her in behind the massive ship, but the grapple line was too short. The next time Blake caught sight of the tiny craft, it was upside-down in the heaving sea. They watched his uncle, the man who had boarded, fight his way up the slowly tilting steps to the next deck, and enter the aft lounge.

"Carson! No! She's here! She's here!" Blake cried.

"Is he crazy? What is he doing?" said Mia.

"He's looking for you. That was his plan, all along."

They clutched each other in silent disbelief as the great *Mother of Harlots* continued her slow death-roll, watching in the desperate hope that Carson would reappear. Three minutes later, the chrome exhaust stacks and spherical radar arrays atop the shattered bridge vanished. The ship's belly appeared for a heart-rending moment before it too disappeared beneath the surging sea.

Blake bit his lip. "Okay. Show's over, kids," he said. Let's get to the raft. It's just a hundred feet. Haul, now!"

"Don't let go of me!"

"You think after all of this, I am ever going to let go of you again?"

"How can you be so calm?" she said, almost accusingly.

"Easy! I'm on drugs! Now come on!" Foot by foot, they made their way back to their little black and orange island.

"It's really roomy inside," Blake said, pushing her up the ramp. "I think you'll like it." With her last ounce of strength, she rolled inside and lay there like a beached seal. Blake pulled himself in, flattening her. She was too fatigued to care. He turned to zip up the portal, but nearly jumped straight through it when something shrieked behind him.

"Zut alors! Merde!"

"Oh my gosh!" Mia cried. "Baby! you're alright!"

Nebby squatted low on the survival bag. She slithered to the center of the raft and curled around it. Nebby nibbled her cheeks as she stroked his back, and muttered sweet things to him.

Blake sealed the portal, shooed the parrot off, and opened the survival bag. *You're welcome,* he thought, bitterly.

The monstrous seas tossed the raft like a plaything, spinning it as it plunged down the waves, and threating to roll it over as it crested the next surge. Blake fought to find the sea anchor in the crowded bag, finally extracting a large piece of folded nylon cloth. He secured it to the towline and chucked it out the portal. Once in the water it opened like a parachute, dragging behind the raft, stabilizing it and making the unbearable ride almost tolerable.

There were Dramamine patches in the kit, and he stuck one on Mia's neck.

***

Nello drove the small boat expertly, taking the big waves without catching too much air. Cain was on his satellite phone with Cumulus, who was guiding them to *Tarshish.* Graffley held on with everything he had, but was taking it well. "First time in my life I really felt alive!" he declared.

At last the black schooner was sighted. "How are we gonna board without a grapple?" shouted Cain.

"We got one. Use the anchor!" Graffley replied.

"Mr. Graffley you are a true American genius! You cover me, okay?"

"Yes sir!"

Cain retrieved the small Danforth anchor and line from the cabin.

"Okay, here we go!" yelled Nello. Orange tracers began to streak overhead, cracking like thunder. Nello used the waves to nip and tuck, making it nearly impossible for Monster to draw a bead on them. But at last he timed a burst well enough, and a quarter of the powerboat's foredeck and bow shattered, fiberglass splinters pelting faces already stinging from the vicious salt spray. Nello swept close behind the schooner's stern and lunged along the starboard side, before Monster could cross the deck with his weapon. Cain slung his makeshift grappling hook, and used the up-roll of *Tarshish* to propel himself over the rail. He rolled against one of the skylights, and scurried toward the bow. Graffley leapt for the line and pulled himself up. He planted his feet on deck, congratulating himself just as Monster staggered around the deckhouse with his big machine gun and caught sight of him. Graffley flew back over the rail in large chunks.

"She's cuttin' to the other side!" Steam cried.

Monster slogged back to the starboard rail, braced his gun, and opened fire. Nello returned the favor, rounds whizzing past to the right and left like angry bumble bees.

Cain staid on his belly, wriggling along the forward skylight, then to the gun locker, finally scuttling to the back of the deck house, just a few yards from Monster.

Monster stopped firing, and when Nello saw him pounding his fist on the top of the big machine gun he knew it was now or never. He fired his last few rounds at his former team mate then drove his craft in a hard turn, attempting to cross behind to the starboard side again.

Monster clenched his teeth and growled "Fell for it!" He pulled the trigger and demolished the motorboat in a cloud of debris, blood, and flame. The bright red dot from a laser-sight flickered across his back. Monster spasmed violently, dropping the big gun, and collapsed. A crimson torrent flowed across the deck. Steam set the auto pilot, and descended through the hatch to the engine room. Cain crept across the deck, fired several shots through the hatch, then peered over its edge.

"Take care what you're shootin' at, Cain," shouted Steam. "Some things down here don't react too good to bullets!"

"C'mon Steam, this is bigger than all of us and you know that, sailor! This is about America. *Your* America!"

"And Monster's America? You got a lot of damned gall, Cain! I just watched you snuff my best friend, and you're lecturin' me about patriotism? You sold us out, you treasonous son of a whore!"

"Give me the bomb, old man!"

"Oh, this here ain't no bomb, this here is Vladimir Putin's alarm clock! It's set to go off any time now!"

"You got your teeth in, Steam? I always hated you when you had your teeth in!"

"I s'pose I should give you a peek at it, since you come all this way. Now, I'll ease out nice and slow; but you mind I figured out the manual override, and Super-Glued my finger to the switch! Now, here I come!"

Cain braced himself, and trained the gun on the door to the work bay. Steam eased into view cradling the foam block and bomb like a baby, his right index finger on the firing switch.

"Steam, think of your country! We don't have to die like this!"

"Oh, I ain't afraid to die, Cain," he grinned. "I've got cancer!"

***

Blake had just spread a Mylar survival blanket over the three of them, when the dim gloom of the windowless raft became brilliant day for several seconds, followed by an unbelievable booming that rolled over them like the last roar of a dying sea god.

"What on earth was that?" Mia groaned, covering her ears.

"About five kilotons," Blake replied.

They were all shivering.

"This is the worst water bed. Ever," she said.

Blake gave a little laugh. "Are you okay?"

"All things considered."

"I can't believe you're really here. I can't believe I am sitting here looking at you. Mia, I love you."

"Yes. Yes, you do," she smiled. "I think the patch is working."

He remained quiet and let her drowse, realizing that he hadn't slept in twenty-four hours. He wondered how many hours he had left, and when the deadly compound would take effect. He touched his chest. The vial was gone. *Must have lost it when Carson tackled me.* He reflected back on those moments. *He saved me. I'd have washed overboard. He had a plan. He was going to go after her.*

When he opened his eyes again, he felt her breath caressing his cheek. Nebuchadnezzar had his head under her chin. It was warm and humid under the silver plastic sheet. The wind wasn't howling anymore, and the ocean was no longer pushing and shoving and heaving from all directions. The rain had let up, and now only spattered the tent in occasional fits.

Blake slipped from under the Mylar and crawled to the portal. He unzipped it a little and peeked out. The waves were running a mere three feet in long easy swells. The wind had dropped to what he guessed to be ten or twelve knots. The sky was still low and gray, but the clouds were beginning to break up in a ragged scudding mess. He wondered what time it was. *The wind has been from the east and southeast, so... That's east,* he speculated. *And it's darker than the west and that's not very bright itself. Wow. We slept all day. I'm betting it's four o'clock. Two hours of daylight left.*

Mia was still sound asleep. Blake inventoried the survival bag, mumbling the contents to himself. "Lots of flares, smoke, pump, repair kit. A bucket! Sponges, couple of knives, flashlight, fishing gear, a solar still, a drinking cup. Protein bars! Water packets! And so much more! Aha! And a handy manual of survival instructions." He opened the booklet and read off a fictional list: "Step 1. Don't die. Seems obvious, but you never know. Step 2. Don't get kidnapped by a maniacal underworld kingpin. Now you tell me? Step 3. Don't get involved with rogue DEA agents. Seriously, I didn't think they existed. Step 4. Do not play with nuclear weapons. These are not toys! Okay, Mom warned me. My bad. Step 5. Don't bluff your uncle with a gun if he can count better than you." Suddenly, it wasn't funny. A chill ran down his back. "Alright, survive now, grieve later. C'mon, Barber, keep it together."

He found another Mylar blanket, wrapped himself in it, and ate a survival bar. "Lemon-vanilla never tasted so good." He curled up against the bag, and slept soundly.

27

Morning was warm. Blake smiled when he saw the wide orange roof glowing with sunshine, and marveled at the ample size of the raft. He unzipped the portal and beheld the endless Atlantic, sparkling under a beautiful blue sky. A long low swell cradled the raft gently, and the light breeze seemed almost apologetic. "Oh, Starbuck! It is a mild, mild wind, and a mild looking sky," he murmured to himself. "Moby Dick. The first thought of home I've had in three weeks, and it's home-*work.* "

The macaw stirred, crawled out from under the foil, and perched on the survival bag. Mia sat up slowly and took a minute to collect herself. "I don't even know what to say."

"Good morning?"

"Is it?"

"Well, I thought that would be less alarming than 'guess what? You're stranded on a raft in the middle of the Atlantic with your boyfriend, three days of food and water, and a foul-mouthed macaw.'"

"Oh fudge, am I?"

"Impossible, yes; but true."

"Well," she said, stroking Nebuchadnezzar. "I still have my baby."

"Yeah, glad he could make it," he said without enthusiasm. He went to the bag. "Here, have something to eat. These bars aren't bad. Four hundred calories each."

Blake gently shooed the bird off and slid the bag to the side. Nebby waddled to the portal, hopped up on the wall, turned his backside to the wind and lifted his tail.

"Good boy!" Cheered Mia! "Baby's potty trained!"

Blake returned to the portal with the scoop-like bailing bucket and rinsed the boarding ramp. He stared out at the great wide sea and tried to console himself with the thought that she was still coping with the shock of the whole affair, still finding her bearings. But, without the Phobolyn, the rising tide of his own anger was becoming difficult to restrain. The fact wasn't lost on her.

"Blake I'm sorry."

"You act like that damned bird was the one who saved your life," he snapped.

"I'm just… I'm, like, just trying to hold it all together, Blake. I am totally beyond my ability to cope with what I…what *we've* been through. Please, try to understand, Okay?"

"Okay," he said, flatly.

She slid over to him. "Blake, when that bird flew in my prison window and said 'Stoof it in yer pookits,' I almost fainted. And then I found the tracker thingy and I thought, 'Oh my God, I'm going to live!' You gave me the will to keep fighting. You gave me hope."

"The tracker was Jayce Mitchell's idea. I kind of liked him. I hope he made it."

"But *you* taught Nebby to say that!"

"He tipped off my uncle, too. Got Newly killed. Which wasn't a bad thing, I guess."

"See! Nebby chewed through my restraints. Otherwise, I would have drowned. You know, I hated him at first? But we kinda got to be buddies."

"Like me?"

"I never hated you, and you know it," she chided, sweetly.

"I'm sorry," Blake said. "For getting you into all of this."

"It's all over. Now we have to pick up the pieces and go on. Trust and go forward. That's your family battle cry, right?"

"What happened to you?"

"I'm… not ready to talk about it."

"I understand. Wow. You've lost a lot of weight."

"You look like you've picked up a few pounds," she smiled, and touched his cheek. "Thank you so much, Blake."

She wrapped her arms around him, and they shared a long hug. "We're gonna make it, Tux."

"We are."

"Oh, crap!" she winced. "Careful, I've got some sore ribs."

"Mia, I'm worried. I'm out of the drug Cotillion gave me. It's supposed to have really nasty withdrawal symptoms."

"I'm here for you."

"I mean, *really* nasty." He couldn't bring himself to tell her.

"We'll burn that bridge when we come to it. Right now we need a plan."

"Ah, you go ahead. The last plans I made sank two ships, and resulted in the detonation of a nuclear weapon."

"Is that what that was?"

"Five Kilotons. It's a wonder we don't glow in the dark."

"Oh, boy," she sighed. "What's in the bag?"

The inflatable Mylar radar reflector provided a couple of hours of welcome relief. Nebby went crazy over the shiny silver cube and, after the portal was zipped up far enough to keep it in, a rowdy game of chase, keep-away, and volley ball ensued. The laughing and shrieking was audible for miles.

"That gives me an idea," said Blake as he unzipped the flap, stood up, and tied the twenty-four inch cube to the peak of the roof. "We make long strips out of one of the blankets, and…"

He sat back down, just in time to see Mia's smile turn to slack-jawed horror.

"OMG! What! Is! That!" she cried.

Blake turned to see a huge black bump-covered cone rising out of the ocean a mere twenty feet away. It spun slowly in place until a big inquisitive eye fixed itself upon their floating home.

"Thar be whales here!" he laughed as he stripped off his shirt and plunged down the short ramp.

"What the hell are you doing? Get back here!" Mia rushed to the portal.

"I'm picking up my vacation, where I left off!"

"Blake! Get back here, you jackass!"

"You're just jealous 'cuz you got a bird, and I got a whale!"

"Do not touch that whale! It's like a federal offense or something."

"Oh yeah. You can kill fifty million babies in the womb, but you sell fresh eggs or touch a whale and they send a SWAT team!"

"Dammit Blake! I need you not to die!"

It was too late. He reached the glistening monolith, and laid hands on it. "It's so amazingly huge! And it's alive! It feels me! It knows I'm here!"

"Blake, there is like a mile of god knows what under your feet right now. I'd feel a lot better if you'd just get back in the raaaaaft!"

The entire raft lifted into the air on a sleek black mound. Blake was laughing his butt off. Nebby flew out of the portal, squawking.

"This is not helping my recovery!" she protested.

The raft splashed back into the water, and quivered. Mia reappeared in the portal. "Blake, Please!"

The spy-hopping leviathan began to submerge. "Blake, look out! Behind you!"

Blake turned his head to see another whale charging straight for him. Suddenly he felt the water rushing up from below, and a great white fin scooped him up. He clung to its edge as the whale rolled over, delivering him from harm's way. His rescuer went all the way around, bringing him back to the surface.

The color had gone out of Mia's face, and she'd stopped shouting.

"I'm good!" Blake called, tentatively. "All good." He patted his new friend's side, and returned to the raft. Nebby landed on the roof, and had a heyday fighting with the reflector ball.

"You idiot!" she shouted, as she clutched Blake's waistband and hauled him back in.

"Yow! Thanks for the mammoth wedgie!" he protested.

Mia thrashed him with Ngandu's shirt. "You could've freakin' died! How could you be so stupid?"

"Okay, that was stupid!" he gasped. "Awesome, but stupid. I'm sorry."

"Not good enough! I don't believe you!"

Blake really didn't want to hear it. But at least now she had the energy for an argument. Mia was getting to be Mia again.

"This is all my fault," he said. "And I'm sorry. That's all I can say."

"You can't say anything, Blake!"

"I know you've suffered."

"No! You! Don't!" she shouted.

Blake's patience finally snapped. "Shut up!" he shouted back, snatching the shirt from her grip with a savage jerk. "*You're* the one with no idea! None! Do you know what Cotillion was going to do to you? Do you?" he shouted in her face. "When he told me, you know what I did? I literally crapped my pants and lost my mind! And then you know what I did? I betrayed my uncle, and Barrett Reynolds, and Monster, and Steam, and Feral Cain and his team. I lied, and I used people to get you back! Oh and, by the way, you're alive and they're all dead. All of them! All! Of! Them!" He panted for a moment. "But I got you back, so mission accomplished—whatever that's worth, now."

He saw the abject fear in her eyes, and backed off, returning to his spot by the portal. "And it makes me sick because I don't know whether I did it because I felt guilty, or because I really loved you."

They were silent for a long time. Mia struggled to keep the welling tide of emotion in check, but it was too much. She cried out as it all came flooding back: Inca, Perla, and Macoute; the terror, the stench, the anguish. Blake did all he could to keep his eyes on the horizon as she bawled and screamed.

Blake took notice of Nebuchadnezzar's roof-top antics, and stood up. "Hey, jerk! Get away from that! You pop that, and I will eat your liver! Now, come on!" He managed to get the macaw by one leg, and eased him onto his arm without falling overboard. "Get inside, you flippin' idiot!" Nebby jumped down and waddled hastily to Mia, looking over his shoulder as if to say "what's *his* problem?"

"Blake, I am so sorry! I am such a selfish bitch," she gasped between sobs. "I told myself a hundred times a day that you were coming to get me. I told them all. I am so sorry!"

He went to her, laid a hand on her back. "Mia. I feel like I'm being torn apart inside. Every minute of every day. I think I'm going crazy. It's too much."

She peeled herself off the floor, and leaned into him. She said nothing for a few minutes, just trying to get the spasmodic sobbing under control. When she caught her breath, she said, "I can't explain it all. I just can't go there right now. I'm not ready."

"All I wanted was to get you out of this. Nothing else mattered."

"And you got me. You got me," her voice trailed off in a whisper, then she sighed heavily. "Oh, hell."

"What?"

"We've got issues."

***

Blake had just inflated the solar still, a teardrop-shaped float with a clear top and yellow bottom. He was desperately trying to keep it away from Nebby, when the first cramp hit him like a Taser in the gut. He shrieked and fell on his side, clutching his belly, Mia rushing to him.

"Get the still!" he groaned. "Don't let 'im pop it!" Blake let out an ear-piercing shriek that startled even the macaw. Mia hastily put the still out the portal and tethered it to a hand line. Blake made hideous retching sound, and sprayed everything near him with vomit. Mia was in a panic.

"No, no, no! Blake what's wrong? Blake!"

"Cotillion's revenge." He began to shake, violently.

"What do I do? Blake, I don't know what to do!"

"Don't...panic," he gasped between moans. He screamed with the next bolt of abdominal lightning. "There! How do you like it, bird? Oh, oh Lord!"

Within an hour he was burning with fever. The electric jolts through his gut continued throughout the afternoon and into the evening. Mia got the bucket and sponge, and sat by him through the night. By morning he was delirious. She was able to get water into him, but it didn't stay down long. She checked the supply. "Two days of water left, but not at this rate. How do we work this still thing? Nebby! Give me that!"

The macaw was gleefully shredding the pretty yellow packet on which the instructions for the solar still were printed. "Bird! You are the worst! Jerk! Ever!" Only half of the diagram remained intact. She pulled the beach ball-sized still inside, and looked it over. "Funnel and a tube. That's gonna be a little awkward. Well, here it goes."

She returned to Blake, and sponged his forehead. He was drenched and shivering.

"Buddy, you can't give up on me. You just can't. Did I tell you about Inca? There was this little girl where they were keeping me…"

By sundown his breathing had become shallow, and he was barely responsive.

"No, not again," Mia whimpered. She went to the portal. "I can't take this again. Please God!" she cried out. "Don't do this to me again!" *Do it to me,* she thought. *There you go.* "Please, I know I am so selfish. I am Me-me Mia. But don't do this. Don't let this happen to Blake. It wouldn't be fair! He thinks this is all his fault. He thinks he killed all those people, but he doesn't think of the ones he saved! He doesn't see that! Fiona's mom told me that you answer prayer. I believe that, now. You have done so much for me I never realized, and I've never thanked you for it. Thank you so much for Blake. He is the best thing that ever happened to me. Please don't take him away. I will stay with him forever." She paused in her supplication, listening to the breeze, watching the ocean and the sky became one in the fading light.

She crawled back to him, and made him drink. It stayed down. She and Nebby nibbled part of a protein bar, and had a little water.

Mia startled awake with the first rays of the sun. The fear that Blake might have died while she slept prevented her from sitting up, for a long time. When finally she did, she held her breath and stared at him. His chest was moving. He was breathing comfortably. She dared a little smile, and slipped to the portal to refill the still's reservoir.

The reflections from the gleaming ball reminded her of something. "You said you had an idea. Now what was it?" She sat down, and pondered. "You're not the only one with a brain in your head, Mr. Professor. Nebby was playing with the radar reflector when you said something about… the survival blankets…which are…Made of the same stuff as the reflector? You said cut them in strips. And what?" Her gaze fell on Nebuchadnezzar. "Nebby," she chuckled at the dawning comprehension. "You need some exercise!"

Fifteen minutes later, Nebby was in the air trailing glinting Mylar streamers twelve feet long, from his legs. She took the other blanket and draped it over one side of the tent. Mia kept Nebby circling the raft for ten minutes before she allowed him back for a passionate fawning over, a good drink, and a snack. Toward noon, Blake began to stir.

"Blake? Sweetheart?" she said, nervously. "Drink some water for me, baby."

"When did you start talking like my mom?" he said, just above a whisper.

She smiled, and took her first deep breath in two days. "How are you doin' buddy?"

"I think...I'm through the worst of it."

"Have some water." She held his head up, and he took a couple of ounces.

"Is it okay?" she asked, looking tentative.

"Yeah. Fine."

"Oh, good. The fresh is gone so I had to use the solar still. There'd be more, but I ran out of pee."

Suddenly, Blake was the one who looked tentative. "Um, that thing is made mainly for seawater, you know?"

Mia's cheeks flushed bright pink. "Oh! Well...uh; let me just fix that right up! Nebby come on. Time for radar duty!"

The still, filled with seawater, turned out almost a quart that afternoon. Blake ate a protein bar, and slept. Mia kept Nebby on a schedule of short, frequent flights. In the meantime she went through the survival kit, and caught a couple of cat naps. When night came, she brought the blanket in and draped it over Blake. She was utterly spent. "Welcome to the ICU," she mused, pulling the survival bag up for a pillow, and covering herself with the remainder of the other blanket. Nebby nestled under her arm.

When morning came, she put Nebby out to fly, filled the still, and fed Blake a whole bar. Her stomach growled loudly. They giggled together.

"You better eat," he said.

"Don't worry about me."

"Don't tell me you haven't been..."

"I said don't worry."

"Mia!"

"I would do anything for you," she said.

"Then eat one of those bars. Nobody likes a martyr."

"Uh! You *are* feeling better, you jerk!" she huffed.

He lowered his eyes. "I'm sorry. I'm so sorry about all of this." But she wasn't listening—to *him*. He looked up. Her head was cocked and her eyes were fixed, but on nothing in particular. She was stock still, in spite of the gentle swaying of the raft. Suddenly she shouted and sprang for the portal. "Oh my God! Here! Here!"

Mia grabbed the paddle and struggled to turn the raft. The gleaming white hulls of a big catamaran swept past like a glorious angel of mercy.

"Oh my gawd! Doreen, it *is* them!" cried the skipper. "Mia, where's Blake?"

Blake recognized the unmistakable New York accent. "Jotty! Jotty!" he laughed. "I'm here!"

Jotty brought *Rachel's Song* into the wind and luffed the sails. Nebby flew down to the raft and started his war with the radar ball, all over again.

"It's alright, Doreen, she didn't eat him! You kids got the whole Caribbean standing on its head looking for you, do you know that?"

Doreen threw Mia a line. She tied it to the raft, shaking her head in ecstatic disbelief.

She ducked back inside. Blake, was sitting up and grinning. She brushed the stray curls out of her face and looked him in the eye. Laying a trembling hand on his cheek, she slid it slowly behind his neck, and pulled his face to hers. The kiss lasted a long time, before she let him come up for air. "No more apologies," she whispered.

28

Ava caressed her son's face and smiled as a nurse checked his IV, and an orderly removed his dinner tray. The debriefings and meetings had gone on all day in his private room at University of Miami Hospital. Agents from the DEA were there bright and early. Eventually, the FBI, the CIA, and DHS all came to call. There would be no end of appointments, interviews, and meetings in the weeks to come—not the least of which would be a trip to Washington D.C. to testify before Congress.

And then there was Daley Dunright, Channel Three Action Reporter—all the way from Richmond, Indiana. She had called her contacts in Washington as soon as she'd gotten Blake's email. A few hours later, the management of the Azure Haven was set upon by an army of DEA agents and local police.

In between all of the poking and prodding from the doctor and his nursing staff, the good news had come that Blake and Mia were not, in fact, radioactive. *Tarshish* had traveled several more miles before the detonation, which the CIA agents had estimated at only one kiloton. The southeasterly gale and heavy rain had kept them well out of the fallout plume. Blake's blood tests turned up negative for toxic compounds, though his hands trembled slightly. He suffered frequent panic attacks and nightmares for another eight weeks. The doctor said something about PTSD, and recommended that he and Mia both see a therapist when they got back home.

There was a knock at the door of his private room. A burly man in white entered.

"Mom, this is Captain Wexler."

"Pleased to meet you, Mrs. Barber," he replied. Wexler loomed over Blake's bed. "You're in a helluva lot of trouble, Mr. Barber."

"Bring it on, sir," Blake said.

Wexler drew a deep breath. "Kid, if you weren't such a mess, I'd kick your butt."

"With all due respect, Captain, if I weren't such a mess..." Blake offered an unmistakably wry smile, lifted his eyebrows, and left it at that.

Captain Wexler suppressed the urge to laugh. He blew a staccato puff out his nose and smirked approvingly. "When you're back on your feet, I expect to see you in the recruiting office." He nodded to Ava, and headed for the door. Mia nearly knocked him over as she burst into the room. "Sorry Captain! Wait, come back here!" She turned on her heel and threw her arms abound him. "Thank you, again." Then she rushed to Blake's bedside, beaming, and gave Ava a big hug.

"I just talked to Perla! You know, the one I gave the tracker to? Captain Wexler said they caught the trafficker's boat just off Haiti. They let me talk to her! They think Immigration is going to let her stay! Is that awesome or what? She said she'd name her children after us."

Blake smiled and nodded. "Awesome! But thank Jayce for that one. How is Serena?"

"Out drinking with Daley and her senator friend, I think. Oh, Nebby has to be in quarantine for thirty days before we can take him home."

"Well, that's something we can be thankful for."

"Uh! Blake, that's our baby!"

"So, did Mom tell you? About Turlow?"

"Don't keep me waiting!"

Ava smiled. "He was escorted off the cruise ship in Cozumel."

Blake supplied a few missing details. "Got tanked up and grabbed some gal's butt. Her ex-NFL husband didn't approve."

"That is too freaking rich!"

"There's something else Mom found out."

Mia looked to Ava and lifted her eyebrows.

"The lion's share of the estate was never in danger," Ava said. "The trust accounts were set up in our names a long time ago. Mom told me when she got back from the Yucatan."

Mia became pensive.

"Mia, I'm so…" Blake began.

"Hush! What did I tell you about that?

***

It was another week before they set foot on the snow-bound soil of their Indiana home. And as Blake had imagined, it was completely surreal. Nobody knew anything of their adventure, except for what they had been permitted to divulge: that their yacht sank in a heavy squall after leaving St. Croix, and that they were lost at sea in a survival raft for seven days. For a short while they were back in the limelight, giving sound-bite interviews and being treated like celebrities. Then it was over. It was all business as usual for the rest of the world, and it expected them to pick up and get on with things.

Blake stood at his attic window in the fading twilight, and stared across the backyard toward the house where Barret Reynolds and his sister Becky Lynn had grown up. Another two inches of snow had fallen, burying under a smooth white blanket the yard where the Urquart and Reynolds children had played.

There had been no memorial for Carson, nor for his shipmates—the *Tarshish* men. Blake struggled against the monstrous emptiness he felt, the grievous loss, the howling questions of fate, faith, and futility. "And I only am escaped alone, to tell thee," he murmured. Blake contemplated how he might locate and contact their families. *They should know,* he thought.

Mia's voice drifted up the stairs. "C'mon, Tux! We don't want to be late to our own party!"

Blake stared for a moment longer, before heading downstairs.

Tripper Gunn had arranged a hearty reception at the sailing club, in recognition of the trio's safe return. Fiona's family had come down from Manitowoc, and the little girl stuck to Mia like glue. Mia didn't seem to mind. When the glad-handing and unanswerable questions finally became too much, Blake took refuge in the locker room. He pulled on his coat and took a postcard from one of its pockets. It featured a staysail schooner. On the back, the anonymous sender had sketched a passable representation of a jay bird. It was postmarked Puerto la Cruz, Venezuela. Blake slipped out of the hilltop clubhouse, retreating from the glowing good cheer, and ambled down the peninsula to the point. There he stood in the cold night and watched the moon rise over the frozen lake, as wisps of snow twisted across the black ice like tormented spirits.

Snowmen of the Serengeti

Sign up for email updates on book 3 in the Uncle Arctica Series!
Coming Soon!
trespassislandbooks.com

Uncle Arctica

Book 1 in the Uncle Arctica series
Sign up for email updates!
trespassislandbooks.com

Glossary of Sailing Terms

You don't have to know anything about sailing to enjoy *The Storms of Tarshish*, but it will help if you become familiar with a few of the following sailing terms.

Aft Toward the rear of a boat.

Astern Behind the boat.

Boom A horizontal pole attached to the mast, and to which the bottom of the main sail is attached. Also the sound it makes when it hits you in the head during a wild jibe.

Bow The front end of a boat.

Bow Pulpit A railing at the bow of a boat which may extend beyond the deck, out over the water.

Buoy A floating marker. Some folks say "boo-ee," some say "boy."

Cleat A device used for securing a line. There are many styles of cleat. Some resemble two horns, around which a line is wrapped in a figure-eight fashion;

some have spring-loaded jaws through which the line passes; "pinch-cleats" trap the line in a tight wedge-shaped groove.

Companionway A ladderway leading through a hatch to the next deck below, or above.

Davit A small shipboard crane, generally used in pairs for suspending or lowering a utility boat, or loading cargo, etc.

Deck The top of the boat covering the hull.

Ease To loosen or let a sail out.

Forward Toward the front of a boat.

Genoa Sail A type of jib or foresail, a genoa is larger than a regular jib, extending back past the mast and overlapping the mainsail. Sometimes called a genny, or jenny.

GPS The acronym for Global Positioning System. GPS is a navigation system that allows users to determine their exact location, velocity, and time 24 hours a day whether on land, in the air, or on the sea. It functions anywhere in the world in all weather conditions. Garmin is a popular brand of GPS.

Halyard A line and/or cable used to raise and lower a sail.

Hard a'lee The warning given by the skipper that he is turning the boat (by pushing the tiller hard to the leeward side.) Usually preceeded by the call "ready about!"

Head A toilet or water closet on a boat or ship.

Heeling When the sailboat leans over as the wind speed (and boat speed) increases. This is usually when the crew hastens to sit on the rail and hike out.

Helm A wheel or tiller used for steering a ship, or the entire apparatus for steering a ship.

Hull The body of a boat.

Jib The sail forward of the mast. In some older boats the jib had a boom, too.

Jibe Changing the direction of the boat while sailing with the wind coming from behind the boat. Same as a Tack, but the wind passes from one side of the stern to the other. This results in the boom swinging—often with dangerous force—to the other side of the boat. Jibing is a "duck or die" proposition.

Leeward The direction which the wind is blowing to. If the wind is blowing right in your face, then your back is facing to leeward. Your back is then on the leeward side of your body.

Lifeline. A cable or wire running along the edge of the deck, supported by stanchions.

Line On a boat, ropes are called "lines." A line is any rope having a specific purpose.

Luff The forward edge of a sail. Also, when a sail collapses because the boat is pointed too close to the wind, the sail is said to be "luffing." Also, a maneuver where one forces a competitor into the wind, causing his or her sails to luff.

Keel A stationary fin or ridge attached to the bottom of the boat which provides stability.

Knot A nautical unit of speed, roughly equal to 1.15 miles per hour. Also, a fastening made by tying two lines together.

Mainsail The large triangular sail attached to aft side of the mast. Usually, the mainsail is also attached to a boom, along its bottom edge.

Mast The vertical pole to which the mainsail and stays are attached.

Mizzen Mast On a boat with multiple masts (like the Terrapin,) the mizzen mast is the next mast aft of the main mast.

Port If you are in a boat facing forward (toward the bow,) port is left side of the boat. Remember: port and left both have four letters.

Radar An electronic apparatus which uses radio waves to determine the range, angle, or velocity of objects (i.e. ships, aircraft, weather formations, terrain, etc.) The word is actually an acronym for Radio Detection And Ranging. The term has since entered the English language as a common noun, losing all capitalization. Simrad is a popular brand of radar.

Rail Not actually a rail, but that part of the deck along the sides of the boat where crew members may sit and hike out.

Rigging The arrangement of sails, sheets, halyards, control lines, and other gear. Often divided into the running rigging (the previous stuff,) and the standing rigging (the mast, boom, shrouds, and stays.)

Rudder A flat piece of wood or metal used to steer the boat.

Saloon A large cabin for the common use of crew or passengers. Contrary to recent assertions, it is pronounced the way it is spelled!

Sheet A line used to control the trim of a sail. Main sheet, jib sheet, spinnaker sheet.

Shrouds Cables which stabilize the mast. Also called side-stays.

Starboard If you are in a boat facing forward (toward the bow,) starboard is the right side of the boat.

Stern The rear end of a boat.

Tack Changing the direction of the boat while sailing with the wind coming from the in front of the boat. The bow of the boat passes through the wind so that it changes from blowing onto one side to the other. For example, if the wind is blowing onto the port side of the boat, you are on "port tack." You turn the boat so the bow passes through the wind (momentarily pointing straight into the wind) until the breeze now blows onto the starboard side of the boat. Now you are on "starboard tack." The sails shift to the other side of the boat as the tack is completed.

Topsides The sides of a boat between the waterline and the deck

Transom The back end of a boat which has a square-stern.

Tell Tale Streamers that indicate the direction the wind is coming from. Often made from old video/audio cassette tape!

Tiller A long handle attached to the rudder for steering the boat.

Trim To tighten or pull a sail in.

Windward The direction the wind is coming from. If the wind is blowing right in your face, you are looking to windward. Your nose is then on the windward side of your head.